# THE UPRISING

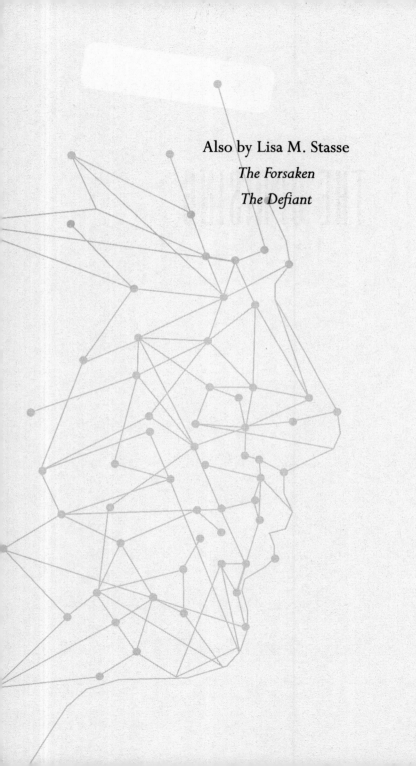

Also by Lisa M. Stasse

*The Forsaken*

*The Defiant*

# THE FORSAKEN TRILOGY

# THE UPRISING

## LISA M. STASSE

SIMON & SCHUSTER BFYR

NEW YORK LONDON TORONTO SYDNEY NEW DELHI

An imprint of Simon & Schuster Children's Publishing Division
1230 Avenue of the Americas, New York, New York 10020
SIMON & SCHUSTER BFYR is a trademark of Simon & Schuster, Inc.
For information about special discounts for bulk purchases, please contact Simon & Schuster Special Sales at 1-866-506-1949 or business@simonandschuster.com.
The Simon & Schuster Speakers Bureau can bring authors to your live event. For more information or to book an event, contact the Simon & Schuster Speakers Bureau at 1-866-248-3049 or visit our website at www.simonspeakers.com.
Also available in a SIMON & SCHUSTER BFYR hardcover edition
Cover design by Lizzy Bromley
Interior design by Hilary Zarycky
The text for this book is set in Perpetua.
Manufactured in the United States of America
First SIMON & SCHUSTER BFYR paperback edition July 2014
2 4 6 8 10 9 7 5 3 1
The Library of Congress has cataloged the hardcover edition as follows:
Stasse, Lisa M.
The uprising / Lisa Stasse.
p. cm.
Summary: "Alenna Shawcross fights to stay alive after she discovers the secrets of the wheel where she has been exiled"—Provided by publisher.
ISBN 978-1-4424-3268-0 (hardcover)
[1. Government, Resistance to—Fiction. 2. Fascism—Fiction. 3. Prisons—Fiction. 4. Survival—Fiction. 5. Science fiction.] I. Title.
PZ7.S7987Upr 2013
[E]—dc23
2012025051
ISBN 978-1-4424-3269-7 (pbk)
ISBN 978-1-4424-3270-3 (eBook)

*For Alex McAulay*
*again and always*

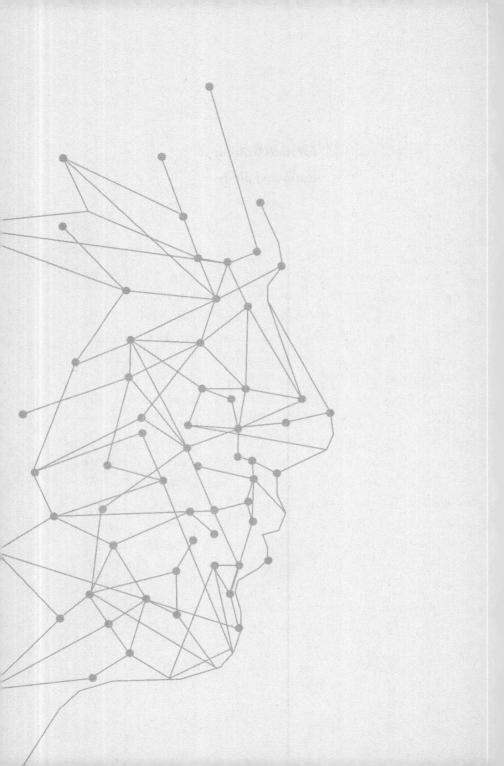

# ACKNOWLEDGMENTS

Massive thanks to my fantastic agent, Mollie Glick. I'm extremely grateful for her excellent advice, her great notes, and for her dedication to the Forsaken series in general. Thanks also to Rachel Hecht, Kathleen Hamblin, Hannah Brown Gordon, Stéphanie Abou, and the entire team at Foundry Literary + Media, as well as Shari Smiley at The Smiley Group, LLC.

Huge thanks also to my brilliant new editor, Zareen Jaffery. Her edits and guidance helped *The Uprising* become the book I knew it could be. Working with her is a true delight, and I look forward to collaborating with her on the next book in the trilogy. Thanks also to Lydia Finn, Lucille Rettino, Julia Maguire, Michelle Fadlalla, Venessa Williams, Dawn Ryan, Bernadette Cruz, Kelly Stidham, Sooji Kim, Mara Anastas, Brian Kelleher, Justin Chanda, Jon Anderson, and everyone else at Simon & Schuster for their amazing support. And a special shout-out to Lizzy Bromley for her spectacular cover designs.

Love and thanks to my family and all my friends. Without you, none of this would be possible.

# 1 SUNLIGHT

I SIT IN AN uncomfortable metal chair, facing a row of six scientists in white lab coats. These are my inquisitors. I'm deep inside Destiny Station, sequestered in a small chamber carved into the massive sandstone mesa that I've called home for the past three weeks. The rebel scientists who run the station use this room for depositions and debriefings. It's one of many such rooms and tunnels dug like burrows into the strange rock formation.

Large digital screens are mounted in a row on the wall behind the scientists. The screens show different images. Many of them display footage of Prison Island Alpha—the colony for banished teens that Liam and I escaped from. A desolate tropical island known as "the wheel," where life expectancy is eighteen years of age. I was only on the wheel for two weeks, but every day was a fight for survival.

Supposedly, we were sent to the wheel after failing a test meant to predict a tendency for future violent and criminal behavior. Instead, we were actually exiled there by our corrupt government, because we were immune to mind-control drugs that they deployed to subdue the population. This meant we were a risk. We might rebel against the government, so they wanted us gone for good. After Liam and I managed to flee the wheel, we were rescued by the rebel scientists in Australia, who gave us refuge in Destiny Station.

I glance up at the digital display screens. They now show an array of faces that I recognize from my time on the wheel. Many of these kids were my friends. I'm wearing a row of electrodes around my left wrist, like a bracelet made of wires and sensors. This is to monitor my subconscious physiological reactions to these images. One of the scientists is crouched over a computer, noting and analyzing my responses.

Dr. Vargas-Ruiz, who helps run Destiny Station, sits directly in front of me, leading the deposition. I've been in this room for two hours already today. And for three hours every afternoon since I arrived here.

The scientists ask me questions about every detail of my life on the wheel. Often, it's the same questions over and over, until I feel like I'm going crazy. The scientists mean well. They're trying to get as much data as they can from those of us who got rescued. But these individual depositions are grueling, like a test that never ends.

I'm struggling to adjust to life in general at the station. After so many years living in the United Northern Alliance—that wretched nation known as the UNA, where most personal freedoms were banned—it's hard to adapt to normal life again. *Not that Destiny Station is anything close to normal.*

Mornings are spent training for the battle ahead when we return to Prison Island Alpha. Nights are spent strategizing. Twelve weeks from now, we will be leaving Destiny Station. The scientists believe this is the optimum time frame for departure. If we leave any sooner than that, we might not be prepared. But if we wait much longer, the scientists fear that the UNA will figure out our plans and bomb Destiny Station.

After we leave Australia, we will join up with other rebel bases scattered around the globe and then return to the wheel. There, we will take control of the island, and then use it as a new home base to launch an assault on the continental UNA.

"Alenna?" Dr. Vargas-Ruiz suddenly says, adjusting her glasses. "Please pay attention. Look at the photos."

"I am," I snap back. "But can't we hurry this up?"

A single face flashes onto all the screens at once. A beautiful, blond-haired girl with wide blue eyes.

"Meira," I say absently, before the scientists can even ask me who it is. "The co-leader of our village on the wheel. Still alive, unless our village has been destroyed."

Dr. Vargas-Ruiz nods. "And you never saw any sign that she was secretly working for the UNA? As a spy?"

"No. I already told you. She was kind of cold and calculating, but she and her boyfriend Veidman kept everything running. They were a few years older than me. I never thought they were spies."

I can picture our village perfectly in my mind. The wooden shacks, the hammocks slung between trees, and the dark river where we bathed. On the wheel, us banished kids formed two tribes: the villagers and the drones. Liam and I were villagers. We only wanted to make the best of things, and find a way to escape the island. In fact, Liam was our village's most respected and fiercest hunter and explorer.

But the drones were wild, and susceptible to new, experimental drugs that the UNA secretly dropped on the wheel. The drones followed a masked prophet who called himself "the Monk"—a man who turned out to be Minister Harka, the exiled leader of the UNA. He had been secretly banished to the wheel by traitors in his own government, and had taken on a new identity there. A body double had taken his place back in the UNA so that no one even knew that he was gone. His followers on the wheel caused chaos and constantly attacked our village in an attempt to gain control of the island. They wanted to enslave us, and make us fight one another for their entertainment.

Another photo appears on the screens. A girl with dyed-blue hair, a sleeve of tattoos down one arm, and a knowing gleam in her dark brown eyes.

"Gadya," I say, swallowing hard. Her absence makes my heart ache the most. She was my best friend on the wheel, and she saved my life more times than I can remember. "I told you, the last time I saw her, she was alive but injured. Do we really have to go through this again?"

Dr. Vargas-Ruiz nods.

I know that the scientists will show me everyone. Including the faces of the other friends we left behind, either trapped or captured, like David, Markus, and Rika. And the faces of the dead, like Veidman and Sinxen. I'm still in mourning for them. Seeing their faces on the screens makes the pain more acute.

But what the scientists show me next surprises me. It's a topographic map of the wheel. From above, it resembles a large, jagged circle. The different sectors, which look like misshapen pie slices, are marked with their respective colors.

Our village was inside a region called the blue sector, which was the last remaining area of the wheel not controlled by drones. The other sectors—orange, purple, yellow, and red—had already been taken over by them. And the gray zone, which houses the machinery that transports kids to and from the island, was uninhabitable.

I lean in for a closer look at the map. I try to imagine what my friends on the wheel are doing right now. Probably some of them are battling the drones. And I know that others are cryogenically frozen in pods in the specimen archive—a giant hive located inside the gray zone. Flying machines called selection units kidnap kids and take them there to store until UNA doctors can dissect their brains.

When I return to the wheel with the rebel scientists, I know we will face battles with both the drones and the selection units before we can conquer the island. I'm not certain that we'll win. Most of us might end up getting killed or getting snatched by the machines.

"Alenna, what are you thinking about? You have to tell us," Dr. Vargas-Ruiz prompts.

"I'm thinking about the specimen archive. About how the UNA will keep dissecting kids until they discover how to synthesize some kind of ultimate drug—one that will brainwash everyone on the planet. And if we fail in stopping them, then no one will be able to prevent the UNA from dominating the entire globe. . . ."

My stomach lurches. Suddenly, I can't take it anymore. All the questions. All the photos of my missing friends. All the stress. I feel the jagged rock walls closing in on me like they want to devour me. I can't catch my breath.

"Tell us more," Dr. Vargas-Ruiz keeps saying.

"Yes—" another scientist begins, excitedly motioning to a colleague to look at the computer screen displaying my reactions. "You think we'll fail in our mission?"

I stand up, shoving back my metal chair with a loud clatter. Everyone stops talking at once. The screens go black. I rip off my electrode wristband and throw it onto the table.

"Alenna?" Vargas-Ruiz asks. "What's wrong?"

"I'm sick of this!" I say. "You already know the answers to everything. You've already asked me these questions before!"

"Depositions are a normal part of life at the station for new arrivals like yourself," Vargas-Ruiz says calmly. "You know that."

"But I've been here almost a month! When are you going to stop?"

"When we're certain that we've learned every detail about your experiences on Island Alpha, and how you feel about them."

A bearded scientist gazes at me balefully over his glasses. "If it weren't for us, you wouldn't be alive right now. You'd be cut up in a UNA lab somewhere. Isn't this a better option?"

I glare back at him. The scientists are just watching me. Staring at me like I'm a lab animal.

"I need to find Liam," I say, the words coming out in a burst. He's the only one who understands exactly what I've been through. No one else shares our bond, or knows how strong it is. "I'm taking a break."

"Alenna, wait—" Vargas-Ruiz begins, but I don't want to hear what she has to say. I just want to get out of this room. I know exactly where Liam is—waiting for me on the roof deck on top of the station.

I spin and head straight for the door. I swing it open and plunge out into the rock tunnel.

The air here is hot and stale. It never feels bright enough in these tunnels, no matter how many lights are turned on. I can't wait to find Liam and get some sunlight.

I start racing down the tunnel, brushing past a group of scientists. They stare at me, frowning, but I don't care. I just keep moving, in case Vargas-Ruiz sends someone after me. I reach a

6

set of rough-hewn rock stairs, and I start running up it.

When I get to the top level of the station, I'm panting for air—both from exhaustion and from an increasing sensation of claustrophobia. I don't know how the scientists living here have managed to cope. Some of them have been here for years inside the mesa. I tear through a tunnel on this level until I reach a metal ladder leading up into a narrow, vertical shaft. My fingers clasp at the rungs.

I start climbing the ladder, determined to reach the roof deck as soon as possible. I feel like I'm crawling up a chimney. I finally see a circular metal hatch above me.

When I reach the hatch, I turn the handle and fling the door open, blinking against the harsh glare of the sun. I crawl up and out of the shaft and onto the surface of the rock.

"Liam!" I call out, looking around for him as I get to my feet.

I close the hatch door behind me, basking in the light. Here, on top of Destiny Station, I'm nearly two hundred feet above the ground. The wind whips through my long, dark hair. I take a deep breath.

"Liam?" I call out again. I don't see him, but the top of the mesa is vast, and it has a few jagged rocks and boulders on it.

I stare out at the horizon. From up here, I can see the harsh Australian outback sprawling in every direction. The splintered rocks and sand dunes below me make it look like the surface of an alien planet. Everything is desolate and abandoned.

"Alenna," a familiar voice says right behind me.

I startle, spinning around. It's Liam. "Thank god! I thought I was alone."

"Yeah, I could tell."

I hug him, wrapping my arms around his lean, muscular body.

I nestle against his chest, fitting my body against his. He puts his arms around me. I shut my eyes for a moment. Falling in love with Liam was the best thing to happen to me on the wheel.

"What are you doing up top?" he asks. "Aren't you supposed to be in a deposition for another hour?"

"I couldn't take it anymore, and I kind of freaked out," I admit. "I had to find you." I sigh. "Everyone's going to be mad at me now. For running out of the room."

"They'll get over it."

I lean up, staring into Liam's beautiful blue eyes. The wind is ruffling his brown hair. I suddenly close my eyes again and kiss him. My lips melt into his, making me shiver, and for a moment I start to lose myself. Then I feel self-conscious, and I pull back, looking around. "There's no one else up here with us, right?"

He smiles. "Worried about your mom catching us?"

"Maybe."

"It's okay. I saw her down on level three, working."

"Why doesn't that surprise me? My mom is always working."

In some ways it's comforting to know that her personality hasn't changed since I was a little kid and she spent her days sequestered in her genetics lab. But in other ways, it's annoying. I was hoping she'd want to spend more time with me after we were separated for six years because of the UNA. Still, I know that the survival of Destiny Station depends on her. Unlike some of the other rebel scientists here, she doesn't take part in the depositions. Her work is too crucial—trying to reverse-engineer the UNA's drugs in order to find an antidote.

I also know that after our recent reunion, things remain awkward between us. When the government snatched her and my dad for being dissidents all those years ago, I thought she was dead and that I was an orphan. I have to get used to the idea that I have a mother again.

"So how was your deposition today?" I ask Liam. He had his a few hours before mine. "Same old stuff?"

He nods. "They showed me a bunch of pictures of Minister Harka and his body doubles." He pauses. "Honestly, I'm not even sure what they want from us anymore."

"Me neither."

We stand there for a moment, getting buffeted by the wind. Then Liam pulls an object from the back pocket of his jeans. "Here, look. I found this for you."

It's an old paperback book. I grin as I take it from him. Because books and most digital media were banned in the UNA, I've been trying to read as much as I can to make up for lost time. There are plenty of books here that the scientists and other refugees pass around among themselves. "Thanks," I tell him.

I glance at the cover, and read its title out loud: "*The Myth of Sisyphus* by Albert Camus."

Liam nods. "I remember how you told me that the myth kept you going on the wheel."

He's right. The story of Sisyphus endlessly pushing his boulder up a mountain, which my dad used to tell me as a child, helped me find meaning in the repetitive, painful journey we faced on the island. I turn the book over in my hand, contemplating it. This thin paperback looks like some kind of strange philosophical essay about the meaning of that Greek myth. I wonder if my dad ever read this book.

"So, are you ready for the concert tonight?" Liam asks me, brushing a strand of hair out of my eyes.

"I've been trying not to think about it," I confess. "I mean, there's a lot more stuff to worry about than that. Besides, holding concerts is just some dumb thing they do here to put us at ease."

"It's not dumb. And I know you'll do great."

"And if I don't?"

Liam flashes me a crooked grin. "I'll still love you."

I hug him again.

Tonight will be the first time that I play guitar in public. And it's the first concert I'll attend since the UNA banned any music not approved by the government back when I was eight. Because the arts were censored and repressed so much in the UNA, the scientists prioritize them here. The concert tonight is a chance for kids to gather and get onstage and perform.

"I wish I had that guitar you made for me," I tell Liam. I'm thinking about the one that he carved out of wood on the wheel. That guitar was what let me know how he really felt about me. *And the night he gave it to me was the first time we kissed.*

"I'll make you another guitar," he says. "A better one. They've got way more tools here. I should have done it already."

He walks to the edge of the mesa and stares down at the barren landscape below. "Might be hard to find any trees around here, though."

"Hey, don't get too close," I call out.

He glances back. "After everything we've been through, you're worried about me falling off this thing?"

"Maybe." I walk over to join him at the edge, staring at the red desert, with its arroyos and dunes. There are no towns or cities here. No roads. Only this stark landscape burning under the sun. There is nothing here but Destiny Station.

I know that Liam and I should make more of an effort to fit in at the base. We've kept mostly to ourselves over the past few weeks, despite the fact that there are three hundred other rescued kids here. But our experiences on the wheel have taught us caution.

In addition, despite what Vargas-Ruiz told us when we first got here, the divisions between the two different tribes on the wheel have not dissolved. The rescued villagers stick together, and so do the rescued drones. It's generally not hard to tell the two groups apart. Often the drones have teeth chiseled into points and short hair from shaving their heads on the wheel. Their eyes often look haunted as well, although I get the sense they barely remember how they once behaved.

I rarely see members of one group interact with the other. Heavy, unspoken tension hangs in the air between them. Now, far from the wheel and the UNA's drugs, us villagers and drones should be able to set our differences aside. But old animosities die hard. I understand why. If it weren't for the drones, a lot more villagers would be alive.

"You okay?" Liam asks, putting his arm around my shoulders.

"Just thinking about the wheel, and our friends. I mean, especially Gadya. They showed me a photo of her again today. I feel guilty that we left her behind in the archive. She probably got frozen, or worse."

"We don't know that. I mean, I got captured once and I survived. The same thing might have happened to her."

"But if no one goes back and saves her, she's never going to make it off the island."

Liam turns to face me. "I know. That's why we have to do something. When we get back to the wheel with the rebels, we have to make it our first priority to rescue everyone from our village who got left behind."

I nod in agreement. "And we need to find David, too."

Liam glances at me, his brow furrowed. "I'm not sure about that kid."

"I am."

I know that Liam thinks my friend David is just a drone, or a spy, so he doesn't trust him. But he doesn't know David like I do. David and I woke up on the wheel together the very same day. I was lucky and got rescued by Gadya and the villagers, but David got captured by drones. The last time Liam saw him, David was escaping from the prison kennels in our village. Liam never saw David save Rika on the frozen lake, or sacrifice himself so that Gadya and I could get inside the specimen archive. *Liam never really got an opportunity to know David at all.*

"David is on our side." I lean into Liam's body. "You have to give him a chance."

It's then I notice an unusual object in the sky. A dark speck flitting across the horizon, miles away from us.

"Hey, do you see that?" I ask Liam.

Then I realize that his eyes are already tracking it, squinting against the sun.

"Is it a transport plane from the wheel?" I hold my book up to shield my eyes against the glare. No planes have arrived since the one that brought me and Liam here. I know that the scientists are expecting another one soon; Vargas-Ruiz mentioned it in a deposition a few days ago. From what I've learned, planes from the wheel turn up roughly every three weeks.

Liam is peering at the approaching speck. "It's too small to be a transport plane. Could be some kind of satellite."

We both keep watching it. For some reason, the object unnerves me. Maybe because it reminds me of the selection units—those flying masses of metallic tentacles that pulled kids

12

into the sky on the wheel. In the village, we called the selection units "feelers," and I still think of them that way.

"It could be some kind of Australian thing," I point out uneasily. "Something their government is testing, like a new aircraft or weapon." The object is larger now, and moving even faster. Getting closer.

It appears to be heading straight at Destiny Station. I know that the scientists inside the rock must already be following it on their radar system. Nothing dangerous can approach Destiny Station without being detected far in advance. So, if no alarms are blaring, we're most likely going to be fine.

But the object keeps heading our way, slicing through the air with incredible speed. I squint at it, struggling to make out its contours. The sunlight sparkles and shimmers off its gleaming surface.

Liam turns to me. "Maybe we should go back inside for a bit. Just in case."

"You're only saying that because I'm out here with you," I reply. "If you were alone, or with your hunter friends on the wheel, you'd never want to go back in. Am I right?"

Our eyes meet. He can't deny it. "What's wrong with being protective?" he asks.

"Nothing," I say. "Except I know I can handle this. Don't forget that I'm a fighter too. Remember, I rescued *you* back at the archive."

Liam grins. "Yeah, and I rescued you from the feeler attack in the forest before that. So we're even." He pauses. "And I'm not just trying to be protective. I figured we should tell someone what we're seeing." His grin fades a bit as he stares out at the sky again. The object is going to pass directly overhead if it keeps moving along the same trajectory.

"It's weird there aren't any sirens yet," I say to Liam.

I've gotten used to warning sirens going off at least twice a day—each time the radar or satellite feeds pick up any suspicious activity. Their loud, wailing sounds echo through the tunnels like the baying of subterranean wolves. The sirens startled me at first, but now I barely notice them.

It's been years since anyone tried to attack Destiny Station, but the scientists are hyper-vigilant right now. *Which makes sense— given that they're hijacking UNA aircrafts from the wheel and landing them here in the desert.* It's only a matter of time before the UNA figures out what's going on and comes after them. This is another reason why the scientists moved up their plan for us to return to Island Alpha, from one year to twelve weeks.

The object in the sky keeps cutting its path toward the station. I finally get a better look at it.

What I see makes my heart nearly stop beating.

It's some kind of military machine. *Similar to a feeler, but even more terrifying.* Tentacles whip out from either side of it, centered around a large spinning disc. To my horror, I watch sharp blades flash out from the tentacles. Even though it hasn't tripped any alarms yet, this is definitely a weapon sent from the UNA.

Liam sees the lacerating blades too. He grabs my arm and yells, "Run!" We both start racing for the closed hatch. My heart pounds in fear.

I hear a faint hissing sound behind me, as the object shoots through the sky down toward us.

Liam and I reach the hatch just as the noise grows even louder. It's the sound of blades slicing through air.

I duck and race sideways, getting another glimpse at the machine. Now I can see the blurry outlines of the UNA's bloodred logo on the bottom of the disc—an eye hovering over a globe. The machine's tentacles have large blades running up and down their lengths. The blades buzz like miniature saws. Like they're meant to cut and destroy anything they come in contact with.

The thing is almost on us now. Liam throws open the door of the hatch leading down into the station. "Go!" he yells at me.

"Not without you!" I scream back. After being kept apart once before on the wheel, I refuse to be separated from him again.

"I'll be right behind you!" he yells, pushing me forward. Trying to save me.

Now I hear the warning sirens start up.

But the sirens are too late.

The disc zooms through the air straight at us. Like it can sense our presence. There's no time to get in the tunnel.

Liam presses me down behind the open door of the hatch, which is sticking upright at a ninety-degree angle. It provides us with some shelter. I feel Liam's warm, protective body over mine. The machine hammers through the air at us, its tentacles slamming against the door. I press myself flat against the rock, shutting my eyes for a second.

Then a loud grinding noise makes me look up. To my shock, the thick metal door to the hatch has been shorn in two. The churning blades on the tentacles have sliced right through it, like chain saws through a tree branch. The machine circles back up into the sky, preparing to attack again.

Liam helps me up. "We have to get back inside!" he yells.

I hear the buzzing sound of the machine. It's descending again.

I fling my legs down into the open hole, grabbing at the ladder rungs with my fingers. But I slip and miss.

15

I start sliding down the shaft, crashing against the rock sides and the metal rungs as I cry out in pain.

There's a flash of light above me, and Liam careens into the shaft as well, right behind me.

Then my legs crash into the rock floor, and I fall backward, hitting my head and elbows. I roll out of the way as Liam comes slamming down after me.

I hear grinding noises above us, and I gaze up, trying to catch my breath. The churning blades of the machine plow into the remains of the hatch. *It's trying to get down into the station with us.* Tentacles whir and gnash, their blades grinding the sandstone into dust and sparking against the metal ladder. The opening isn't wide enough for the machine. It's trying to expand the hole.

I struggle to sit up. Liam is right there next to me. We start crawling away from the bottom of the shaft.

"You okay?" Liam asks, staggering to his feet and giving me a hand.

"Yeah," I gasp. "You?"

"Fine."

We stand there in the tunnel, both gazing up at the dust and debris raining down from the roof of the station. The sirens continue to wail. Men rush past us, heading toward the shaft. They are all wearing helmets and carrying guns.

More figures race toward us, including Dr. Terry Elliott, one of the other chief scientists here, specializing in anthropology. He's tall, with thinning gray hair. "What did you see up there?" he calls out urgently.

"I don't know!" I tell him. "It was kind of like a feeler. I mean, a selection unit. But with blades on its tentacles." My knees and elbows are throbbing. I can hear the machine grinding away above us, mindlessly trying to cut through metal and rock.

Then a volley of gunshots begins.

The noise explodes through the tunnels. The guards are firing at the machine, trying to destroy it. It squeals in mechanical agony as the men blast away.

The tunnel starts filling with dust and smoke. "We need to get out of here, and deeper into the station," Liam says.

I nod. We start stumbling away, heading down the tunnel, both of us dazed. More gunshots ring out behind us.

Vargas-Ruiz rushes out of another tunnel that intersects with ours. Her eyes are wide and her curly hair is disheveled. This attack clearly took everyone by surprise. "What's going on?"

"You should know," Liam says. "Alenna and I were up on the roof deck. Something came after us." He gestures toward the tunnel behind us. "And it's still here."

"Our radar failed to track it," Vargas-Ruiz says, staring at us. "It appeared out of nowhere."

"We wanted to fight it," I tell her. "But we weren't ready."

"I'm glad you didn't fight," Vargas-Ruiz replies. "You're not trained, and you don't have any weapons. Let our security team deal with events like this."

"You could give us weapons if you wanted," Liam points out.

Vargas-Ruiz doesn't respond.

"So what does this mean?" I ask her. "Why did that thing come here from the UNA? Why now?"

"I don't know," she replies. "And it could mean nothing. Or it could be the start of an onslaught. I won't know until I see it. Until we can take it apart and study it in the lab, and find out exactly what it is."

The words "an onslaught" are still ringing in my ears. I thought that Liam and I were safe in Australia, at least for a while. *Clearly, I was wrong.*

Vargas-Ruiz sees the look on my face and sighs. "Don't worry. It could just be an exploratory probe. We've been concerned that the UNA would send something out to follow the hijacked planes, and relay data back." She pauses. "We're planning on realigning our radar and satellite controls so that nothing like this can happen again."

"What do we do until then?" I ask.

"Nothing. Destiny Station is safe. But this isn't the first time we've been attacked, and it won't be the last. Until we leave to join the other rebel bases and go back to Prison Island Alpha, you're stuck here." She starts to walk away. But then she stops and turns back to us. "Just be careful about going up top from now on. And, Alenna, you shouldn't have left the deposition room today. I expect a lot better from you."

Before I can think of a good response, she turns away again, heading toward the crowd of people and guards. The machine is silent now, and there are no more gunshots. I take a deep breath and try to calm down.

"So what do you think?" I ask Liam softly as we begin walking down the tunnel.

"I wish we could leave and fight the UNA right now." He looks at me, his blue eyes flashing for an instant. "I don't want to sit on the sidelines anymore. But there's nothing we can do right now. When the time comes, we'll get out of this rock and back to the wheel." He kisses me on the forehead. "Then we'll give it everything we have."

A voice suddenly calls out, "Hey!"

I turn my head, startled. Liam turns too.

A girl is standing there in the tunnel behind us. She's pretty, with gentle brown eyes, dark skin, and a thin, lithe physique that makes her look taller than she really is. She has short-cropped black hair, only an inch long at most, and she's wearing a black tank top and jeans. I've seen this girl around, but never spoken to her. She's a year or so older than I am.

I know that she's a former drone. On the wheel she probably lived in a frenzy of madness, her mind clouded by UNA drugs and enthralled by the Monk's deranged teachings. In the dim light, I can see long, raised scars on both of her wrists.

Liam and I stare at her. It's hard for us to trust anyone who was once a drone, after we fought them so many times in battle. Even though the drugs are gone from their systems, it has become an ingrained response for me to think of them as enemies.

But this girl is smiling, and her eyes look lucid and kind. She walks closer and holds something out to me. I glance down and see that it's the book that Liam gave me. *The Myth of Sisyphus.* I must have dropped it during the attack. I take it from her, grateful but a bit confused. The cover is scorched on one corner.

"You're safe now," the girl says. "They blasted that machine into confetti. And a guard found your book on the rocks up top. I thought I'd give it back."

"Thanks."

"My name's Cass." The girl looks from me to Liam and back again. "Cass Henning. I know it's a weird time for you guys right now. I mean, you probably just see me as some crazy drone. But that's not who I really am." She pauses. "I've been here for two months. Everything on the wheel just seems like a dream to me now. Like it didn't actually happen . . ." Her words trail off awkwardly. She crosses her arms, looking a bit nervous. I wonder what the other former drones here would think of her talking to us like this.

"It's okay," I tell her. "My name's Alenna."

"I know. Your mom works here, right?"

I nod. The girl seems relieved that I'm being nice to her.

Cass glances at Liam. He's remained silent this whole time. He spent much longer on the wheel than I did. More than a year. And he lost many more friends at the hands of the drones. I haven't seen him talk to one of them yet.

"Go on," I prod him gently. I can tell that this girl isn't a threat to us. At least not right now.

"I'm Liam," he says, reluctantly shaking her hand.

Cass nods. "Nice to meet you." Then she looks back at me. "You ready for the concert tonight?"

"They're still going to have it?" I ask her. "Even after what just happened? Seriously?"

"Of course. That's how they do things here. They just keep going, no matter what. Pretending everything's normal."

"Like we did on the wheel," Liam says. "We just kept going—no matter how many times your kind destroyed our village."

Cass looks at him. "I'm sorry. For the insane stuff that happened on Island Alpha. But you'll see that things are different here. I'll prove it to you, and so will the other ex-drones. We've detoxed from the UNA drugs, and we know that the Monk was a fake. And the scientists make us ex-drones go through counseling sessions, in addition to the depositions. I'm a totally different person than I was on the wheel."

Liam nods, relenting a little. "Okay."

Cass glances back at me. "I'm a musician too. So I'll be seeing you tonight at the concert."

Before I can respond, I hear a boy's voice calling her name from another tunnel.

I peer down its depths and see the boy, dimly lit by some yellow utility lights hanging along the wall. He's just a shadowy figure, but if he's one of her friends, he's most likely a former drone.

"I'd better get going," Cass says, turning away from us. "Good talking to you."

She heads down the tunnel toward the boy. Liam and I stand there, watching her retreating figure. The boy waits for Cass. When she reaches him, the two of them turn and walk off down another side tunnel together, out of view.

"I never thought I'd shake a drone's hand," Liam says to me, sounding thoughtful. "No matter what they say, I still don't trust them."

I hold up my book. "She brought me this. She can't be all bad."

Liam and I start walking down the tunnel again, heading to the stairs that lead back to our quarters down on level two. Despite Liam's reaction to Cass, I'm comforted by how nice she was. I know that eventually we'll have to put aside our tribalism if we want any chance at reclaiming the wheel and freeing our friends.

"C'mon. Let's go," I say to Liam, taking his hand and leading him forward. "If we're stuck here, we need to make the best of it."

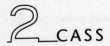

# 2 CASS

LATER THAT AFTERNOON, I'M sitting on my small bunk, strumming a borrowed guitar. Liam and I have been given our own small living quarters—two tiny adjoining rooms with a sliding door that opens between them. We keep the door open most of the time, except when the scientists make us lock it at night.

Liam lies across from me on his bunk, looking at maps and images of the wheel on a portable computer screen. I finger some chords on the frets of my guitar, trying to practice for later tonight. The concert is at seven.

"Sounding good," Liam says, looking up at me and grinning through the doorway.

"It's easy to play when it's just you and me. It'll be different when a whole crowd is watching." I play another chord, but then a knock comes at the front door of my room. "Come in," I call out, instantly muting the strings.

The door swings open. Vargas-Ruiz is standing in the hall just outside. Liam gets up and walks over to the doorway between our rooms.

"You want to see the machine that attacked you?" Vargas-Ruiz asks both of us. "We're disassembling it in one of the mechanical engineering labs on the fifth level. You can come and look at it with me if you want."

I'm already getting to my feet.

"So what is it?" Liam asks Vargas-Ruiz. "Some new model of selection unit?"

"We're not exactly sure. Just come with me."

I put the guitar down gently on my mattress. Then Liam and I follow Vargas-Ruiz out of the room and into the narrow rock tunnel.

"Alenna, you were one of the only people to ever bring down a selection unit," Vargas-Ruiz says, as we start walking down the tunnel. "During your battle on the ice in the gray zone. And both you and Liam encountered miniature ones inside the specimen archive and managed to evade them. That's why I want you to take a look at this one. And tell us if it's anything like the machines on the wheel."

"It was worse," Liam says.

"*Way* worse," I add.

"The feelers on the wheel were designed to capture people," Liam continues. "This one was designed to kill."

Vargas-Ruiz nods. "That's what I feared."

We follow her over to a narrow freight elevator, one that works on a primitive system of pulleys and weights. We step onto it, and she yanks a long, wooden lever. We quickly begin moving upward to level five, as the rickety platform and ropes groan under our weight. The rock walls rush past us until we eventually come to a jolting stop.

Liam and I step out after Vargas-Ruiz. This level looks different from the others. I haven't been up here much before, and I don't think Liam has either. There are more steel beams buttressing the sandstone around us. And the floor is covered with sheets of metal soldered together.

"This way," Vargas-Ruiz says, briskly walking along the tunnel. Her shoes clack on the metal floor.

Eventually, we reach the entrance to a large laboratory. It has glass walls several inches thick, set deep into the sandstone walls. I peer inside, curious. Masked scientists are at work behind the glass, leaning over computers and strange white gurneys. I'm eager to see the remains of the machine.

Vargas-Ruiz hands both of us light-blue surgical masks to wear. "Just in case," she says, before putting a mask over her own face.

"In case of what?" I ask, but she doesn't reply.

Liam and I exchange puzzled glances. Then I put my mask on as Liam does the same. Vargas-Ruiz taps a code into an electronic panel near a slate-gray metal door. The door instantly slides open, and we follow her inside.

The door shuts behind us, locking us in. We're inside a small metal antechamber, facing another door. It's like being in an air lock. I grasp Liam's hand. Vargas-Ruiz taps more buttons on the wall, and the second door opens. We walk right through it and into the lab.

The air here feels different—colder and cleaner. Almost sterile. I glance over and see large metal vents installed into the rock. I can hear the hum of some kind of air purification system.

"We keep the lab climate controlled," Vargas-Ruiz explains, noticing my gaze. "At least when the generators are working."

"So where's the machine that came after us?" Liam asks, his voice muffled by his mask.

Vargas-Ruiz nods. "Over here."

She leads us toward a huge metal table surrounded by a group of twenty scientists. They are wearing masks, white gowns, and green surgical gloves. The remnants of the machine lie on the table in front of them.

The scientists glance our way when they hear us coming. Many of them are holding sharp instruments, including metal shears and titanium scalpels.

"Why are *they* here?" one of them asks Vargas-Ruiz.

"These two kids have more experience dealing with selection units than the rest of you put together," she replies sharply. "Alenna pulled one out of the sky, and Liam was taken by one— and lived. Think of them as elite consultants on UNA technology."

We reach the metal table. I lean in to take a closer look at the thing that tried to kill us. I'm drawn by an uncanny sense of fascination and dread.

The machine is sprawled on the table like a large mechanical octopus. Its central disc looks smaller than it did when it was in the air. Wires, computer chips, and pieces of metal surround it, neatly arranged on white towels. The machine is damaged from the gunshots, missing a few tentacles, and leaking greenish-white hydraulic fluid. Otherwise, it looks surprisingly intact.

I thought it would be completely blown to pieces. I'm confused for a moment, until I see a gloved hand reach out with tweezers and place a charred microchip back inside some kind of internal sensor array.

These scientists are not taking the machine apart.

They're putting it back together.

Reassembling it. Repairing the damage.

"You're fixing it?" I ask. "That's crazy! Why?"

"So we can learn how it works," Vargas-Ruiz says. "If we know how to put it together, then we can figure out the best way to destroy it."

"The guns seemed pretty effective," Liam says.

None of the scientists replies.

I keep looking down at the thing on the metal table. It gives me the creeps. Its blades, now stationary, glint under the bright fluorescent lights hanging overhead.

Then a tentacle twitches.

It's a barely perceptible movement. No one else seems to notice. I tell myself that I must be imagining things.

*But a second later, the tentacle whips sideways.*

I leap back, shocked. The tentacle knocks bits of stray metal off the table with a clatter. Liam is right there, instantly stepping between me and the tentacle to protect me.

"It still has power?" Liam asks the scientists.

"Barely," one of them says from behind his mask. "Nothing to worry about."

"You should have drained its battery," Liam says.

"If it gets loose in the tunnels, it's going to hurt a lot of people!" I add.

"We've been unable to fully power it down," Vargas-Ruiz explains. "It runs on layers of diffracted energy cells, which means there's no central power source to isolate. Each limb has its own energy reserve. It's draining down over time."

"Take a look at its tentacles," another scientist prompts. The masks make everyone hard to differentiate, and vaguely sinister. "Do they look similar to the ones on the selection units?"

Liam and I stare at the machine warily. "I've never seen anything exactly like it," Liam says. "Not even when I explored the gray zone. It's smaller and faster than the selection units, and the blades make it deadlier." He scrutinizes it. "It's not made of metal, right? It's something else."

The scientist nods. "Good eye. A silicone-plastic hybrid. Like a much denser version of the polymer that the cooling barrier is made of back on Island Alpha. Its blades are sharper than diamonds, but they don't show up on radar too easily."

I look over at Vargas-Ruiz. "Why would the UNA build something like this? What's its purpose?"

She peers at us over her glasses. "We don't know yet."

Right then, Liam leans over the table and reaches out a hand.

"Don't—" one of the scientists gasps.

But it's too late. Liam has grabbed one of the loose tentacles. He holds it up to his face, inspecting it. The tentacle bends slightly in his grasp, motors whirring as its blades spin lazily.

"Put that thing down!" I snap at Liam, afraid it's going to cut him.

"I just need to know what we're up against," he says, peering closely at the tentacle. "This machine looks more advanced than the feelers back on the wheel, but it's a similar technology." He holds the tentacle out so we can see. "More wires inside. Looks like an updated model, if I had to guess." The tentacle keeps curling and bending, even though it's severed from its body.

Liam tosses it back down like he's disgusted by it. I can't believe he picked it up like that, without a second thought. One of the things I love about Liam is his fearlessness and his skill as a warrior. But I don't want him to be so reckless. I nudge him hard in the ribs. "Don't do that again," I whisper.

He nods. "Okay. Sorry."

I gaze at the scientists. "Please don't put this machine back together," I implore them. "You're making a huge mistake. On the wheel, whenever one feeler showed up, others followed. This thing could be sending out a distress signal. A thousand more of them could be headed our way."

Liam nods in agreement. "You should destroy it right now."

The scientists ignore us, inscrutable behind their masks. I can tell that no matter what we say or do, they're going to continue their work. I have a sudden urge to just get out of here. To get away from this killing machine. I glance around, looking for my mom. Maybe I can get her to intervene on our behalf. But she's not in the lab.

"We're going to tighten our security," Vargas-Ruiz finally says. "Make sure the hatches are locked. We won't let any machines get inside our tunnels." She steps back from the table and addresses the scientists. "I expect a full briefing on your progress before nineteen hundred hours." Then she turns toward us. "Come with me. It's time to go."

We rapidly follow her through the homemade air lock, out of the lab, and into the tunnel. The gray door slides shut behind us.

"What's going to happen now?" I ask her, pulling off my mask. She and Liam do the same.

"The scientists will run a series of tests on the machine. They'll try to figure out when it was built, and why. The UNA has some of the best scientists in the world at their disposal—many of them working at gunpoint. They also have far more resources than we do. We have to be smarter and stay one step ahead of them."

"More machines are probably headed our way, right?" Liam asks. "Give us the odds."

"Be honest," I add. "We're not afraid to fight."

"It's possible that more are coming," Vargas-Ruiz admits. "But they might be the least of our problems. If the UNA launches an assault on Destiny Station, they could use weapons far worse than this one. They could even use a contained nuclear device, although they know that Australia would retaliate." She pauses. "Of course, any attack, even a minor one, could interfere with our plan to leave on schedule and reach Island Alpha."

"What can we do to help?" Liam asks her.

"Right now, just go about your regular activities. We've only survived here by sticking to our routines, no matter what gets thrown our way." She sighs. "Look, I have to go now, but I'll come and get you later if there's any news." She turns and begins walking away from us, in her typically abrupt fashion. Then she calls out behind her: "Alenna, I know your mom is looking forward to seeing you play in the concert tonight. . . ."

"I can't think about music right now!" I say.

I feel a hand on my arm. It's Liam. "It's okay," he says. "I want to hear you play too." He brushes back my hair with his fingers, trying to calm me down. "Vargas-Ruiz is right. We're safe for now. Let's enjoy it while it lasts."

I take his hand and hold it tightly. I'm not sure if he actually feels this way, or if he's just trying to make me feel better. "I guess you're right."

He squeezes my hand back. "Aren't I always?" he asks, kidding around.

I glance back at him. "No."

We start walking down the tunnel again toward the elevator. Vargas-Ruiz has disappeared already, so now it's just the two of us.

The noises of the station are all around me, and I can smell food grilling somewhere, wafting up from another level. But this long tunnel is mostly deserted. Only occasionally does someone cross our path, and it's usually one of the scientists.

We're almost at the rickety elevator, when three large figures step out from a cross tunnel.

They stand there, twenty feet away, blocking our path. Three stocky boys about Liam's age. Refugees from the wheel, like us. They're wearing jeans, old black T-shirts, and combat boots. All of them have shaved heads.

"Drones," Liam whispers to me, slowing his pace. I slow down too.

"Hey there," one of the boys calls out gruffly. His words echo down the tunnel. "Liam and Alenna, right?"

Liam nods. "Who wants to know?"

"I do. We need to talk to you guys."

"About what?" I ask.

We walk closer, on guard. We stop five paces away from them. I've never seen these boys before. But it's clear they were waiting here for us to show up. I see old homemade tattoos on their arms. One of them has the remnants of multiple facial piercings around his lips and nose. Another has a black patch over his right eye.

"If you don't let us past, there's gonna be trouble," Liam says to them calmly. I sense his muscles tensing. My heart starts racing faster. My mind flashes back to the many battles on the wheel, and to my training with Gadya. I feel my hands start balling into fists.

The drones don't respond to Liam's words. They just keep staring at us. Liam stares back, completely fearless. I almost get the feeling he wants to fight them. I glance behind us, fearing an ambush. But the tunnel is empty. We could walk away right now—but I know that we'd just be postponing an inevitable confrontation.

I look back at the silent, menacing drones. "Tell us what you want, or leave us alone," I say finally. My voice is loud and strong in the tunnel.

I'm just about to speak again, when another figure emerges behind the boys, smoothly sliding her way between them. It's a girl. The boys move aside rapidly to let her pass. She stands there in front of them, in the glare of the utility lights hanging on the wall.

"Cass!" I say when I see her, feeling relieved. She's already changed her outfit, no doubt in preparation for the concert later tonight. She's wearing a black dress, heels, and a thin silver necklace. Silver bracelets cover the scars on her wrists.

"I've been looking for you two," she says, running a hand through her short hair. I see that her fingernails are now painted black. Then she notices how fiercely Liam and the boys are staring one another down. "Wait, is there a problem here?"

"Not unless your friends start one," Liam says.

Cass glances back at the boys. "Jeez, relax. Okay?" she tells them.

"What's going on?" I ask her warily. "Why are you here on this level? Have you been following us?"

"Kind of," Cass admits.

"Why?" Liam asks her.

"Listen, after the concert tonight, we're going to hold a meeting. Just some of us kids. It's a chance to talk. You could use some friends." She pauses and then lowers her voice. "We're planning on sneaking out of the station for a few hours, to a secret meeting place that we know about in the dunes."

"Outside the station?" I ask. "Really?"

"Yes."

"I knew it," Liam mutters. "Once a drone, always a drone. Let me guess—you want to sneak out so you can get wasted and set stuff on fire? Or maybe even try to attack me and Alenna?"

"It's not like that," Cass protests. "We just like to go outside at night for fresh air, and we can't get access to the roof deck after today's attack. Dr. Elliott sealed the hatch." She adjusts her necklace. "After the concert, the scientists will be preoccupied with getting back to work. It's an opportunity for us to speak in private, where no one can overhear us. Sound travels through these tunnels and air vents like you wouldn't believe."

I look at the three boys standing behind her. They're staring at us with intense, brooding eyes.

"Count us out," Liam finally says, starting to walk forward again.

I'm right at his side. The last thing I want to do is sneak outside Destiny Station and risk death. *According to my mom, going outside at night was exactly how my father got killed several years ago.* The station provides us with some degree of protection, even if it's not perfect. Going outside for no reason seems foolish. It would be easy to get spotted by UNA technology. I'm sure they're watching the station somehow.

Cass steps forward, blocking us. "Listen," she says. "You have friends stuck back on the wheel, and so do we. Forget about the drama that went down between our tribes. We have to work together now, while we still can."

"What do you mean?" I ask, pausing for a moment.

She fixes me with her brown eyes. They don't look so gentle now. They look resolute. "Vargas-Ruiz and the other scientists don't really care about us," she whispers. "Sure, they care about bringing down the UNA. And so do we. But they're moving way too slowly. By the time we get back to the wheel, it's going to be too late. You saw the thing that attacked us today. More will come—both to the wheel and to this place as well. Destiny Station's days are numbered."

"What can we do about it?" I ask.

"That's what I want to talk to you about tonight," Cass continues, glancing back at the boys. "We're working on our own plan, in case things go wrong here. One that will ensure that our friends and yours get rescued from the specimen archive. We know what you two managed to do on the wheel, and we respect it." She gestures at the boys behind her. "They do too, even if they won't admit it. We want you on our side."

"I'll never be on the same side as you," Liam says. "How many villagers did your friends kill on the wheel?"

"How many of my friends did *you* kill?" she snaps back. "How we acted wasn't completely our fault. We just responded differently to the UNA drugs than you did." The boys behind her start shifting their weight, like they're about to move forward.

Liam tenses up. I can tell he's getting ready to fight again.

"We'll think about it," I say quickly, taking hold of Liam's hand. My mind is racing. I don't want to turn down an opportunity to talk about rescuing our friends. Even if it involves working with drones. Or sneaking outside.

Cass nods. She motions for the boys behind her to back down. "If you decide you want to meet, then follow me after the concert tonight." She pauses. "There's a secret set of underground tunnels. They open into a nearby cave in the dunes. The scientists don't know that we use it to meet. I'll take you both there."

"Sounds like a good place to get ambushed," Liam says.

"Actually, there'll be some villagers there too. You'll see. If you're willing to take the chance." She glances at me. "And I might even have some information about your friend David Aberley."

I can't hide my shocked expression. "David? How do you know about him?"

Cass gives me an enigmatic smile. "Meet us tonight if you want to find out. We really need your help—or we wouldn't be asking." She pivots on one heel, turning back to the boys. With a final glare, the boys turn around too. The group slowly starts walking away.

I look over at Liam. "I assume we're going to meet them tonight?" I ask softly. "Given what they seem to know."

He nods reluctantly. "They could have a trap waiting. We'll need to come prepared." He's staring after them. "But I hope they're telling the truth. If they're not, I'll make sure they pay for everything that happened to us back on the wheel."

"Same here." But I'm also thinking that if they're telling the truth, then we're in more trouble than I thought. They've been at Destiny Station longer than we have. And if they don't believe that the scientists are going to liberate the wheel in time, then they might have good reason to think so. I need to talk to my mom and see if I can get some answers. Cass doesn't seem crazy or brainwashed to me. And she knows about David somehow.

"I want to hear these kids out," I tell Liam. "But I'm ready to fight if things go haywire. We should bring some knives."

Liam suddenly smiles at my words, like he can't help it. "That sounds like something I would say. We can grab a couple from the kitchen." His smile fades. "I'm sure the drones will have weapons too."

We start walking to the elevator again. I don't have long before the concert, until I'm on stage in front of everyone with my guitar. *And music is the very last thing I'm thinking about.*

Instead, I'm thinking about David. On the wheel, after he was taken by a feeler, he just vanished. There was no sign of him on any computer system when we reached the observation deck at the specimen archive. It was like he'd completely fallen off the grid. If Cass has any answers about his disappearance, I need to hear them. Not a day goes by that I don't think about him.

I exhale slowly, realizing that I've been holding my breath. Between the machine attacking us today and the ex-drones, I'm starting to realize that the politics of Destiny Station might be just as complicated as those on the wheel—and staying here might prove just as deadly.

# 3 DESCENT

AN HOUR LATER, I still can't stop thinking about our encounter with Cass and her friends. I know that I'm going to have to clear my mind for a while, or the concert is going to be a disaster. It's only half an hour away, and I've just finished getting dressed. I walk across my living quarters, my bare feet padding on the cold rock floor.

I tap on the sliding door between my room and Liam's. "I'm ready," I say. "C'mon."

Liam slides the door open.

"Wow," he says, hesitating for a moment when he sees me.

"What? Is something wrong?"

He doesn't move. "You look beautiful."

I feel myself starting to blush. "Cut it out. I do not. Get over here and zip me up."

He steps into my room and slides the door shut. He walks up behind me. Then I feel his strong hands brush against my back as he slowly zips up my dress. It's one that my mother gave me the first week I arrived here, when she was helping me gather some clothing. I don't know where or how she found something so luxurious. Maybe someone here made it. Or maybe it was donated years ago by the Australian government.

I adjust myself in the dress, trying to get comfortable. It feels too tight in the wrong places. "I look terrible," I mutter. I push back my hair, trying to flatten it. Shampoo is limited here, like so many other things. "I'm a mess."

Liam gently takes my elbow and steers me over to a small circular mirror hanging on one of the rock walls. "Look," he says softly.

I gaze into the mirror and lower my hands.

The girl staring back at me doesn't look like one I've known very much. Not in the UNA, and definitely not on the wheel. The girl in the mirror has surprisingly decent hair, and is wearing a knee-length, flowing blue dress with a beaded neckline. The girl almost looks glamorous. *Almost.*

"Okay, I'm officially embarrassed," I mumble, glancing away.

Liam pulls me toward him. "Don't be. You look fantastic."

"You better not expect me to always look this good," I tell him. "It's not like I'm Meira or something." I can't help but think of her right now. Meira was the only girl in our village on the wheel who always looked good—with spotless clothes, perfect skin, and sleek blond hair.

"You're way better-looking than Meira." Liam gazes into my eyes. "To me, you always look great."

I lean up and kiss him. Softly at first, my lips pressing gently against his. He kisses me back, hungrily. I pull him closer to me, feeling the muscles under his shirt. I also feel his hands moving up and down my body, caressing me.

But then I tear myself away from him, worried. I can't lose track of time now.

"What is it?" he asks, looking bemused.

"I'm nervous. I've never played in public before, and some of these other kids have. I really don't want to screw up."

"There's no chance of that happening, believe me." Liam looks around, like he has just remembered something important. "Wait— Do I need to get dressed up too? Is this like some fancy dress thing?"

I laugh. "No, you're fine. Unless you want to join me onstage. Only the performers get dressed up."

He looks relieved. "Good. I don't have any clothes except jeans and T-shirts."

"You think I don't know that?" I tease him. "Besides, that's your choice. They've got plenty of decent old clothes here in the stockroom. Or one of the scientists could loan you something." Then I glance at the clock on the wooden bedside table. "It's six forty. We better get going."

My mouth is starting to go dry. And not just because of the concert. I'm nervous about what's going to happen afterward— when we meet up with Cass. Liam managed to sneak two sharp knives from the kitchen, and he's hidden them both in a homemade ankle sheath.

I pick up my guitar from the bed with one hand, wishing I had a case for it. But there isn't one. I just feel lucky that there are any instruments here at all.

Liam holds out his hand and I take it.

"Come this way," he says.

He leads me out of the room and into the rock tunnel. The tunnels are more crowded than before, with a mix of kids and adults. A lot of people are heading for the cavernous underground space where the concert will be held. It's the size of an auditorium. The scientists often use it for meetings and presentations, but tonight it will be our theater.

"Look," Liam says, noticing someone up ahead in the tunnel. "It's her."

I follow his gaze and see Cass. She's walking side by side with another girl. One with long, dirty-blond hair, wearing a yellow dress. Possibly a former villager. There's no sign of the three menacing boys that accompanied Cass earlier.

"Let me go talk to her," I tell Liam quickly, sensing an opportunity. "I'll see if I can find out more about their plan for tonight."

"I'll come with you."

"No, stay. Cass might be more open if it's just us girls."

Liam nods. "Okay. But be careful, because I definitely don't trust her yet. Just look for me in the audience." He shoots me a grin. "Front row, of course."

I smile back and give him a quick kiss. Then I move forward, negotiating the rock tunnel with my bulky guitar. "Cass!" I call out, trying to catch up to her. "Wait for me!"

She turns around when she finally hears my voice, and she pauses for a second with her friend. "So, have you decided?" she whispers when I reach her. "Are you and Liam coming tonight?"

I nod. "Yeah. Why not?"

Her friend glances my way, pushing blond hair away from her oval face. She has friendly green eyes, and she's wearing tortoise-shell glasses. "I'm Emma Sivertson," she says with a shy wave. "From a village in the blue sector, just north of you."

As we start walking again, I introduce myself. But it turns out she already knows my name from Cass. We head toward a flight of narrow stairs, chiseled into the rocks, leading down to the lowest level.

"I'm glad you and Liam are going to hang out with us tonight," Emma murmurs.

"So you and Cass are friends?" I ask her, unable to suppress my curiosity.

Cass laughs slightly. "Yeah. Imagine that. A drone and a villager. Shocking, I know."

"Things are really different here than on the wheel," Emma adds. "Honest."

"I hope that's true," I tell her.

We start descending the staircase. I hold my guitar close to my chest so that it doesn't bang against the rock walls and get damaged. I glance back, trying to catch a glimpse of Liam. But he's gone from view in the crowd.

I notice that Emma is gripping a small wooden case with one hand. She sees me looking at it. "Flute," she says. She gestures at Cass. "Cassie's a singer. Doesn't need anything but a microphone."

"And an audience," Cass adds.

"Yeah, that helps," Emma replies.

I can sense the closeness between these two girls, despite their different backgrounds on the wheel. Their friendship makes me optimistic. It also makes me miss Gadya more than ever. I wish that she were here with me and Liam right now. She didn't deserve to get stranded on the wheel. Not after everything she did to help us.

We enter a wider hallway, with a mob of kids and adults surging around us. Up ahead, I see the entrance to the large auditorium. Everyone is heading inside. I want to ask Cass more questions about our upcoming meeting tonight, but there are just too many people around. So I stay silent.

I walk through the open metal doors with the rest of the crowd, side by side with Cass and Emma. The space beyond the doors is large and warm. According to Vargas-Ruiz, it's a natural cavern that the scientists discovered years ago under a section of the mesa, when they were digging their tunnels.

The chamber is about forty feet deep and sixty feet wide. Lights have been hung in clusters above us in the ceiling, like primitive chandeliers. And benches have been cut into the rock to provide seats. At the other end of the cave is a raised wooden platform. It's painted black and resembles a stage.

I glance up and see that beyond the lights, huge metal rafters support the ceiling. The walls are also buttressed by riveted steel beams, much like the ones I saw on level five. It looks safe here. I get the feeling that this cave could be used as a bunker against assaults or bombing raids.

I walk down one of the aisles alongside Cass and Emma. An older man is guiding all of us performers to an area behind the stage.

"They're trying to make us feel like we're regular kids again," Cass mutters. "But we've been on the wheel. We've seen what life is really about."

I know exactly what Cass means. It's uncomfortable to act normal again, like I'm putting on a fake personality.

"I really don't want to be here right now," Cass continues, sounding frustrated. "It's a waste of time."

"Didn't you sign up for this?" I ask.

Cass laughs. "Yeah, but I'm regretting it right about now."

Emma just looks at me. "Don't be fooled by her bad attitude, Alenna. Cass loves singing. But she loves grumbling and complaining about stuff even more."

Cass snorts, but she doesn't contradict Emma.

The three of us keep walking down the aisle until we reach the steps leading to the backstage area. "This way, girls," the older man says, guiding us up the stairs toward the room.

It's another natural cave—one that's much smaller than the auditorium. A black curtain has been pulled partway in front of the opening to give us some privacy. I wonder if these caves are connected to the tunnel that Cass mentioned. *The one that provides a secret passage out of Destiny Station.* The scientists must know that the tunnel exists. They probably just don't think anyone would be reckless enough to use it.

As I step into the smaller cave, I look back. I catch a glimpse of Liam. He's entered the auditorium, and is striding up to the front. Probably headed for the front row, just like he said. I wave at him, but he doesn't see me. He looks preoccupied about something. Maybe even worried.

Then I'm swept along backstage, and I lose sight of him. Maybe he's thinking about our meeting tonight. Or maybe he's thinking about his father, Octavio.

Octavio was once a famous rebel leader, but he got kidnapped by UNA soldiers and disappeared. According to Vargas-Ruiz, there's a chance he escaped and might be alive—living in another secret rebel base in the Highveld of South Africa. But no one has confirmed that to us yet. Communications between the rebel bases are sporadic and heavily encrypted, so that they don't get intercepted by the UNA, or another government. The entire world remains at war, mainly due to the UNA's ravenous desire to conquer the globe. Liam has been waiting for any news about his dad the whole time we've been at Destiny Station.

I realize then that I don't see any sign of my mom. She said she was coming tonight, but I also know that time becomes meaningless to her when she's working. Just like it did when I was ten years old. Still, I hold out hope that she'll make it. I want her to be proud of me. And I want to feel like I have a mother again.

I take a seat backstage on a small bench. Cass and Emma settle on either side of me. Handwoven tapestries line the walls to keep this cave warm.

"How are you feeling?" Cass asks me. "Got the jitters yet?"

"I've had them for a while," I admit. "You?"

"Sure. This is only my third time onstage. Ever." Then she leans in closer, her voice going to a whisper. "Don't forget about our plan, okay? I mean, if you and Liam are really coming."

"How could I forget?" I ask. Then I pause. "Are you sure you know something about David? Like, what happened to him? Or where he is?"

She nods. "Not everything. But something. You'll see tonight in the caves."

"Can't you tell me now?"

"No, because then maybe you and Liam won't show up."

Emma hushes us both. "Keep it down, Cass. The walls have ears." She opens her carrying case and takes out her flute.

Cass and I exchange a final glance. Then I start tuning my guitar, getting ready for my big debut.

Twenty minutes later, I find myself walking onstage with my guitar and guitar pick, my heart caught in my throat. The order of performers has been chosen randomly, by picking numbers out of a ceramic bowl. I'm the second person to go on. I was hoping I'd be closer to the end.

The audience applauds as I reach the center of the stage, where a wooden stool awaits me, sitting in front of a microphone. I peer out and see Liam. He gives me a thumbs-up. I can't help but smile back at him.

It's hard to see much beyond Liam. Two work lights have been propped up on either side of the stage like spotlights, to illuminate the performers. But they're blinding. From what I can tell, the auditorium is about two thirds of the way full.

I keep gazing beyond the lights as best I can, scanning the benches for my mom. There's no sign of her. *Typical,* I think.

But then I see the door at the back of the auditorium slide open, and a figure steps through the opening. I can tell right away that it's her. I watch her take a seat as the door closes behind her. I'm relieved and grateful that she's here. But now I'm even more nervous.

I sit down on the stool and bring the microphone forward, up to my lips. There's a brief snarl of feedback over the PA system. It dies down almost immediately.

"Hey there," I say tentatively into the microphone. My voice booms out into the echoey space. "I'm Alenna Shawcross. I'm new here. . . . And this is the very first time I've ever played for a crowd." I'm not sure what else to say.

The audience claps again. I lock eyes with Liam. I'm amazed that I'm so nervous. *How can it feel harder to play music to a crowd than face down death on the wheel?* I swallow hard, telling myself that it's incredibly stupid to feel like this when so many serious things are going on in the outside world.

I glance back into the smaller cave where the other kids are waiting to go on. The curtain is pulled back a few feet so that they can watch the show. I see Cass inside, smiling encouragingly. I still can't tell if she's going to turn out to be an ally or an enemy.

I bring the microphone forward again, even closer to my mouth. "Okay, here we go," I murmur, as my fingertips find their places on the frets. I stare at Liam again.

My thoughts are tumbling into a nervous swirl. *Maybe I shouldn't be up here. Maybe I'm not good enough.* I try to calm myself by taking slower breaths.

I decide to just focus on Liam when I play, and pretend that the crowd isn't there. That way, it will feel a lot easier. I know that Liam is on my side, no matter what. I sit back a bit on the stool and bring the guitar pick up to the strings.

"This song is called 'Reynardine,'" I say, my words ringing out in the silence. "It's an old Celtic folk song about a fox, written a long time before the UNA got formed. I learned it from my dad when I was a little girl. I'm going to play it now as an instrumental, in his memory."

I lower the microphone on its stand, adjusting it so it will pick up the sound of my guitar. Then I shut my eyes and strike the first haunting chord, the noise echoing loudly against the rocks of the cave, amplified by the microphone. My nervousness starts to melt away the instant I begin playing and the music overwhelms me.

The song is second nature to me. I remember practicing it with my dad, when I was only ten. It's like no time has passed at all since then.

I open my eyes, looking only at Liam over the work lights. I'm conscious of the other people watching me, but except for Liam and my mom, no one else really matters. It feels like I'm playing this song just for them. *And for my dad as well.*

I'm in the middle of the first chorus, and I haven't screwed up yet, when something strange begins to happen. I feel a slight vibration underneath my feet. It's faint at first, but slowly intensifies. I try to ignore it, thinking that it's just the scientists working on something in one of their labs.

No one in the audience seems to notice it. I keep playing,

putting the sensation out of my mind and focusing on the song. But I can feel the vibration getting even stronger.

I'm not sure what to do. I see a few heads in the audience turning around, like some of them are starting to feel the vibration too.

Then, above Liam, one of the chandeliers in the ceiling begins swaying slightly. I've never seen or felt anything like this in the weeks I've been at Destiny Station.

At the same instant, my microphone cuts off. Wailing sirens slice through the air. The floor is shaking more now, much worse than before. I stop playing and stand up. The audience starts standing up too.

I hear a deep creaking, groaning noise, and then a harsh splintering sound. In horror, I watch a large crack appear across the rock wall to my left. Then another fissure appears, bursting across the opposite wall of the cavern, lightning-fast. People start yelling out to one another.

Movement catches my eye. Faster than I thought possible, Liam has scrambled up onstage, rushing to my side. Everything is sliding into pandemonium, as debris begins raining down on us from the ceiling.

"You okay?" Liam yells over the noise.

"Yeah, but what's going on?" I clutch on to him with one hand, and grip my guitar with the other.

As if in response to my question, the lights flicker and then dim.

Then everything goes totally dark, plunging the cavern into blackness. People call out instructions to one another.

A few battery-powered emergency lights near the exits snap on, bathing everything in a spooky red glow. The noise of the

crowd gets louder. People are trying to guide everyone t[o]
exits at the back of the cave.

"We need to get out of here right now," Liam says. We start
heading down the steps off the stage.

Suddenly, a figure dashes out of the darkness, making me
jump. It's Cass. She tugs at my arm, trying to pull me sideways.

"What are you doing?" I ask.

"This way!" she says. Behind her, I see other dark figures waiting at the side of the stage. Other former drones, and Emma too.
"Staying in here isn't safe," Cass continues, yanking off her heels
and tossing them off the stage. "Trust me! If the station's being
attacked, then you're safer coming with us." I realize then that
they're heading for the secret cave.

More bits of rock rain down. There's an explosive noise as a
chunk of sandstone breaks loose and crashes down in the center
of the cavern, decimating some of the empty rock benches. The
air is already thick with dust. With the power out, there's no air
circulation, as well as almost no light. More rocks come tumbling
loose. It looks too dangerous to run through the cave now. Our
best option might be to follow Cass after all.

Liam has seen the falling rocks too. "Let's go!"

"Stay close behind me," Cass says to both of us. "Don't get lost.
I move fast!"

"So do we!" I retort.

Cass races across the stage toward the smaller cave, with both
of us in tow. Ahead of her, I already see her friends moving quickly
through the dim light. We barrel into the small cave. The metal
beams creak wildly behind us. I hope they can bear the weight of
whatever's happening, or else this entire cavern is going to collapse.

I look up ahead. Cass is headed for a narrow opening in the side of the cave wall. I'm startled that I didn't notice it before. It must have been hidden by a hanging tapestry.

I realize then that I'm going to have to let go of my guitar. I can't take it into this narrow tunnel with me. I pause for a millisecond, setting it down on a wooden table with a pang of regret. And then I'm running again with Liam, right into the darkness of the hidden tunnel.

"It gets pretty tight!" Cass yells back at us, from up ahead. The earth feels like it's shaking around us now. I'm worried about my mom. *Did she make it out in time?*

"You first," Liam says into my ear, letting me slip past him. "I'll be right behind you. You'll be safest in the middle."

I keep moving, sheer momentum driving me forward. It's almost pitch black in here. I can barely catch a glimpse of Cass in front of me. I struggle to keep up. Liam is just a step behind me.

The narrow tunnel takes a sharp turn—but I don't see it in time. I slam against the rocks, scraping my arm. I cry out in surprise, but I keep moving. So does everyone else. Behind us, I can hear increasingly loud noises that sound as though more of the rock ceiling is collapsing into the main cavern.

"Hurry!" Cass yells.

We keep following her, plowing forward in the darkness. The tunnel seems to go on for forever. It continues to twist and turn, and I keep banging my elbows and knees. And then it starts to get even narrower.

After the machine attack on the roof deck, I knew it was likely that something else bad would happen to Destiny Station. I just didn't think it would come so soon, or be so drastic. I keep running.

"Careful up ahead!" Cass's voice calls out.

And right then, I slam my head hard into a low piece of rock. I stop for a second, stunned. Liam stops too, right behind me. White stars flash and sparkle across my vision. I blink my eyes, reaching up a hand to touch my head.

"What's wrong?" Liam asks. "You okay?"

"Yeah," I tell him, probing my forehead. I can already feel a hard lump forming. But I shake it off, and we start moving forward again.

"C'mon!" Cass calls back to us impatiently. Her voice sounds fainter, like she's farther up ahead now.

"Maybe we shouldn't have gone with them," I say to Liam. "These tunnels are like a labyrinth."

"If there's trouble, we can always head back and take our chances in the station. Or if we actually get outside, we can run and hide in the dunes together."

"Okay." Ignoring my throbbing head, I move even faster. The roof of the tunnel is lower here, but it's finally starting to widen at the sides. Of course, there's no sign of Cass anymore. Or of anyone else.

Then our tunnel starts moving upward. I feel like we're running up a sharp incline, and the air is getting thinner and cleaner.

"Cass?" I call out.

"Alenna!" a voice drifts back to me, sounding frustrated. "What's taking you guys so long?"

A moment later, Liam and I burst out of the tunnel and into another cave. Both of us are panting for air.

This cave is partway open to the outdoors. The front half has collapsed into a pile of rock and sand, obviously a long time ago. It now resembles the shell of an amphitheater.

From here, I can see the gentle curve of sand dunes under the stars and moonlight, and beyond them, Destiny Station itself, about a quarter of a mile away.

Scattered around this cave are flickering torches, casting a yellow glow. There are also some maps and other documents spread out on low rocks, presumably in preparation for our meeting.

Kids stand there inside the mouth of the cave, staring out at Destiny Station. Their backs are to us as they watch the besieged mesa. Most of them don't even notice our arrival, except for Cass. She's waiting for us.

"You made it," she says. "And I thought you said you were fast!"

"You know these tunnels. We don't," I tell her.

I stare past Cass at Destiny Station. I see flames blazing out a few of the lower air shafts. *What is happening to it?* I think of my mom again, and my heart seizes up.

"What's causing the fires?" I ask Cass. "Why did everything start shaking?"

"We don't know."

She leads us over to the group of other kids. There's at least twenty of them here in the cave. Other than Cass and Emma, and the three glowering boys with shaved heads, they are strangers. Ex-drones. Liam and I stand there with them, watching the station. It appears to still be shaking, like it's at the epicenter of some strange localized earthquake.

Under the moonlight, I see people streaming out of the large opening at the base of the station. Running for safety. But I don't see any sign of machines or bombs—or of anything attacking the base at all.

"Maybe this is some kind of accident," I say. "Maybe something went wrong in one of the labs? Maybe they fixed that machine and it got loose."

Emma turns to me, pushing her glasses up her nose. "The scientists have way too many safety protocols."

"Then, what?" Liam asks.

"Some kind of weapon," another voice says. "The UNA is behind this. They have to be." The voice belongs to one of the three boys who blocked our path in the tunnel earlier. The one with the eye patch.

"I'm not sure it's the UNA this time," another boy pipes up. "Could be the Aussies. Could be they finally want us off their land." Heated voices start talking over him.

Liam and I stand there as the kids around us begin to argue. I still can't take my eyes off the fires burning inside Destiny Station. *How much of the station is going to be engulfed before the flames get put out?*

"Quiet!" Cass yells at the crowd. "I feel like I'm back on the wheel!" She pauses, as her friends stop yelling. "It's obviously the UNA, just like I was afraid of. It must be some new kind of weapon that we don't know about yet. Could be subsonic or electromagnetic, beamed down from a satellite."

"Or someone could have sabotaged the station from within," Liam says in the ensuing silence. "That's another possibility."

"No one would do that," Emma says.

Liam gazes around at the crowd. "No villager would do it."

"None of us would either," Cass says. "This place is our home too."

A sudden explosion makes everyone startle. I watch as a fireball bursts out of one of the upper vents on the fifth level, blasting the metal grate into the air. More people stream out below. Destiny Station is being completely evacuated.

51

"We need to go and help them," I say, stepping forward. "We can't just sit here and do nothing while people get hurt!"

"It's too dangerous," another boy says. "It's better if—"

"We don't have a choice," Liam interrupts him. "The scientists will be looking for all of us. If they can't find us, they might think we're trapped inside the station."

"We'll tell everyone where you are," I add. "In case they want to know."

Together, Liam and I start walking out of the cave opening, stepping over fallen rocks.

Cass moves forward and holds out an arm to stop me. "Alenna, wait—"

I brush past her, my eyes fixed on the ever-growing crowd of scientists and kids fleeing the burning station. My mom is in there somewhere. I need to find her.

Liam and I make it out of the cave entrance and onto the sand.

*And that's when it happens.*

An object plummets down from the sky, dive-bombing straight into the crowd in front of Destiny Station. At first I think it's a giant chunk of sandstone, shaken loose by the explosions. But then the screaming starts, and I realize that it's something far deadlier.

Another object zooms down after it. Followed by another. And another one after that—like a whole buzzing swarm descending at once.

They're killing machines. Just like the one Liam and I battled on top of the rock.

"No!" shocked voices yell behind us.

"The machines were waiting until everyone was out of the station," I say to Liam. "Waiting to massacre them!" I feel like I'm going to throw up.

Liam and I start moving forward again even faster, still ready to fight, no matter the odds. But then even more machines burst down from the sky, plowing into the crowd.

I start hearing gunshots, as guards fire back at them, trying to blast them out of the sky. A machine gets hit and explodes in a flare of white light. A piece of it crashes down into a nearby dune, kicking up a massive spray of red sand.

Liam pauses for a moment, and so do I, blinking sand from our eyes.

"There's nothing we can do," Cass's voice calls out behind us. "At least not right now . . ."

I keep watching the machines in horror, barely listening to her words.

"Look!" Liam says, pointing out at the dunes.

A small group of figures are racing away from Destiny Station. They're running across the sand straight toward us, like they know exactly where we are. They're clearly scientists from the station. Some of them are waving at us urgently.

I move forward again to help them, heading rapidly in their direction with Liam as more machines blaze paths of destruction down from the night sky.

# 4 ESCAPE

WE GET CLOSER TO the figures in the sand. I can't see their faces yet. But then a voice cries out, "Alenna, is that you?"

"Mom!" I yell back, my heart surging with relief as I recognize her voice. I rush forward with Liam. I finally reach my mother and we hug.

"Thank god you're all right," she says. Her face is pale and worried in the moonlight. Her dark hair, streaked with gray, is dusty with bits of sandstone. Her eyes—which look so much like mine—are wide and frightened. We hug again. She feels fragile.

Five other scientists are with her, including Dr. Elliott. Two of them are carrying shotguns. I hear more gunshots as the scientists at the station continue to fight the machines, and try to survive this terrible night.

I glance behind me. Cass and the other kids are just watching us from the cave entrance. They don't come to our aid. They just stand there—like they're unwilling to risk their own lives. I can't believe they're not helping us.

My mom looks at me. "It's not safe at Destiny Station anymore. We have to leave right now. I came to get you, and Liam too."

"How did you know where we were?"

"You think that we'd rescue you from Island Alpha but not keep an eye on you once you got here? Cass and her crew don't think we know about this cave, but we've always known they meet here. We've got hidden cameras mounted in the ceiling."

"Hurry," Dr. Elliott says. "To the cave." We follow his lead, racing back toward the cavern opening.

"What's happening?" I ask my mom as we scramble over the low dunes. "How are we going to rebuild from this?"

"We can't." My mom glances at me and Liam. "But we have an escape route. We've always had one, in case something like this happened. You kids didn't know about it for your own safety."

"You mean you didn't trust us," I say.

"We trust some of you, just not others," my mom replies.

When we reach the opening of the cave where Cass and her friends are waiting, we rush inside, seeking shelter. The sound of the machines attacking the station continues.

Everyone is talking and asking questions. Cass looks pretty surprised to see the scientists here. Voices echo off the walls, mixing with the distant sounds of gunshots.

"So what's the plan? What do we do?" Liam asks the scientists, his voice cutting through the noise.

My mom turns to him. Dr. Elliott gestures sharply for the rest of the crowd to be silent. "Underneath these natural tunnels is a man-made one," my mom explains. "We built it three years ago. It stretches from here to an underground lake, which leads directly into the ocean."

"How's that going to help us?" Cass asks. "I don't—"

Another loud explosion in the station startles us all. The impact shakes my bones, even from this distance. Small pieces of rock and grit fall from the ceiling of our cave. Everyone looks up nervously.

Someone starts crying. It's a girl I don't know. A former drone with red tattoos on her face, and teeth filed into sharp points. She's huddled in the corner. Emma moves over to console her.

"So many people are dying!" the girl sobs. "It's not fair!"

Liam starts pacing back and forth. "We should be fighting. Doing something!" I feel the same way.

More explosions fill the air. I try to block out the tragedy of what's going on at Destiny Station. Bleak thoughts rush through my mind. *Maybe after they've killed everyone at the station, they'll come after us next.*

"We have to go now," Dr. Elliott says. "I'll lead the way into the escape tunnel."

Outside, I continue to hear screams and see flashes of gunfire. I also see the endless shadows of machines shrieking down from the sky to claim fresh victims.

Dr. Elliott quickly extracts a remote control device from his pocket and presses some buttons. Immediately, with a creaking groan, part of the rock wall behind us starts opening up on hinges, revealing a circular metal portal. Cass and her friends look stunned.

"Unbelievable," Cass mutters.

My mom rushes over to the side of the portal and types a code into a computer panel. There's a loud click as the metal portal unlatches itself. It automatically opens outward, revealing a wide, man-made tunnel hidden behind it. We cluster around the opening. The two scientists with guns are guarding the cave, in case any machines head our way. Liam takes hold of my hand.

"The people who got trapped at the station are the unlucky

ones, but many of them will survive," my mom says, glancing back at us and seeing our concern. "All the scientists here know about this escape tunnel. Many of them will find their way to it. Some of them probably already have. There are other hatches besides this one."

"Why did you hide this from us?" Cass asks, sounding indignant.

"You would have tried to use it if you knew it was here." My mom pauses, scanning the crowd of kids. "I know how desperate you are to get back to Island Alpha. We couldn't let you know."

"You should have told us," another voice calls out.

"What does it matter now?" I yell back. "Stop arguing and listen!" The crowd falls silent again.

"We don't have long," Dr. Elliott says. "The machines will find us soon. We better start moving." He ducks his head and steps through the portal into the tunnel beyond.

Moments later, all of us are inside the dark tunnel. Liam and I are still holding hands. I don't want to get separated from him if anything goes wrong.

Dr. Elliott quickly swings the hatch shut behind us and locks it. He taps a button on the remote, and a grinding noise starts up. It's the false rock wall descending again, cloaking the hatch. The sounds from outside are muffled now. Just quiet thuds.

My mom moves over to a panel on the wall and taps more keys. Lights snap on around us, lining the bottom of both sides of the walkway. They have the dim, green glow of emergency beacons.

I'm startled by what the lights reveal. Rather than another rough-hewn rock tunnel, natural or otherwise, this one is gleaming, with shiny metal walls. The floor is smooth and metallic too.

The tunnel extends into the distance. The green lights stretch off as far as I can see.

"This tunnel was one of the projects that your father helped oversee," my mom says softly to me. "This is what he was working on in the dunes, before he lost his life."

I nod, trying to fight back my emotions. I bet my dad never could have predicted that this tunnel would one day save my life.

Liam cocks his head to one side, like he's listening for something. Then I hear the noise too. It's the faint sound of panicked voices ahead of us, farther along in the tunnel.

"Good," Dr. Elliott says. "Others have made it." He starts moving forward, about to stride down the long metal hall.

"Wait!" Liam calls out. "You haven't told us where we're going. Or what's even going on."

"He's right," I add.

"We're leaving Australia for good," Dr. Elliott says, as he starts walking. All of us follow him.

"What?" Cass asks, startled.

"This tunnel goes to a saltwater lake. And in the lake, there are two large vessels that will transport us out of here. They have room enough for everyone. We anticipated that we might need them to escape. From here, we'll navigate south through the Indian Ocean, to a top secret rebel base on the coast of Antarctica."

I can hardly believe what I'm hearing. I never thought we'd be heading anywhere except Island Alpha.

"What kind of vessels?" a boy asks Dr. Elliott nervously as we walk. "Boats? If we turn up on radar, we'll get bombed."

"It's not radar we have to worry about," Dr. Elliott replies. "It's sonar. The crafts are submersible vehicles. Able to stay underwater for weeks at a time. But there's no time to talk now—we have to go faster. You'll see what I mean when we get there."

"Stay close by," Liam whispers as we keep walking. "I'm not sure what's going on yet."

"Me neither," I murmur back. No one here ever seems to tell the whole truth about anything. *Just like it was back on the wheel.*

We continue walking rapidly down the tunnel with everyone else, heading toward the sound of the other voices. As we move, there are booming noises overhead. Every now and then, the tunnel shakes slightly.

It makes my heart ache to picture what's happening to Destiny Station right now, and to anyone who got stuck there, either inside or out. *How many people will die tonight, burned by flames or torn apart by the blades of the machines?* Simply because of the UNA's desire to crush any group that might pose a threat to it. Even here, thousands of miles away from the UNA, they came after us. It feels like there's no escape from their grip on the globe.

"Hey!" voices call out, as we get closer to the other group in the tunnel. They've finally heard us.

A few minutes later, we catch up with them. This group is much larger than ours, consisting of about a hundred kids and adults. They stand there, looking terrified and dirty.

"Is this all of you?" my mom asks.

"More are coming," a bearded man answers her. I recognize him as one of the scientists who helped move our pod into the station, on the first day that we arrived here. "Many have died."

"Vargas-Ruiz?" my mom asks.

"I was hoping she was with you," the man replies.

"We're headed for the submersibles in the lake," Dr. Elliott says. Everyone is quiet, trying to listen to the conversation.

The bearded man nods. "Are they primed? Stocked?"

"As much as they're going to be. We think we can reach Southern Arc in three days."

"Southern Arc?" I ask. "What's that?"

"The name of the base in Antarctica. It's the sister base to Northern Arc—the one in the Arctic. From Southern Arc we can contact the other bases around the globe and try to launch our assault on Island Alpha right away." Dr. Elliott turns to Cass and the other former drones. "So, you get your wish after all. For things to move faster."

Cass and her friends look like they don't know what to say.

The thud of a detonation above us makes me flinch. Here in the tunnel, we're protected from the impact. But I know that this tunnel could collapse if it receives a direct hit.

"We need to keep moving," the bearded scientist says, pushing forward. The crowd follows him, our group merging with the others. Liam and I walk next to each other. Cass and Emma are right in front of us.

It's a long journey to the underground lake. We just keep heading down the tunnel, seemingly for miles. At three different places, we meet up with other groups of people. There are now at least five hundred of us in the tunnel.

Even in this moment of crisis, I notice that the different tribes are separating out. The ex-drones form groups of their own, splitting from the other kids. But at least Cass is still walking near me and Liam.

I no longer hear the sounds of the battle. We've gone too deep, and we're too far away from the station. I only hear the noise of hundreds of footsteps.

I realize this is my chance to ask Cass about David. She promised me information about him, and I'm still determined to get it.

"Cass," I call out. She hears me and turns around. "What were you going to tell me earlier?" I ask. "About David Aberley?"

She looks at me. "He's alive. Did you know that?"

"No." I desperately want to believe her, but I can't be sure. We keep walking. "How do you know?"

Cass looks around to make sure that none of the scientists are listening. "I've seen a video dispatch from him," she whispers.

"What do you mean?" I ask, startled. "When?" I glance over at Liam. He's listening too.

"On a screen in one of the reconciliation rooms," she continues softly. "Late at night last week. There were some scientists in there—including Dr. Elliott. They were watching live footage from the wheel." She lowers her voice even more, so that it's barely audible. "They were communicating with David somehow. Talking back and forth. I only caught a glimpse, but I saw his full name and an ID number at the bottom of the screen. Then, later, I heard you and Liam talking about him. I figured you must have known him on the wheel."

I'm shocked. "But he was taken by a feeler! I saw it."

"Then he survived and got free of it somehow."

"How do we know you're not lying?" Liam asks her. "It's impossible that David was communicating with Destiny Station like that. There aren't any microphones on the wheel."

"There must be. We just didn't find them." Cass falls silent for a second as we keep walking. "You have to trust me. Why would I lie about David? I'm doing you a favor by telling you about your friend. And I helped save you after the concert, too."

"What did David say?" I ask Cass. "Assuming that you're telling the truth."

"Something about being in a resistance cell back home in the UNA. He was reading the scientists a bunch of data. Numbers and letters, like a code."

Liam and I look at each other. Cass might be telling the truth if she knows about David being in a resistance cell. Still, I know that she could have learned about that from someone else.

If it's true, I'm not sure what to make of it yet. "Where would David have found a microphone? And how would he know how to communicate with Destiny Station? It doesn't make sense that he and the scientists would be talking to each other."

"I agree," Cass continues. "I wanted to hear more so I could figure it out, but I couldn't stay any longer. I was afraid I'd get caught so I just sneaked back to my room."

We keep walking. My mind is racing. I knew that something strange must have happened to David when he didn't turn up in the specimen archive. But I don't understand how he escaped from the feeler, or what he was telling the scientists. He's always been so mysterious. Able to move within any group of people like a chameleon. Able to escape any bad situation. I wish he were here right now to help us, but also to give us some explanations.

Eventually, the mob of people stops moving. I try to see up ahead, but there are too many people in front of us and I'm not tall enough. "Liam?" I ask.

"We're at another door," Liam tells me, craning his head to look over the crowd. "A giant portal." There's a loud clanking noise. "It's opening up . . ."

A second later, the crowd starts surging forward again. I grip Liam's hand.

"It's going to be okay," he says. "We're going to get out of here and down to Southern Arc."

"I know."

Then the crowd jostles us, and we're forced to keep moving.

"Form two lines!" a man begins yelling in an officious voice. For a second, the words remind me of that terrible day when I took the GPPT in the scanning arena, back home in New Providence. The GPPT was the name of the government personality profile test that I supposedly failed. *The one that got me sent to the wheel in the first place.*

But of course if I hadn't failed the test, I never would have met Liam. Or ended up here with the other rebels, including my mom. I would have spent my life stuck in the UNA, never knowing the truth about the government, about my own parents, or about myself. I guess I'm glad that things turned out the way they did. I just wish Destiny Station hadn't been destroyed, because now one less safe haven exists in the world for rebels like us.

The tunnel widens, and Liam and I reach the huge metal portal. It's at least fifteen feet wide. We walk through it, stepping out onto a large stone platform lit with lanterns.

Beyond the platform is a vast underground lake of opaque, milky-green water. It stretches out a hundred yards in every direction before running off through subterranean channels. Steel barricades at the edges of the platform prevent people from falling into it.

"Two lines!" the voice keeps yelling. Other voices pick up the cry.

In the underground lake, I see the gray decks of two submarines, sitting side by side. Their towers and periscopes rise up like dual steel monoliths. I'm startled by the sight. The rest of the vessels are mostly concealed under the water. Metal catwalks stretch down to their decks from the stone platform. People are being led down the catwalks and helped on board through hatches.

Liam and I move forward again with the crowd. The scientists in charge of loading everyone onto the submarines are trying to get an even distribution of people in both.

Everyone keeps walking. I don't know how these vessels are going to fit five hundred people between them. I hope they're larger than they look from the surface.

"How far do you think it is to the Antarctic?" I ask Liam.

"Maybe three thousand miles," he replies. "Could be even farther. I'm not sure."

*Three thousand miles of slicing through the cold ocean.* So many things could go wrong during a journey like that.

I glance at Cass. For the first time, she doesn't look so confident. In fact, she looks like she feels sick.

"You okay?" I ask her.

"Yeah." She swallows hard, eyeing the submarines. "No big deal. I can't swim. But that's not a problem, right?"

"You'll be fine," I tell her, trying to reassure her.

"Two lines!" the voice yells at us. "Get moving!"

Liam and I slip sideways into one line. Cass and Emma follow. Other kids get herded into another line.

"Faster!" Dr. Elliott yells. Some nearby kids are crying, upset about friends who haven't made it. I understand exactly how they feel. I look around for my mom, suddenly worried for her. I don't see her anymore.

"What's going to happen to the people who don't get here in time?" I ask Liam. "You think they'll be left behind?"

Cass speaks before Liam can even answer. "Yes," she says. "That's how they do things here. The scientists are cold. Not evil like the UNA, but hard. That's what I meant earlier, when I said they didn't care about anyone."

"Maybe the people who get left behind will try to rebuild the station after all," Liam says. "Or maybe there's another escape vessel hidden somewhere. The scientists might be cold, but they definitely know how to stay alive."

I nod in agreement. "We don't know everything that goes on around here."

"Keep telling yourself that," Cass says, sounding doubtful.

"You didn't know that they were watching you in the cave," I say. "And you didn't know about these submarines either. Maybe you just need more faith in the scientists."

"I'm through putting my faith in anyone except myself."

"Now who sounds cold?" Liam asks her.

Cass flashes him an angry look, but Emma puts a gentle hand on her shoulder. Cass doesn't say anything more.

Our line moves forward.

Soon we're standing on the catwalks, heading down to the submarine on the right-hand side. I'm standing on my toes and scanning the crowd for my mom, but I can't find her. I wonder if she's already on board one of the submarines, but maybe she's helping orchestrate everything somewhere.

"Liam, do you see my mom?" I ask.

He shakes his head. "Not yet."

One by one, we step off the catwalk and onto the deck of the submarine. The corrugated steel is slick with water. Emma almost slips, but catches herself at the last second, grabbing on to a railing. I help her up.

"Careful," Cass says.

The four of us walk over to the nearest open hatch and ladder.

I look down inside. I can't see anything except glowing white light.

I crouch down and grab the top rung of the metal ladder.

"I'll be right behind you," Liam says.

"You better be." I take a deep breath. Then I start descending the ladder, heading into the belly of the submarine.

# 5 SUBMERGED

When I step down off the ladder, I'm standing in a vast cylindrical chamber. Inexplicably, everything around me is made of gleaming metal and glass. The floor is made of thin marbled tiles. Despite the low ceilings, it's oddly plush and opulent in here—the exact opposite of what I expected.

I'm still standing there, gazing around in wonder, when Liam steps off the ladder next to me.

"There's no way the scientists built this thing," he says.

He's right. The chamber is gigantic. Large glass portholes, nearly as thick as the glass in the specimen archive, are set into the rounded hull. I can see the milky-green water outside. Recessed lights in the ceiling provide a bright, comforting glow.

"They must have hijacked the sub from another nation," I reply, looking around. We move away from the ladder, farther into the chamber. I can see winding stairways descending to lower levels.

I notice some text inscribed along one side of a gilded metal railing. Although I can't read it, I recognize the writing as either Chinese or Japanese. "Look," I say to Liam, pointing it out.

He leans in. "So the sub comes from the Asian Alliance. I bet the scientists modified it, though. To be able to get under the ice when we reach the Antarctic."

More people keep entering the space, including Cass and Emma, so we keep stepping aside to make room.

A voice crackles to life over hidden loudspeakers. I assume it belongs to the captain. "Vessel One will be leaving in five minutes. Please move calmly away from the hatch and down to levels two and three."

I see scientists walking around, helping get everyone situated. Liam and I head for a stairway.

"What did this thing used to be?" I ask, thinking out loud.

"An escape vehicle for the emperor of the Asian Alliance," a voice declares behind me. I turn and see Emma standing there. Cass is next to her.

"How do you know that?" I ask.

"I can read Japanese." Emma sees my surprised expression and smiles. "My parents were diplomats. At least before Minister Harka's government took over the UNA. My dad taught me Japanese in secret." She looks around. "According to the writing, this submarine was built in 2024, probably so the emperor would have a way out of Japan if things went wrong over there—which they did. I'm guessing the other ship was a decoy vessel so nobody would know which one he was in."

"Tell us more," I say, as we begin to walk down a flight of stairs.

She nods. "I'll read whatever I see. Earlier there was a sign that said this submarine's maximum capacity is three hundred people. Probably for his family members and rich friends."

"I never knew you could read Japanese," Cass mutters.

"You never asked. Besides, it's not a very useful skill in Australia."

The four of us exit the wide stairway and step out onto the lower level. Here it's a bit more narrow, but mainly because there are lots of rooms off this hallway. I catch a glimpse of rows of stacked bunk beds inside one of them.

"How long do you think we'll be on this thing?" I ask Liam. "Best guess?"

"Depends how fast we go. I'm guessing the sub's nuclear-powered. But maybe the scientists found a way to harness some other power source. It could be a day or two at full speed. Or a week, if it's slow."

I look at him. "How do you even know all that?"

"I read about nuclear submarines when I was studying how to defeat the UNA last week. There was a whole digital file about them at Destiny Station."

We pass a series of round portholes through which I can faintly see the gray hull of the other submarine. It sits about twenty feet away from us in the murky water.

"Find seats if you can," the voice on the loudspeaker blares. "We're preparing to move out."

Liam and I sit down in leather seats in front of one of the portholes, across from Cass and Emma. Other kids and adults are flooding into the space, making it even more crowded. The massive engines come to life, and everything starts shaking.

I stare out the porthole, feeling like I'm in a state of shock. I'm still wearing my blue dress from the concert. I wonder if my mom is on this vessel or on the other submarine. She has to be on one or the other. I also wonder about David—and if Cass knows more than she's saying about him. I need a chance to talk to her alone. Maybe she'll open up in private.

The engine gets louder. The floor starts thrumming under my

feet. I can't believe this is happening so fast. I feel a jolt, as if we're about to start moving forward. The other submarine is just sitting there.

Next to us, Emma is trying to calm Cass down. Cass is freaking out about the water, and worrying what will happen if the sub breaks down and we have to swim.

I reach out and take hold of Liam's hand. "So, we're on the run again," I say.

"Could be worse."

"I know. At least we're together."

He pauses for a moment. "I never said how great you were onstage tonight, did I?"

"Please. That's the last thing I'm thinking about right now."

"I just wanted you to know how amazing you were." He gazes into my eyes, like he can see right inside me. "I'm sorry about what happened. And I know you're worried about your mom. We'll find her."

I nod.

"I promise you that we're going to be okay. In fact, we'll end up getting back to the wheel faster than before, and——"

His words cut off.

I'm confused for a moment. Then I notice that he has shifted his gaze and he's looking past me, straight out the porthole.

"What's wrong?" I ask.

"I thought I saw something in the water."

Cass and Emma overhear him. They instantly lean forward, looking out the porthole too. "Did someone fall in?" Cass asks. Liam doesn't answer. He's staring out the glass.

Then I see a flash of motion too. It's something black and fast, churning through the water. For a moment, I think that maybe it's a shark. One that has swum in from the ocean. Or some strange kind of underwater creature, just living down here in the subterranean lake.

But then it flashes past the porthole again, and I can tell exactly what it is.

*It's a killing machine.*

One of them has found the submarines.

"No," I breathe, watching in horror as it darts back across the porthole for a third time. Its blade-covered tentacles cut through the water, creating spiraling wakes around its central disc. I had no idea these things could operate underwater.

"Oh god," Emma murmurs next to me in shock. She's seen it too. So has Cass, who looks catatonic.

Piercing alarms instantly start sounding. And other people begin to notice what's happening outside the glass. I hear a few startled screams.

"Keep away from the portholes!" a voice blares over the loudspeakers. But no one listens to it. Everyone is trying to get a good look at what's going on.

"Is there more than one of them?" a voice asks.

"I can't tell!" another voice calls out.

"Can they get inside here?" a girl cries.

Liam and I keep staring at the water. My heart is in my throat. *How did this thing even find us down here? How did it get into the lake?*

The noise of the engine increases to a roar. We start moving downward and forward, slowly pulling away from the dock. But there's no way to outrun this machine, and I know that its blades can slice through our hull and cause serious damage. Maybe even sink us, or force us to evacuate.

I see the second submarine pulling out too, gliding down alongside us through the greenish water.

"If we can get to the open sea, we can navigate away from it—" Cass starts saying hopefully. Her fingers are clenching the armrests of her seat.

But her words are interrupted by a grinding jolt, like we've hit something. A few people cry out in surprise, and a few others nearly lose their balance.

Our submarine and its companion both start moving faster. But we're not going fast enough to evade the machine. I see its tentacles whipping and darting around in the water. For some reason, it seems more interested in the other submarine than in ours.

It slams itself against the side of the other vessel without any warning. Its blades slice right into the metal shell, sending out a spew of air bubbles. The other submarine veers closer to ours.

I can now faintly see terrified faces behind its portholes. The machine is using its tentacles to slide sideways across the surface of the other submarine and onto the glass of a porthole. Air keeps leaking from the holes in the hull.

"We have to do something!" Liam calls out. We're both already on our feet.

But there's nothing we can do but watch, trapped behind our own porthole. I stand there transfixed, as the machine begins gnashing at the glass of the other submarine.

The faint figures are scrambling away from their portholes now. Trying to get back up top and off the submarine, if they can. I feel another flash of fear. My mom could be on that vessel. Both submarines are still moving side by side. Going faster. Our red navigation lights now illuminate the side of the other craft, casting an eerie glow in the water.

"They're going to have to evacuate," I say to Liam over the noise of the alarms.

But my words come too late. I watch as the machine continues assaulting the foot-thick glass of the other submarine, until a crack appears in the porthole. And then another.

"I can't believe this is happening," Cass mutters.

At the same instant, I see the cracks on the submarine's porthole grow and splinter. The glass starts to buckle inward.

It caves completely a second later, in a massive implosion of water that sucks the machine inside along with it. I see the vague shadows of people inside fleeing from the flood and the grinding blades on the tentacles.

Our submarine keeps moving faster. But the other one instantly slows down, as more water gushes into the gaping hole in its side.

"I hope my mom isn't on there," I say to Liam numbly. I know that more machines might be out here in the water somewhere. I'm afraid that we're going to be next.

But we keep moving forward, picking up speed. I glance around. Everyone looks shocked—like they're also expecting the worst. Yet it never comes.

"We're going to be okay," Liam says after a minute or two passes. "We're going fast enough now. We're going to get out of here."

"What about the people on that other sub?" I ask.

"Maybe they can get back to the surface of the lake, and climb onto the deck."

"Then what?" Cass challenges him. "They'll be stuck there with the machine."

"As long as they stay alive, there's hope," I tell her. She looks unconvinced. "They have guns, remember? They can fight back."

Our vessel keeps moving in silence, heading through the water.

With nothing else to do, Liam and I finally sit back down, staring out the porthole. A few moments later, the alarms cut off. I want to go look for my mom, but it's so crowded. And I know she could even be in the cabin with the submarine pilots—impossible to get to.

The voice begins talking over the loudspeakers again. It makes no reference to the horror that we just witnessed. "We are now on course to Southern Arc, a journey of 2,962 miles. At our speed, it will only take nineteen hours before we arrive there. Our engine and reactor core have been modified and our hull has been reshaped for maximum hydrodynamics, allowing for rapid passage through the ocean at one hundred and sixty miles per hour." The voice pauses. "We are not fully stocked with provisions, but there is enough water for everyone to comfortably make the journey."

"You really think we'll make it?" I whisper to Liam.

"We've made it out of worse situations than this one."

I nod, but I know that he's just trying to cheer me up.

Then three dark shadows fall across us. I look up. The boys with shaved heads, Cass's friends, are standing there staring down at us.

"Hey guys," Cass says to them. But for once, they completely ignore her.

"You made this happen," the stockiest one of them snarls at me and Liam. "You brought the machines here. They followed your airplane."

Liam stands up, eyes blazing, ready to fight. "No, they didn't. Why would you say that? Besides, we got here the same way you did!"

"We had friends on that other sub," a second boy says, the one with the holes in his face left over from too many piercings. "They might be dead now. Because of you."

"Guess what? My mom might be on that submarine!" I snap back at him, standing up too. "We need to work together and stop fighting! We're not on the wheel anymore. And Liam and I don't control the machines. If they'd followed our airplane, they would have gotten here three weeks ago, right?"

"We don't trust you, no matter what anyone says," the first boy adds. "We know what you think of us."

I make a huge effort to calm myself down. "Let's not argue," I say. "Not now. We just need to get to Southern Arc. The UNA is our enemy. Not each other."

"Alenna's right," Cass says sharply to the boys. She stands up, staring at them fiercely. "Liam is too. For all we know, the UNA has been on to us since *our* plane landed. It might have nothing to do with them."

The boys keep glaring at us. "All I know is that everything was fine until these two turned up," the first one says to Cass. Only the boy with the eye patch stays silent.

The voice on the loudspeaker crackles to life again: "You will be assigned rooms and sleeping bunks for the duration of our journey. Please go down to the cafeteria on level three to receive your assignments and register for your food and water allotments."

I look at Liam. We both already know it doesn't matter what rooms we get assigned. We're going to stick together no matter what.

I stare out the porthole again, ignoring Cass and the three boys, wondering what happened to the other submarine. I hope everyone made it out okay, as doubtful as that is. Of course, the survivors will be stuck at the ruined station. But maybe with enough weapons they can defeat the machines and reclaim it as their own.

Either way, it means our numbers have already been cut in half. We will be arriving at Southern Arc with only two hundred and fifty people.

"Let's go get some water," I say to Liam.

We quickly move away from the boys and Cass. The four of them are now arguing among themselves as Emma watches dejectedly. Liam and I head toward a staircase that goes farther down to the next level.

As we start moving down the steps, the thrumming of the engines becomes much louder. So does the noise of the crowd. There are more people down here, and we push through the mob, searching for some sign of organization.

I no longer feel the submarine moving. It's like I've already become used to the sensation. I'm scanning around for my mom, desperately hoping she's somewhere on board with us. *But I'm starting to get the feeling that she's not.* I don't know who to ask or where to go to find out. I try not to panic. I force myself to focus on other things.

"If Cass is telling the truth about David, I wonder if there's a way for us to contact him ourselves," I say. "I mean, from the submarine. They must have some kind of communication system so they can talk to Southern Arc."

Liam nods reluctantly. "Look, you know how I feel about David. But if there is a way to contact him, then I'm in favor of finding it. At this point, we need any information we can get."

We keep walking. I grip one of the smooth oak balustrades to keep from stumbling in the crowd. I still have no idea what David was doing talking to the scientists in the first place—but I know that we need to find out.

I feel like I'm at the center of some gigantic puzzle. One that I possess all the pieces to, but I can't fit them together yet.

There's got to be a way for us—the drones, the villagers, the scientists, and David—to work together and figure out how to defeat the UNA. And if there is, we need to find it very soon, while we still have a chance.

# 6  CITY OF ICE

LIAM AND I SPEND that night in a room crammed with eight metal bunks that fold down from the walls. We're in there with other former villagers, but I don't know any of them.

I was hoping to get more information from Cass and Emma, but both of them have disappeared back into their group of friends. Clearly, the scientists were smart enough not to force any former drones and villagers to bunk together.

I'm increasingly worried about my mom. From Dr. Elliott, I learned that she isn't on board this submarine. But according to him, she wasn't on the other one either.

"I don't know where she is, but I'm certain that she's safe," he told me brusquely, when I caught him for a second in the hall. Then he kept walking rapidly away from me.

It doesn't make any sense. For some reason, my mom must have stayed behind at Destiny Station. I can only hope there was another vessel hidden somewhere. I tell myself that if she's survived this long, then she must have had a good escape plan for herself. *She has to be alive.* I refuse to go back to being an orphan again.

The farther we get from Australia, the more my worries about another assault from one of the machines fade away. I know that it's possible the UNA is tracking our submarine, but I've also overhead scientists talking about how they're jamming as many sonar frequencies as possible. I'm hoping that we've made a clean getaway.

The night passes quickly, blending seamlessly into the next day. Here, deep under the surface of the ocean on level three, I can't even tell which is which.

"Alenna," Liam says gently, waking me up in the morning. I struggle to open my eyes. I've slept in my dress, and now the fabric is crumpled and marked with creases. Liam leans over my bunk and touches my arm. "Want to grab some breakfast?"

I reach up and hug him, pulling him in and holding him close. "Sure."

Without Liam, I'd be lost. *I wonder if he feels the same way about me.* I look deep into his gentle, intelligent eyes. I don't say anything. We just stare at each other for a long moment, until it becomes sort of awkward.

He finally laughs. "You feeling okay?"

I break into a smile and then let him go. "I'm just grateful for what I have."

I slide off the bunk. Liam has found some regular clothes for me from a storage locker—jeans, a gray blouse, an army-green jacket, and a pair of boots. The jacket is a bit too large for me, but the other clothes fit fine.

"And I've got something else," he says, holding up my charred copy of *The Myth of Sisyphus*.

"What? How do you have this?" I ask, taking it from him, confused but glad.

"I brought it with me to the concert, in my pocket. Thought I might flip through it if the show took a while to start. I was curious after you talked so much about the Greek myth."

I nod, happy to have the book back.

After I get dressed, and slip the book into my jacket pocket, we head out of the room, walking down a narrow hallway. I see a group of scientists conferring with one another. We move past them, stopping only when we reach a wide chamber lined with portholes and Japanese symbols.

I glance out one of the portholes, and startle. Instead of water rushing by outside the glass, I see that we're zooming past the base of a massive white iceberg. It looms only a hundred feet away from us.

"Wow," I say, in both wonderment and fear.

Liam stares out the porthole too. "Polar ice fields. We must be getting closer to Southern Arc."

Our submarine is gliding so fast that it quickly moves past the huge iceberg. But another mass of ice soon takes its place.

"We better eat breakfast before the food is gone," Liam says. We walk over to a chrome table where silver packets of food are being handed out by a woman with gray hair. They're stale Japanese military rations from years ago. Little tan-colored protein bars wrapped in tinfoil.

Liam takes one and holds it up. "Better than what we had on the wheel." He takes a bite, and then makes a face as he chews. "On second thought, maybe not."

I can tell he's trying to make me laugh. He knows how worried I am about my mom—and everything else that's going on. I take one of the protein bars and open it.

Liam keeps munching on his. "I guess it's not terrible," he says encouragingly as I bite into mine. "No worse than hoofer meat."

The protein bar tastes chalky and dry, and it's as hard as concrete. But I'm starving, so I eat it anyway.

After that, we get our ration of water. It's doled out into small paper cups for us. I swig it down, wishing there were more. I tell myself that soon we'll be off this submarine.

I look around for Cass or Emma, but I don't see either of them anywhere, or the boys. I wonder where they are, and if they're deliberately avoiding me and Liam for some reason. It's mostly just scientists around us now. They are talking earnestly about what comes next when we reach Southern Arc.

Then the voice on the loudspeaker comes to life. The room falls silent, except for the omnipresent thrum of the engines.

"We've made excellent time, and we will reach Southern Arc within the next three hours," the voice says. "Start preparing yourselves, and gather your possessions. Please be ready to disembark the vessel swiftly when the moment comes."

"I wonder what Southern Arc is going to be like," I murmur to Liam. I'm picturing something barren and frozen. Tunnels dug into the ice of a glacier, like the tunnels in the mesa at Destiny Station. Except bitterly cold, and even more vulnerable to attack. The UNA is forcing us to live underground like rats. *Is this really the price of freedom?* "I hope it's not more tunnels," I grouse.

One of the scientists overhears me. He's slightly chubby and wears wire-rimmed glasses. He turns our way. "You haven't seen pictures of Southern Arc?"

"No," Liam says. "I thought they were classified."

"None of that matters anymore." The man walks over to a digital display screen on the wall, hanging between two portholes. A few other people start glancing his way. He taps in a code, and the screen comes to life. "Take a look at Southern Arc," he tells us.

Liam and I crowd around the screen. We're looking at some kind of live video feed, not a photograph. It must be coming from a camera mounted outside Southern Arc, and being broadcast to us here. I'm surprised by what I see——but not in a bad way.

Southern Arc is an actual building. A huge one. In the gray light of the Antarctic, I see massive concrete walls rising up from a landscape of snow and ice. The building is vast, like a gigantic bunker complex from a past era, at least six stories high. Windows jut out at angles from the thick slabs of concrete.

"The place we call Southern Arc was once a research station belonging to the United States in the late 1990s," the scientist explains. "It was filled with scientists, monitoring the ice, and doing valuable polar research. But then everything fell to pieces. . . ."

I continue gazing at the screen.

"When the UNA formed, they cut their ties with the station," the scientist continues. "They left the researchers behind to freeze. They didn't want to spend the money to come and get them, and they had no interest in polar research. They left them to die, without a second thought."

"But they didn't die," a voice breaks in. It's a younger, thin woman, with curly red hair. Another scientist. "In fact, they managed to survive by growing food in an underground greenhouse. From there, they formed the nucleus of Southern Arc. It's the hardest base to infiltrate or attack, because of its location. The UNA has tried to send submarines full of soldiers there, but the rebels at Southern Arc have destroyed them. And they've shot incoming missiles out of the sky. The base is essentially a fortress. It's filled with a mix of six hundred refugees from the UNA, and run by the sole surviving American scientist from the late twentieth century."

The woman pauses. "It's the most militaristic of the bases, too. It was intended as a place of retreat, if our attempt to reclaim the wheel failed. Now it's the only safe place we can get to."

Everyone in the room is watching the screen now, kids and scientists alike. The male scientist punches in numbers, and the screen goes black. Then a face appears from the darkness. It's a photograph of an ancient, gaunt man with a long white beard and stringy white hair. His face is heavily lined and pockmarked with frostbite scars. His deep-set gray eyes look haunted.

"Dr. Neil Barrett," the scientist says. "Seventy-three years old. He controls every element of life at the station. He agreed to give us shelter."

Movement catches my eye out the porthole, and I look away from the screen. We're rocketing through the water, past another group of large icebergs. Some of them are now only thirty feet from the submarine. I feel the engines turn our vessel slightly, altering our course. The entire submarine groans from the pressure and the motion. I glance back at the screen, but it goes dark again as Dr. Barrett's face disappears from view.

The pinging of an electronic warning system begins to sound. The captain's voice bursts over the loudspeakers: "We are nearing the base of the ice field. The water may get rough. Please find seats and secure yourselves for the duration of our journey."

People immediately start moving around. Liam and I take seats near a wall. There are no seat belts, so I just grip the armrests. I can feel the currents of the water making the engine noises change and shift. My stomach flip-flops. The submarine continues its rapid passage forward. Increasingly large chunks of ice are visible from the portholes.

Liam and I sit there for the next few hours. The ride is

increasingly bumpy, and sometimes terrifying. But finally, we draw nearer to the station.

"We're coming up," Liam says, glancing out the nearest porthole. "Look."

"It's going to be so cold," I say. Despite the heated air in the submarine, I can sense the freezing temperatures behind the metal and glass hull.

A current of water buffets our vessel. Everyone sways in their seats. Minutes fly past as we sit there, navigating the ice field, moving even closer to the base.

Finally, the voice on the loudspeaker says, "We are nearly there. Prepare for—"

Right then, the submarine shakes again, and everyone slides sideways. A few people gasp.

I fall into Liam. The lights flicker for an instant and then come back on. I stare out the porthole. I see a mountainous slab of ice just a few feet away from us in the water. "That was way too close," I murmur. We keep moving, but we're rapidly slowing down. "Did we hit something?"

"No, I think we've arrived," Liam replies. "This must be Southern Arc."

I keep looking out the porthole. Liam is right. This isn't an iceberg but the base of some larger frozen landmass. The lights flicker again, and the submarine starts slowing even more.

I feel farther away from the wheel and our friends than ever before. And I'm desperate to know if my mom is okay, and where she is. I know that coming here to the Antarctic is a necessary step to prepare for our assault on Island Alpha. But I want to be back on the wheel, saving Gadya, David, Rika, and everyone else whom I care about.

I think about my dad and his stories about Sisyphus. About how it's important to find meaning in repetitive suffering. Those stories kept me going on the wheel. But I feel like I've passed beyond the boundaries of that Greek myth. Sisyphus was stuck pushing his boulder up the same mountain over and over, but Liam and I managed to actually make it off the wheel. I just don't know what to do next. *Maybe I need to find a new myth to get me through each day.*

I think about the book by Camus in my pocket. Maybe I'll find some answers in its pages somewhere—if I ever get a chance to read it.

Warning signals keep pinging from the loudspeakers. Outside, I only see whitish-blue ice, as though we're moving along a narrow water-filled channel, right into the frozen heart of Southern Arc.

Eventually, the submarine comes to a complete stop in a rush of water and icy slush. I watch it foaming outside the portholes.

The engines cut off. I'd grown used to their sound, and without it everything is eerily silent except for some creaking noises. I can't tell if they're coming from the submarine or from the ice outside.

Then there's a loud metallic crash above us. The submarine's hatches are being thrown open.

*We're finally here.*

Liam and I both get to our feet, along with the rest of the passengers around us. Everyone starts moving toward the stairways.

When Liam and I reach the top level, we walk to one of the open hatches and ladders. Hands swiftly help us up and out of the vessel. Soon, both of us are standing there on the deck of the submarine.

I was expecting that we'd be inside a giant, icy cavern. Instead, we're inside a strange domed structure. Around and above us is a mosaic of colorful tiles, arranged in a checkered pattern. It's almost like we've entered a huge swimming chamber. It's not what I imagined. Banks of flickering fluorescent lights illuminate the space.

"Hey, it's not that cold in here," I say to Liam, startled. While the air is definitely cool, it's far from freezing.

Bodies quickly force us forward. Liam and I start walking along the surface of the submarine. The submarine is surrounded by a tiled deck. Metal walkways stretch out to it, much like the ones back at the underground lake near Destiny Station. We reach one of the walkways and head up it. In the tile walls, I now see large openings. Wide arches lead into other massive spaces. Each space is lit by more fluorescent lights.

Voices call out on either side of us. I look around and get my first glimpse at the people who live and work at Southern Arc. They look very different from the scientists at Destiny Station. They're wearing military-style green and black outfits. And all of them have guns strapped to their leather belts. They look more like unsmiling UNA military police officers than fellow rebels.

I can tell that Liam is observing everything too. Sizing up the situation. "This is pretty weird," he whispers to me.

I nod. "Let's be careful."

We follow a group of refugees from the submarine down a tile pathway and through a huge concrete arch. I now see Cass and Emma in the crowd. I want to talk to them, but they're too far ahead of us right now to reach.

All of us enter into a massive, heated circular chamber. There are even more military-type men and women in here, hustling everyone along. These denizens of the Antarctic don't exactly look thrilled to see us. I haven't seen one of them smile yet.

Video screens on the tiled walls display outside views of Southern Arc. I see windswept glacial expanses of ice and cold. The images suggest great solitude and emptiness. *This is, literally, the end of the earth.* There's no farther place that any of us can run.

As we keep walking, I look up and see a balcony high above us. It runs around the circumference of the large tiled space, right at the top. Nearly thirty feet above our heads.

A figure stands up there in front of some kind of digital console, peering down at us. From his white beard and hair, I instantly recognize him as Dr. Neil Barrett. I only get a brief glimpse of him as we walk, but his face is oddly expressionless.

Liam notices him too. "If he's been here since the 1990s, then that's more than forty years," he says. "This place must feel like a prison to him."

"I know. I'm surprised he hasn't gone crazy." I wonder what it would feel like to spend forty years in a place like this. That's two and a half times longer than I've been alive. And more than half of Dr. Barrett's entire life. *It must seem like an eternity.*

Liam and I keep walking. Dr. Barrett passes out of view.

Our group reaches another huge chamber. This one has long oak tables inside, arranged in rows. And at one end of the room is a massive window, staring out into the barren wasteland of the Antarctic. Beyond the window I see large satellite dishes and arrays of tall ice-covered antennas.

I think about what Cass said, about the scientists talking to David back at Destiny Station. I wonder if there's a way to use these antennas to communicate with him now. I know it's possible that Cass was lying, or mistaken, but it didn't seem that way to me.

People stand everywhere in the crowded chamber, with an air of nervous expectation. Loud voices are all around me. Everyone sounds tense and afraid, even the scientists. Many of them are talking to the militaristic guards.

"Welcome to Southern Arc," a deep, gravelly voice suddenly intones. I look up and see Dr. Barrett again, standing up high on the balcony, which continues into this room above us. Now he's flanked by two armed guards. The noise of the crowd quiets immediately as we watch him.

"As you know, my name is Neil Barrett," he says. "You are my guests here." He scans the crowd below him with piercing gray eyes. "I have just received word that the other rebel bases have been bombed—most of them completely destroyed with heavy casualties."

The crowd starts murmuring again. My heart sinks. I look over at Liam.

"My dad," Liam says to me, sounding worried. "What if he was alive after all, at the Highveld base?"

I take his hand in mine. "It's going to be okay."

Dr. Barrett gestures for silence. "I will be sending out rescue parties to find the survivors from the damaged bases. Some of them have already fled, and they are stranded partway here." He pauses. "Our mission is now clear. I have been waiting and preparing a very long time for this moment. We must return to Island Alpha and liberate its inhabitants as soon as possible. We will fight anyone there who opposes us, and we will turn the island into our sanctuary. Then we will continue onward to the UNA, and destroy it!" He stares out at the crowd, eyes burning. "And from the ashes, we will create a new world order. One that is fair, and does not try to enslave its own citizens!"

88

Some people around us start applauding, but there's something about Dr. Barrett that makes me uneasy. I agree with every single word he's saying, but there's a fanatical zeal in his eyes—one that reminds me a bit of Minister Harka. I can only guess how much anger he feels about being banished here for so long. Will his desire for revenge cloud his judgment?

Dr. Barrett ignores the noise of the crowd and keeps talking. "Southern Arc has limited resources. That means everyone is under strict rationing orders from this day forth. One quart of water per person each day. We melt water from snow, but that takes time and energy." He gazes at us sternly. "Time and energy are mankind's most precious resources. Here you will only be served two meals daily—at least for now. We don't know how many more refugees will turn up on our icy doorstep. We must conserve our resources, so that we'll have the ability to return to the wheel and conquer it."

I just want to get out of here as soon as possible and back to the wheel. I tell myself that even if I feel uneasy, I can't lose sight of my goals. And it's up to me and Liam to make sure that they happen. Even if it's hard, I just have to hope that Dr. Barrett can be trusted—and that he won't lead us astray on the long journey ahead.

# 7 THE DECISION

WHEN DR. BARRETT'S BRIEFING is over, Liam and I decide to explore as much of Southern Arc as we can. But uniformed guards block off certain areas, with folded arms and pistols. Dr. Barrett seems just as worried about spies as Veidman was on the wheel. Still, there are certain rooms and halls that we are able to move about in freely. Many are filled with other refugees—not from the submarine but from previous incidents over the years. Most of the people here look thin and tired. Lost. Some of them lie listlessly on bunks in small rooms. Others talk among themselves.

Liam and I follow a tiled staircase and try to enter an observation level, but a guard turns us away.

"You're not allowed up here," he snarls.

"C'mon. We're on the same side," Liam tells him.

"We just want to look out the windows," I add.

The guard shakes his head, "Go back with the other refugees." His face is like stone. He barely makes eye contact with us. He just stares straight ahead.

Liam and I turn and walk away, back down the staircase. A lot of Southern Arc is built underground, presumably to conserve heat.

"They're so friendly here," Liam jokes, shaking his head.

"I guess it's better than getting injected with truth serum," I point out. "The villagers weren't too friendly when I first got to the wheel either."

Liam smiles. "I'd forgotten about that."

Turning serious, I say, "It's weird, though. The guards are treating us like we're a big annoyance. They should be happy that we survived and made it here."

Liam nods. "And I bet most of the guards were once refugees themselves, ones that Dr. Barrett probably trained."

We reach the end of the staircase and turn a bend into a wide hallway. There, we nearly run straight into Cass. I stop walking, surprised to see her.

"Where have you been?" I ask. For once, she's by herself. She's changed clothes, and she's now wearing jeans, boots, and a black hoodie. "Why have you been avoiding us?"

"I didn't want to cause any trouble on the sub," she admits, after a moment of hesitation. "My friends don't like you. The boys, I mean. Not Emma—she's nice, and she pretty much likes everyone." She pauses again. "But I've been looking for you since we got here, Alenna. I need to talk to you about something."

"Then go right ahead," I tell her.

"Alone."

"Just tell me here and now," I say, guessing that it must have something to do with David.

Cass glances at Liam. He's standing right next to me. "Don't you know what 'alone' means?" Cass asks him.

Liam just stares at her, looking both amused and kind of annoyed by her attitude.

"The boys made me promise I wouldn't talk to you," Cass

finally explains to him. "That's why it has to be me and Alenna alone."

"Fine," I say. I look at Cass. "We'll do it your way." I glance back at Liam. "Just stay nearby, okay?"

"I'll wait at the end of the hall," he says with a shrug, heading toward a small alcove with some video screens in it, about twenty feet away.

"I'll keep it quick," Cass replies. Then she turns to me and lowers her voice. "It's about David Aberley."

"I figured as much. Tell me everything you know."

"Better yet, I'll show you." She slides an object out of her back pocket. It's a digital device as thin as a sheet of paper, with moving images on it.

"Where did you get that?" I ask, startled.

"I swiped it from one of the scientists when he wasn't looking."

I glance down the hall and see Liam. He's looking at the video screens, pretending to be distracted. Pressing various buttons to get different views of the ice fields outside the station. He's acting like he can't hear Cass, but I'm pretty sure that he can.

"Your friend David is in real trouble," Cass whispers.

I glance down at the digital image in Cass's hands. At first I can barely make out what I'm seeing. It's just a gray, distorted mass of moving pixels. And there's no audio. Then I see a pale face emerge from the darkness.

*David.*

The breath catches in my chest. This is the first proof I've seen that he might be alive. I feel a surge of relief that makes my legs weak for a second. Since the moment that David and I arrived on the wheel together, our fates have taken such different paths.

I keep staring down at the moving image. Behind David, I see a mass of squirming metal tentacles. *A feeler*. David is racing away from it, running through the trees. The camera appears to be attached to his body somehow, filming his face and whatever is directly behind him.

"How is this possible?" I breathe, horrified by what I'm seeing. "When is this even from?"

The image breaks apart for a second, and then I see David's face again. The feeler has pulled away, back into the sky, and David is churning through thick underbrush. His glasses are askew, and he looks desperate.

"Two days ago." Cass swipes her hand across the image and it transforms into a list of data, including dates. "This is a log of his dispatches from the wheel. One every couple days." She presses a button. "But the data is corrupted. I think someone tried to wipe it from this reader, and only partially succeeded. There's no sound, and most of these video files are full of glitches, and only a few seconds long. The one I showed you is the most recent one listed on here."

I keep watching. The image judders and then the sequence restarts again, like it's playing on an infinite loop. It doesn't look like David is in the gray zone anymore, and I wonder how he escaped from it. I feel an ache in the pit of my stomach. David is alone on the wheel, battling feelers by himself. His situation is worse than being frozen in the specimen archive.

"Why are you showing me this?" I ask Cass. "I mean, I'm grateful. But I don't understand. Why do you care about David so much?" I stare at her closely, trying to figure it out. "It's more than just because you heard I'm friends with him. Am I right?"

She doesn't answer. Just rolls up the digital display in silence.

I look down the hallway at Liam. He glances over at me.

93

"Don't tell him what I showed you," Cass says softly. "I know he doesn't trust me, and he probably doesn't trust David either."

"Liam and I share everything," I tell her. "And any enemy of the UNA is a friend of his, believe me."

She shrugs. "Fine, then. But I'm afraid he'll start a fight with the boys—or vice versa." She slides the folding display back into her pocket. "Look, if you really want, you two can come eat with us tonight. We need to start planning how to reach our friends when we get to the wheel." She starts walking away. "Just tell Liam not to pick any fights, and I'll tell the boys to control themselves too."

"Wait," I call out softly. She stops. "Is there any way for us to contact David directly from Southern Arc?"

"I'm working on that." She starts walking again, disappearing around the bend of the hallway, her boots clicking on the tiles.

I turn back to Liam, heading toward him.

"What was that about?" he asks when I reach him. "I heard some of it, but not everything. David's alive, huh?"

"Cass has actual footage of him from the wheel," I reply. "New footage, from after we escaped the island. The feelers were after him."

"Are you sure the footage is real?"

"Pretty sure. Cass thinks there's a way for us to contact him."

"I hope so." Liam glances back at the video screens on the wall. "Check this out." He presses a series of arrows, and the image shifts. Now we're looking at an overhead view of the station. It resembles a massive rectangular box in the center of a field of ice. "We can see this place from almost any angle. There must be cameras mounted everywhere outside. At least sixty of them. It's good security."

The stark image makes me understand just how truly alone we are out here. Unlike at Destiny Station, or even in our village on the wheel, we are probably the only inhabitants on this entire landmass.

"It wouldn't be that hard to nuke this place," I mutter, feeling a sudden chill of fear.

"Southern Arc's got pretty good defenses," Liam says. "I think some of those antennas outside are used to control old war satellites. That's how Dr. Barrett has the capability to shoot incoming weapons out of the sky."

I look over at Liam. "Cass wants us to have dinner with her and her friends tonight. They need our help."

Liam nods. "I'll have dinner with them, but I don't really want to help them. They'll take our help now, but as soon as we're back on the wheel, they'll turn on us. Drones can't help how they act. It's in their DNA. We should use them to get information but nothing more."

"Not all drones are bad people—" I begin to say.

But then I hear a loud noise coming down the hallway toward us. It sounds like an army of footsteps echoing on the tiles. Liam and I turn in the direction of the sound.

A group of twelve uniformed guards comes into view. They are carrying guns. At the front, leading the group, is a tall, thin, bearded figure dressed in white robes.

It's Dr. Barrett.

Liam and I move aside, pressing ourselves against the wall. I assume that Dr. Barrett and his men are just passing through, on their way to somewhere important. But his eyes are fixed on us. *And he's headed directly our way.*

Dr. Barrett and his men slow down as they reach us. They

come to a stop just a few feet away. I stare back at them, not sure what to do or say.

"Alenna Shawcross and Liam Bernal," Dr. Barrett says. His voice is simultaneously hard and raspy. "Correct?"

I nod. Up close, his face looks even older. More ravaged by time and weather than it looked in the photograph. The bones nearly poke out of his damaged skin. Only his gray eyes look curiously youthful.

"Alenna, I wanted to tell you that your mother is safe," he says. "She boarded a third submersible vessel. A smaller one, meant for the top scientists. She's on her way here with a few other survivors."

I feel a flood of emotion. "I knew there had to be another way out of the station!"

Liam puts his arm around my shoulders.

Dr. Barrett nods. "Indeed." He turns his intense gaze to Liam. "But it's you I need to talk to most of all."

"About what?"

"About your father. Octavio."

Liam looks startled. He lowers his arm. I take his hand in mine in case it's bad news. "Is he alive?" Liam asks. "Is he at one of the other bases, like Vargas-Ruiz said?"

"He's alive, but he's not at another base. Right now, he's stranded in a craft in the Indian Ocean with fifty other survivors. He's halfway between Southern Arc and the tip of South Africa."

I feel Liam's hand tighten in mine. "But he's alive?" Liam sounds stunned, even though I can tell he's trying to hide it. I know exactly how he's feeling. I went through the same thing when I learned my own mother was alive, years after I'd given up hope.

"He won't be alive for long," Dr. Barrett continues flatly. "Not unless we do something right away. Base Lerato, in the Highveld of South Africa, was attacked by the same type of machines that decimated Destiny Station. The survivors, including your father, escaped in a reconditioned hydrofoil. But they didn't have enough fuel to make the journey all the way here—and of course the ice fields would have prevented them from reaching us anyway." He pauses. "They're now a thousand miles away, floating adrift. They will soon get picked up by some government or another. Or a storm will hit and sink their craft."

"What can I do? I'll do anything," Liam says, the words tumbling out in an urgent rush.

"Your father has a reputation as a fierce fighter and rebel leader," Dr. Barrett says. "So we're planning a rescue mission for him and his men." He pauses again. "But we need volunteers."

"I'll go," Liam says. "If that's what you mean."

"So will I," I say without a second thought.

Dr. Barrett turns his unblinking gaze toward me. "It's not as simple as that. The group that travels out to rescue the survivors from Base Lerato will not be returning to Southern Arc. They will continue directly to Island Alpha. They will meet up with everyone else there, as part of our coordinated assault." His gray eyes look like steel. "This is a dangerous mission. I know you must want to rescue your friends from the specimen archive. Perhaps it is better for them if the two of you travel separately . . ."

He doesn't finish his thought, but I know what he means. *There's a chance that whoever goes to rescue Octavio won't make it back to the wheel alive.*

"Can't you just send some of your men?" I ask, gesturing at the armed guards that surround him. "Why do you need volunteers like us? Just send a hundred guards to make sure everything goes well!"

"Some of my men will be coming too. But more must stay here. I cannot force people to sacrifice their lives, or I would be no better than the UNA. I can only ask that they volunteer." He looks at Liam again. "Besides, I know that Liam is an accomplished warrior, like his father. I could use someone young like him on the journey fighting by my side."

"You're going as well?" I ask Dr. Barrett, surprised.

"Yes. My second lieutenant will be in charge until we regroup on the wheel."

Liam and I look at each other. I'm not sure what to say.

"You have time to think it over," Dr. Barrett tells us in his strange, hoarse voice. "Two hours. Make your decisions and let one of my men know—but do not tell anyone else. I don't want the others refugees to know about the mission, in case there are spies in our midst. We leave today, in secret, to rescue Octavio and the other survivors." He steps back, gathering his white robes. His men cluster around him with their weapons. "Victory is within our grasp," he says to us. "So we must claim it." Then his group walks off rapidly down the tunnel, shouldering their guns. Liam and I are left standing there alone.

"My dad is alive," Liam murmurs, sounding like he's still in shock. "Vargas-Ruiz said there was a possibility . . ." He turns to me. "But I didn't really believe her."

"I know."

"So what should we do?"

"What do you mean? We have to go after him!"

Liam looks into my eyes. "I can't ask you to do that. If something bad happens, then I'd risk losing the most important person in the world to me."

"You're not asking me to go. I *want* to go."

He shakes his head. "But I don't want you to. It's going to be way too dangerous."

"Like it isn't dangerous here?"

"You're safer here than out on the open ocean."

"Are you sure about that? Look at what happened to Destiny Station." I realize that we're about to start arguing. "Why are you being so stubborn right now?"

"Because I can't let you risk your life when you don't need to! Besides, you heard what Dr. Barrett said. If we both went, and didn't make it, what would happen to Gadya and everyone in the archive?"

"Liam, I can make my own choices."

"So can I."

There's a moment of tense silence.

If it weren't for Gadya and the other kids on the wheel who need our help, I would go with Liam—no matter what he wanted. I am a warrior now too. But as the shock of Dr. Barrett's words starts to wear off, I think that maybe Liam is right after all. We can't let our friends down. If we both go to rescue Octavio and we get hurt or captured—or worse—then the others might never get rescued.

"Let's make the right choice," I say. "You have to go alone. I'll stay here after all."

It hurts me so much to say those words, like a knife is twisting into my heart. If I'm not going, then I want to beg Liam to stay too. But I know this is the right thing to do. If Liam's father died because of me, I wouldn't be able to live with myself. *And it would inevitably come between us.* "It's your dad. You need to be there for him."

"Do I?" I can see the torture written on Liam's face. He looks surprised by my words. "I can't leave you here alone," he says. "We have to stick together. We'll both stay, then. That's the answer."

I take his face in my hands, trying not to cry. "Liam, come on. I'm going to be okay here without you. We'll meet back up on the wheel, like Dr. Barrett said."

"I can't do it," he murmurs. "I just can't leave you. Not even for my dad."

I lean back and gaze into his warm eyes. I can't bear the thought of him leaving either. But I also know that he must. "I love you, but you have to take the risk." My voice cracks, and I swipe at my eyes. "And then we'll go save Gadya, Rika, and all our other friends on the wheel."

He nods. "Are you sure this is what you want?"

"Yes."

"I don't know what I'd do if something happened to you."

"I feel the same way—so you better stay safe out there." I pull back from him, wiping my eyes a final time. "Two hours isn't long," I say. "We better let Dr. Barrett know that you're going with him, so he can get you ready for the journey. Maybe he'll give you some real weapons."

He smiles. "It's going to be okay," he says. "You know that, right?"

"I know," I reply. And in that moment, I feel hopeful that things are going to work out. That Liam is going to save his dad, and then we're going to liberate the wheel together.

Liam leans down and kisses me. I fall into his embrace. *We can't afford to fail—everyone is depending on us.* And everything is happening so fast. I vow that no matter what comes my way, I will fight and overcome it, until I am safe and reunited with Liam again.

# ⚮ DEPARTURE

TWO HOURS LATER, LIAM is ready to go. He's been stocked with a gun and a black and green uniform, just like the ones that Dr. Barrett's guards wear. Both of us stand there in a small tiled antechamber. Waiting for one of the guards to come and get us.

Liam glances at himself in a mirror and frowns. "This makes me look like a UNA soldier."

"No, you look good—sort of."

I straighten his collar. We both laugh a little. But the laughter is barely disguising my nervousness and fear.

Liam picks up a bulky fur-lined jacket that one of the guards gave him. He sticks it under his arm.

I don't even know what vessel they're going to use to reach Octavio's hydrofoil. *Maybe one of the submarines that we traveled here on?* But I'm guessing Southern Arc must have its own ships. I just haven't seen any of them yet, mainly because Dr. Barrett is so secretive, and he's keeping the whole place tightly locked down.

At least Dr. Barrett will be leading the expedition. Despite his gruff personality, if he's survived for four decades in the freezing wilderness—since before there even was a UNA—then he must be doing something right.

I still can't believe that I encouraged Liam to go on the expedition. I try to find any positives in the bleak situation. I guess that with Dr. Barrett gone, maybe there will be more of an opportunity to move around the base, and to try to find a way to interface with David. Assuming David is still alive.

I'll need to work with Cass. For whatever reason, she seems interested in helping David too. And although I don't fully trust her yet, or her friends, she definitely has information that I need.

The door to our chamber abruptly opens, without a knock. I turn around. A grim-faced guard is standing there. He looks Liam up and down, barely glancing at me.

"It's time," the guard says to Liam. "Dr. Barrett is waiting for you."

Liam and I follow the guard out of the room and into the tiled hallway. We walk quickly past the other people. Some of them glance our way, no doubt wondering why Liam is dressed in a uniform and holding a gun.

"Who's going to run things here with Dr. Barrett gone?" Liam asks the guard as we walk. "He mentioned his second lieutenant? Where is he?"

"I'm sure you'll meet him at some point. Dr. Barrett will be monitoring everything remotely."

"Why is he even going himself?" I ask the guard. "I mean, I'm glad that he is, but why exactly?"

"Dr. Barrett would never ask any man to do something that he himself isn't willing to do," the guard intones. "That's the reason we follow him." He pauses for a moment. We stop walking as well. He turns to look at us. "Dr. Barrett has stared into many an abyss. Each time, he has conquered it. There is no person on earth I would rather follow than Neil Barrett." The guard turns around again and keeps walking.

I nod, but I'm disconcerted by his cult-like devotion. It reminds me too much of the drones following the Monk. Liam has noticed it too. He looks at me and raises an eyebrow.

We keep walking in silence until we reach a tiled door. The guard unlocks it, swinging the door open to reveal a long tunnel, sloping upward. I start walking forward with Liam, but the guard blocks my path.

"You can't go any farther," he says. "You have to wait here because—"

"She's coming with me," Liam interrupts. "To say good-bye."

The guard lowers his hand and looks at me. "You sure you want to?"

"Of course," I tell him. "Why not?"

He shrugs. "Fine. This way, then. But don't say I didn't warn you about the cold." With those words, he starts walking again, up the tunnel. Liam and I follow close behind.

"Are we traveling by boat? Submarine? Helicopter?" Liam asks him.

"You'll see soon enough," the guard calls back to us.

"I'm getting sick of hearing that," I mutter.

As we keep walking, I feel the air getting colder. Liam puts his arm around me, and I snuggle into him.

The hall comes to a dead end in a small room with a low ceiling. It has black-and-white checkered tiles on the walls and the floor. I glance around. Ancient-looking electrical switches hang on the wall to our left, with red wires dangling loose from them. The guard presses a black button attached to a metal switch box.

"Get ready," he says.

And then, a moment later, the entire ceiling of the room begins sliding back, letting in drifts of snow and chunks of ice. Freezing air instantly floods the space, blowing back my hair. It's nearly as cold in here as it was inside the gray zone back on the wheel.

The guard folds a metal ladder down from one of the walls. "Up and out," he says. "No time to waste." Liam moves over to the ladder and helps me up. He and the guard are right behind me as I climb to the surface. I curl my fingers up inside the sleeves of my thin jacket, so I don't touch the metal with my bare skin.

I crawl out onto the ice and stand up. The biting wind cuts through my clothing, making me shiver.

I look around, my eyes narrowed against the light. It's not sunny—just gray. But the light is reflected off the white landscape, making everything overwhelming bright. My teeth are already chattering.

Liam is at my side. He gives me his heavy jacket, and I put it around my shoulders.

I glance behind me and see the massive concrete walls of Southern Arc a few hundred feet away. The strange tiled tunnels must stretch well beyond the confines of its walls. I wonder how far the tunnels run underneath these ice fields.

"Check it out," Liam says, nudging me, and I follow his gaze.

To our left, a huge, black military-style helicopter with two sets of rotors sits on the ice. It looks old, like maybe it's been here since the base was founded. I see metal patches riveted onto one side. They look like they're covering old bullet holes.

Guards move around the helicopter, brushing off snow and ice. And in their midst, dressed in white furs, black gloves, and boots, stands Dr. Barrett, barking out orders to his men.

"Come on," the guard says to Liam, heading in the direction of the waiting helicopter. "It's time." But I'm not ready for Liam to leave yet.

"I can't believe we're saying good-bye to each other," I murmur, huddling against the freezing wind, suddenly realizing what we're doing. *Am I crazy to let Liam go?* More than anything, I want him to stay—or I want to go with him on the journey. I didn't know that making the right choice would feel this hard. I wonder if it's too late to change my mind or make Liam change his.

"If you want me to stay, I'll stay," Liam says, like he's heard my thoughts. His breath is warm against my cheek.

I hug him tighter. "I know. But you'd end up hating me for it."

"I could never hate you."

"Maybe not. But I'd hate myself." I pull back from him. "So I'm not giving you a choice." I begin stripping off the coat he gave me, despite the cold. "You'll need this on your trip."

The helicopter rotors start up with a clatter, kicking up bits of ice.

"Liam!" Dr. Barrett calls out, his voice barely audible over the noise. "Aren't you coming?"

"Go," I prompt, handing him the coat. "Find your dad. I'll see you back on the wheel."

We kiss. His lips are warm and soft. I could stay like this forever. But the moment comes to an end.

"Be safe," he tells me, staring into my eyes. "I don't know what kind of communication system they'll have on the helicopter, or on my dad's hydrofoil, but I'll try to contact you and send a message. And don't be too trusting when it comes to Cass, or anyone else. Keep your guard up, like you did when you first got to the wheel."

"I will. But only if you do the same when it comes to Dr. Barrett," I tell him.

"Agreed."

The noise of the helicopter gets louder. The guards are waving impatiently for Liam to get on board.

"You better go back inside where it's warm," Liam says, slipping his coat on.

We kiss a final time.

Then we let go of each other, and Liam starts jogging toward the waiting helicopter.

Without him there, the cold wind kicks back in. It's so intense that I crouch down, trying to shield myself from it. Liam reaches the helicopter, turns back and waves at me, and then climbs on board. I see the helicopter door swing shut behind him.

Almost immediately, the helicopter begins to lift off from the ice. I stand up and wave, hoping that Liam can see me through the windows. I can't see him anymore. The light of the sky reflects off the curved glass. I keep waving anyway. The helicopter flies higher, heading due north.

I stand there watching it depart.

Soon, the helicopter is just a speck in the clouds. I can't believe that Liam is gone. I shut my eyes, telling myself that it's going to be okay. That Liam will help save his dad, and that we'll reconvene on the wheel without any problems. I'm just not sure that I believe it.

A guard emerges from the hole in the ground behind me. "You'll get frostbite," he says. "Come back inside."

Freezing, I trudge over to the opening. I quickly descend the icy ladder, glad to be out of the wind.

I step onto the tiled floor, barely able to feel my fingers and toes. I glance back at the guard. He's closing the opening to the outside world. Sealing us inside Southern Arc again.

I begin walking back down the tunnel toward the rest of the station.

As I walk, Liam's absence hits me like a physical pain in my chest. *Liam is really gone.* I want to race back up and out of the base, and chase after the helicopter—as crazy as that sounds.

I'm crying, but I fight the tears back down. I vow that I will save my tears for when Liam and I are reunited again, and they will be tears of happiness.

I reach the main hallway. My arms and legs are tingling from the warmth of the station. I take a deep breath. I feel very alone and out of place here now. I haven't been this alone since I first woke up on the wheel, before I met David. And that was a terrifying time.

I step into the hallway and start walking down it, heading to one of the large chambers. I decide that I need to find Cass and Emma. The least I can do while Liam is away is try to learn as much as I can about what's happened on the wheel since we left it. And the key to doing that involves finding out more about David.

It doesn't take me long to locate Cass. She's in the cafeteria, sitting at a table next to one of the three thuggish boys with shaved heads. The one with the eye patch. Cass sees me coming and nudges him with her elbow. He looks up at me.

"Hey there," I say, feeling awkward. Before, I always had Liam at my side.

"'Hey' yourself," Cass says. The boy doesn't say anything.

I slowly take a seat across from them. "You heard anything more from David?" I ask.

"Maybe." She pauses. "Where's Liam?"

I hesitate. I'm about to lie, but then I realize that she'll learn the truth soon enough. "He left the station. He's gone with Dr. Barrett to find his dad, who got stranded halfway here after Base Lerato was bombed."

Cass nods somberly. "I hope he succeeds."

The boy next to her suddenly reaches out a hand across the table, startling me. "My name's Alun," he says. "Spelled with a *u*."

I shake his hand. He grins sheepishly. His unexpected smile makes him look sort of goofy and endearing instead of bulky and menacing. "Sorry if I've been kind of rude to you. Cass told me not to say much when Liam was around. Not to make Liam mad. He's got a reputation."

I want to laugh. If they knew Liam like I do, then they'd know that there was nothing to worry about. But of course to the drones, Liam is a fearsome warrior. A killer. "No problem," I say to Alun, nodding. "You drones have a reputation too."

"Former drones," Cass corrects me. She runs a hand through her short hair. I see more old scars on the insides of her arms. They're the remnants of deep horizontal cuts, and they look self-inflicted. "We're still going to meet tonight," she continues. "But later than dinner. Just a few of us. To talk about David, and about the scientists' plan for Island Alpha."

"Can't you just tell me now?"

She gestures at the tiled walls. "I learned my lesson at Destiny Station. Someone might be listening—or watching."

I follow her gaze. I only see the omnipresent checkered tiles. But I'm sure she's right. I feel like no matter where we are, we're constantly under some kind of surveillance. Why should it be any different here?

I nod. "Fine. Tell me what you can."

Cass leans forward, and gestures for me to do the same. "I'll come and get you late tonight, at two-fifteen in the morning," she whispers in my ear, her words barely audible. "We're going to break into one of the communication centers and meet up there."

"Break in?" I say. "Are you serious?"

Cass shushes me.

I lower my voice. "We'll get caught," I whisper. "They'll think we're spies and lock us up! Dr. Barrett's guards are incredibly paranoid, or haven't you noticed?"

"Breaking into places and stealing stuff is something I do pretty well," Cass says. She doesn't sound proud of these skills, but she doesn't sound guilty either. Just matter-of-fact. "Be ready at two fifteen, okay? If you're interested, that is."

I glance over at Alun. He smiles at me encouragingly.

"I'm taking a risk here," I say to Cass. "This could be a trap."

Cass sighs. "Listen, most of us drones acted the way we did on the wheel because of the UNA drugs. You got lucky, and the drugs didn't affect you the same way. But do we seem crazy or wild to you now?"

"Breaking into a control room here sounds kind of crazy, or at least pretty dangerous."

"We want the same things you do," Alun adds softly, sounding almost wistful. He gazes at me with his one good eye. "To get our friends back from the jungle and from the archive. We think that David is the only person on the entire wheel who the scientists are able to communicate with."

"How do you know that?" I ask.

"It's just what we've heard," he replies cryptically. "We don't know why, or how exactly."

Cass leans forward and whispers, "Tonight, we're going to try to get the communication system up and running ourselves. See if we can talk to David directly."

"How will we get past the guards? I assume the communication center is watched around the clock."

"I'll take care of that."

"And if we do get caught? We'll need a good excuse."

Cass nods. "I'll create a distraction and take the blame. The rest of you can run."

I look at her and then at Alun. "Okay," I sigh. "I'm in."

Cass grins. "I knew you would be."

Alun gestures at the refectory behind us. "Want some food?"

"I'm not hungry," I tell him. My stomach feels sick over Liam.

"You should eat now, before they tighten the rationing," Cass says. "I heard that's coming next." She stands up.

Alun does too, swigging the last of his water.

"See you tonight," Cass says. Then she pauses and adds, "But if you tell anyone about our plan, we'll find out. And then everything's off."

"I don't have anyone here to tell," I murmur honestly.

I watch as Cass and Alun walk away from me. Right now, I'm missing Liam more than ever. *And Gadya, Rika, David, Markus, and everyone else.* Even Meira. Not to mention my own mom. I still don't know if she's really safe, despite Dr. Barrett's words. I wonder when she'll arrive here. I feel like at Destiny Station I was just getting used to being alive and free again, and it was ripped out from under me before I could enjoy it.

I walk over to one of the canteens and get my ration of water. I drink it down in a few gulps. I hope Cass is right about being able to communicate with David. A million questions for him run through my mind.

110

First, I want to know if he's okay. Second, I want to know how he escaped from that feeler. And third, I want to know how he's in communication with the scientists and the guards at Southern Arc. The more secrets we can figure out together, the greater our chance of success when we return to the wheel.

As I leave the cafeteria, I look around for Emma—or anyone else I know—but I don't see any familiar faces. So I decide to use the rest of the day to explore as much of the station as I can without getting stopped by the guards. I stroll down the tiled halls, trying to project an air of confidence. I'm looking for the underground greenhouse, desperate to get a glimpse of something green and alive in this barren place.

The hallways seem endless, all lit by naked fluorescent lightbulbs. Every now and then, guards on patrol pass me by, as do other residents of the base and streams of refugees from Destiny Station.

I occasionally see groups of kids too. Former villagers, but no one that I know. For a moment, I'm tempted to join up with some of them. Most of them look pretty friendly. But I don't want to waste any time right now.

I keep walking, descending a short staircase.

I arrive at a low, narrow tunnel, curved on either side. There are fewer people here, and a loud thrumming noise fills the air. It gets louder the farther I walk. I eventually reach a series of large steel doors, guarded by men with AK-47 assault rifles.

"What are you doing down here?" one of the guards calls out to me, as I try to blithely stroll past him.

"Going for a walk," I say.

"You can't be down here."

"Why not?" I glance at the steel doors. "What's behind there?"

"Generators and batteries," the guard says warily.

"Where does the fuel for Southern Arc even come from?" I ask, realizing that it must take a huge amount of energy to power this station.

"Everyone always asks that," the guard says. "It's from renewable sources. Solar power, turbines, and water. We have a windmill array not far from here, and underwater turbines offshore. Our generators convert the power harnessed by those sources into electricity."

I nod.

"Now get back to wherever you came from." He gestures up the short flight of stairs dismissively. "Go."

I want to keep moving forward. I can see that the tunnel extends farther into the distance. And the noise of the generators gets even louder down there. But now other guards are watching me closely, and I don't want to draw too much attention to myself.

"Thanks a bunch," I say, faking politeness, as I head back toward the stairs.

I wonder if the communication rooms are somewhere down this hallway, past the generators. I haven't stumbled across them so far.

But I know that tonight I will have my chance to find them. And if everything goes well, I will get an opportunity to talk to David again and try to unravel some of the mysteries that haunt me so deeply.

# 9 TRANSMISSION

THAT NIGHT, I SIT huddled on a bunk bed in a room with twelve other refugees from Destiny Station. I'm unable to sleep, knowing that Cass and Alun will be coming for me at two fifteen. For a while, I'm worried that the other occupants of the room won't be asleep at that hour either. They shuffle and twist, flailing on narrow bunks as they try to find sleep. Some of them have nightmares, crying out and then waking up, just to repeat the cycle again.

I can't stop thinking about Liam. I wonder where he is right now, and if he's okay. *Is he close to finding his father yet?* I hope he's thinking about me, too.

I wonder what he would advise me to do right now. Maybe I'm making a huge mistake by listening to Cass. I could always ignore her and pretend to be asleep tonight. But my need to find out more about what happened to David outweighs my fear.

To pass the time, I flip through some pages of *The Myth of Sisyphus*, hoping to find some guidance there. The paperback copy is old and some of the pages are missing. As I skim through it, a phrase catches my eye: "There is scarcely any passion without struggle." From my experiences on the wheel, I know this to be true.

I'm about to read more, but the fluorescent lights only stay on until eleven, when they abruptly cut off. We're plunged into semidarkness. Only a red exit light above the door provides any light. I assume this is a way to conserve power. I can barely see the hands of the old analog clock hanging on the wall near the exit, so I close my book and put it down.

Finally, one by one, the other people in the room fall asleep. I can hear their deep breathing and their snores. I lie there on the bunk under a thin gray blanket. My clothes are on, including my boots.

I grow increasingly nervous as two fifteen grows near. I keep staring at the clock. I feel like my adrenaline is the only thing keeping me awake and alert. *I wonder if Cass will even show up for me.* Maybe she'll have second thoughts about inviting me along.

But then, precisely at two fifteen, there's a soft knock at the door. I pull the blanket off me and sit up slowly on my bunk, making as little noise as possible. I gently lower my boots onto the ground.

The knock comes again. It's so soft that if I weren't waiting for it, I might not have heard it. I stand up and walk to the door as quietly as I can. I take hold of the handle and turn it, swinging the door inward.

I peer out into the hall. It's lit only by red emergency lights on the walls, spaced twenty feet apart. Cass's face appears from the darkness, looking ghostly in the crimson shadows. "You ready, Alenna?" she whispers.

I look behind her and see a group of eight other kids, including Alun and Emma. I didn't think there would be so many of them.

I swallow hard and nod.

"Then c'mon," Cass whispers. She glances down. "But take off your boots first, or you'll make too much noise."

I notice that all of them are barefoot, so I do what she says.

Then I open the door a bit more and slide through the opening. I step out into the hall. The station seems colder now without the bright lights on, and without any people around. The tiles are icy on my feet, even with my socks on.

I gently close the door behind me. "Lead the way," I tell Cass, peering around the dim hallways.

"Hey there," Emma whispers, coming over to my side. "Is this spooky enough for you, or what?"

I smile a bit. "It's better than the wheel at nighttime," I whisper back. "You sure we won't get caught?"

"Don't worry," Alun says, overhearing. "Cass knows what she's doing."

"I hope so," I reply. "Or we're all gonna get locked up." I can't imagine what the punishment is at Southern Arc for breaking into a locked communication center. I'm guessing it's pretty harsh. Dr. Barrett seems like the kind of person who would relish running a maximum security prison as much as a rebel base.

We start walking quickly down the hall. Everything is bathed in the red glow.

"Let me do the talking if we run into any guards," Cass says to the group. "But hopefully, we won't. We just have to move fast."

We keep walking, rounding the corner and heading into another hallway. Every sound is magnified—the rustling of our clothing, the sound of our feet on the tiles, and even our breathing.

"Check it out," Emma whispers, holding up a small white object as we walk. In the dim light, it resembles some sort of remote control.

"What is that?"

"A key to the communication center. Cass took it off a guard earlier today. He obviously hasn't noticed it's missing yet."

Cass holds up a hand. Everyone immediately stops walking. I almost stumble into Alun, but I stop just in time.

"What?" one of the other boys hisses at Cass.

"Shhh," she says back. "Listen."

I listen closely, but I don't hear anything. Only the silence of the station at night.

"I think we're okay," I finally say.

"Just being careful," Cass murmurs in response. We start moving again, more cautiously than before.

A few minutes later we reach our destination. It's a section of the base that I haven't seen yet—a newer wing built underground. Shiny tiles gleam in the red light. We stop in front of a thick metal door, huddling around it. The door is painted black, and it looks like the entrance to a bank vault.

"We're right under the satellite arrays here," Emma explains to me. "This is the communication wing."

"And no one guards this place at night?" I ask, incredulous.

"They should, but they're on a secret smoke break between shifts. Dr. Barrett doesn't know about it, but it's common knowledge among the refugees here. We asked around. But we have to move fast. The guards will be back in ten minutes."

"Ten minutes?" I'm surprised. "That's how long we have?"

Emma nods. "Probably less. I thought Cass told you."

"It's an in-and-out job," Cass mutters. "We don't need long. Emma, get the door."

Emma presses the button on the remote control, and the black door unlatches automatically and glides open, revealing a dark space within. The door is about a foot thick. We quickly slip inside the opening. The door slides shut behind us with a dull clank.

We move past a bank of computer screens, heading into the heart of a technological wonderland. Everywhere I look are computers and cables, and glowing plasma screens displaying colorful streams of data. I follow after Cass, sliding past Emma and the boys so that I'm right behind her. If we only have ten minutes at most, I need to make them count.

Cass goes over to a touch-screen pad near a computer and starts rapidly entering numbers. She catches my gaze and says, "I memorized the code they use to contact him. I watched when they punched it in at Destiny Station."

Emma is behind me. "This code will send a signal over the satellite, hopefully straight to David."

"I'm confused. What device will he pick up the signal on?" I ask. "He doesn't have a computer with him."

Cass and Emma look at each other. Finally Cass speaks, as she returns her gaze to the screen: "Maybe he had more than matches hidden on him when he got to the wheel. I'm not sure."

I freeze, startled.

"Wait— How can you know about that?" When David showed his hidden matches to me, that first day on the wheel, we were completely alone together. No one was watching us. And I certainly never told anyone about it.

"Perhaps we have our own reasons for wanting to contact David," Cass says.

I realize then that Cass and the others must definitely know David somehow. Maybe from his resistance cell back in New Providence. Or from some other place entirely. I half-suspected this. I'm just surprised that they didn't tell me earlier.

Just as I'm about to ask them what's really going on, a loud beeping noise starts coming from the computer.

"Turn that off!" one of the boys hisses.

"I'm trying!" Cass replies, tapping the keys even faster.

The beeping stops. We stand there without moving.

"You think anyone heard?" Emma whispers. Everyone is silent except for Cass. She starts typing in numbers again.

"The door's shut, and this room is soundproofed," she explains.

Right then, the screen nearest to us flares to life.

"Look," I say.

Cass nods. "We're in."

I stare at the screen. The black-and-white image is slightly pixilated, as though the satellite feed is malfunctioning. But it's good enough that I can tell what I'm looking at.

*It's David's face.*

He's lying sideways on the ground, curled up under a hand-woven blanket. For a moment, I'm sure that he's dead and we're watching his corpse. His angular face is battered, cut and bruised. But then I see his chest rise and fall. He's sleeping.

"David?" Cass asks, speaking into a microphone in front of the computer.

"It's me, Alenna!" I add, leaning in before anyone can stop me. "Can you hear me? Liam and I got off the wheel!"

I see movement. David opens his almond-shaped brown eyes, and stares blearily into the camera lens.

"David," I say again, as the others crowd around the computer, their voices chiming in as well.

"Alenna?" David asks, sounding dazed. His voice reaches me as a distorted crackle. He grabs for the camera and holds it closer to his face. I have no idea how we're talking to each other right now.

David smiles. It feels like he's looking straight at me through the screen. "You made it," he says. "I thought you would." He pauses. "I wasn't so lucky."

"We're here too," Cass adds.

David nods. "I know—I can hear you."

"Someone tell me what's going on," I say, frustrated. "How do you guys know each other? And David, how did you get away from the feeler? I don't understand anything that's happening right now."

"Alenna, we don't have time for—" Cass begins.

"No. I need to know. It's important."

"I got the feeler to drop me," David says, sounding tired. His voice is barely audible. "When we brought that other one down on the lake, I thought I saw a battery latch on its underbelly, hidden beneath the eye in the UNA logo. It matched some schematics I'd seen before in New Providence in my resistance cell. So when the feelers grabbed me, I climbed up the tentacles and held on to the battery. I managed to rip it out when it flew lower to the ground. The feeler crashed back down onto the pipes."

I listen in stunned silence. Is that even possible? Is David telling the truth?

"I hit my head and blacked out," he continues. "When I woke up, I hid before another feeler could find me. Then I found a different way out of the city on the shore, around the lake, and back into the forest. By accident, I found a tunnel that went underneath the barrier—one we didn't know about. I've been running ever since." He pauses. "Cass probably already told you, but I know her from my resistance cell back home."

"She didn't tell me," I say, shooting her a glance. "But I guessed as much."

"David, we don't have long," Cass says. "How are you talking to the scientists? Did you find some sort of communication device on the wheel?"

"I discovered that every feeler has a camera, a microphone, and speakers on it, mounted in a bracket at the front. I took that stuff from the one that dropped me and crashed on the pipes. I started trying to broadcast distress signals. I knew the UNA would pick them up, of course. But I also hoped that some rebels had managed to hijack the feed and were monitoring it. Turns out I was right." He pauses for breath. "The scientists at Destiny Station picked up on it and routed me to a different frequency, one that the UNA can't trace. That's how I got in touch with them. So now I can talk to you guys, and you can see me, but I can only hear you."

"Amazing," Alun murmurs, adjusting his eye patch.

"Alenna, what about the others?" David asks me. "The ones who made it to the gray zone with us?"

"Rika and Markus got taken by feelers too. So did James, the Monk's drone. They're inside the specimen archive. Gadya is stuck there too, if she's even alive—"

Cass interrupts: "What are things like on the wheel right now? Give us your coordinates and we'll try to find you as soon as we land there."

"I can't stay in one place. The feelers and the drones keep me on the run." His image flickers and dims.

One of the boys moves in to adjust the screen. Other boys are scrambling to grab data off hard drives, and collect it on portable readers they've scavenged.

"So were you ever really a drone?" I whisper to Cass. "If you were in a resistance cell in the UNA, doesn't that make you a rebel?" All these different allegiances and secrets make me feel like I'm standing on shifting sand.

"I was both," she says.

We look back at the screen again as David's image reappears. "Where are you, roughly?" I ask David. "What sector?"

"I don't know. By the sun, I think I've made it into the purple sector. The scientists have my data logged for the past two weeks, though. Just get it off the computers if you can."

"We will," Cass says. "We've already tapped into the system. They're asking you to give them reports on the wheel, right?"

David nods. "I'm doing surveillance and sending them geographic coordinates. So they know where it's safe to land when they get here."

One of the boys behind us speaks up: "Only three more minutes left."

"We'll get your data, and we'll find out where you are," I tell David. "Just try to stay in the same sector."

The image flickers and rolls on the screen again. I'm afraid that we're going to lose contact with him for good.

"David, the signal's breaking up," I say.

"Alenna, I don't think what the scientists and Dr. Barrett are telling everyone is completely true," he says, his voice crackling in an abrupt burst of static.

"What do you mean?" I ask.

"I don't know if they plan on freeing the kids in the specimen archive. At least not for a very long time."

"Why not?" Cass asks urgently.

"They think the kids are safe there in stasis, and won't cause them any problems. They don't think they need to deal with them for years. They're just telling us they're going to save them first, so we'll do what they want. At least that's what I think."

I lean forward, worried about what other lies Dr. Barrett and the scientists might have told us. "David, Liam's gone to find his dad, Octavio. They're stranded on a hydrofoil a thousand miles from here. Have any of the scientists talked about that?"

"No. At least not in front of me. They're just using me to give them data."

"Two more minutes," the boy behind us warns. "We gotta leave soon."

Cass turns away from the screen, looking toward Emma, Alun, and the other boys. "Grab all the data you can," she hisses. "And then let's get the hell out of here." She turns back to David. "We'll try to contact you again. But next time we see you might be on the wheel."

"I hope so."

"Ninety seconds!" one of the boys says, sounding panicked.

I press my hand against the screen. David's image flickers there, in ghostly black and white. "David, we're coming for you," I tell him. "Just hang on, okay?"

He smiles tiredly. "Just get here soon, Alenna." He gives the camera a small wave and a rueful smile.

And then the screen flares and goes black. David is gone. Time is nearly up.

"Let's go!" I whisper.

We start racing back through the room, heading toward the black sliding door. Alun has Emma's remote control in his hand. He's already pushing the button with his wide fingers. But the door doesn't move.

"C'mon!" Cass says.

"It's not working!" Alun replies, pounding on the button

harder. "Maybe it only works from the outside!"

We reach the door and stand there. There's no doorknob or latch. Just an electronic key-swipe. And we don't have a key. We're trapped inside.

"We're gonna get caught!" another boy yelps. "Sixty seconds left until the guard comes back!"

Suddenly, I see something: a red emergency alert button near the door. I lunge forward and slam it with my palm.

The door instantly slides open with a hiss. But at the same time, warning alarms start blaring at maximum volume. I'm not sure whether I've saved us or doomed us.

"Run!" I yell, darting out of the room.

We barge into the hallway. Alun turns back and hits the button on the remote, making the door slide shut behind us. But the alarms keep wailing. Louder than the ones in Destiny Station. The red lights that line the hallway begin flashing, too. Everyone's movements look strange and jagged, like we're caught in strobe lights. The footsteps of nearby guards rush in our direction.

We start running down the hall as fast as we can. As we get farther along, I see one door pop open, and then another one opens too. People step out, scared and confused. I freeze for a second, but then see that these are just other refugees, not guards. Some of the refugees must have been given rooms on this wing. The alarm is now waking the whole station up.

I feel Cass's hand grip my arm. "Nice work," she whispers. "I think we're safe." We start walking again.

More refugees wander into the halls around us, calling out and asking questions. The guards are here now, guns drawn, trying to determine what's going on and attempting to restore order. But the crowd gets in their way. We deliberately blend in with them, pretending that we just woke up. The sirens cut off.

"Won't they have us on surveillance tape?" I ask Cass, suddenly paranoid. I'm afraid that if they catch us, they won't let us go back to the wheel. *And then I won't get to see Liam again.* I can't let anything jeopardize that.

Cass smiles, her eyes glinting in the flashing red lights. "The surveillance data for the entire station is recorded in that one communication center." She opens her palm and shows me a small data drive. "Guess it's gone missing . . ."

"Hey, you there!" a guard calls out to us, as our group starts to disperse. "You guys!" The drive disappears from Cass's hand like magic as she slips it back into her pocket. I still don't know how she had time to grab it in the first place.

"Yes?" I ask the guard, trying to sound as innocent as possible.

"Back to your rooms!" The guard looks around, then calls out, louder, "Back to your rooms, everyone! False alarm."

Breathing a sigh of relief, Cass and I start heading in the same direction, just the two of us. The others have scattered.

"So you were in David's resistance cell?" I ask softly as we walk. "Tell me everything."

"I wasn't in his cell. Not technically. I'm not from New Providence. I'm from Dayton, Ohio." She pauses. "I mean, the place that used to be called Dayton before Minister Harka and the UNA ruined everything. But sometimes the different cells would work together. I met David more than a year and a half ago on an encrypted online connection. A group of cells scattered across the country were trying to learn more about how the GPPT actually works. They trained me how to get into secret places, and how to snatch things without being caught. They also taught me and David how to subvert certain UNA technologies."

"You've never met David in person, then? Back in the UNA or on the wheel?"

She shakes her head. "No, just online. But I trust him more than I'd trust members of my own family. I was already frozen in the specimen archive by the time you and David got to the wheel. He probably didn't even know that I was there. I mean, he knew I'd failed the GPPT the year before. But he couldn't have known I'd get taken by a feeler."

We keep walking. "How come I didn't know about these resistance cells when I was living in New Providence?" I ask.

Cass squints at me. "Would you really have joined one if you did? Before you failed the GPPT?"

After a moment's thought, I tell her, "No, probably not. But back then I didn't know what was really going on in the UNA."

"I wouldn't have known about the cells either, except my older brother Vincent failed the GPPT, too. My parents believed the UNA's lies. That he must have been harboring subversive tendencies, and was some kind of latent psycho. They took his photos down off the walls, and pretended he didn't exist. But I knew the truth. He never did anything wrong. *Nothing*. My parents wouldn't listen to me, and none of my other relatives would listen either. That's what made me stop trusting adults—and made me start questioning everything around me. I got really depressed. Angry. Eventually I got contacted by a local cell." She shrugs. "Not that we really accomplished much. We just got sent to the wheel."

"Any resistance to the UNA is worth something," I tell her. "And I'm sure there are more resistance cells out there. Maybe even ones that nobody knows about yet."

She looks at me. "You think so?"

I nod. "There must be."

We finally reach the door to my room. My roommates are awake from the sirens, milling around in the hallway. The red lights are on, but they've stopped flashing.

"Did you ever find your brother on the wheel?" I ask Cass.

"Yes." She pauses. "But not alive. He was killed by some villagers in the orange sector—before the drones took control of that area." I can see the pain in her eyes, like a raw wound in her soul. "I found his grave."

"I'm sorry."

She glances away. "Me too."

We stand there awkwardly for a moment. Maybe this is part of the reason why Cass joined the drones. *To avenge her brother's death.*

"I better get going," Cass says finally. "I need to hide the data drive before anyone finds it on me. Let's talk more in the morning."

"Definitely."

Cass turns to leave. I stand there in the hall for a moment, staring down the long tunnel looking after her as she walks away. The red lights reflect off the tiles, creating strange, hypnotic patterns.

Then I head back into my room and find my bunk. Soon it will be morning, and there will be plans to make. I go to sleep that night dreaming of the wheel, and longing for the moment when Liam and I are reunited on that treacherous island.

# 10 THE AIRSHIPS

I WAKE UP TO harsh fluorescent lights glaring into my face. It feels like only a few seconds since I went to sleep, but night has already passed. I check the clock on the wall. It's already seven in the morning.

I push the blanket off me and stagger out of bed, fully dressed. I feel exhausted and thirsty. I smooth down my hair. Then I put my boots on and grab my jacket, with its copy of my book in it. I head out of the room, passing the bunks that still hold sleeping occupants, and step out into the empty hallway.

It seems like we got away with breaking into the communication center last night. I figure that if anyone was going to catch us, they would have done it already. I start walking down the hall, headed to get my ration of water and food. I can't wait to tell Liam everything that I've learned—about David, the wheel, and Cass. I miss him so much. By now, hopefully he has found his father.

I wish there were some way to communicate with Liam, like there was with David. But I'm guessing that communications between Dr. Barrett's helicopter and Octavio's hydrofoil will be almost impossible to intercept, and heavily protected.

As I near the refectory, I look around for Cass. I don't see her anywhere. I only see guards and adults lounging around near the walls.

"Alenna?" a voice calls out behind me. I turn around and see Emma standing there. Her hair is up in a tangled bun.

"Hey," I say.

"The others are sleeping. Except for Cass, but she barely ever sleeps. Want to grab some food together?"

"Sure." We walk over to get our rations. "So how did you end up hanging out with Cass and her friends?" I ask.

"You mean, why don't I hate her because she was a drone?"

"Exactly."

She laughs. "Well, you're friends with David, right? And everyone thought he was a drone on the wheel. Identity isn't always as straightforward as people think."

"David's different. He was forced into it. And he was just acting."

Emma looks at me. "Maybe the same is true of my friends. But even if it's not, it's okay. We're fighting for the same cause now. Once we get back to the wheel, and stop the drones' exposure to the mind-control drugs, most of them will come to their senses."

I think about the kids on the wheel who are sick—villagers and drones alike. On the wheel, we called this disease the Suffering. It was a bad reaction to new UNA test drugs, and it caused people's flesh to slowly disintegrate. It was always fatal. I look at Emma. "What about the Ones Who Suffer? Is there anything we can do to help them?"

"The scientists are working on some kind of vaccine," Emma replies. "At least that's what Cass says." She pauses. "I was actually a nurse for the Ones Who Suffer in my village. That was my task."

"I didn't know that," I tell her, surprised. "That must have been hard."

"It was. I volunteered for it. I didn't know what I was getting into." She glances away. "But it was worth it. I don't usually talk about it much."

I want to ask her more questions about the Suffering, but she seems reticent. I understand why. She probably knows more kids who died than the rest of us combined. So I don't push her. There's something gentle and sympathetic about Emma. I can see the kindness—and sadness—in her pale green eyes.

We go over and get our food and drink—one protein bar and a cup of water each, just like on the submarine. Then we head toward a metal table set close against the wall. There, we sit across from each other and talk softly, so that no one can overhear.

"Now that Minister Harka is dead, I bet the drones' hierarchy is already falling apart," Emma continues, taking off her glasses and setting them on the table. "They've lost their whole reason to exist. Without a leader, they'll go into a downward spiral . . ."

For an instant, I have a flashback to the depravity of the drones' encampment. My head fills with images of diseased kids, of girls selling themselves for food, and the smell of rotting meat. "That might not be a good thing," I point out.

"True," Emma replies thoughtfully.

I think about our return to the wheel as I take a bite of my protein bar. I definitely don't want to walk into a situation that's even worse than the one we left. "I wish we'd had time to ask David about relations between the villagers and the drones. If things are better or worse." I sigh, feeling scared for him. "I hope he can survive until we get there."

"His resistance cell obviously trained him for survival in tough circumstances. I think he's going to be okay."

I take another bite of my dry protein bar, washing it down with a gulp of water. "Were you in a resistance cell too?"

She laughs. "No. I was oblivious to all of that."

"Yeah. Same here."

"I didn't even find out they existed until other kids told me about them on the wheel."

I nod. "Me too. Where were you from? I mean, originally?"

"Los Angeles Three," she says. Her eyes get a faraway look in them. "I miss it there. Not life in the UNA, but just my family, y'know? Going to the beach. Hanging out. The good stuff." She pauses. For a moment I almost envy her memories. I wonder what it would have been like to have had my parents with me growing up, instead of being sent to the government orphanage.

"I don't miss New Providence," I tell her. "There's not too much for me to be nostalgic about."

She looks at me. "I know. And I'm sorry about your dad. I heard people talking about him back at Destiny Station."

I nod. "It's okay. It happened a long time ago. I'm worried about my mom, though. She's supposed to be on her way here, but she hasn't turned up yet."

Right then, Alun and a brown-haired boy appear at the table, holding their rations. I haven't seen this other boy before. He's thin and bony, with a sharp chin and floppy brown hair parted in the middle. He wasn't with us last night. I can't tell if he was a drone or a villager on the wheel, but I'm guessing villager.

"Hey," Emma says to them.

"Hi," I second.

"Did you really bring down one of the feelers?" the brown-haired boy asks me, with no introduction. "On a frozen lake?" The words burst out of him like he's been waiting a while to pose this question.

"Yeah," I tell him. "I mean, me and a bunch of other kids."

"For real? It's not just a story?"

I nod. "We overpowered it and dragged it onto the ice." I think about what David told me about the feelers and their battery packs. "The feelers aren't as infallible as everyone thinks."

"I told you she killed a feeler," Alun says to the boy. "Now pay up." The other kid hands Alun his protein bar.

I look at Emma, confused, as the two boys head off, bickering. "What was that about?"

"They're betting on you," Emma says, smiling a little. "You and Liam are sort of legendary around here, for the stuff you did on the wheel."

"All we did was try to survive."

"Well, you did it better than almost everyone else." She pauses. "I wish I'd been able to take down a feeler. But one of them got me and froze me. I just woke up at Destiny Station when the scientists thawed me out. Months had passed since I'd been taken. It was awful—like a whole chunk of my life had been stolen."

"Do you remember any of it?" I ask her, curious. "Like how it felt to get frozen? Or what happened after the feeler took you?"

She shakes her head. "No. I just remember flying through the air with those tentacles wrapped around me. I couldn't breathe. Couldn't move. And then I either passed out, or it injected me with something. Everything went black. And the next time I saw light again, I was inside the medical lab in Destiny Station." She shudders. "I don't want to think about what would have happened to me if the scientists hadn't hijacked my plane."

131

A nearby bank of video screens embedded in the tiles comes to life. At the same time, a warning siren starts pinging. Everyone in the dining hall instantly goes quiet, including me and Emma.

Dr. Barrett's gaunt and grizzled face appears on every screen, emerging from the darkness. It's a live video feed.

I half stand up, trying to see if I can find Liam behind him in the shot. But it just remains a close-up of Dr. Barrett. Emma puts her glasses back on to watch.

"There is no time for formalities or niceties," Dr. Barrett begins, staring directly into the camera. "Things out here on the ocean are worse than we expected. We have encountered— and defeated—two enemy crafts sent from the southern UNA." He pauses. "I am talking to you right now from the Base Lerato hydrofoil. We have found and rescued Octavio Bernal, and what remains of his crew. And we have refueled his craft. So far, none of my men has been killed. We are safe for the moment. But we are low on resources, and we need your assistance. We cannot withstand many more attacks." His hooded eyes stare at us from under furrowed brows. "The time has come to begin our assault on Island Alpha. We cannot wait any longer."

Around us, voices start murmuring in surprise. Emma and I look at each other. I didn't think this day would come so soon— but at the same time, I can't wait to be reunited with Liam. I feel terrified but also strangely exhilarated.

"My men know what to do," Dr. Barrett continues. "They will initiate the procedure for everyone to leave Southern Arc, and head to Island Alpha immediately."

The voices around us get louder. Both Emma and I stand up, watching the screens. I'm suddenly worried about my mom. What will happen if we leave here before her vessel arrives? I still don't know why it's taking so long. I assume her submarine can't move as fast as ours—but I'm afraid that something has gone wrong.

On the screen, the signal breaks up for a second and then reconfigures itself.

"Obey the guards," Dr. Barrett continues. "They will lead you onto crafts that will take you directly to Island Alpha. They will also brief you on our military strategy."

"I gotta find Cass," Emma whispers nervously.

On-screen, Dr. Barrett keeps talking. "The time has arrived to storm the island and take it from the drones and the feelers. Octavio and I will be meeting you there when you land. You must keep your wits, and gather every ounce of courage that you possess." His eyes burn with a passion that encourages and disturbs me. "*We cannot fail*. Our entire future depends on successfully recapturing Island Alpha."

The image flickers again. We're about to lose the signal. The screen abruptly goes dark, but Dr. Barrett's disembodied voice continues to speak.

"Soon, Island Alpha will be ours. We must never give up, until we have taken the island as our own. By any means necessary . . ."

His words disappear in a wave of angry distortion. Then the audio cuts to silence. Around us, everyone is talking loudly, buzzing about what Dr. Barrett just said. No one expected this kind of message today. A lot of people seem upset, but I'm relieved to know that Liam is alive, and that my journey back to him is beginning.

I hear heavy footsteps and turn my head to see guards entering the refectory. "This way!" one of them calls out to everyone. "You heard Dr. Barrett! The time has come!"

"We'll brief you when we get on the airships!" another guard yells. "Every second you waste now could mean a life lost later on."

I see guards start grabbing startled people by the arms, pushing them forward. "Go! To the airships!"

"Airships?" I ask Emma. I'm picturing large cargo planes, like the one that took me and Liam off the wheel and brought us to Destiny Station.

Emma looks at me, equally confused. "If they have airplanes here, they've been hiding them pretty well."

She's right. Other than Dr. Barrett's helicopter, I've seen nothing around the station anywhere except ice.

We quickly join the group of people heading to the exits, following the guards. The guards are everywhere now. It's clear that they're well-prepared for this moment, like they've practiced it many times.

We reach a guard. I can't help but ask him, "Where are we going exactly?"

He gestures brusquely with his hand. "Up and out of the station. Now move it!"

"But I need to get my things!" Emma says, realizing that he means we're leaving this instant. "Everything's still in my bunk."

"Too late," he replies. "Just keep moving."

"What? That's crazy! But——"

The crowd surges forward, and we're forced past the guard. People flood down the hallway, and we get caught up with them. It's like the whole station is being evacuated.

I wonder what Dr. Barrett meant when he said things were worse than he'd thought. I long to feel Liam's arms holding me again. I never should have let him go. I feel a knot in my stomach. *What if he's alive, but injured?* Dr. Barrett said that no one had been killed, but he didn't say if anyone had gotten hurt. I start to feel panicked again.

"This way!" a guard calls out.

We're being guided up a flight of tiled stairs. Heading out of Southern Arc and into the freezing cold. I can already feel blasts of icy wind hitting us, even though we're inside the station. The doors, hatches, and ports leading outside must have all been thrown open. I button my jacket, glad that I have it with me. Emma pulls up the collar of her own jacket against the wind.

Both of us are looking around for Cass and her other friends. There are so many people here, Cass could be anywhere.

We reach another wide staircase, and we walk up it. The air is getting even colder and thinner. The stairs seem to go on forever. Above us is a wide opening with sunlight filtering through it.

"Wow," Emma breathes. Something has caught her attention. I follow her gaze, peering out the opening as we walk.

A huge cylindrical object moves across the sky for a moment, blotting out the sun. It's like some kind of massive UNA warship. Startled, I stop walking, and get jostled by the crowd. Then the object moves out of view. I stare after it, craning my neck.

"What was that?" I ask Emma.

"I don't know."

"I guess we better find out." We start walking again.

I reach the top of the stairs with Emma at my side. We step out onto the ice and into the bitterly cold air. I can feel the hairs inside my nose already starting to freeze. I shove my hands into my jacket pockets. Emma is shivering next to me. The sun now reflects off the ice so brightly that my eyes ache. There are guards everywhere, yelling to one another.

But what gets my attention is the object in the sky. It's floating above us in the subarctic air. A massive gray airship, like some kind of gas-filled dirigible. It's easily half the length of a football field, and drifting about twenty feet above the ground. Ropes tie it down to large metal stakes that have been driven into the ice.

Under the cylindrical hull hangs a huge compartment, clearly meant to carry passengers. Machine guns stick out from turrets placed between narrow windows. And attached to the back of the craft is a complex system of engines and giant propellers.

"This is the way off Southern Arc?" I ask, startled and confused. I guess I was expecting something more high-tech.

"We're going to get shot right out of the sky!" Emma says, echoing my dismay. "We won't even make it to the wheel."

I see Alun forcing his way through the crowd. A wool cap covers his shaved head. Emma and I both call out to him. He hears us and starts heading our way.

"Check it out!" he exclaims when he reaches us. His breath is visible in the air and his cheeks are flushed. He gestures at the airship drifting in the sky above us. "Can you believe this?"

"It's not going to fit everyone," I say. "I don't understand."

"Me neither," Emma adds.

"Let me show you something." Alun leads us through the crowd, cutting a hasty path, practically knocking people out of the way with his bulk. Some people have jackets on and some don't. The guards have rushed us out here so quickly that no one seems prepared. This harsh, abrupt way of doing things is apparently just part of life at Southern Arc. We follow Alun, our feet crunching on the ice, until we reach the edge of the mob.

I now have a clear view of our surroundings, and I stare out across the ice in surprise.

For several miles, I see an armada of gray dirigibles, lying deflated on the ice. Their soft hulls are collapsed over the passenger compartments. But guards move between them, with giant metal machines on sleds, rapidly filling their air compartments with whatever gas keeps these strange crafts aloft.

"They've got ten of these things," Alun explains. "Inflatable ships, with a skin made from synthetic fibers. Each one can carry almost a hundred people, plus supplies."

"And one simple bullet, or a firework, could take each one out of the sky," I say.

"She's right," Emma agrees. "They're going to become fireballs."

"Naw, they're using a new form of inert helium to fill them. I asked a guard. They're not flammable," Alun replies. "And each one has hundreds of individual compartments inside, with valves. If one compartment gets hit and leaks, the others instantly seal off from it. And the leaky compartment repairs itself—the synthetic fibers close up and heal. Plus, the machine guns will take care of any attack ships. These things are actually pretty hard to bring down. Cass got her hands on the technical specs a few hours ago and told me about them."

"This seems insane," I murmur.

"Does it really?" Cass's voice says from behind me.

By now I'm used to her sneaking up on us, catlike. I turn around. She has a thick black jacket on, and a black cap. They both look like they've been stolen from an unwitting guard.

"These airships won't show up on radar," she continues. "No metal. Everything's made from radar-absorbent fiberglass and polymers, even the guns. And they can fly really low to the ground. No one knows that these ships exist. Dr. Barrett's men have been building them under the ice for the past eight years. There's no other way to get so many of us across the ocean undetected."

"What about when we get to the wheel?" I ask. "People will see us then. Drones will inevitably try to fight us, and so will the feelers."

"That's true," she concedes. "But I think we'll be landing in a desolate spot in the purple sector. It's a safe place that David scouted for the scientists—based on what I can piece together from his dispatches."

"Isn't the purple sector overrun by drones?" Emma asks.

Cass nods. "Some of it. But maybe that's the only large flat surface David could find. We need someplace like that to land."

I glance up at the airship swaying in the sky. The huge gas-filled cylinder still looks unwieldy and unsafe. I don't know how it will fare in the cold temperatures. At least its guns are reassuring.

The four of us stand there in the ice field as the wind blows through our clothes. People bustle around us, getting ready for our departure. I rub my hands together and stamp my feet, trying to stay warm.

I have no doubt that the drones will come at us with everything in their arsenal. I wonder how Cass feels about fighting her former tribe when we get there. Or maybe Cass really never did think of herself as a drone. I can't tell for sure.

I overhear Emma asking Alun how long the journey back to the wheel is going to take. I lean in to hear the answer. I know that we're thousands of miles away from the wheel right now. I can't imagine that these airships travel very fast.

"Probably a week," Alun guesses, over the hubbub of the crowd and the noise of the wind.

I try not to think about it. I shut my eyes for a moment, worrying about Liam. I just need to hear his voice and make sure that he's okay. But the only way that's going to happen is if we both make it to the wheel safely.

"C'mon," I say. "Let's try to get on board."

Less than an hour later, we're boarding one of the inflated dirigibles. Almost everyone is leaving Southern Arc for good. Only a skeleton crew of guards will remain behind, to keep the station running and wait for the third vessel coming from Destiny Station. The vessel that my mom is on. If we fail, they will likely be the sole survivors of the rebellion against the UNA.

As I step onto a shaky folding staircase, heading up into the passenger cabin of the airship, I see a guard standing at the top of the steps. He's handing out a small white object to each person getting on board the craft. I see a man ahead of me pop the object into his mouth. It's some kind of pill. I'm instantly on high alert.

"What is that?" I ask Cass. She's on the step ahead of me, clutching the railings. I figure that if anyone knows what the pill is, it's her.

She leans back. "An antidote to the new drugs in the air and water on the wheel. So that no one will turn back into a drone. Or get exposed to the Suffering. The pill inhibits the body from absorbing the UNA's toxins, supposedly."

I nod. "You trust it?"

She shakes her head. "Not really. But they won't let us on board until we take one. The scientists at Destiny Station developed it, and brought the pills here on the submarine."

"Really." I feel nervous. I wonder if this is a pill that my mother helped design.

Cass nods. "The guards and scientists are taking the pills too. No one wants to get the Suffering."

We keep moving up the folding stairs until we reach the top. Cass grabs her pill, and then pops it into her mouth showily.

Next, it's my turn. The guard places the pill in my hand. This pill could be absolutely anything. I hesitate, holding it up to look at it more closely. It looks deceptively innocuous. It's tiny, round, and white, and it doesn't have any markings on it.

I'm essentially trusting my life to the scientists and Dr. Barrett, but I don't feel like I have a choice. *Who knows what other kinds of drugs the UNA has been dumping on the wheel in our absence?*

"If you don't take it, then you gotta stay behind," the guard says to me wearily, hoisting his gun. "What's it gonna be?"

Without thinking about it any more, I put the pill into my mouth. For a second, I'm tempted to hide it under my tongue, but in the end I decide to take it. *If I don't, I won't be able to get back to Liam.* And I don't want to risk getting the Suffering. There's no water, so I choke the pill down dry. I just hope there aren't any awful side effects.

I open my mouth to show the guard that I've swallowed it. He gestures at me to board the craft.

I keep moving until I'm fully inside the spacious passenger compartment, which hangs below the main body of the airship. Everything is made of hard plastic. I can feel it shifting slightly in the wind. The motion gives me a seasick feeling. It's surprisingly warm in the space, like it's heated.

I peer out one of the slitlike windows, gazing down at the people below us as they move around on the ice. I see other ships nearby too, floating in the air like surreal gray clouds.

I look around the compartment again. It's one huge space, with cots built into the walls. In the back are some doors leading to narrow bathrooms. It's clear that this airship has been designed to be as minimally functional as possible. It's already half full with refugees, with more coming up the stairs.

There are six separate gun stations. Two on each side of the compartment, plus one near the front and one at the back. Guards are at each of them, their eyes glued to electronic viewfinders. The guns are mounted outside, and operated by computer controls. This way, there's no direct opening into the compartment for cold air to rush through.

At the very front of the compartment, off to one side, is a separate glass control booth. Two men sit in it—our pilots. In front of them are levers and steering mechanisms. I also see arrays of switches and flashing digital displays. I can't even imagine how much work went into building one of these crafts, let alone ten of them. I'm surprised Dr. Barrett didn't use them to get out of Southern Arc sooner, but maybe he was waiting for the shipment of antidote pills from Destiny Station.

Plastic seats line the center of the space. *And I thought the submarine was bad.* I can't imagine spending an entire week in here, with almost no privacy, and a feeling of endless, grinding tension in my stomach.

Cass and I find seats, and Emma and Alun join us. I wonder where the other two boys with shaved heads are, but I don't see them. Across from us is a video screen on the wall. Like a large window, it displays images of the icy wilderness, broadcast from cameras attached to the exterior front of the airship.

I lean forward, trying to see. In the corner of the frame, I can glimpse the edge of the massive concrete structure of Southern Arc.

I turn to Cass. "You still have the data on David, right?" I ask softly.

She nods, patting her coat pocket. "Everything's in here, including a GPS I stole from a guard this morning. We can track David when we land—or at least I hope we can."

We both stare at the video screen, watching the other airships on the ice. I see one of the ships start to lift upward a bit. I think it's an accident at first, but then I notice that the guards down below are cutting the ropes that bind it to the stakes. They're about to release it.

"Look," I say, pointing at the screen. "It'll be our turn soon."

We watch as another airship starts rising nearby, heading up above us and nearly out of view. The ships move slowly, drifting aimlessly into the sky. Their propellers aren't moving because the pilots haven't turned on the engines yet. They're waiting until the ships drift up even higher, to avoid any dangerous air currents near the ground.

"Okay, everyone!" a tall, wiry guard at the front calls out loudly, cutting through the din of voices. Our compartment is now full, and the door is closed. "Take your seats if you don't already have them."

"Guess we're ahead of the curve," Cass mutters.

Right then I feel gentle motion as we start to move upward. Our journey has begun.

Everyone inside the compartment falls silent for a moment. I glance around at the worried faces of both kids and adults. We are all refugees, at the mercy of these airships and Dr. Barrett's plans. Guards stand at their guns, peering down at their view screens, on constant alert.

"Our voyage will take between five and eleven days," the guard continues. "These dirigibles are designed to go at a top speed of ninety-five miles per hour, but that depends on the wind and other factors. Get prepared for a long, uncomfortable ride."

The crowd just stares back at him.

"In addition," the guard says, "you should know that Dr. Barrett has prohibited us from stopping and helping any other airship if there is an emergency. If one of our fleet falters, then we have to leave it behind, along with everyone on board. Making it to Island Alpha is our sole priority."

Feeling sick, I brush hair back from my eyes. The airship is swaying more now. "I feel like I've been on the run ever since the day I failed the GPPT," I murmur to Cass. "Like I'm in some kind of nightmare loop, and it's never going to stop. I just wish we were back on the wheel already."

"Me too," Emma says, overhearing me.

"Same," Alun mutters.

Cass is looking at the video screen like she's hypnotized.

"You okay?" I ask her.

She nods.

The ground is getting smaller beneath us. Southern Arc is now just a few feet in size. I can't even make out the people down there anymore. The engines start up with a clanking noise, as the propellers in the back begin to turn.

"The running stops when we get to the wheel," I say, staring around at the others.

"Agreed," Cass says, glancing over at me.

"We make our stand there together," I continue. "And we don't give up. No matter what happens. We find Liam and David and everyone else."

The others nod.

The clank of the propellers becomes a roaring, buzzing hum.

Our ship begins moving forward through the air. Slowly at first, but then faster. I stare at the video screen as Southern Arc fades into the distance, and we move toward whatever future awaits us on the wheel.

# 11 THE RETURN

THE SIX DAYS ON board the airship pass more slowly than any other days in my entire life. On the one hand, there's a constant feeling of terror that we're going to be attacked and torn from the skies. But on the other hand, there's also the relentless boredom of sailing above a monotonous ocean, trapped inside a space with a bunch of other people, most of whom are strangers.

My thoughts constantly turn to Liam. I was hoping we would get another dispatch from Dr. Barrett, but so far there has been no news. I try not to obsess about it, although this seems like a bad sign. I just tell myself that it's going to be fine. That it has to be. *Liam is going to meet me as soon as we land in the purple sector.* I can't bear to think of any other possibility.

I also wonder if my mom has made it to Southern Arc yet. I'm hoping there'll be some way to contact her once we reach the wheel.

Here, trapped on the airship, Cass can't hack into the computer system to find out more details about anything. We no longer have access to any of David's new dispatches either. Although, at night, hiding in the bathroom, I've watched the old ones on Cass's stolen folding screen.

What I've seen has been incredibly disturbing. David looks bruised and battered, and he's constantly on the move. Trying to stay ahead of the feelers and the drones. He seems frightened and exhausted. But it's the images behind him that provide the true horrors. Things on the wheel look like they're getting much worse, at least from the pixilated glimpses I catch on the screen.

Occasionally, I see massive forest fires burning out of control. Or teeming feelers descending from the sky, slamming their tentacles down at the trees. David is adept at hiding himself, but I know he can't survive this onslaught forever.

I tell myself that at least our airships haven't been attacked on the journey. The guards have maintained their positions at the guns twenty-four hours per day, in rotation, but they haven't had to fire a single shot. We haven't even run into much bad weather, other than some bumpy air pressure transitions when we moved away from the cold of the Antarctic and over the open ocean.

During our journey, the guards have briefed us on the plan, and held a series of meetings. The plan is simple. The ten airships are going to land in a cleared area in the purple sector, where we will meet up with Dr. Barrett and his men. We will then establish a perimeter and make that area our fortified base camp. After that, we will push outward each day, armed with weapons. There are numerous handguns and bullets on board each airship.

However, we are only supposed to use force if we have to. The guards and the scientists are hoping that we can convince the villagers and drones that we are there to rescue them. That we are not some hostile, invading force sent from the UNA. I know that the villagers will understand this instantly—but the drones will be much harder to deal with.

The plan is to keep pressing onward until our base in the

purple sector becomes a new hub for the island, a safe haven. And slowly we can restore order, shoot down the feelers, give out the antidote pills, and stop the warring of the tribes.

I'm worried that the UNA will try to bomb us once they realize that we've overtaken the island, but the scientists believe the UNA would never risk destroying their own prison colony. The scientists, thanks to Dr. Barrett, also have the means to jam radar systems and hopefully shoot down any missiles. The UNA's military is stretched so thin, no one believes they will actually send a fleet of soldiers to the wheel.

Only after the island is under our control are we supposedly going to free the inhabitants of the specimen archive. But of course that's where our plans and the scientists' plans differ slightly. I have my own hopes about getting to the archive much sooner than that, if possible, and figuring out how to free our friends. Cass and Emma feel the same way. I know we can get our friends out, even if we have to do it one by one, like I did with Liam.

I've been reading more of *The Myth of Sisyphus* to pass the time, and take my mind off the stress. In a way it makes me feel closer to the memory of my dad. Inside the book, I find the line he always used to say to me about the importance of perseverance in tough times: "One must imagine Sisyphus happy." It's oddly comforting to see it in this book.

But I also find passages that make me uneasy. According to Camus, both religious faith and science are equally inadequate at explaining the world. To Camus, the world seems like a frightening and absurd place. One where people can do terrible things to one another, but face no consequences.

On the back cover of the book, a black-and-white photo of Camus stares out at me, looking vaguely ominous. In a brief biography of him on the back, it says that he was a French philosopher who became a member of the resistance against the Nazis in World War II. *A rebel, just like us.* He must know a thing or two about life during wartime. And how to fight fascism.

Now, on the morning of the sixth day in the airship, we finally have the wheel in sight. It's visible in the distance on the video screens.

My heart feels like it stops for a beat when I see Island Alpha emerge from the water and clouds, under overcast skies.

I've been lying on my narrow bunk, reading, with Cass above me. I put my book down and instantly leap up, rushing over to the screen when the wheel first appears.

"We're here!" I say. I intend to yell the words, but they come out more as a breathy gasp. Cass hears me anyway, as do some of the other passengers. They rush over, and we huddle around the screens.

From this distance, the wheel looks desolate. But I know that is not the case. The island rises up from the water in isolated grandeur, with craggy tree-covered cliffs. Inhospitable and severe. *This must be the coast of the purple sector.* The airship rapidly moves closer, and more details come into view.

Other than the cliffs, the wheel looks just like I remembered it. A dense, tropical island with colorful flowers blooming everywhere in the jungle. The only difference is that in this sector, thick wisps of white fog roil over the landscape. But other than that, this could be the blue or orange sector. Teeming with animals and birds of great beauty—but hiding within it the madness and chaos created by the UNA and the drones.

"Home sweet home," Cass says sarcastically, as Emma joins us. Alun is right behind her.

Our airship slows, now that we're close to the island. I see the other nearby airships doing the same thing. Our compartment shakes for a moment and then settles down again. The speed of the propellers decreases even more.

I'm scanning the sky for feelers. I'm also looking at the wheel for any sign of Dr. Barrett's helicopter or Octavio's hydrofoil. So far, I see nothing.

I tell myself that they have to be down there somewhere, unless we've beaten them to the wheel. *Maybe they're hiding themselves until we arrive.*

I exhale, trying to force the fear out of my body. I'm shaking a bit, and my mouth is dry.

I've been refusing to think about what life would be like for me if Liam didn't make it back. I need to be strong now, or I'm not going to survive. I haven't forgotten what a harsh, unforgiving place the wheel is. Liam and I barely escaped with our lives the last time we were on it.

"Nervous?" Emma asks me gently.

"Yeah. You?"

She nods. "Very. Do you see our landing site yet?"

I shake my head. "No."

She leans in and squints at the screen through her glasses. "Me neither."

Our craft keeps moving forward, over the shore and then over the cliffs. We're trying to figure out where our fleet of airships will be touching down. We're coming in low, so we can't see everything clearly yet.

Suddenly, there's a loud cracking noise outside our compartment. Alarms start going off. I haven't heard any alarms on this airship, not during the whole six days that I've been on it. *This is not a good sign.*

"Feelers?" Cass asks urgently. "Or maybe fireworks from the drones?"

I keep watching the screen. Everyone is rushing around, trying to see out the windows. The noise didn't sound like feelers or fireworks to me.

The sound comes again. Louder this time. A few people get frightened by it, and they cry out. The alarms continue blaring.

"Take your seats!" one of the guards yells.

"What's going on?" I ask him.

He doesn't answer. Our airship just keeps moving forward. The pilot lowers our altitude even more.

"Birds!" Alun exclaims in a rush of understanding. "It's just birds. Look." He starts laughing with relief.

I stare at the screen, and then feel a flood of relief too. He's right. We're passing through a flock of seagulls. They're hitting against the skin of the airship, making the strange thumping sounds that echo down to us in the compartment.

Emma looks pale. She wipes sweat from her forehead.

"Deep breaths," Cass is telling her.

We keep moving lower. Our ship is in the lead now, heading down to the wheel with the others trailing behind and above us.

"Look down there," I say. We're rushing past the tops of green trees shrouded in banks of white fog. I'm amazed that we haven't been attacked by feelers yet.

I finally see something far ahead of us. It's a gigantic open patch of land in the jungle nearly a mile long, and at least half a mile wide. It has a cliff covered with trees on the left-hand side of it, and thick jungle surrounding the other sides below.

This must be our landing site.

As we get closer, I see why this area is so flat and empty. The whole region has been burned to the ground. The trees have been incinerated, and transformed into ash and rubble. Even some of the ones left standing around the edges of the clearing are blackened and dead.

Our airship keeps moving forward, coming in lower. Everyone is staring out the windows or at the view screens. I'm waiting for a feeler to locate us and explode into action. But it doesn't happen.

As I peer at the view screen, I suddenly see a ragged figure emerge from the dead trees and stumble into the scorched wilderness. My heart instantly starts beating faster. The figure staggers through the thin fog that drifts across the field, and begins waving at our airship. *Is it Liam? David?* I squint to see, my heart pounding.

The figure keeps waving. Signaling for us to land. The person is obviously trying to steer us into position. He can barely stand up, and his clothes are tattered.

As we get closer, I realize who it is with certainty.

"David!" I say.

"No way!" Cass says, leaning in to look at the figure. "You're right. It's him. He's helping us down."

Our airship moves closer to the ground. This whole area is completely deserted, except for David and the tendrils of fog. *Maybe the fire drove everyone else out.* Or maybe this is one of those desolate patches on the wheel that David once told me about, when he suggested that we run away together and form our own colony. The kind of place that few drones or villagers call home. I sometimes still think about David's offer, although I'm not sure why.

"Steady yourselves!" a guard yells, as our airship lists to one side. I grab on to a nearby railing. "We're coming down fast!"

I glance at the screen and see the other airships near us descending as well. We're going to be landing in this huge, scorched field. I can't wait to get off this ship and see David again. I've missed him so much. Against the odds, he has survived.

We keep moving until we near the ground. Guards fling open hatches beneath the gun turrets and start throwing down ropes with pointed weights attached to the bottom. I watch as some of the guards slide down the ropes to the ground below. They work to plow the weights into the earth and secure the crafts.

The warm, humid air of the wheel instantly starts flooding into the passenger compartment. It smells just like I remember— musty and dank, like rotting leaves.

Cass stands up. "I guess we won't have to go looking for David after all."

I gaze out one of the open hatches at the sprawling landscape stretching beyond us. The fog is very thin here, but gets thicker around the edges of the jungle. Liam and his dad have to be around here somewhere, even if I can't see them yet.

Guards start lowering the steps in the front of the compartment. Everyone is rushing forward.

On the video screens, I can see David in the distance, signaling at the other airships. They are in the process of landing on the burned field. There still aren't any feelers here, nor any drones. Just David. I don't understand what's going on, but I'm so relieved to see him that it doesn't matter. Hopefully, he'll know where Liam is.

I join the throng of people exiting the airship, eager to get into the fresh air after so many days on board this craft. Cass and Emma are at my side, trailed by Alun. We reach the stairs, and I step out onto them.

The air feels good on my skin. A warm breeze dances across my face and through my hair as I descend the steps. I try not to think about the fact that I'm returning to the very island that I spent so long trying to escape. I tell myself that things are different now. That I'm with a large group of heavily armed rebels. That I'm safe. But I'm not sure I believe it.

I reach the bottom of the stairs and step onto the charred earth. My feet disappear into the thin layer of drifting fog. I stare down at them. It's like standing on a field of cinders and ash. The jungle looms around us at the edges, except for the large, gray cliff face to our left rising up about sixty feet in the air. I move to one side, to let people past.

Cass joins me and hesitates for a moment. Like Emma, I know that Cass's last memories of being on the wheel probably involve getting snatched by a feeler. She looks dazed.

I glance around. Some of the other kids wear the same stunned look, like they can't believe they've returned. It doesn't matter whether they were villagers or drones—they look shell-shocked. A few of them kneel on the ground, trying to steady themselves. Some are crying. For them, returning is far worse than it is for me. I left on my own terms, but they didn't. Also, Liam is here somewhere waiting for me. I would rather be on the wheel with him than safe but alone in Southern Arc.

Cass still isn't moving.

"At least there aren't any feelers here," I say to her. I glance up at the gray sky. "And the guards have guns. It's not going to be like it was before. You don't have to worry about being taken again."

She looks over at me. "I'm not afraid of the feelers."

"Then let's go find David. C'mon." I can see him ahead of us in the distance, signaling to people. But Cass just stands there near the stairs. "What's wrong?"

"I'm afraid of turning back into who I was," she says softly. "When I was here before, I wasn't thinking clearly. I mean, at first, I chose the drones' side because of what happened to Vincent. And because I thought I could always switch sides again if I wanted to. But then my thoughts got muddled, and I felt half crazy. I guess it was the drugs. It's like some kind of nightmare. I'm scared it's going to happen to me again." She turns to me with anguished eyes. "I'm afraid I'll lose my mind."

"Cass, you're going to be fine. They gave us an antidote to any drugs here, remember?"

"Yeah, and it better work or I'm going to be really pissed off." She glances down at the scars on her wrists. "I bet you noticed these, right?"

I nod.

"I don't even remember doing that to myself. That's how messed-up I was. Apparently, I did it with pieces of broken glass one night. I'm lucky that I survived." She glances back at Alun. "And he lost his eye when he was drunk and setting off fireworks. Life for the drones means nothing."

"The antidote will work," I tell her, wanting to reassure her. Wanting to help her feel better, and make the pain and fear go away.

People keep moving around us, pushing past. Emma and Alun are waiting nearby. "Will you watch me in case the pill doesn't work? Let me know if I start acting weird?" Cass asks.

I nod. "Promise." I see David moving farther away from us. "But right now, we have to focus on getting to David. You're going to be okay. I'll make sure of it." I start moving forward, pulling Cass with me.

Half of the other ships have landed now, all of them near our end of the field, and the area is getting crowded with kids and adults. Guards are already moving out, guns drawn, to form a perimeter around our landing site.

Emma and Alun join me and Cass as we head toward David. Between the people and the encroaching fog, he's becoming increasingly hard to see. An elusive figure in the mist.

We race directly toward him, darting through the throng of refugees and guards. I'm afraid he'll disappear before we can reach him. I speed up my pace.

"David!" I call out, rushing the final yards toward him.

He hears my voice and turns. "Alenna?" he yells back, hobbling to meet us. Then he sees Cass, Emma, and Alun behind me. "You guys made it!"

"Of course we did!" I yell, as we finally reach him. He leans forward and hugs me. I hold him tight for a moment. "I'm so glad you're okay!" Then I let him go. He's wearing his glasses, but he looks wirier and tougher than I remembered.

"Nice to meet you in person," he says to Cass.

"Likewise. You're shorter than I expected," she replies.

"Thanks for that," David says. The two of them hug.

"You're hurt," I point out to him. David has scratches down one cheek, and burn marks across his forearms. Not to mention scabs and bruises over the rest of his body.

"It's nothing," he says. "Just life on the wheel."

We stand there watching each other. Emma and Alun both introduce themselves to him. Nearly all the airships are on the ground now, being secured by ropes, weights, and stakes. People flood the field. The guards are barely able to contain the crowd. Voices yell in a cacophony as the guards try to organize everyone.

"So how much does Alenna know?" David asks Cass.

"Everything," Cass says.

"Why didn't you tell me about you and Cass, and about the resistance cells in the UNA all communicating with each other?" I ask David.

"I wanted to, but I knew if stuff like that came out, no one would trust me at the village. Especially not Veidman and Meira."

"The scientists at Destiny Station said both of them might be spies," I add.

"I wondered the same thing," he says.

"Have you seen Liam?" I ask. "He left Southern Arc with Dr. Barrett, to find his father. They're supposed to meet us here."

For an instant, I think I see something dark flicker behind his eyes. *Like he knows more information and just doesn't want to say.* But maybe I'm imagining it. The moment passes.

"They're not here yet," he says, his eyes completely clear again.

I try to calm my rising panic. "But they left before we did. We got a dispatch that they'd encountered some UNA crafts. Maybe—" I break off. I can't even say the words. *Maybe they didn't make it.* But that's not possible. I refuse to let myself believe it for a second. "Maybe they're just taking longer."

"They could have landed someplace else in the purple sector," Cass points out. "Maybe they're headed our way right now."

"I gave them the same coordinates that I gave you," David replies.

"Hey, how come there aren't any drones around here?" Emma asks him. She's been pretty quiet since we arrived here.

"Yeah, and how did you find this clearing?" I ask David.

"I found it when I was running from the feelers—and scouting for a place large enough for the airships to land," he says. "Must be the remnants of some fires that the drones set. The only other option was one of the beaches, but most of those are full of drones now. Except for the beach in the gray zone, and obviously you couldn't land and set up camp there because of the cold temperatures." He pauses. "And most of the other sectors have too many feelers in them."

I glance up automatically at the mention of feelers. But there's nothing in the sky. I guess Dr. Barrett knew what he was doing when he designed the airships. I was sure that our arrival would trigger hidden motion detectors and set off a wave of feeler assaults, but somehow we've sailed through the air unnoticed.

"But why aren't there any drones here at all?" Emma presses David, frowning. "Back in the villages, we thought this sector had been conquered by them. Were we totally wrong?"

David doesn't answer.

Suddenly, people start surging forward around us. I get buffeted by the noisy crowd. It feels like everyone is on the move at once for some reason.

"I have to go," David calls out abruptly. "I'm supposed to talk to the captains of each ship and Dr. Barrett's second lieutenant, too. I need to coordinate everything and let them know what I've learned."

"We'll come with you," I say.

David shakes his head. "It's better that I do this alone."

I don't understand why, but I assume he has his reasons. Maybe it's part of Dr. Barrett's security protocol. I know that there will be plenty of time to catch up with David later. "I need to look for Liam, anyway," I tell him. We hug a final time. Then he starts moving away.

A moment later comes a sharp crack. A loud pop. Everyone

hears it, and the volume of the crowd increases. I glance up at the sky again, expecting to see a firework display from the drones. But the gray sky remains clear of anything but clouds.

*Then the screaming starts.*

I hear more sharp pops.

And I remember that this time around, people on the wheel have guns. I'm not hearing fireworks—I'm hearing gunshots.

"Get down!" voices start yelling.

I sink to the charred earth in the fog, ducking behind a set of steps descending from one of the airships. Cass and Emma stay with me, but Alun dashes off somewhere else nearby for shelter. He's too large for the steps to shield him.

I hear more gunshots. They sound like they're coming from the other end of the rectangular field. I squint between people and airships. Our guards are firing into the jungle beyond the clearing, although I don't know why.

People are starting to panic, and they're using anything they can to shield themselves, in case a drone attack is imminent. Some run back up the steps to seek shelter in the ships.

Emma is hiding her face. Cass looks startled, but alert. I try to locate David, but I don't see him anymore. I stand and move a few feet to my left to get a better view. I see more of our guards rushing down the length of the field, firing at something unseen in the trees ahead of them. The thin fog makes it hard to see anything distinctly.

Then there's a burst of noise, as the airship closest to the other side of the field unleashes its machine guns, pointed away from us in the direction of the forest. The bullets spray into the jungle, lashing at the tropical leaves and branches like a hailstorm.

I'm filled with the sudden fear that maybe this is a mistake.

Maybe Dr. Barrett is leading Liam and Octavio's men toward us through the forest right now, and the guards have mistaken them for an army of drones. I almost scream out for the guards to stop shooting.

But then the guns stop for a moment, and in the deafening silence, a loud, distorted voice slices through the air. It's coming from within the jungle, amplified by some hidden mechanism. All of us can hear it clearly.

"Heathens! Hold your fire!" the voice says, booming across the landscape. "We have captured your leader, Dr. Neil Barrett, and the other infidels with him!" The voice is strange and metallic-sounding. I don't recognize it at all, but I know it must belong to a drone. Perhaps a watcher or leader from this sector. "If you fire on us again, we will kill the infidels. They are now our prisoners of war."

I feel my legs get shaky.

*This can't be happening.*

"He's bluffing," Cass says to me.

I can't even respond.

My knees give out and I crouch down. If the voice isn't lying, then it means that the drones have taken Liam. That he's being held captive—and might be killed. I knew that the journey here was a risk, but I was certain that Dr. Barrett and Octavio would keep Liam and themselves safe. *How could I have been so wrong?*

I expect the guards and the airships to start firing again, but their guns remain still. There's only silence. The guards near the forest have their assault rifles out, but they've paused to listen.

"You are surrounded by ten thousand of my soldiers," the amplified voice continues. "We have been waiting for your arrival. If you fire one single shot, we will consider it a declaration of war.

159

You have the guns, but we have your leader, and we outnumber you more than ten to one."

"I can't believe this," I whisper numbly.

"Your guns will be useless when thousands of us overrun this land with spears and arrows," the voice continues. "None of us will hesitate to sacrifice our lives. You are heathens! You must be punished."

I remember what happened when we got surrounded by drones like this once before, in the orange sector. That was the battle in which Liam got taken, and half our warriors were killed.

"It was a trap," I say to Cass, shutting my eyes. "This sector. This field. Everything." I turn to her. "They were waiting for us here. Don't you see that? Somehow they knew exactly where we were landing."

Cass doesn't say anything. I can tell she knows I'm right.

"Who are you?" a guard calls out, his voice loud and brittle in the silence. His uniform is decorated with gold stripes on the sleeves. I wonder if this is Dr. Barrett's second lieutenant.

"My name is not important," the voice replies. "Lay down your weapons and surrender to our will. This is not your land; it is ours. And you are all prisoners now. Accept your fate, and you will live. Resist, and you will die. Your guns are no advantage—we know this terrain well and you do not."

I hear strange noises, and I glance up. Standing up high on the edge of the cliff, I see a line of at least a thousand drones appear. They are pointing arrows straight down at us. I also hear noises in the jungle around us. The sounds of a huge army. This is definitely not a bluff.

Cass and I look at each other. My own desperation is reflected in her eyes. Around our feet, the fog grows thicker.

Our mission to liberate the wheel has become imperiled before it even began. I feel like crying, but I can't afford the luxury. If Liam is still alive, even if he's a captive somewhere, then there's hope.

*I have to find him.* Then we can work together to turn this around. We have no other choice except giving up, and that will never be an option. A line from *The Myth of Sisyphus* springs into my mind. That only the warrior truly understands the real nature of existence and the universe—and that one must always choose action over contemplation. I gather my strength. For Liam, I will fight. For Liam, I will do anything.

# 12 BETRAYED

FOR A MOMENT, I'M worried that our guards are going to start shooting anyway. I'm guessing that the guns on the airships could take out a lot of these drones. But the sheer numbers would eventually overwhelm us, and the drones have a strategic advantage. Also, these guards work for Dr. Barrett. I'm not sure if they're willing to put his life in danger.

But surrendering to the drones will probably mean death anyway. If these drones hadn't kidnapped Liam, I'd want the guards to open fire right away.

"If you attempt to reboard your ships, we will destroy the passenger compartments with flaming arrows," the distorted voice continues calmly. "Your only option is to surrender and live under our rules, in our domain."

"They want to make us their slaves," Cass hisses. "I know how their minds work. They'll make us serve them and do hard labor. And worse!"

"I know." I'm torn between my desire to fight for what I know is right, and my love for Liam. I don't want anything to jeopardize his life.

Seconds pass like hours. Neither side makes a move. I try to think about what Liam would do. Or Gadya. They would definitely want to fight. But at the same time, I know they wouldn't put the lives of someone they love in danger if there were a smarter way to do things.

"How did the drones know that we'd land here? Or that we'd be arriving in airships?" I ask Cass, trying to figure it out.

"They must have intercepted some of our transmissions. Or maybe someone ratted us out."

"Who would do that?"

Cass doesn't answer. Neither of us wants to think about how terrible it would be if someone we trusted betrayed us.

We suddenly hear rustling noises from the jungle. I watch as our guards start backing away in the fog. Then I see them turn and run toward us, back to safety. The rustling noises turn into an even more ominous sound. *The noise of thousands of footsteps headed our way.*

I wish I had a weapon on me right now. I look around for something to use, but I see nothing.

A moment later, a line of drones steps out from the trees, followed by another line, and yet another. They march through the fog across the field in our direction. They are all wearing home-made black robes.

Startled, I notice that the drones are arranged in some kind of strange military-style phalanx. I've never seen anything like it before on the wheel. The drones march in line toward us, like a well-trained army of UNA soldiers.

None of them are screaming profanities or throwing fireworks. They don't seem crazy at all—not like they used to. If anything, they seem kind of mindless. Like robots following a computer program. Some carry spears, and others carry bows and arrows.

Their army just keeps moving toward us. I see no sign of their leader. He's still hiding in the trees.

"Something's changed with the drones," Cass whispers to me, sounding as shocked as I feel.

We watch as the army walks closer.

The drones stop about a hundred paces away from our ships and our end of the field. It's like they all received an invisible signal at once. Almost like they're wearing UNA earpieces giving them commands or something—as impossible as that would be. There are at least a couple thousand of them here on the burned field.

It's a true standoff. We huddle between the huge airships, watching this massive enemy force. Waiting in dread.

The amplified voice of their leader booms over us again. "This is merely a fraction of my army. You are surrounded by equal numbers on all sides, not to mention my warriors on the cliff."

I look around. It seems like no one knows what to do. The guards clearly expected Dr. Barrett to meet them here and guide them. I'm not sure whether we're about to do battle, or surrender our freedom to this army. Either way, Liam's life, and mine as well, hang in the balance.

"The choice is yours," the voice continues. "You have sixty seconds to decide. If you fire one shot, you die. If you lay down your weapons, you live."

Movement abruptly catches my eye.

I see a lone figure striding swiftly across the field, cutting a path through the wisps of fog. He's walking across from our side of the field to theirs.

I'm confused. *Is this person crazy?* He's going to get killed!

Then, stunned, I realize that it's David.

I don't understand what he's doing.

Without thinking, I stand up and yell out his name. Cass starts calling for him too. Is he going to sacrifice his life in some kind of deranged attempt to bargain with the drones?

"David!" Cass and I keep yelling. "Come back!"

Other people try to hush us.

David doesn't turn or glance behind him. Maybe he didn't hear us. He just keeps moving rapidly.

"David!" I scream again, ignoring the guards telling me to be quiet. I don't want David to make a martyr of himself. A single arrow from a drone could kill him instantly.

I start to move forward. I'm ready to run out into the field and grab him if I have to. To rescue him from what's about to happen. He once saved Rika on the ice. Now it's he who needs saving. Cass is just one step behind me.

"David, don't do it!" I yell, not even sure what he's about to do.

But then, as I watch, David raises both of his hands above his head. He makes a strange forward motion with his index fingers.

It's not a gesture of surrender, or of war. Instead, he's signaling to the army. The drones in the front row raise their hands and signal back to him in the same way.

And then, in a flash, I understand the awful truth.

David is not on our side.

*He is on theirs.*

I can't speak. I feel sick. I just keep watching in stunned disbelief, as I sink back down to the ground.

"No!" Cass yells next to me, sounding enraged. "That's impossible! Not David!"

I watch David keep walking, hobbling quickly over the blackened earth, heading straight toward the waiting army.

I can't believe it either.

"He betrayed us," I say, spitting out each word painfully. It should have been obvious to me all along. But I just didn't want to see the warning signs. He set up this landing site to trap us. He lied to us again and again. And he sent us those misleading dispatches. *But why?*

David reaches the drones. They instantly part for him. He walks down the line, completely untouched.

"He's the one who told them where we'd be landing," I say tiredly. "The drones didn't intercept any transmissions. It was a setup."

"I'm going to kill him," Cass breathes. "I'm going to break his scrawny neck!" She sounds close to tears. "All this time I wanted to get back here and help him! But he was just playing us for fools!"

"I know," I say helplessly.

Because of David's actions, Liam might die. How could David have done such a terrible thing to his friends? I trusted him with everything! Maybe someone is forcing David to do this. But that still wouldn't explain his betrayal. David has sabotaged our entire plan.

*Was Liam right all along?* And everyone else who thought David was a spy for the Monk? Was David manipulating me the entire time? It's hard to accept, but the evidence is right in front of me.

"Your sixty seconds are up," the voice intones loudly from the trees. "Make your decision or face your doom."

David continues to glide down the rows of armed drones. He disappears through the fog into the shadows of the jungle.

At the same time, the army of drones in front of us raises its spears and arrows. More noises come from the trees. And above us, even more drones appear at the top of the cliff. They line it, pressed tightly shoulder to shoulder, with another line of rein-forcements behind them. If we fire our guns, then thousands of precisely aimed arrows will zoom down at us.

"Prepare for battle!" the leader of the drones calls out to his army. Arrows are slotted into bows.

A split second later, the second lieutenant screams out to the leader: "Wait! Stop! Hold your fire! We agree to your terms."

"No!" Cass yells. Some voices join her. "Don't surrender! They'll kill us either way!" Others shout her down.

But it's too late.

The muzzles of the guns in the airships are being lowered.

Is this the right decision? I'm not sure. There would have been no way to survive the waves of arrows from above. Most of the drones would have been shot by our guns, but most of our group would have died as well. *But it doesn't feel like the right decision to me.* I tell myself that at least it doesn't put Liam in danger for the moment, unless the voice is lying.

The army of drones on the field starts marching forward. More drones flood out from the trees around us. The whole time, the drones above us keep their arrows trained on us.

Their behavior is almost as startling as David's. How did these drones become so well-trained and disciplined in only a month? It seems impossible.

"We could still fight," Cass whispers into my ear. "We don't have to do what the guards say. We could fight and then make a break for it!"

I nod, looking around for any avenue of escape.

But right then, a scientist from Destiny Station splits away from the crowd and grabs one of the guard's handguns. He grapples with it, wrenching it away from the guard. Before anyone can stop him, he points it in the direction of the drones.

For a moment, I think this is the start of a rebellion.

But within half a second, he has five arrows sticking out of his torso. His body topples to the ground.

He didn't even have time to fire a shot.

Silence falls over the landscape. Two scientists rush out to grab his corpse.

"Anyone who tries to fire on us will be killed," the voice of the drone leader intones, matter-of-factly. "Lay down your weapons. Put your hands above your heads. This is your only path to survival."

The army of drones keeps marching forward. Soon they will reach us.

I look at Cass. "It's over for now," I say softly. "We can't fight them, or we'll be killed. We have to survive this day, so we can strategize and get revenge later on. When we're not outnumbered so badly."

"As soon as I can, I'm going to make them pay," Cass says, her brown eyes flashing with anger. "Especially David."

We share a long look. I never thought that David would betray me. I believed in him with all of my heart, when almost no one else did. Back at the village, I was his sole defender. "David will pay most of all," I reply. "What he's done is unforgivable. When we get our chance, we'll go after him first."

Cass is about to say something else, but then the drones reach our group.

"Kneel!" one of them commands, pointing his spear at us.

Both Cass and I go down to our knees reluctantly, along with the other refugees around us.

I stare up at the drone. His eyes are oddly dull and glassy. His face is puffy and his short hair has fallen out in patches. I remember the drones being wild and nearly psychotic, driven by bloodlust. But this drone seems dispassionate. Like he's not even fully here, like he's some brainwashed UNA bureaucrat.

More drones reach us. This is not what I expected upon returning to the wheel. In fact, it's pretty much the worst thing I could imagine. I only hope that I'll be able to find Liam again soon—and that he's alive.

I feel the hands of a drone dragging me upward. I go limp. I don't struggle or fight. I need to seem docile now. *That way, when I do fight back later on, they'll never see it coming.* I notice that Cass is doing the same thing. There's no point drawing attention to ourselves any more than we've already done. At least not until we have a good plan.

The drones pat us down, checking for weapons. They also strip us of our jackets. They find Cass's hidden data drives and her GPS, and they smash them on the ground with their spears.

Cass and I are then pushed and prodded along with everyone else—kids, scientists, older refugees, and guards. The drones start leading us away from the landing site and into the jungle.

I wonder who their leader is now that Minister Harka is dead. There must be one—there's no way these crazed kids got so organized on their own. Is their leader the voice in the forest?

"Faster," one of the drones says, shoving me in the back. I've noticed that most of them talk monosyllabically now. Like speech is difficult for them.

There's a sudden explosion behind me, and I flinch. The noise of the crowd grows louder as everyone turns back to look at what's going on.

A large orange fireball rises up from the field and into the air. It's followed by a plume of thick black smoke. I smell the acrid odor of burning plastic.

Another concussion detonates across the landscape. I see a second fireball rising up into the sky.

"They're destroying the airships!" one of the scientists yells.

The gas inside the airships might not have been flammable, but the ammunition and fuel stored on board the passenger compartments clearly were. I also realize that the antidote pills are being destroyed.

I should have guessed that the drones would do this to the airships. Even though they could have used the ships to get off the wheel themselves, they would rather destroy them completely. I'd forgotten that the drones don't even want to leave this island. That they're happy here amidst the death and destruction.

"That was our only way off the wheel," Cass mutters, as we hear more explosions. We keep moving forward, deeper into the forest. I know that the drones won't stop until the airships are completely destroyed. I wish I knew whose orders they were acting on.

Some of the kids and adults are crying. But most are walking stoically.

"How are we going to save anyone when we can't even save ourselves?" Cass asks as we walk. She's right next to me. I glance back and see Emma and Alun farther behind us. One of the drones has taken away Alun's eye patch, so he has made a new one by ripping off part of his T-shirt and tying it around his head like a ribbon.

We walk faster, guided deeper into the verdant jungle. Even though we've been taken captive right now, I know that we'll fight to free the wheel when the time comes. *Even if we die trying.*

As we walk through the forest, I think about the last time I was captured by the drones. Back then, the drones were frenzied and manic, wearing face paint and cackling and leaping around. Torturing us just for the fun of it.

It was terrifying at the time, but at least there was something human about their behavior. These new drones are almost scarier. They display no emotions whatsoever. None of them talk to each other. And they rarely talk to us, other than to tell us to keep moving.

Maybe some new kind of drug is being dropped on the wheel. *Some new UNA formula intended to pacify the drones.* Something has obviously turned this tribe into a formidable, quasi-lobotomized army. Their lack of facial expressions is as disturbing as their relentless uniformity.

Perhaps the UNA has finally found the perfect drug that it has been looking for—the kind of drug that renders even the most rebellious minds docile. Maybe even David has been affected by it. Only that would explain his actions.

The drones keep leading us through the trees. We walk for at least an hour, trudging through the jungle. I feel hot, sweaty, and exhausted. I'm starting to despair.

Finally, the drones slow down a bit.

We've reached some kind of gigantic building that resembles a massive, abandoned cathedral. I see it rising up from the trees. It's a vast structure, made of weathered red brick, with a rotting wooden roof. A large, round stained-glass window adorns one of the walls—an image of a lamb facing a tiger. The other windows are mostly smashed. There are holes in the roof, and ropy green vines grow up and around the sides of the building. Despite its disrepair, it's huge and imposing.

I stumble over a tree root, and then steady myself and keep walking. I gaze up at the brick building again as we get closer. It must be some kind of relic from an earlier era on the wheel. From the time when my parents were here, or even from before that.

Apparently, it will now become our prison. The drones clearly intend to keep us inside this building while they figure out what to do with us.

They herd us up a wide cobblestone path. Weeds and small white flowers grow through cracks between the stones. Everywhere I look are drones, watching us with arrows drawn, pointed in our direction. I know that they won't hesitate to fire on anyone who tries to run, or who fights back. Some of the drones also hold pistols and rifles now, confiscated from Dr. Barrett's guards.

"Move," drones say, as they gesture for us to enter the decaying structure. I keep walking next to Cass. Both of us are silent. We pass underneath a huge brick archway and into the cavernous building.

Nervous voices echo against the stones. Shafts of gray light shine down from the holes in the roof, at least forty feet above our heads. Birds flutter about inside, nesting in the remains of the rafters.

Refugees keep streaming into the space. The old cathedral is so huge that there is plenty of room for us. The floor is just rubble and dirt.

A scuffle breaks out nearby. Several of Dr. Barrett's guards have grabbed one of the drones. They're trying to take his gun. Instinctively, I get ready to help. I'm hoping for a rebellion once again.

But arrows hammer down instantly from above, making me gasp. Dr. Barrett's guards fall back. Dead.

Shocked, I glance up.

Only then do I see painted figures high in the shadows, moving around on rickety wooden catwalks. The place is crawling with drones.

I wonder if Liam is being held here, or somewhere else. Is he with Dr. Barrett and Octavio? I look around for him desperately, but it's so crowded that there's no way to find him.

I glance back at the front doors of the cathedral. Refugees continue flooding into the space. Although we number nearly a thousand people, we are nothing compared to the drones. I've never been outnumbered this badly on the wheel before.

The crowd is silent now, after the murder of the guards. The loudest voices are just whispers. I hear the sounds of the jungle outside, and the squawking of birds overhead.

Then there's a loud concussion. I turn to see that the thick wooden doors of the building have been slammed shut behind us, and bolted. The broken windows on this level have been boarded over with planks, so there's no other way out. I stand there next to Cass, looking around. I don't know what the drones are going to do next.

They could set fire to this building. Kill us with flames and smoke. Then again, they could have killed us already if they wanted to.

Inexplicably, I notice the drones among us start dropping down to their knees. They keep their weapons pointed at us, but they crouch down in the dirt like they're about to begin praying.

"What the hell are they doing?" Cass whispers.

"I don't know!"

Completely confused, I look around. Again, it's like the drones are acting as one cohesive unit. I catch an unexpected glimpse of Dr. Elliott in the crowd. I haven't seen him for a long time. He must have traveled here on another airship. He's studying the drones closely. The scientists seem as shocked by the drones' behavior as we are.

"Prisoners of war!" a voice suddenly booms out, making me startle. It's the same amplified voice we heard in the forest. "Welcome to your new home. Confinement House Four, in the center of the purple sector."

The noise of the crowd gets louder. Everyone starts looking around. The voice seems to be coming from everywhere and nowhere.

"Where is this bastard?" Cass mutters next to me, craning to look.

"I'll let you know when I find him," I whisper back, searching the crowd.

"What do you want with us?" Dr. Elliott calls out loudly. He's risking his life just by speaking. "We're here to free the wheel. To free all of you!"

Voices rise up in support from the crowd:

"We're on the same side!"

"We hate the UNA just like you do!"

"Let's work together," another scientist near me starts to implore. The butt of a spear crashes down on his head, silencing him.

I'd forgotten that reasoning with the drones is futile. To them, we're as much of a threat to their way of life as the UNA is.

I hear creaking footsteps on one of the catwalks above us, and I look up. A row of drones is nimbly striding across it. They're headed toward a large wooden balcony at one end of the cathedral. It's shrouded in shadows, twenty feet up.

The balcony was once an organ or choir loft. It has old, rotting blue silk curtains hanging down on either side of it, and a wooden railing at the front. I see dark openings leading into other spaces at the sides. But most of the balcony is boarded up with sheets of plywood.

"We will never be on the same side," the hidden voice declares. "You are here to destroy the wheel! To destroy our chance at eternal life. We know about your plans. We cannot let them happen." The drones start chattering on cue, as they begin praying rapidly.

*Don't they know that the Monk is dead? And that he wasn't even a monk—that he was Minister Harka in disguise?* David obviously hasn't told them about any of that. There are more creaking noises above us.

I look up as I suddenly realize something. I nudge Cass. "The balcony," I whisper. "I think that's where the voice is coming from."

We stare up at the balcony just in time to see a group of drones reach it on the catwalks. Everyone around me is looking up, too. The drones on the balcony ignite torches, which provide the shadowy space with warm, yellow light. I actually see the remains of the old organ, shattered and destroyed.

Other drones begin moving sheets of plywood aside, revealing a black, cavernous hole behind them.

And then, a figure steps out of the darkness, heading right to the front of the balcony.

What I see makes my heart stop.

I hear people around me gasp. Most of the drones near us are still praying. I feel Cass grip me for support.

Standing there in the balcony is a figure I thought I would never see again. A person who died on the shore of an icy lake, right in front of my eyes. Its sneering wooden mask flashes in the torchlight, as the crowd murmurs in horror and recognition. Everyone knows exactly who this is.

"Oh my god," I breathe.

The drones continue genuflecting in worshipful prayer, as everyone else looks at one another in terror.

Standing there on the balcony, dressed in heavy black robes and a cowl, surrounded by armed drones, is the Monk.

# 13 MASKS

I STARE UP AT the masked figure. "You're dead," I murmur to myself in disbelief. "I saw you die. . . ."

But as I gaze at the figure, my initial shock quickly fades. This isn't the Monk at all—at least not Minister Harka.

This man isn't confined to being carried. He is standing there on his own two feet, like he's younger and lither. The Monk couldn't even walk, and could barely talk near the end. But this man has no trouble doing either of those things.

"How is this possible?" Cass asks me, as the crowd noise grows louder. "You said he was dead!"

"It's someone else. Wearing the same mask." Most of the drones probably don't realize that their original Monk is dead. Or maybe there was always more than one Monk. Perhaps this is even one of the Monk's body doubles. If Minister Harka had them back in the UNA, maybe he also had them here on the wheel.

I eye the masked figure carefully. His voice isn't familiar, but it's being distorted and amplified. Perhaps deliberately, so that no one will recognize him. There must be a microphone hidden on him somewhere and speakers hidden in the balcony. For a moment I wonder if it's Dr. Barrett in disguise, and that he's the real traitor, but this figure is just too short to be him. A terrible thought occurs to me then:

"Could it be—" I break off, not wanting to even say his name.

*"David?"* Cass whispers softly.

We squint up at the figure. It could be him, but I'm not certain. We're too far away, and the mask and the robes obscure the wearer's body. It also wouldn't explain how we heard the Monk's voice in the trees when David was among us—but maybe that voice was a recording. Anything is possible on the wheel.

"Bring out the leader of the heathens," the masked figure intones as we keep watching.

At his words, a white-haired, shirtless old man is brought forth from the darkness on the balcony. He's supported on either side by two drones. His head lolls downward to his chest, and I can tell he's been badly beaten. His bearded face is bruised and marred with cuts. So are his chest and arms. I recognize him instantly.

It's Dr. Barrett.

My heart leaps. *If Dr. Barrett is here, then so is Liam!* Perhaps even somewhere nearby.

I stare around, trying to find him. I long to call out for him. To scream his name. But that would put both of us in extreme danger.

"This is your leader?" the masked figure asks us rhetorically. "This sad excuse for a human? Ancient and forgotten. A man who placed science above belief." He pauses. "This man treated faith like an infection to be stamped out. He was not satisfied with his own domain in the Antarctic, but came here trying to colonize our land."

"It's not like that!" a scientist yells. "We're here to save you!"

"We are not the ones who need saving," the Monk continues.

His drones keep murmuring deranged mockeries of prayer under their breath. "You are." He pauses again. I sense a cruel smile hiding behind the mask. "We are going to help you understand that, starting with Dr. Barrett."

The drones on the balcony bring Dr. Barrett forward. He struggles to speak, but he's too exhausted and weak to say any words. I wonder how long they've been torturing him. I never expected to see Dr. Barrett so broken and frail like this. *I wonder if they've tortured Liam as well.* How could David stand to be a part of such cruelty?

The drones press Dr. Barrett against the balcony railing. For a moment, I'm afraid that they're going to toss him over the edge and into the crowd below. But then, a drone steps forward. A tall, thin boy. He holds up an object for everyone to see.

It's another mask. Glittering and metallic. There are holes for the eyes, but none for the mouth or nose. Then he turns it around. The inside of the mask has inch-long metal spikes embedded in it. They're as sharp as knives.

The drones in our midst begin to cheer. The noise is deafening and overwhelming. It's the first time I've seen them display any kind of loud emotion. They pump their fists in the air as they shriek. But even now, there's something programmatic about their actions. They're more like automatons than human beings.

"Put it on!" the Monk insists, his amplified voice loud and jagged over the noise of the mob. "Put it on!"

The drone raises the mask. Dr. Barrett recoils, trying to shove the drone away. Other drones grab him from behind. Dr. Barrett opens his mouth to scream, but the crowd is so noisy now, I can't even hear him.

I get jostled from behind, as the throng starts moving. Drones are laughing and hollering, like they've gone insane. Finally releasing their pent-up madness and fury. At least this is closer to what I expected. Maybe now that the drones feel like they've won, they are free to act crazy again. Everyone else is screaming and yelling too, as the floor of the cathedral turns into a melee.

As I duck a random elbow, I try to keep my eyes fixed on Dr. Barrett. The drone raises the mask even higher, right up to Dr. Barrett's face. The old scientist writhes, trying to buckle away. But the drones are relentless.

The drone holding the mask steps forward and presses it onto Dr. Barrett's face as hard as he can. At the same instant, another drone behind Dr. Barrett latches the mask at the back, tightly. Dr. Barrett screams in absolute agony as the spikes enter his flesh. The mask is now locked onto his face.

The drones on the balcony step away from him. Dr. Barrett claws at his face with trembling hands. Blood starts dripping down onto his chest.

"This is not your land!" the Monk cries out over the commotion below. "You are invaders. Trespassers! If you wish to set foot on the wheel, then you must join us. We control each of the sectors now, and the gray zone too. There are no more villages. The blue sector is ours. The villagers are all dead!"

With a sick feeling, I remember the threat that a drone once made to me. On my first day on the wheel. That the drones would soon overrun the entire island, and drive us villagers into the ocean. *That threat, which once seemed impossible, has now become our reality.*

On the balcony, Dr. Barrett is struggling with his metal mask. But there's no way for him to get it off. His blood continues to flow.

"We offer the only path to escaping from the wheel," the Monk continues. "Life after death. The wheel is a testing ground for the soul. Science has no place here."

Dr. Barrett sinks to one knee, staggering. Drones reappear and grab him by either arm. They pull him roughly back into the shadows. I doubt that he'll survive much longer.

"Forget your past. Forget your future plans. Forget who you are. Join us, and you will live forever," the Monk declares. The army of drones begins to cheer again, in a monotonous roar. "Unless you join us, you will remain imprisoned here until you starve."

I turn to Cass. "We're going to have to find Liam and anyone else we can, and then get the hell out of here!"

Cass nods, but she's looking dazed.

"Cass?" I prompt.

"Was I really like this?" she asks. "Was this what it was like when I was a drone?"

"This is much worse," I tell her honestly. "It must be some new kind of drug. And while Minister Harka was a total sham, I'm scared this new Monk actually believes what he's saying!"

I see Emma and Alun nearby. We've gotten separated from them by the crowd, but they're slowly making their way back over to us without drawing attention to themselves. Everyone is moving and yelling.

"Join us, and you can go free!" the Monk continues to decree from his perch high above us. I wish I could see his eyes through the mask, but the distance is too great. I don't think it's David—but I can no longer trust my own judgment about him.

"We'll never join you!" a nearby kid screams. It's a former villager from Destiny Station. "I fought your kind before. I'll fight them again!"

Drones move forward and begin beating him. He falls down, lost in a sea of bodies.

"We'd rather die than become like you," someone else yells. It's a bookish, middle-aged scientist with glasses. "What you've done here is as bad as the UNA! You have to listen to us. You must understand that—"

The drones descend on him with their spears. The crowd surges again.

I snap my head around, thinking that with this commotion, we can find an escape route. But the exit is heavily guarded, and the Monk and his drones are watching over everything from the balcony.

Fingers suddenly brush against my arm. I yank my arm away, startled. I glance up to see a tall drone standing in front of me, dressed in black robes with a cowl hiding his face. He's gripping a spear. I pull back in fear and anger.

But when I look closer, I see that this man is much too old to be a drone. All of them are my age, or just a bit older, but this man is in his forties or early fifties. He's handsome, with olive skin and kind, dark eyes. He looks oddly familiar. Cass is right there next to me, glaring at the man.

"Alenna Shawcross?" the man asks me softly, keeping his head lowered so that no one close by can see his face.

I nod.

"Come with me."

"Who are you?"

He doesn't answer my question. "We're not safe here. Follow me. I'll take you to Liam."

My heart surges. "He's alive? He's okay?"

The man nods. And right then I realize who this stranger must be.

"You're Octavio!" I whisper. "Liam's dad."

He brings a finger to his lips. "Don't say my name. Just follow."

He turns and quickly walks away through the crowd. Like he doesn't want anyone to notice our interaction.

Startled, I immediately head after him. Cass is just one step behind, trailed by Emma and Alun.

"Did you hear?" I whisper to Cass, my chest bursting with happiness and relief. "Liam's alive! That's his dad!"

"I heard. Does he know a way out of here?"

"I hope so."

We keep walking. Octavio continues to keep his head down, waving his spear in the air. With his robes and his cowl, he manages to pass for one of the drones. No one challenges him. *They must think we're his prisoners.*

We continue pushing our way through the crowd. The Monk is still exhorting everyone to follow his ways, while his drones savagely beat anyone who calls out in opposition to him.

I see that we're headed toward the left-hand wall of the cathedral, where a group of kids cower under the remnants of a partially collapsed brick staircase.

"Can we trust him?" Cass whispers into my ear as we walk.

"Yes," I reply. Then I add, "I think." After what happened with David, I'm far from certain. I'm not even sure this man *is* Octavio. I only have his word and his resemblance to Liam. For now, that will have to be enough.

We keep walking until we reach the ruined staircase, forcing our way through kids and adults, and past drones. Everyone is clamoring.

Octavio stops. He turns to face us. "We don't have long," he whispers. "They were holding me in a torture cell underneath this building. Someone threw weapons and keys into our cell to help us get out. I killed a guard, and took his cloak and spear. I left the guard's corpse in my clothes, but soon they'll figure out I've escaped."

"Is Liam down there too?" I ask urgently.

"No. He also killed a guard and took his robes. We overpowered the guards together and escaped up into this cathedral. Some of my other men were able to do the same thing." Octavio stares at me. "We've been looking for you. Liam said you could fight. Is that true?"

"Yes, he helped train me."

Octavio nods. "Good."

"I can fight too," Cass adds.

Alun nods. "Same here."

"Me too, if I really have to," Emma whispers.

"So Liam's in the crowd somewhere?" I ask Octavio. I'm staring around desperately at the drones in robes, trying to find Liam. But there are hundreds of drones in here. How am I ever going to find him?

Suddenly, a voice cuts through the noise. "You!"

I turn and see three drones standing there, watching me and Octavio with their dead eyes. Octavio has his back to them. If they see his face, they'll know he's an interloper.

"Yeah?" I say, trying to hide my fear.

At the same moment, Cass snarls at them, "What do you want?"

But none of these drones have eyes for us. They are now only staring at Octavio. They must already suspect that something is wrong. "Turn around," one of them instructs him. Another raises a bow and slots an arrow into it.

Octavio just stands there with his back to them. He doesn't respond to their words. Cass and I try to edge our way between him and the drones, but one of the drones shoves us aside.

"Show yourself," the third drone commands Octavio.

Around us, the crowd surges as people cry out for help. The drones move around, beating the refugees. I look up at the balcony. The Monk is watching everything with approval.

"Turn around right now!" the drone with the bow insists. He aims the arrow directly at the back of Octavio's neck. "Or face our wrath!"

Slowly, Octavio begins to turn his body. He moves deliberately, so as not to startle the three drones. Cass and I step out of the way. If Octavio is anything like Liam, then I have a feeling I know what's coming next.

I hear one of the drones gasp when he sees Octavio's face.

He's about to call out in warning, when the spear flies from Octavio's hand straight into the drone's chest. It flies faster than I've ever seen a spear fly before. The tip plows directly into the drone's heart, toppling him to the ground.

At the same instant, the drone with the bow unleashes his arrow directly at Octavio's face. There is no room for Octavio to duck. I scream, expecting the worst. But Octavio throws up an arm, his robes swirling, and the arrow gets caught in the fabric, tumbling harmlessly off to one side. The drone looks startled.

Octavio leaps three steps forward and grabs the drone by the throat, crushing his larynx with his strong fingers. The third drone tries to run. Octavio whips a knife off the belt of the strangled drone and throws it at him. The knife hits directly in the center of the drone's back, and he goes straight down to the ground as the crowd parts.

I'm stunned.

Within two seconds, Octavio has defeated—and killed—all three of the drones. I've never seen anyone move that fast, except maybe Liam. But our troubles have just begun, because everyone has noticed the commotion. Drones are heading in our direction.

"Run!" Octavio calls out, yanking his spear from the drone's body, and using the bloody weapon to clear a path through the crowd. Arrows fly straight at him, but he bats them away with the spear and his robes.

Cass, Emma, Alun, and I follow after him, barely missing getting hit by arrows ourselves.

Octavio's actions have started a violent revolt. I see other scientists and villagers begin fighting back. Arrows rain down, along with spears.

A drone appears in our path, baring his sharp teeth. He grins at us. A moment later, my fist plows into the side of his head, knocking him out of the way.

I leap up onto his body, feeling my boot crunch down on his ribs as he howls in pain. Arrows fly down from the catwalk. One barely nicks my shoulder, but I keep going.

I glance up as I hear screaming high on the balcony. The drones are amassing around the Monk, protecting him. This is because an intruder has appeared on the balcony with them.

To my surprise, I see that it's a tall figure dressed in robes. He's standing on the balcony with long knives in both hands, advancing on the Monk. I can't see his face, but I recognize the way he moves.

*It's Liam!*

He's alive.

And he has gone straight after the Monk without any hesitation. Somehow he's managed to get onto the balcony. A hailstorm of arrows comes his way from the drones on the ground. He leaps up onto a nearby balustrade to avoid them.

"Liam!" I call out over the screams of the crowd, unable to stop myself. "It's me!"

Then I feel something crash into my back. I stagger forward. For a moment, I think I've been hit by a spear. But then I realize it's just the body of a drone falling off one of the catwalks.

I shake off the blow and keep moving. For a moment, I allow myself to think that maybe we can somehow overcome the drones and take control of the cathedral. But as arrows rain down, I see the main doors burst open. More drones flood inside the cathedral— hundreds of them. And there are thousands outside. The numbers are just too great. We can't fight them here. We need to find a way to escape into the jungle and regroup.

More of Octavio's men have appeared, throwing off their robes to reveal themselves. They are skilled and brutal fighters. They cut a path of carnage through the startled drones that surround us.

"Liam!" I scream again, as loudly as I can.

This time Liam hears me and glances down.

"Alenna!" he yells back, dodging arrows. The onslaught has become too much. He's going to get hit soon. The Monk and his drones are backing away into a small, dark corridor behind the balcony. It's some kind of escape route.

Liam grabs hold of one of the old, rotting curtains near the balcony's edge. I duck blows as I watch him swing out onto the curtain. It starts to tear. He slides down it, crashing toward the ground. He lashes out at drones with his feet, scattering them.

The entire cathedral has turned into complete, terrifying

chaos. Arrows and spears fly through the air nonstop. Some of Octavio's men have gotten up on the catwalks and are tossing more drones over the edge.

I try to fight my way over to Liam, but there are too many people in the way. Then Liam sees me again. He starts using his knives to forge a path straight in my direction. The blades are long and sharp, like swords.

A few seconds later, Liam reaches me.

"Thank god you're alive!" he yells. He grabs me and hugs me tight.

*I never thought this moment would come.*

I grab him right back. I was terrified that I would never see him again. Now I never want to let him go. And I never will.

"Where are we going?" I yell. "What's the plan?"

"My dad knows a way out," he says, leading me forward as the battle rages on. Liam lashes out with a knife, slashing at a drone, making him retreat. Now that we're fighting back, the drones seem flustered and confused. But there are so many of them, they will win any fight, simply because of their overwhelming numbers.

Liam and I keep moving, following after Octavio. Cass, Emma, and Alun are doing the same thing, as are Octavio's men. They're a few paces ahead of us now, barging their way through the rioting crowd. I see blood on the back of Alun's neck. He must have been sliced by an arrow. I'm surprised that none of us has been killed or badly wounded.

Octavio is heading straight for one of the red brick cathedral walls. I don't understand what he's aiming for. There's no sign of an exit here. Just solid bricks.

"Liam?" I ask as we run.

"It's okay! Keep going."

I glance up at the balcony. The Monk is gone. There's no sign he was even up there. *Who is this new Monk?* And how did he take power so rapidly?

I turn back to stare at where Octavio was, but now there's no sign of him either. I'm confused. Then I see Cass reach the same place at the wall.

She disappears, her head slipping down beneath the crowd. It takes me a second to realize that there must be some kind of opening here. Perhaps one that goes underneath the wall of the building and leads into the jungle. Of course there are thousands of drones out there. But outside, we'll have a better chance of survival than if we're trapped in here.

Liam and I race toward the brick wall. I see Emma and Alun disappear from view too. More drones step into our path. We savagely disarm them in a few simple movements.

We reach the wall. I slam against it with Liam. I glance down and see a round hole in the dirt floor near my feet. It's the opening to a concrete sewer pipe. A metal manhole cover has been pushed aside. This is obviously where the others went.

The hole doesn't appear to lead outside. It just plunges deeper into the earth, perhaps down to the torture cells beneath us.

Right then, a wave of arrows flies over our heads, plowing into the brick wall. Liam and I duck.

The arrowheads clatter against the bricks and drop down harmlessly. But I know that more will follow. The screams of injured drones, kids, refugees, and scientists intermingle into one giant, deafening roar.

"Go!" Liam says. "I've got your back!"

"Okay!"

I stagger to my feet. More arrows whisk through the air around me. I feel them brush my hair.

Without thinking too much, I leap straight into the hole—ready to face whatever awaits us down there in the dark.

# 14 MAPS

I CRASH DOWN ONTO concrete. Liam jumps right after me, and we tumble into each other. I stand up, dazed, looking around in every direction. Liam stands up too. We're inside a large, horizontal tunnel. One that appears to run in either direction, both under the cathedral and also out into the jungle.

Octavio and his men are standing there in the dark a few feet away, waiting for us. Cass, Emma, and Alun are already racing off down the length of the tunnel in the direction of the jungle. Their feet splash in a stream of oily water.

"You need to run," Octavio says, his voice echoing against the curved concrete walls. "Now, while you have the chance."

"Dad, I'm not leaving you here," Liam says. He's stripping off his robes, revealing jeans and a T-shirt beneath. He slips his knives into leather sheaths strapped to his back.

"Some of my men are still in danger, and I've sworn to protect their lives. You know that. And I want to see if I can rescue Dr. Barrett. Now go!" He gestures down the tunnel. "Take Alenna to safety. And save yourself as well. I'll be fine. When the time is right, I'll find you again."

Liam nods. "How?"

"I have my ways," Octavio says.

"C'mon," I say to Liam.

"Stay safe," he tells his dad, hesitating for a second.

Octavio nods in return. "You too." They clutch each other's hands tightly for a moment, and then they let go.

Liam and I begin racing after the other kids. The sound of the battle is audible overhead. Scattered gunshots now punctuate the howling and the screaming.

"I thought you might be dead!" I confess as we run. I'm panting out the words through ragged breaths. "I was so scared! What happened out there?"

His hand finds mine, and I clutch it. It's amazing to feel his touch again.

"My dad's boat didn't have enough fuel," he explains. "They were adrift. When Dr. Barrett and the rest of us got there, we had fuel, but we'd had to fight several battles. We didn't have much else."

Liam and I continue running. I glance back. More of Octavio's men have found the tunnel, and he's helping them into it.

"Eventually, we made it back to the wheel," Liam continues, "but we were ambushed by thousands of drones as soon as our helicopter and the hydrofoil landed here on a beach. It was like they knew we were coming."

"They did," I say. "David told them."

"I knew not to trust that kid!"

"You were right. He's been working both sides. When we landed here in airships from Southern Arc, he led us straight into a trap. Drones came right out of the trees, took us hostage, and destroyed the airships."

"That figures." We turn a bend in the tunnel and keep running.

"They firebombed the helicopter and sunk the hydrofoil. So, we're stuck here. Again." His hand tightens on mine. "But at least we're together. I never should have left you alone at Southern Arc. I regretted it the instant the helicopter took off!"

"Me too! I never should have told you to go!"

There's so much to talk about, but hopefully there will be time later. For now, we just have to survive.

I stare down the tunnel as we run. "Where does this thing go?"

"It should lead outside the cathedral. Whoever threw weapons into our cells also put a map of this sector in mine. It's in my pocket. I haven't had time to study it yet."

We run faster, moving in earnest. My boots are soaked from the cold water beneath our feet.

"I'm sorry I didn't believe you about David," I say, gasping for air. The tunnel seems to go on forever. "I don't know if he was always a spy, or if they tortured and brainwashed him until he betrayed us. Either way, I shouldn't have trusted him."

"It's okay. What matters is that you're safe, and we're together. At least the drones didn't attack the airships while they were still in the air."

"The new Monk must want us alive for some reason."

"Probably for the same reason we want the drones alive—to convert them to our way of thinking and to increase our numbers."

I'm breathing so hard from exertion, it's hard to talk anymore. I just put my head down and try to run faster. In the distance, I finally see a circle of white light, and the silhouettes of our friends rushing toward it.

Behind me, gunshots suddenly explode down the length of the tunnel. Liam and I both duck. I glance back.

I hear more shots and see the flash of a muzzle. I can't tell if someone is shooting at us, or if Octavio and his men have gotten guns somehow and are shooting at the drones.

Liam and I just keep running toward the light. I hope that there aren't any drones wherever this tunnel ends. If there are, we could get trapped down here.

Eventually, we catch up to Cass, Emma, and Alun. They can barely breathe, and they're going much slower now. Alun has lost a lot of blood from the wound on his neck. Blood is covering his long-sleeve shirt.

"Hey, Liam," Cass says. Emma is holding on to her for support.

Liam nods. "Hey."

Emma and Alun both look terrified. Alun reaches up a hand to probe the laceration on his neck.

"You okay?" I ask him.

He nods. "Yeah."

Together, we race the final distance until we reach the very end of the tunnel. It opens directly outside, into the forest. I can see green jungle and daylight beyond it.

But our path is blocked by an iron grating. It's wide enough to stick an arm or leg through, but not wide enough to fit an entire body. The iron is embedded into the concrete, so there's no way to pull it loose. For a moment I feel sick. *We're trapped down here after all.*

We stand there for a moment in front of the grating, crouching and trying to recover our breath. The stale air in the tunnel is putrid.

I hear more gunshots behind us.

Liam grabs the iron grating, trying to feel for a weak spot. I start doing the same thing, and the others follow. The iron feels pretty solid. Then Liam steps back and takes both of his knives out, raising them up.

"This might not work," he says. "Depends how strong the iron is."

"Try it," I say, encouraging him.

He pauses and then holds out one of his long knives. "Try it with me?"

I smile and take the blade. "Thanks."

Liam swings his blade outward as he lunges at the grating. His blade flashes against the iron, metal sparking against metal. For a second, I'm afraid that his knife is going to break. I move forward and swing my blade, too. The blow makes my arm throb as the blade clashes against the thick iron bars.

At first, it seems like this is not going to work. But the iron grate is old, and as we keep hitting it, one of the iron beams snaps in two and clatters to the ground. I shield my eyes as Liam and I strike at the grating again and again. We manage to shatter another piece of it. Bits of iron skitter through the air and across the tunnel floor.

With a few more strokes, enough iron is gone that there's a hole large enough for us to sneak through. Liam and I are breathing hard from the exertion. He sheaths his blade. "Let's go," he says. I keep hold of my knife, relieved to have a weapon back in my hands.

We start climbing through the hole, one after another. Liam and I are at the end, together. I climb outside right before he does, the jagged iron railings slicing at my clothes and skin. But within a second, I'm through. I stand there in the jungle heat with everyone else. Liam comes out of the opening a moment later.

All of us look around cautiously. There are no drones here, or if there are, they are well hidden in the verdant trees. I'm not sure which way to go, or what to do. I can't see the cathedral anymore.

I hear faint gunshots coming from the tunnel.

"We can't just stand here," I say. "We have to run."

Cass nods.

"Which way?" Alun asks, sounding exhausted. "If we make the wrong choice, we'll be caught. . . ."

Liam reaches back and takes a folded sheet of crumpled paper out of his pocket. This must be the map. "Check it out," he explains to the others. "Someone threw this into my cell to help us, along with some weapons."

We crowd around him as he unfolds the paper. I think that we're going to hear more gunshots at any second, or that drones will leap from the trees. Or worse—that feelers will appear from the sky to snatch us.

I stare down at the sheet of paper. It's an old-fashioned hand-drawn map. I tilt my head, trying to make sense of it.

"So where are we?" Cass asks.

"Look," I say, pointing at a small $X$ that marks an area of the forest. It's at the end of a dotted line leading out of a large square. "I bet that's where we are right now. I bet the square is the cathedral, and the dotted line is the tunnel."

"How can you be sure?" Cass asks. "The $X$ could mark our destination, not our location."

"There's no other $X$ on the map anywhere," I tell her.

"But how could the person who gave Liam this map know that we'd end up here?" Emma asks, straightening her glasses and peering at the map again.

"Probably because there's no other way out of the tunnels," Liam answers. He gazes around. "Alenna's right. Some of these landmarks even match up." He points at a massive pile of rocks ahead of us, to the right. Then he points to a small triangle marked on the map. "Look. The triangle could signify the rock pile."

We're all studying the confusing map now. The *X* orients us, possibly, but it doesn't explain where to go. Nothing is labeled. The map just shows areas of forest, with strange demarcations, grid lines, and numbers on them. There are also additional small squares and rectangles drawn in. But without a key to the map, it's hard to understand. *And I'm not sure we can even trust this map.* I wish Cass still had the GPS.

I take the paper from Liam.

"The squares are probably all buildings," Cass says over my shoulder.

I nod.

Liam points at another square, one with thick black lines emanating from two sides of it. The lines run in either direction, off the map on both edges of the page. "If this square is another building, then it's the largest one near us, other than the cathedral. Let's go there and check it out. If the drones are preoccupied with the cathedral, maybe we can explore this sector and try to find more weapons."

"It could be another trap," Emma says nervously. "Or another confinement house, or whatever they called it."

"If it's a trap, then we'll run again," I tell her. "Back into the forest." I hand the map to Liam.

"Maybe we can find some supplies in the building, or something else to help us," Liam says.

"Let's do it," I agree.

We begin running through the trees, with Liam using the map to guide us. I start to see a few wisps of fog on the ground again.

The fog must be endemic to this sector. If it keeps getting thicker, it might help to obscure us, but it will also make it harder to see anyone heading in our direction.

As we move, I worry about Octavio. I hope that he'll be able to fight his way out of the tunnels. I know he told us to run, but maybe we should have waited for him. I don't want anyone else to sacrifice themselves for me—let alone Liam's dad. I'm trying hard not to think about what might have happened to my own mom. But maybe she's safer not being on the wheel.

The trees look stark and menacing in the increasingly thick fog. We run as close together as we can. None of us want to get lost out here. Liam and I are next to each other, leading the way with Cass. Alun lags behind because of his injury, but Emma is helping him. I see her inspect the gash on his neck. Hopefully her experience nursing the Ones who Suffer means that she can help him. Every now and then we stop and consult the map in detail.

There are still no signs of any drones. I'm guessing that most of them are back at the cathedral. But I know that the masked figure will send some out after us.

"Stop. Wait!" Liam calls out.

Our group huddles around him.

"What?" I ask.

"I think we're close."

We're all looking at the map again. The fog drifts around us in banks, getting denser than ever. Liam points to our right. "The building should be over here somewhere, if it exists."

We stare around in the fog. A bird takes off from a nearby tree, squawking and startling us.

"I hate this place," Cass mutters to Emma.

We start hiking to our right, forging our own trail through the underbrush between huge mangrove trees. Liam's knife is raised, and so is mine.

We keep walking for a few minutes.

"I think I see something," I finally say, hesitating for a moment. The others pause too.

"Where?" Liam asks me softly.

"Up there." I point ahead at the trees. Everyone looks, trying to see through the foliage and the fog.

"What the hell?" Cass mutters, as fog drifts past us and gives us a better view for a second.

There is indeed some kind of concrete structure ahead of us. But it's not a building on the ground. It's about thirty feet above our heads, running through the trees. I squint, trying to understand what I'm looking at.

Liam has the map out again. "Look," he says to me. "The building we're headed toward has lines coming off it." He glances up at the thing in the trees. "The lines could be some sort of roads. Like elevated highways, or even a train system."

As crazy as it sounds, that's what this thing reminds me of—the giant elevated highways back home in the UNA. The ones that passed over the poor neighborhoods in New Providence, and cast shadows across the streets. But this road looks completely incongruous here. "It's probably some artifact from when the UNA built everything on the wheel," I say. "Something that got abandoned."

"If it's a train line, there's no way it's gonna be working," Cass replies.

"Who knows. In the gray zone, a lot of things were working," I tell her. "They were just automated."

"Even if it's only a road, we need to get up there somehow and walk along it," Liam says. "We can get our bearings, and get a better view of the wheel too."

"What if the drones control it?" Emma asks, eyeing the elevated roadway uneasily as she helps support Alun. He's looking even paler than before. "What if they're up there waiting for us already?"

"Then we'd better hope for some good luck," Cass replies.

We look around at one another in the fog. I know we don't have too long before someone finds us. "First, we have to find a way up there," I point out.

Liam is consulting the map again. "The square is to our right some more. And it might not be a building. It might just be a way up to the road, like a huge staircase or a passenger terminal."

"Let's find out," I tell him.

We begin walking forward again, blades out.

The soil and underbrush feel mushy and swampy here. The fog is even thicker. The air is so damp and muggy that it's hard to breathe.

We keep walking. After another few minutes, I see a solid structure emerge from the fog, on ground level this time. We head toward it. My senses are on alert for any nearby drones or feelers.

As the structure continues to emerge, I see that it's made of cracked slabs of concrete. It's partially disintegrated, even more than the cathedral was. Pieces of rebar stick out of it in places. Chunks of concrete litter the ground around us. It's like the building—or whatever it is—got hit by a bomb at some point in the distant past.

"It's in ruins," Emma says. She pauses for a moment. Alun is at her side. His breathing is ragged.

"Everything is in ruins on the wheel," I tell her. "That doesn't necessarily mean anything."

"Yeah. C'mon, Emma," Cass says, striding forward.

Liam and I keep walking too. The others follow. Holes are blown into the sides of the concrete structure. When we reach the largest opening, we stop. There's nothing but silence. I know it's possible that drones are waiting to ambush us here, but it doesn't feel that way. I sense no presence but our own.

Slowly, one by one, we slip inside the opening. It's not a building, exactly. It appears to be an old access tower for the elevated highway. One that provides a way up to the road from the forest, most likely for maintenance workers. To our left, I see an elevator. It's ancient, and partially melted. Like it was destroyed in a fire. But to the other side, I see a set of narrow stone steps, leading upward.

The steps are cracked, but they look secure. I can't see where they go, because there's a bend in the staircase, as it winds its way up to the highway.

"This way," I say, gesturing toward the steps. Dust covers everything here, and tendrils of fog have sneaked their way inside. I glance up and see tangled vines growing through holes in the concrete above our heads.

Liam and I walk over to the stairs. Cass, Emma, and Alun are right behind us. Cass kicks the lowest step. The noise of the blow echoes through the space.

"Careful," I say. "Don't be too loud."

Cass nods. "Just testing the concrete."

"I can't wait to get out of this fog," Alun mumbles, shivering, even though it's not cold. The wound on his neck is raw and continues oozing blood.

Liam steps onto the first stair. I take his hand and he helps me up. We walk up another step. Cass is right behind us with Emma and Alun.

We rapidly head upward. The stairs keep winding around, like a spiral staircase. In places, pieces of concrete are missing. But fortunately, the stairs don't give way. Soon, we will be at the top, and onto the elevated highway—or whatever this road is.

This was not what I expected would happen when we returned to the wheel. I thought Liam and I would come back with a huge army led by the scientists to liberate everyone. Instead, we've been reduced to a group of five, stumbling around on the wheel alone. Just trying to survive and find a way to keep going.

We must continue forward, no matter what gets thrown our way. I think of another line from *The Myth of Sisyphus*. One that has been rattling around in my head: "A reason for living is also an excellent reason for dying." It scares me, but I know it to be true. I keep holding Liam's hand. As long as we're together, then I know that everything is going to be okay—or at least that's what I tell myself as we reach the top of the stairs.

# 15 ELEVATED

LIAM STEPS OFF THE staircase one second before I do. His knife is out, ready to strike anyone who's up here.

I step out behind him, prepared for the worst as well. Prepared to encounter another silent army of drones.

But no one is standing up here but us. A cracked concrete roadway extends in either direction. We are indeed on some sort of abandoned, elevated highway.

Up here, we're above the fog and higher than many of the trees. I gaze out over a surreal landscape. Milky fog obscures much of it. The tops of trees poke through in places. I was hoping we'd get a better view of the wheel, but that won't be possible unless the road goes even higher or the fog clears.

Cass, Emma, and Alun step out behind us.

"Wow," Cass says sarcastically. "If only we had a car, this would be awesome."

"We have our feet," Liam says. "We're going to have to walk out of here. Get out of this sector and far away from the drones. Then figure out a new plan of attack."

I'm looking around. On the side of the road closest to us, I see a long metal rail, like the kind used by local trams in the UNA.

Next to it is a shallow concrete gulley, filled with old leaves. "We might not need a car," I say, gesturing at the rail.

Alun staggers over to the rail to check it out. His bleeding has stopped again, at least for the moment. "Track's useless without a train," he says.

Liam and I follow him and stare down at the foot-thick metal rail ourselves. It's rusty in places, and has dirt on it, but it looks intact. Liam suddenly kneels down and touches it before I can stop him.

"Careful!" I say, afraid the rail is electrified. But nothing happens to him. Liam taps it a few times with his fingers.

Then he leans over even more, putting his ear flat against the metal. He's listening to see if there's a vehicle on the track.

"Anything?" I ask.

"No," he says, leaning back. He gets to his feet and comes over to my side.

"Maybe something's farther along. Just sitting there," I say.

"It's possible." Liam takes out the map and we both stare at it.

The others are looking around at the trees. Everything is silent and still.

"There's another small square marked along this path," Liam says to me. "Look." I see the square that he means. Dashed arrows come out of it, too. "Could be some kind of transportation center. Maybe there's a tram there."

"There's no way it'll be working," Cass calls out, heading over to us. "It's just wishful thinking."

"We need to walk up to it," I tell her, as Liam folds the map back up. "That's the direction we have to go, right? We need to get away from the cathedral, like Liam said. Maybe we can even find our way to the specimen archive eventually—or look for surviving villagers in the blue sector. Now that we're on the wheel, and everything has gone wrong, we need to come up with a new way to achieve our goals."

"Fine." Cass stares ahead, gazing up the desolate road that leads far into the distance. "Then what are you waiting for?"

She starts walking away from us, like she's angry.

Liam and I exchange glances. Then we follow after her, with Emma and Alun beside us.

Soon, we've caught up to Cass, and we're walking side by side with her. The road is wide, like a deserted eight-lane highway, with the metal rail running alongside one edge. But there are no markings on the road, other than old tire tracks.

"I bet the UNA built this road when they were constructing the specimen archive, and the other stuff in the gray zone," Liam says to me as we walk. "Seems like an easy way to transport materials across the wheel, or inland from the coast."

"Definitely." This road is clearly too large to have been built by the exiled scientists. And my mom never mentioned anything about roads or cars being on the island. Neither did any villager or drone. The old tire marks beneath our feet are faded and wide, suggesting that long ago, industrial trucks and machines traveled this route.

"Why aren't the drones up here?" I ask Liam. "This would be a great place to watch everything from. I mean, if the fog weren't so bad."

"I don't know. But maybe it's always foggy here or something. Or maybe they're scared of the feelers."

"I haven't seen any feelers since we've been back on the wheel."

He looks at me. "It's weird, right? Maybe they're not in this sector. It doesn't really make sense." He grins. "Not that I miss them, or anything."

Our blades are still out, and we're scanning the treetops as we walk. Just in case there is another ambush.

"Can I see the map again?" I ask Liam.

He takes it out and hands it to me. I stare down at it. Because there's no scale, I can't tell how far we have to go. But so far, most of the things on the map have been nearby. So I'm hoping that the next building along this road isn't going to take too long to reach.

Cass is walking by the edge of the road opposite the metal rail and the gulley. She's peering into the distance.

"See anything?" I call out.

She turns back. "Fog and tree branches. Nothing too exciting."

"As long as there are no feelers or drones, that's good enough for me," Emma murmurs, adjusting her glasses again. She's keeping a close eye on Alun. Hopefully she'll take good care of him if he starts to collapse on us.

Alun stays silent. I know that his blood loss is making him feel incredibly sick. But he's being stoic about it.

We keep walking. Cass eventually comes back from the edge of the highway and walks with the rest of us. The total desolation here is surprising, but it means that we can keep moving rapidly.

Finally, I notice something at the edge of the highway, on the side with the metal rail. Before I can speak, Cass cries out, "Up ahead! See that?"

I nod.

We start walking faster.

Even before we reach the object, it's very clear what it is: a small, gray vehicle sitting right there on the rail. I can see the outline of its shape against the sky.

It's abandoned, like everything else. As we approach, I worry that it will be completely destroyed, just like the elevator we passed earlier.

We slow down right before we reach it, in case someone's hiding inside. I can see now that it's definitely some sort of conveyance. Like a small industrial trolley, meant to transport people or supplies across the wheel. It's facing away from us, in the direction that we want to go.

The sides are made of thick chrome, with large, clear windows. A few of the windows are cracked, but none have been completely broken. The vehicle is firmly mounted on the metal track. It has no wheels, and no weapons jut out of it.

I can't believe that the villagers or drones haven't found it and used it yet. Or maybe they tried, and it simply doesn't work. But I'm surprised they didn't take it apart and use the raw materials for weapons.

We walk around to the front. The sliding door is open, revealing a surprisingly clean metal interior with about six narrow rows of seats. We walk closer.

I gaze inside. There's no steering wheel or driver's seat. It's clearly automated, like the trams they had at the Scanning Arena in New Providence. The front of the vehicle is just a giant pane of glass.

Liam is leaning down, checking the undercarriage. "It's still aligned on the rail," he says.

"Is there any power?" I ask.

"I don't think so."

All of us are walking around it, inspecting it.

I pause for a moment when I hear a distant howl. Then I realize it's just the sound of a hoofer, those genetically modified animals that provide one of the wheel's main food sources. Loud but harmless. I'd almost forgotten about them. Their screams once scared me so much, but now I barely notice them. I glance around again, looking for any sign of drones, but I find none.

Cass barges inside the tram with a sudden crash. Startled, I move forward, but Liam touches my arm. "Let her be."

I stand back as Cass moves around in the vehicle, searching in vain for any way to make it move. "There's nothing in here! There's no way it's going anywhere!" She kicks at the metal wall in frustration and anger, and then slumps down on one of the chairs.

I remember her warning me to tell her if she started acting weird or crazy, like a drone. I almost want to say something to her now, but I think this is just normal frustration for Cass. Or at least that's what I hope it is.

Liam and I climb in through the open door to look around inside with her, while Emma and Alun keep watch outside. The only thing I notice is a series of six buttons on the interior of the tram near the door. They are arranged in vertical lines, divided by color. Each button is an inch in diameter. Three of them are black, two are red, and one is white. "Try those," I tell Cass.

"I already did," she says.

Liam reaches over and pushes the buttons himself. Nothing happens. The tram is dead.

I step back. "We better start walking again."

Cass sighs and gets out of the vehicle. But Liam and I stay inside for a moment longer together. He runs his hands over the surfaces, looking for any way to bring the tram to life. He keeps coming back to the buttons.

I stand near the doorway. Cass is muttering and cursing outside with the others.

"You really think we can get this thing running?" I ask Liam softly. "If not, we should probably forget about it and get going. I don't want to waste time."

"Yeah, I think it's fried," he murmurs back. "If it's anything like the trams in the UNA, then it's powered by an electromagnetic drive. But I can't find a way to activate it. Even if I could, its batteries might have died a long time ago."

"How far do you think we are from the gray zone? Or to the border of another sector?"

"A long way." He glances at me. "We might need to make camp in this sector tonight."

I nod.

"Let me try," Emma's voice rings out, surprising me. She's appeared behind me in the doorway of the tram. She's leaning in and staring at the buttons. "In my village, our hunters found something like this once. I mean, not exactly like this, but it had buttons on it."

I move aside, making room for her to climb on board with us. I can see Alun and Cass talking outside. He's sitting cross-legged on the concrete, resting with one hand pressed against his neck.

Emma brushes back her blond hair and stands in front of the buttons. Liam is now keeping watch for drones and feelers out the front window.

"So what did you find in your village?" I ask Emma, as she scrutinizes the buttons.

"Some kind of old UNA hovercraft. Just large enough for one person at a time. We kept it hidden, until the drones turned up and destroyed it with fireworks one night." She reaches out a finger and starts pushing the black buttons. "We didn't know how to start it at first, but then we figured out that the buttons worked in sequence." She holds the black ones down. Nothing happens.

"But out of six buttons, it could be any combination," I point out.

"It wasn't really a code, or anything like that. It was more like a starter mechanism. I don't think it was meant to be hard to operate. You just held down all three black buttons, and then pushed the white one." Her fingers find the white button and hold it down. "And then you let go and push both the red ones."

She releases the black and white buttons, and then reaches out and touches the red ones.

"Like this," she says. She pushes the red buttons down hard.

Instantly, a humming noise sizzles out from underneath us, and from around the tram. Liam turns toward me and Emma, startled.

"I think she did it," I say in amazement, staring at Emma. She looks just as surprised as I feel. Out the window, I see Cass and Alun staring at us.

"I guess this is more useful than knowing Japanese," Emma muses.

The tram starts to vibrate. The walls rattle as the noise gets louder. I smell the odor of burning dust, as though old electric coils are coming to life again. Giving the vehicle power.

"How can this thing still be working?" Liam wonders out loud.

"Maybe it's like the machines in the gray zone," I tell him. "It just keeps running forever, even after the people are gone. Or maybe it's solar powered."

We stand there for a second, looking at each other. Then the tram starts to move forward. Slowly at first, just inching along the rail in a hesitant, jerky manner, nearly making me lose my balance. Then the vehicle starts to glide faster. Sliding along the rail, making a loud buzzing noise.

I can't believe it. I feel jubilant.

Then I suddenly realize that Cass and Alun are stuck outside.

"Wait!" I call out.

Emma quickly presses the buttons again, trying to make the vehicle stop or slow down. But it keeps moving even faster. Now that it's been activated, it's going to keep heading forward until it reaches its destination. *Wherever that is.*

Liam leans out the open door. "C'mon!" he yells to Cass and Alun.

We're picking up speed with every passing second. I'm startled by how quickly the landscape is now moving past. I lean out behind Liam, and I see that Cass and Alun are both racing after the tram.

"Faster!" I yell at them. Soon we're going to be moving too rapidly for them to even have a chance to catch up. We're already going about fifteen miles per hour.

From somewhere, Cass summons up a hidden reserve of energy. She manages to reach the door. Alun is right behind her, but he's struggling. Liam and I crouch down, gripping thick metal handles on either side of the doorway. We throw out our arms, trying to grab Cass.

She finds my fingers. "Help me!" she yells.

"That's what I'm doing!" I yell right back at her. I grip her hand as hard as I can. She's now running and being half-dragged along.

I lean back, pulling even harder. For a moment, my grasp on her hand almost slips, but then it catches. She lunges forward and topples into the vehicle. We both fall back onto the metal floor with a painful crash.

I stare past her to see Liam leaning all the way out the doorway, trying to save Alun. Cass rolls to one side and I struggle up, grabbing at Liam's legs. I'm terrified that he's going to fall out. More of his body is outside the vehicle than in. And we're moving even faster.

He nearly has Alun's hand in his. "Run!" he's yelling at Alun. "You can make it!"

I grab on to Liam tightly, trying to support him. He stretches out even farther. I can feel his taut muscles. I hold him as hard as I can. Cass and Emma are behind me, screaming at Alun to run. If he doesn't go faster, he's going to get left behind. All by himself, out here on the open road.

Then, suddenly, Liam has him and is gripping his wrist. Alun's torso slams hard against the side of the tram. But then he gets yanked inside. We fall back into the metal space. I stagger up, clutching the back of one of the seats.

"That was *way* too close," I say, struggling to catch my breath. My legs feel shaky. Liam picks himself up and puts his arm around me. Emma is helping Alun to his feet. He looks as though he's going to throw up. The gash on his neck is bleeding again.

Then the noises from outside cut out. I look over and see that Cass has swung the tram door shut.

"Thanks for helping me," she says, noticing my gaze.

I nod. "No problem."

Alun is rubbing his side from where he hit the tram. I can tell that he's in a lot of pain.

"You okay?" Liam asks him.

Alun nods. "Bruised."

"Bruised ego, probably," Cass says, joking, but also with an edge of concern. "Why'd you run so slowly? You could have been killed."

"You try taking an arrow in your neck and see how fast you run," he snaps back, annoyed. He readjusts his homemade eye patch.

Emma shushes him and tries to tend to the wound on his neck.

"So how'd you get this thing to start up?" Cass asks me and Liam.

"We didn't," I say. "Emma did." I gesture at the buttons. "She figured it out."

Cass grins at Emma. "Nice work, girl."

Emma grins back.

We stand there in the tram, gazing out the front windshield. We're going about forty miles an hour now, and continuing to move faster.

I know that we've put ourselves in danger. We have no clue where this tram actually ends up. And for all we know, the track could be damaged up ahead and we could get derailed. But we're going too fast to leap off the tram now. If we tried to jump onto the concrete, we might break our legs. The buttons only started it moving—there's no way to make it stop.

Ahead of us stretches the highway, heading into the horizon. It looks endless as it unspools into the distance. On either side are trees as far as I can see. The fog has almost disappeared now. I wonder if we've crossed into another sector already. The trees are taller, and more of them grow up above the road, although most remain below us. The road is even higher now, elevated as much as forty feet above the ground in places.

I squint into the distance, but there's a slight curve to the road, so I can't quite see what's ahead of us. I have no idea where we are on the wheel. Or why this place is deserted.

"We should keep a lookout for feelers," I say, realizing that one could come down, out of sight, and strike us from above.

I keep staring out the windshield, mesmerized by the view. We're passing right through the forest untouched. I wonder how many different sectors we'll end up cutting through. Or perhaps we're still inside the purple sector. There's no way to know.

"Where do you think we are right now?" Emma murmurs, giving voice to my thoughts. Nobody has an answer. She leans down to inspect Alun's bruised rib cage.

Liam takes out the map and holds it up so that we can see. "I think this black line indicates the road that we're on."

"So where does it go?" I ask him.

"Off the map."

"Seriously?" Cass mutters.

I peer at the map more closely. He's right. This is one of the lines that continues off the page. And there's nothing on the back of the piece of paper.

"So we have no clue where we're even going?" Cass asks.

"We had to escape from the drones and the cathedral anyway," I tell her, staring out into the wilderness. "This will take us far away from them."

"But also far away from the scientists and Octavio's men," Alun speaks up. He has one hand pressed against his side now. "Is that a good idea?"

Liam looks at him. "We would have been captured by drones if we stayed behind." He pauses. "And my dad will be fine. Maybe by now he's even taken over the cathedral." I hear the mixture of hope and worry in Liam's voice. I take his hand in mine.

"Exactly," I say, before anyone else can speak. "We want to rescue our friends. This is the only chance we have right now." I pause. "If we can regroup, maybe others will find us. Eventually we can get to the specimen archive somehow. Inside, there's a potential army of thousands. They might be our best chance against the new Monk and his drones—or at least the frozen villagers will be."

"How are we going to rescue anyone anyway?" Alun asks glumly. "We don't have supplies. And there's only five of us."

"Fewer people than that rescued me," Liam says. "It was only Alenna and Gadya who came and managed to get me out. There's always hope as long as we keep fighting."

I glance over at Cass. She's staring out the window with brooding eyes, like she feels uneasy.

We just keep gliding smoothly down the track. I stare out the window like the others, tightening my grip on Liam's hand. The trees fly past on either side of us, as we move deeper into the unknown heart of the wheel.

# 16 REUNITED

WE KEEP MOVING FOR another half an hour. Our speed stabilizes at what feels like fifty or sixty miles per hour, but it's hard to tell. I don't see any drones or any feelers. Everything remains empty and abandoned.

I sit in one of the seats next to Liam, watching the jungle out the window. I don't see any familiar landmarks. Only tree-tops.

Just as I'm wondering where our journey will end, I see something strange up ahead. Not off to the side of the road this time, but laying directly across it, and across our track as well. Liam and I stand up instantly.

Cass notices too. "What the hell is that?" she asks, standing up as well.

"I don't know." I'm afraid that we're going to hit it. If we keep going at this speed, we certainly will.

But at the same moment, the tram begins rapidly decelerating. I cling to Liam's shoulder to steady myself. The others grab on to chairs and handles. A soft warning beep starts sounding, and the two red buttons on the wall begin to flash.

We slow down even more.

"What's going on?" Emma asks, helping Alun up. He looks even worse than before—kind of groggy.

The object on the road is coming into view more clearly. We're only a few hundred feet away from it now. It just resembles a mass of rubble. Rotting hoofer carcasses and chunks of concrete are strewn across the highway.

I'm confused for a moment. *But then I see that this is a deliberate barrier.* Someone has purposefully placed this stuff here. The carcasses and rocks are piled three feet high across the track and the entire road, blocking anyone from passing.

"It's a trap," Liam says, as he scans the barricade with his piercing blue eyes.

"Another ambush," I agree, as my stomach flip-flops.

"We don't know how long this thing has been here. Maybe it's really old," Emma says. "Maybe whoever set it up has moved on. Or died."

"I don't want to bet on that," I reply.

The hoofer carcasses look too fresh. I'm expecting drones to burst out and open fire with arrows at any moment.

"We stick together," Liam says to everyone. "We fight, if we can." He's scanning the road and the forest on either side, just like I am.

The tram slows down even more. The soft alarm keeps pinging and the red lights keep flashing.

Soon we come to a complete stop. We're just fifteen feet away from the barrier. The lights and the noise abruptly cut off. The tram is silent and still.

"I guess this is where we get off," Cass says.

We stand there for a moment. There's still no sign of anyone. I know that there's no point staying inside the tram—it wouldn't provide enough protection from an assault, and even worse, we could get trapped inside. And clearly we can't keep going on it unless we clear the debris off the track.

I reach over and slide open the door.

"Let's go," I say.

Liam nods. He takes out his knife and steps off the tram, onto the side of the road. I follow.

"Watch your back," he says quietly as I step down next to him. "I feel like someone's watching us, but I'm not sure."

"Drones?"

"Could be."

I hear the others disembark from the vehicle behind us. Liam and I keep walking cautiously up to the barricade, our blades raised. I can smell the decaying hoofer meat from here. "Only drones would build something this gross," I say.

"Maybe we can move it out of the way, if we do it fast." Liam glances at me. "It's possible Emma's right. An ambush should have happened by now."

I stare at the wall of dead hoofers and rocks. "It's going to take a while to clear the rail. You think we can get the tram to start up again?"

"I'm guessing it has a laser sensor that tells it if anything's in its way. If we clear the track, I bet it'll start running."

The others reach us. We stand there at the wall of debris. There's nothing on the other side of the wall—just more road. If we can get this junk out of the way, we can continue our journey. *Assuming there aren't more roadblocks.*

"We better get to work," Liam says, stepping right up to the barricade.

I join him, about to help.

It's then that I'm struck with a strange feeling. I can't describe it. I just get the sense all of a sudden that we're not alone. It's more than a hunch; it's a certainty. I just know that someone is watching us. It must be the feeling that Liam was talking about.

"Liam——" I start to say.

*And right then, a figure rises up from the center of the barricade, ten feet to our right.*

I'm too shocked to move.

Liam stands his ground as the others scatter in horror.

The figure is huge and terrifying.

It's cloaked in bloody hoofer skins, and holds long thin knives in either hand. It wears the dead, dried skin of a hoofer over its face for camouflage, like it's half man and half beast. If this is a drone, then it's a new kind of drone. Scarier than I've ever seen.

Before I can scream, I see other sections of the barricade start shaking. More figures start standing up from the rubble.

They've hidden themselves in the barricade. They probably knew that the tram was coming, by sensing vibrations in the rail. They're all wearing hoofer skins, dripping with decayed flesh, and flashing sharp knives. Their exposed flesh is painted dark gray with dried mud.

The figures begin howling as they scramble toward us. I can't tell how many there are. At least fifteen or twenty.

It takes every ounce of courage I possess not to turn and flee. I stand my ground next to Liam. I raise my blade, ready to do battle.

Liam strikes at the first figure, his blade sparking as it hits the figure's knife. There's no way we're going to win this fight. But I leap forward anyway, trying to strike out at another one of the figures, right next to the one that Liam is fighting.

I see Cass off to one side, struggling with one of them too. There's no sign of Emma and Alun. They're probably running away back down the road. I don't blame them. But I know I can't do the same thing.

I see one of the figures slam Cass to the ground. It stands over her, poised to strike.

"No!" I scream, finding my voice. "Don't touch her!"

Liam is fending off four of these terrifying apparitions at once. Another one comes at me, with fierce eyes blazing, swinging a long jagged knife in one hand like a baseball bat.

I raise my blade to defend myself against the onslaught.

But then, at the last second, the figure inexplicably stops short.

Confused, I lunge forward with my knife, aiming right for its heart.

But the figure manages to dance out of the way. The tip of my blade just grazes its hoofer skins, tearing off a chunk of animal hair.

"Come on!" I yell, knowing that our lives might end right here and now. "What are you waiting for?"

We don't have anything to lose by fighting. We might as well take some of these drones down with us—assuming that's what they even are. I hear screams behind me in the distance. Emma and Alun must have been caught.

"Stop!" the crazed figure in front of me suddenly yells. Its voice is loud and clear, ringing out over the noise of the battle.

To my surprise, I realize that it's a girl.

The figure stares at me. Then she raises her blade above her head, holding it sideways with both hands, to signal that she means no harm.

I stare back, trying to figure out what's going on. Liam pauses too, backing away from the four figures he's been fighting. They stare him down. Their weapons are at the ready, but they've halted their attack.

I glance over and see that the figure who was about to stab Cass has paused too. His blade hovers just an inch above her neck. A second more, and he would have cut her throat.

"Who are you?" Liam calls out. We stand there, glaring at these warriors.

The girl who stopped the fight steps forward.

Then she grins, the mud around her eyes crinkling. "Don't you recognize your old friend?"

*And in that moment, I do recognize her.*

"No way!" I say, shocked.

She tears off her headdress of hoofer skins to reveal her own hair, dyed through with vivid blue streaks.

*"Gadya!"* I yell.

It seems impossible.

But somehow it's happening.

Liam looks as stunned as I feel. Cass is slowly getting to her feet. The man who nearly sliced through her throat is now helping her up.

"Who's Gadya?" Cass asks, rubbing her neck.

I lean forward and hug Gadya as hard as I can. I feel her arms wrap around me. She smells of hoofer blood, mud, and sweat. I can't believe that we've been reunited like this. This entire time, I've been worried about finding her and saving her, but here she is right in front of me.

"I never thought I'd see you again!" she whispers, her voice close to breaking.

"Me neither!" I'm close to tears myself. The last thing I

expected was to find Gadya alive and well on this desolate road.

"How did you get out of the specimen archive?" I ask her. "I thought you'd been frozen, or worse! We were coming to rescue you and everyone else, but we got ambushed."

"I already got rescued," she says, gesturing around at the dirty figures surrounding us. Some of them are taking off their hoofer-skin disguises, and rubbing mud off themselves. I don't recognize any of them. In fact, they look slightly older than most other kids that I've seen on the wheel. Maybe as old as Veidman was. Eighteen or nineteen at the least.

Alun and Emma have rejoined us, dragged back to the barricade. Both of them look confused, but relieved to be alive.

"You know these people?" one of the figures asks Gadya gruffly.

"Yes!" she exclaims. "Some of them." She casts her eyes over our group. "Liam!" she yells excitedly when she sees him.

"Gad!" he calls back. "It's really you!"

"It is!" She turns to the figures watching us. "Alenna and Liam are from my village in the blue sector. They're the ones who escaped from the wheel—the ones I told you about!"

"That's right," one of the figures says, nodding. He has a huge scar across his shoulder, and the lower lobe of his left ear is missing. "You hijacked a pod and got off Island Alpha. If what Gadya says is true."

Liam looks at him. "It's true."

"Why'd you come back?" another one asks us, with a mixture of suspicion and respect.

"We came back to rescue everyone, and to take back the wheel from the UNA and make the drones sane again," I explain. "The UNA destroyed most of the rebel bases around the globe. So we came here to free everyone in the specimen archive, and to stop the villagers and drones from fighting. We were going to make this island our new home base, and use it to mount an attack on the UNA."

"Then where is everyone else?" Gadya asks. "It's just the five of you? I was hoping you'd come back with a bigger army!"

"Our army got captured by drones," Liam says. "David led everyone into an ambush when they landed here in airships."

"For real?" Gadya looks shocked. "Why would he do that?"

"Oh, it gets worse," I continue. "There's a new Monk, and—"

"We know," one of the figures says.

"Then who is it?" Liam asks. "Minister Harka is dead."

"Nobody knows," Gadya says. "But he's taken over and reorganized the drones in just a few weeks. They obviously think it's the same Monk—miraculously healed or something." She pauses. "So do you think David was a spy all along?"

"It looks that way," I tell Gadya.

"Disgusting," she replies. She spits into the dirt. "I'm gonna kill him!"

"Get in line." I still feel sick about what happened. "He fled and joined the army of drones. We haven't seen him since then. Maybe he has some crazy reason, but maybe he doesn't. Either way, it's impossible to trust him. He betrayed us all. We almost died because of him, and the scientists got trapped."

"We better move," one of the other figures says, hoisting up his hoofer skins and his knives. I glance behind me. Emma stands there, looking overwhelmed. Alun is close to collapsing. The strange figures bustle around us, repairing the barricade.

"You're going to have to introduce us to your new friends," I tell Gadya.

"I will. It's gonna blow your mind." She smiles. "And I'll

explain how I got out of the gray zone. I'm so happy you came back! I kind of can't believe it."

"Me neither."

"So, I'll tell you and Liam everything as we go . . ." She glances at Cass, Emma, and Alun, her words trailing off.

"They're okay. They're with us," I tell her.

Liam nods in agreement.

"Let's hope they're more trustworthy than David," Gadya adds. "Now, come on. I'll show you where we're living."

Around us, the figures are nearly finished fixing the barricade. Making sure it will effectively block anything else that comes this way.

We start walking to the edge of the highway. For once, I'm not worried about whatever is going to happen next. I know that I can trust Gadya with my life, unlike David. And with her and Liam next to me, anything seems possible again.

The three of us walk side by side. Cass, Emma, and Alun trail behind. The figures escort them, watching them more closely than us because Gadya doesn't know any of them.

*Maybe fate is on our side for once,* I muse. Trying to find Gadya was one of my most important reasons for coming back to the wheel. And now Liam and I have achieved that, completely by accident.

"How's your ankle?" I ask her. The last time I was with her, it looked broken. She couldn't even walk on it.

She bends down and pulls up the pant leg of her torn, muddy jeans. "It's not pretty."

"Ouch," I say when I see her skin. "Does it hurt?"

"Every day."

There's a painful-looking metal brace around the lower half of

Gadya's left leg, and some sort of homemade splint on her ankle. A huge, jagged scar snakes its way up from it, nearly to her knee. "They fixed me up. It's not one hundred percent, but it's getting there."

"Who are these people?" Liam asks her. "Is there a village we didn't know about hidden in this sector?"

Gadya shakes her head. "They're not villagers or drones. It's a whole other tribe. They've made their own secret world on the wheel."

"David mentioned something about that once," I say. "I mean, not that his words mean anything now. But he said that there were people on the wheel who just went off into the jungle, and did their own thing. He wanted me to come with him."

"I'm glad you didn't," Liam says, glancing over at me.

"Yeah, no kidding."

"David might have been wrong about a lot of things, but he wasn't wrong about people living way out in the jungle," Gadya says.

We reach the short concrete wall at the edge of the highway. I'm not sure how we're going to get down to the forest below. It's about sixty feet below us. I hadn't realized how high up we'd gotten.

I peer over the edge. I see five long, knotted ropes dangling to the ground. No safety harnesses. No equipment. Just ropes.

"Wow," I say. "That's a pretty big drop."

"I wish there were an easier way," Gadya says. "But it'll be all right. Only thirty or forty feet."

I nod. "It looks higher." People are already rapidly descending some of the ropes. I watch them slide down to the green under-brush.

"Ropes are the only way on and off the road near the barricade," Gadya says. "C'mon. Let's get down there and I'll show you around."

Liam and I look at each other. Neither of us can believe that we've found Gadya—let alone been rescued by her and this new tribe.

Liam glances over the edge. "We can go down next to each other," he says to me encouragingly. "The ropes have knots all the way down to put our feet on."

He leans over, grabs a rope, and gives it to me. Then he sits down on the raised edge of the road and grabs one for himself. "This would be easier with carabineers and harnesses," he says to Gadya.

"You'll get used to roughing it after a while," Gadya says, sounding slightly amused. *Typical Gadya.* "That's how they do things around here. As simply as possible."

"So does this tribe have a name?" I ask her. Meanwhile, I'm scrutinizing the rope. Trying to make sure it's not going to snap on me.

"The tribe calls themselves the travelers. They're nomads. They avoid conflicts if they can, and they settle down wherever it's most peaceful."

"Setting up ambushes and attacking people on the road doesn't seem too peaceful," I say, still looking at my rope.

Gadya stares at me. "On the wheel, being peaceful is relative, remember? The travelers do what they have to do, in order to survive."

Liam touches my hand lightly. "You ready?"

I nod. "Sure. If you are."

He takes off one of his sheaths and gives it to me. I stick my blade in it and sling it over my shoulder.

I glance down the length of the highway. Some travelers are helping Cass, Emma, and Alun to nearby ropes.

"There's no climbing harnesses?" Emma asks. "No helmets? Nothing?" The travelers ignore her.

"Yeah, helmets would be nice," I murmur.

"Don't think too much about it," Liam says to me. "Just let your body be your guide. Watch."

He grabs his rope tightly and edges himself toward the lip of the short wall at the edge of the road. Then he swings out with both hands, like he's about to rappel down the side of the highway.

"Be careful!" I call out, but I can tell that he's enjoying himself.

Slowly, he starts moving down a bit. His feet find the first knot and rest on it. He holds onto the rope, swaying back and forth.

"Your turn!" he yells.

I sit on the wall at the edge of the road and swing my legs over it.

"Anyone ever fall off this highway?" I ask Gadya.

"No. So don't break our winning streak."

I take a deep breath. I see travelers sliding down the ropes with ease. At the bottom they slow down and land gently in the underbrush beneath the massive elevated highway.

I see that Cass is already on a rope, dangling there without moving, like a fly caught in a web. She's yelling and arguing with the travelers who are trying to help her. At least she's on a rope, though. *If Cass can do this, then so can I.*

I turn my body around so that I'm facing the highway. I clutch the rope as hard as I can. Then I slowly inch myself off the side of the road.

For a second, I'm afraid that I'm going to fall. My weight drags me down, and I clench my hands around the rope. I barely catch myself. I swing there, my heart pounding rapidly as my feet search for a knot.

"Good job!" Liam is saying. "You're doing great . . ."

My right foot finally finds a knot. I manage to turn and face Liam. He's hanging directly opposite me.

"This sucks," I tell him. "I didn't know I was so afraid of heights until now!"

"We'll be on the ground in no time," he says. "On the count of three, we'll start moving. Okay?"

I nod. He counts down, and then together, we both slowly descend to the next knot. Then the next one. And the one after that.

I look up and see that Cass is still arguing with everyone. She hasn't moved an inch. Emma and Alun aren't even on the ropes yet.

I keep moving along with Liam. Going slowly, but making progress. Then a gust of wind startles me, and makes my rope sway. I make the mistake of glancing down, and I instantly freeze up.

"Just look at me," Liam says calmly. "Don't worry about anything else. Okay?"

"Okay." I keep my eyes fixed on him. We continue descending.

Soon we're halfway there. My breath comes more easily now. Occasionally, I almost miss a knot, but I manage to stay on the rope.

We get even closer to the ground. It's just fifteen feet away, so I'm no longer scared. I glance up and see the roadway high above us. Cass has started coming down, and so have the others.

I hang there for a moment, taking a break. Liam stops too. We stare at each other as we dangle from the ropes.

"What do you think about all of this?" I ask him. We finally have a moment to talk alone, without anyone overhearing us. "Did you know that there were other tribes on the wheel?"

"No. I mean, I heard rumors sometimes, just like you did. But I've never heard of the travelers. Not from Veidman or anyone else."

"If they rescued Gadya and fixed her leg, they must have supplies," I whisper back to him. "And they can't be bad people. Gadya wouldn't be here with them if she didn't think she could trust them."

He nods. "True, but she might not have a choice. They rescued her. She might want to believe in them because there's nowhere else for her to go." He starts moving slowly again. "Let's get down there and find out. Who knows. Maybe they'll know something about how to locate my dad and his men."

I nod, thinking about my own mother. Then I begin to move again too. Soon we'll be at the bottom, and in the travelers' camp. I just hope they're who they seem to be. And I also hope that they have the resources we need to continue our ultimate mission—to return to the speciman archive and bring liberty to the wheel.

# 17 THE TRAVELERS

I REACH THE BOTTOM of the ropes. Liam hits the ground a few seconds before me. He stands there, waiting to help me with his arms outstretched. I hop the final few feet down into lush undergrowth and dirt.

I stare back at the ropes, dangling there like giant snakes. The road is far above us. "That looks a lot farther than forty feet."

"It sure does," Liam says, smiling a little. "My guess is closer to fifty or sixty. I think Gadya just told everyone it was lower, so we wouldn't freak out on her."

"Seriously? You knew that and you didn't tell me?" I punch him in the arm, annoyed. "Jerk."

He smiles back. "Looks like it worked."

I can't help but smile too. Then I hear loud voices drifting down from the highway. I stare up. "It worked for some of us, maybe."

Cass is near the top, screaming at the travelers about something. Alun and Emma are descending slowly. Both of them are hanging on to the backs of travelers, who climb down the ropes with confident ease.

"Without your help, I'm worried I'd be just like them," I tell him.

"Without yours, I would have died in the specimen archive." He leans over and kisses me.

Sometimes, in moments like these, I wish it could just be the two of us out here. Alone on the wheel, but without having to fight anyone or struggle to survive. I don't know what lies ahead of us. I just hope that one day we can find the peace that we're looking for.

Liam pulls back and looks around. "Now let's find out what's going on around here."

"Definitely."

We begin walking through the brush together. Travelers are moving around us. I see Gadya off to one side, talking to some of the figures near the base of an oak tree. We head in her direction.

"Hey!" I call out. "Gadya!" She turns and walks over to us rapidly. She only has a mild limp from her leg injury. It's barely noticeable. I can't believe her leg has healed so quickly.

"You survived the ropes," she says with a grin. "Told you they weren't so bad."

"You go up and down them every day?" I ask.

"Naw. We usually have a sentry or two posted on the highway. He watches the road and checks the tram line. If he sees or hears anything suspicious, then more of us go up. But it doesn't happen too often. You're the first ones to get that tram working. But sometimes, drones find the road on foot. Then we go up there and deal with 'em. Most of them are too scared to come up here, though. They think this road is haunted by ghosts or demons—they don't know it's the travelers. For some reason, the Monk doesn't ever force the drones to come up here."

"So how did you get out of the archive? I was so worried about you!"

"After you two climbed into the pod and got put on the plane in the specimen archive, I just waited up there in the observation deck in the cold. At first, I thought some of those tiny feelers would turn up and catch me. But they didn't. So then I figured I was just going to freeze to death unless I did something drastic." Her eyes go faraway, like she's reliving the painful memory. "I crawled across the floor and managed to get back outside. I was hoping one of the big feelers would come down from the sky and take me and freeze me, like they took everyone else—" She suddenly looks like she's trying not to cry.

"I feel so bad about leaving you," I tell her, leaning forward and hugging her again.

"I wanted you to leave, remember? I told you and Liam to go. It was our best hope for survival."

"What happened after that?" Liam asks her softly. "How did the travelers find you?"

"I got lucky. Occasionally, they send scouts through the gray zone. There are a lot more tunnels under the barrier into that zone than we ever knew about. We just couldn't get to them because the entrances are hidden in different sectors. But a scout found me inside the zone." Unexpectedly, she smiles. "I thought I was hallucinating at first, 'cause he was dressed in hoofer skins. I thought it was a monster. But it was a traveler. He wrapped me in skins and carried me out of the gray zone, down into a secret tunnel leading into the purple sector." She brushes back her blue-streaked hair. "It took me a while to heal. The travelers used special potions and herbal remedies, and they set the bone in my leg. The whole time I was thinking about you guys—where you were, if you'd made it, and what you were doing."

"We were thinking about you," I tell her. "Planning how to get back here and find you, and everyone else. That airplane we left the wheel in was hijacked by rebel scientists. They flew us to a secret base in Australia, but it got destroyed by UNA weapons. So we traveled to another base in the Antarctic, and then I flew here in an airship, and Liam and his dad came on a hydrofoil. That's the short version of how we ended up here."

Gadya looks startled. "Wow. That's some crazy journey!"

"I know."

"So you really came back to rescue me, and everyone else?"

I nod.

"And the rebels have airships and hydrofoils? I didn't know they were so well prepared."

"They used to have them," I say. "Until the drones got them and wrecked them. Now we have to start from scratch."

"Great," Gadya says, her shoulders slumping.

"So where is the travelers' camp?" Liam asks, looking around. "You said they were nomads?"

"Yeah, but only when they have to be. They've been living here for four months." She waves us forward. "C'mon. I'll show you."

We start walking.

"If there are other tunnels, then we can get back inside the gray zone and rescue some captured villagers," Liam says. "Who's the leader here? Can we talk to him or her? Make some plans?"

Gadya turns back to look at him as we walk. "There's no leader. It's not like at the village with Veidman and Meira, or the drones and their Monk. Everyone just works together."

"But without a leader, isn't it just total chaos?" I ask.

She shakes her head. "No. These kids are older than us. They've been here the longest. They're the ones who have the best survival skills—and they've also avoided getting the Suffering. That's why they've survived past eighteen. They don't need, or want, a leader. They take votes on stuff, but no one gets mad if they don't get their way. Everything's pretty peaceful." She lowers her voice. "They don't usually take in refugees like me or you guys. They keep to themselves. But just before they found me, a group of them got trapped by drones in the forest and killed. So they're looking for new recruits to join them."

"How did they evolve? Where did they come from?" I ask.

"They don't even know who started the movement. It supposedly just came from a few kids who formed their own small groups. Kids who deliberately wandered away from different villages a few years ago. Since then, the tribe has just grown."

I nod.

"You two will fit in fine, but I'm not sure about your friends," Gadya continues. "Cass was a drone, right? I can tell. Maybe Alun was too."

"Yeah, both of them," Liam replies.

"They've been given counseling and antidotes to the UNA drugs on the wheel," I tell Gadya quickly. "By the scientists who helped save us at the rebel base. So they're not going to act crazy—or at least I don't think they will. Besides, villagers killed Cass's older brother before she even got here. That's one of the reasons she became a drone."

"She better not act crazy, or the travelers will just vote to abandon her in the jungle."

"So if the travelers can get into the gray zone, why don't they get off the wheel?" Liam asks Gadya as we keep walking. Ahead of us I see nothing but the gigantic concrete support pillars of the highway, and more trees and tall grass.

"They've accepted their life here. They don't see a point in leaving. Besides, where would they go back to?"

I think about Camus's book again, and his emphasis on the importance of fighting for freedom and passion. What would Camus make of the travelers? "So they've given up hope?" I ask. "That's pretty depressing."

"No, they just found out it's possible to avoid conflict and live on the wheel in harmony with nature and their environment."

"And you feel this way too?" I ask, startled. I notice Liam gazing at Gadya in surprise as well.

Gadya stares at us for a second in silence.

"Hell, no!" she finally whispers, looking around to make sure no one's listening. "But I can't tell them that. They don't want to hear it. They're happy. And they realize there aren't enough of them to take over the wheel, anyway. So I keep my mouth shut."

"They're going to get slaughtered eventually," Liam says. "The drones are organized now, like the UNA military. We saw their armies. They're going to sweep through the wheel."

Gadya shrugs. "The travelers will survive. They've made it through more bad stuff than we can imagine. You'll see."

"So where's their camp?" I ask, looking around.

Gadya smiles. "We've been walking through it for the past couple minutes."

I pause, and so does Liam. There is literally nothing around us except trees, underbrush, and concrete.

"Look closer," Gadya prompts. "I told you they lived as one with the land and the environment, remember?"

Liam and I stare around. I walk over to a shrub, thinking maybe there's a hatch hidden underneath. But I see nothing.

"Tunnels?" Liam guesses. "Burrows?"

235

Gadya shakes her head. "Look up."

Our heads tilt up at the same moment.

"Wow," I say. Above us, I see the travelers' camp. It's built up high in the shadows directly underneath the elevated highway, and in some of the trees off to our left.

Everything is made of wooden beams and slats, disguised to look like part of the underside of the road. Platforms hang down on ropes and chains from the highway, attached to the concrete. I see a few figures moving around up there, high above us, watching. For a moment, it reminds me of the drones on the catwalks in the cathedral. But then I shake off the memory.

In the trees, wooden platforms are built up high as well, like birds' nests. They're barely visible. Concealed with leaves and branches. I only see them because I'm searching for them. Otherwise, I wouldn't have noticed.

"Pretty impressive, right?" Gadya asks, enjoying our surprise.

"Yeah, it's incredible," I tell her. "But how do we get up there?"

"How do you think?" Her smile widens.

"Ropes," Liam says.

I follow his gaze. I see some ropes painted gray with dried mud, dangling down from these strange hanging platforms attached under the road.

"The travelers stay off the ground as much as they can. It's the best way to avoid trouble."

"What about the feelers?" I ask. "If the travelers are nomadic and cross over into different sectors, don't the feelers attack them?"

"The feelers leave them alone. I don't know why," Gadya says. "The travelers are pretty careful."

"We haven't even seen any feelers since we've been back on the wheel," Liam adds. "Are they working?"

"I hear them in the distance occasionally," Gadya replies. "I don't know why there aren't more of them."

"Are we still in the purple sector?"

She nods. "Yeah."

Gadya could be right about the feelers, but I know that they have to be somewhere. It makes me nervous that things have changed so much on the wheel since Liam and I escaped from it. If the rules keep shifting, I don't know how we're ever going to win control of the island.

"If you're hungry or thirsty, there's food up there," Gadya says, gesturing to the platforms under the highway. "Nothing compared to what Rika could cook at the village, but it's decent."

"Rika," I say, murmuring the name of our friend. I haven't thought about her in a while. *It's frighteningly easy to forget about people out here.* I never want to let that happen. "We need to figure out how to get back to the specimen archive and find her."

"We'll talk about that when we're up in the camp," Gadya says. "But alone. I don't want any of the travelers to hear us. If they think we're planning something like that, they'll ditch us the next time they move their location. And right now, we need them."

"Fine, but Alenna and I came here to save everyone," Liam says. "Not hide out under a highway."

"Maybe we can try to rally the travelers and get them on our side?" I ask.

Gadya shoots me a skeptical look. "Good luck with that. You don't think I've tried?" She keeps walking closer to one of the roadway supports. We follow her. "Now how about some ropes?"

Fifteen minutes later, we've made it up the ropes and onto the platforms. I stand there, panting for air. We're on part of the strange, wooden scaffolding that hangs about fifteen feet underneath the road. Although everything looks rickety and handmade, the wooden platforms feel surprisingly sturdy. As long as I remember not to look down, I feel fine. A few birds nest up here too. They squawk angrily as we displace them.

Travelers are walking around on the creaking beams that stretch between platforms. Some are resting on beds made of underbrush. All of them are dirty. Their hair is long, often woven into dreadlocks. Some of them look as old as twenty. Because of the grime and the hair, it's hard to even tell the girls and boys apart, but it's a mix of both. Their eyes watch us cautiously.

We walk along a narrow platform, only three feet wide. It has no guardrails. Gadya is in the lead, with me in the middle, and Liam behind.

A few of the travelers acknowledge us with nods, but many of them studiously ignore us. I understand why. This is their domain. And we haven't proven ourselves to them yet.

We keep walking. I smell food, and I glance around. Some nearby travelers are eating something that looks revolting—like egg-shaped, crusty brown oranges. Yet the smell is strangely spicy and enticing.

Everyone looks fairly relaxed. That was something I never saw on the wheel before. Not at the village, and definitely not in the drones' camp.

I wonder what would have happened if David and I had been found by travelers that first day on the wheel, instead of by drones and then Gadya.

Would David still have ended up switching sides and betraying us like he did? *And would I be who I am today?* I don't regret anything I've been through or done, but I wish I hadn't seen so much bloodshed. And I wish that so many of my friends hadn't died or gotten frozen in the archive.

"Alenna?" Liam asks.

"Just thinking about the past," I tell him.

"You guys want some food and water?" Gadya asks. She moves nimbly across the platform, which gets even narrower here. I'm taking tentative steps. Even Liam is proceeding slowly, trying to get his bearings.

"Sure," I tell her. "I'm dying of thirst. And I can't even remember the last time I ate."

"Good. The travelers have plenty of food."

Right then, I almost trip on an uneven slat of wood, but Liam puts out an arm to steady me.

Gadya notices. "Careful. It's tricky at first."

I'm relieved that she doesn't seem angry at me, or weird about me and Liam being together. I was worried that seeing us as a couple might be too much for her, given her history with Liam. The two of them once dated, before I even got sent to the wheel. But she just seems happy to have us back, which is exactly how I feel about her.

We follow Gadya onto a large octagonal wooden platform. I glance up at the concrete underside of the road, which is our roof now. I'm expecting to find some hoofer meat hanging somewhere, or even a primitive kitchen like we had at the village. Instead, Gadya leads us over to a group of discolored wooden buckets at the edge of the platform.

"What is this stuff?" I ask when we reach them, glancing down at their contents. Inside the buckets is an array of strange-looking fruits and vegetables. I can't identify any of them, except for some coconuts. There are also some lumpy white things that look like roots.

"Breakfast, lunch, and dinner," Gadya says. "The travelers don't eat meat."

"Why not?" I ask, as Liam scrutinizes the food as well.

"Health reasons. They think it's contaminated."

"How do they know this other stuff isn't?" Liam asks.

"Because the travelers are still alive and none of them has the Suffering." She pauses. "Also, they don't believe in eating meat in general. They only eat fruits and vegetables, and nuts too."

I reach into one of the buckets. I take out the object that looks like a small, brown orange. It feels slightly furry. "What is this? I saw some of the travelers eating them earlier."

"It looks genetically modified," Liam muses, picking one up too. "I think I'd rather stick with hoofers."

"It's not modified—it's natural," Gadya says. "It's called a langsat. It's a tropical fruit."

I probe the object's skin. It's leathery and vaguely translucent.

"You gotta peel it first," Gadya says. "Put the peel in that bucket there." She points out an empty container.

I nod, gouging my fingernails into the fruit's skin and stripping it off. Underneath, the flesh of the fruit is pinkish-white. I raise it up and take a bite. It's tangy and acidic, with a hint of sweetness. "Tastes kind of like a grapefruit," I say. I take another bite.

Gadya smiles. "I know. Pretty good, right?"

Liam peels his langsat swiftly and takes a bite too. "Tastes a lot better than it looks," he says as he chews.

"So how come we didn't have these at the village?" I ask Gadya.

"They only grow in this sector, I think. Someone must have brought them here and cultivated them. The travelers told me that they grow anyplace that's warm and humid. Apparently they're pretty common in New Hawaii, and on other islands too."

Liam is looking back down into the buckets, holding the half-eaten langsat in his hand. "So the travelers live off this stuff?"

"Yep," Gadya tells him. "Even tubers. Everything's natural."

I turn to see a traveler passing behind us. He's short, and his skin has been darkened by the sun. There are premature wrinkles in the corners of his eyes.

"Hey there," he says to us. He sounds friendly but guarded. He reaches out and grabs an unidentifiable green vegetable from a bucket. Then he keeps on moving, walking off down one of the wooden platforms.

"So they don't have a plan? Or anything?" Liam asks.

Gadya shrugs. "Their plan is to stay alive."

"I'm not sure that's enough," I say softly. "I wouldn't be happy just living on the wheel, especially when so many people are being killed."

"Alenna's right," Liam says. "We can do better than that."

Gadya looks from him to me. "Then let's figure something out together. If——" She's interrupted by loud footsteps. I turn and see Cass heading our way, trailed by Emma.

"Where's Alun?" I ask.

"He lost too much blood to climb the ropes," Emma calls out. "He's back on the ground. The travelers are tending to him for now. I wanted to stay and help him, but they made me come up here."

When Cass and Emma reach us, Cass glances into the buckets.

"Langsats," she says. "Nice." She reaches down and plucks one up. She instantly starts eating it without even bothering to take off the peel. Liam and I just stare at her. She pauses, noticing our gaze.

"You know what these things are?" I ask her.

"Sure. There were a few langsat trees in the orange sector.

People would fight to the death over the fruit." She blinks. "It seems like a crazy nightmare now." She takes another bite. Emma grabs a langsat too.

We sit down on the octagonal wooden platform near the buckets, cross-legged. I glance around. I don't see any travelers in this area right now. The ones that are up here are keeping to themselves. I'm guessing that a lot of them are out in the forest, scavenging and keeping lookout.

"So what do we do?" Cass asks, wiping her mouth. "What's going on?"

"We're trying to figure out how to complete our mission," I explain. "How to take back the island."

"That looks doubtful," Cass says. She pauses, "But I'm in, if you have a good enough plan."

"So am I," Emma adds.

"We have no amazing plan yet," I admit. "We just have goals. We still want to get to the archive. We want to rescue our friends and defeat the new Monk. But we don't know how to do it."

"Would the travelers let us clear a path and keep going forward on that tram?" Liam asks Gadya.

She shakes her head. "They would, but the line doesn't go much farther. The road is collapsed about ten miles from here. Scouts explored it already. The tram would just stop again."

"Then we need to find some of those other tunnels into the gray zone. If the travelers used them to find you, we can use them to get back inside there."

"And what would we do inside, Liam?" Gadya asks, sounding annoyed. "You were in a pod most of the time you were there. Alenna and I did all the work. We'd freeze before we could unthaw more than a handful of kids."

"There has to be some way to release everyone at once. Like an emergency protocol." I look around at everyone. "I'm sure there is. The UNA wouldn't want their carefully collected specimens dying if a missile were aimed at the place, would they? There's probably some kind of quick release for the whole archive."

"Maybe," Gadya says. "We have to decide if that's worth risking our lives for right now. We owe it to Rika and Markus to get back there, but we have to be smart about it."

"Can we even do it?" Emma points out. "Without the travelers' help, how will we find the tunnels into the zone?"

"We'll do it ourselves, if they won't help," Liam says, standing up. "We either find some fireworks and blast our way through the barrier, or we find the tunnels on our own." He pauses. "Maybe we can find my dad out here somehow. He would help us."

"Or we could convince the travelers to help," Cass says.

I stand up. I'm about to respond, when I hear a distant noise. It sounds a lot like thunder. But it's actually something I haven't heard in a long while:

*The sound of feelers.*

I freeze. So do the others.

All except Gadya. She just sits there, taking another bite of langsat. "They're just passing nearby," she says blithely. "They never attack us. They'll be gone in a few minutes."

I glance at Liam. A look of warning passes across his eyes. We keep listening closely. The noise of the feelers is getting louder. Despite what Gadya said, nothing can be predicted on the wheel.

To me, it doesn't sound like the feelers are moving away from us. *It sounds like they're getting closer.*

And then travelers start yelling and jumping up, making the wooden platforms shake. I realize these feelers aren't going to pass us by after all. They're coming right after us—and they're going to snatch us up if we don't fight back.

# 18 DOWN FROM THE SKY

LIAM IS CLEARLY THINKING the same thing that I am. He rushes to his feet, moving over to me. "Gadya, you sure about these feelers?" he calls out. The noise is loud enough now that we have to yell over it.

Gadya looks less certain than she was just seconds earlier. "They'll pass. They always do!" She cocks her head to one side. "There are three of them. You learn to count them by the sounds they make!"

The noise continues to get louder. We're all standing now.

Then I start to hear raw screaming. More travelers rush around us on the platforms.

"The feelers are here on the road!" a voice calls out. "And it sounds like they've got someone!"

I see movement far below us in the brush. Travelers are bursting out and dashing through the foliage. They're heading for the ropes leading up to the highway near where the barricade is.

I stare at Gadya. She looks surprised. "The feelers have always gone overhead until now!"

"And I thought the travelers didn't fight," I say.

"I told you that they pick their battles!" Gadya snaps.

I grip the wooden edge of our platform. I feel a slight vibration in it.

"But what about us? Do we stay up here?" Emma asks. "Hide?"

Although that's tempting, I know we can't do that. "The feeler's tentacles could reach us under here," I say.

Gadya is standing there, looking around for weapons. But there are none up here. "We go up," she says. "Onto the highway. The travelers have taken down feelers before, just like we did that time on the ice."

"Then let's go!" Liam says.

"This way," Gadya replies. "There are some emergency ropes we can climb up. They go directly to the road."

We start racing down the platforms, headed toward the ropes. The travelers have thrown them up and hooked them on to the edge of the highway to provide direct access to it. There's no time to be scared of heights anymore.

When we reach the ropes, I grab one, loop my foot around it, and leap out into the air. I start pulling myself up, using the knots to help. Liam is right next to me on another rope. I try not to think about the drop beneath us.

Liam and I are soon clambering up and over the side of the highway, nearly falling into the gulley near the tram railing. The others aren't far behind us, even Emma.

I crouch near the metal tram rail, stunned by what I see. I expected to witness the beginnings of a battle—with travelers trying to rescue one of their own from a feeler. Instead, I see four feelers just hanging there in the cloudy sky.

They look like they're in some kind of formation. Three of the feelers form a triangle, with the fourth one in the center. Their tentacles are hanging loosely down, and their black helicopter-like bodies aren't hidden in the clouds. They're out in the open—completely exposed. I can see the spinning rotors that keep them aloft. These feelers hover in the desolate sky above the middle of the highway.

The downdraft of their rotors blows my hair back. The noise is deafening and terrifying. Travelers watch from the edges of the road. They're prepared to fight, but they're not taking any action yet.

"So much for your counting!" Cass yells at Gadya. "There are four of them!"

Gadya glares at her. "You're only alive because of me, drone! Besides, these feelers aren't acting like normal ones!"

"Shhh!" I hiss at both of them.

I turn my gaze back to the feelers. My eyes focus on the fourth feeler. The one in the center of the triangle. Its tentacles are curled around an object, obscuring it from view.

"What are the feelers doing?" I ask Liam.

"I don't know. I've never seen anything like this!"

"Have the feelers taken a traveler? Is that a body inside the tentacles?" I call out to Gadya.

She shakes her head. "If they'd taken someone, the travelers would be fighting to get them back." She squints at the fourth feeler. "Maybe it's carrying a bag of chemicals to release. Or a bomb."

My blood goes cold for a second. I look at her, startled. I hadn't thought how easy it would be for the feelers to bring a weapon like that here. *If it's a bomb, they could detonate it and kill us all.*

I feel Liam's arm around me. I glance over at him.

"It's going to be okay," he whispers in my ear. "There are five hundred travelers around us. I've been watching—a lot of them are hidden in the trees. If the feelers attack, they'll pull them onto the road and smash them." He pauses. "And if it's a bomb, then we can duck in the tram gulley. It'll give us some protection."

I nod and gaze at the feelers hanging there, lifeless.

Then the one in the center starts to move.

Everyone shifts slightly, getting ready to fight. But the three feelers on the edges just hang there in the sky, as the fourth one slowly descends. It gets lower to the ground, hovering twenty feet above it.

I watch, mesmerized, as it begins to uncoil its black, metallic tentacles. It's about to reveal the object held within.

I lean forward, trying to get a closer look. Even before the tentacles have unwound all the way, I see that it is indeed holding a body. Everyone around me is yelling to one another.

The tentacles separate more, like they're about to drop this corpse onto the desolate concrete road.

"Stay down," Liam says. "Just in case."

But I keep my head up. Watching.

And then I see a pale hand move.

The person inside the metal tentacles is still alive. In fact, it looks like he's holding on to the tentacles. Or maybe the tentacles are looped around his arms and legs, supporting them. But I can't see the person's face.

"He's alive!" a voice screams.

I sense that the travelers are about to begin moving forward, to try to rescue this person. Liam's muscles tense too as he prepares to help them. I'm ready to battle these feelers as well.

If the person is alive, there's a chance we can save him. I have no idea why the feelers have carried him here instead of to the specimen archive, but maybe there's been some kind of malfunction.

Or maybe these feelers have stopped to attack us on their way to the archive, and they're planning on snatching three more kids to go along with him.

But then, the tentacles pull away from the person's face, revealing his identity.

*I feel like I've been slapped.*

For an instant, I think I'm going to pass out.

Then the blood rushes back into my head, pounding like a wave. My mind is throbbing with anger and the desire for revenge. And the desire to get some answers.

"That bastard!" Gadya's voice cries out in shock.

The person hanging in the tentacles turns his head in our direction and stares directly at us.

*It's David.*

"I'm going to kill him," Liam says, standing up and drawing his blade from its sheath.

"Me too!" Cass screams.

For a moment, I want nothing more than to join them. To race forward with Liam and make David pay for his outrageous act of betrayal. I know exactly how Liam is feeling. His dad's life and everyone else's are in jeopardy because of David.

But then I force myself to stop and pause. "Wait!" I call out. I don't want the desire for revenge to blind us. "Stop!" I grab at Liam. He turns to look at me.

"Are you protecting him?" he asks.

"No!" I yell. "I just don't want you to get hurt! I don't trust David. He could have a gun on him! He betrayed us before!"

"He sure did!" Gadya yells.

"Let the travelers get him," I say. "We don't need to risk our lives again for him, just to get vengeance. He's not worth it!"

Suddenly, the noise of the three feelers surrounding David cuts off. I'm startled. Their rotors have completely stopped spinning. For a moment, the three feelers forming the triangle hang there in the gray sky. But then they drop straight down to the road. They plummet onto the concrete, where they hit and disintegrate with an explosion of noise.

Everyone ducks, as metal pieces of the feelers fly in all directions. I barely have time to shield my face from debris.

"What's going on?" one traveler screams to another.

It's almost like the three feelers have just committed suicide. But of course they're only machines. They can't think. They probably just ran out of power or something. I blink grit out of my eyes.

When I look up again, only one feeler remains in the sky. *The one that David is hanging from.* It moves even lower to the highway, hovering only five feet above the concrete.

The tentacles release his arms. David raises his hands above his head. He holds them there in a gesture that looks oddly like surrender. He stares at us with a blank expression, from behind his glasses.

I sense nothing but seething hatred and hostility coming from Liam and the others. Everyone who knows what David did completely hates him now. If it weren't for David, we might have already overtaken the archive, and gained control of the wheel.

The travelers rush forward to rescue him from the feelers, now that the odds are in their favor.

But Liam, Gadya, and Cass rush forward too—with less kind motives. If the feelers aren't going to have him, then they will. I race after them.

I gave David the benefit of the doubt so many times. I was

always his champion before—sometimes his only one. But after stranding us on the field, and leaving us to be enslaved by the drones and their new Monk, I can't imagine finding such forgiveness in my heart again. *David has lost my trust.* I don't believe in him anymore.

I wonder why he's even come here right now. Maybe the new Monk banished him, as some kind of sick punishment.

As we head forward, the tentacles abruptly release him. David drops onto the concrete, landing in a crouch on the balls of his feet. The helicopter portion of the feeler drops a few feet lower, hovering above his head. The tentacles fan out around him, creating a whirling, whipping frenzy.

The first few travelers who were about to reach him are now forced backward. They leap away to avoid being struck by tentacles.

Over the violent frenzy, David yells out to them, "Stay back!"

The tentacles keep lashing around. It's almost like they're protecting him. *But how is that possible?* Liam, Gadya, Cass, and I keep running closer. We're only about twenty paces away.

"Listen!" David calls out again to us. "I'm here to help you!"

"Shut up!" Gadya screams. She bursts free of our pack and races straight at the tentacles. Travelers try to stop her, grabbing at her hoofer-skin jacket, but she barges past them roughly. She has murder in her eyes.

"We need him alive," I yell. "To get answers!"

Liam and I are both one step behind her. Travelers are mobbing the tentacles now. David is about to be overrun. He keeps yelling at us to listen to him, but no one does. Travelers knock against the tentacles, trying to grip them.

Gadya is almost upon him. I see her slide a short knife out of an ankle sheath and raise it up, ready to slice David's throat. But then a tentacle crashes into her, knocking her sideways. She staggers across the road, the knife skittering out of her hand.

At the same time, enough travelers grab on to the other tentacles. Their weight drags the feeler sideways across the road. David is left standing there, exposed.

"Hey, David!" Liam calls out, racing straight at him.

David looks up. For a moment, his eyes find mine and they widen. "Alenna! There you are! I don't—"

And then Liam's fist strikes David right in the face.

David stumbles backward, his glasses flying off. He falls back onto the road, slamming onto the concrete, instantly unconscious. Liam stands over his body, looking down at him.

I run forward to Liam's side, as do the others. The travelers continue dragging the feeler down, farther along the highway.

"What are you doing?" a traveler yells at Liam angrily.

"His name's David Aberley," Liam says. "He's the one who betrayed us. The one who led everyone into an ambush. My dad might be dead because of what he did."

"Is this true?" the traveler asks me.

I nod. "A lot of people lost their lives because of David. He helped the Monk instead of us."

More travelers surround us. Everyone is talking at once.

I crouch down by David's body. His eyes are shut, like he's asleep.

Another traveler leans down. "He's out cold," the traveler says.

"Tie him up," Liam instructs. "He can't be trusted."

"Who can be, in this place?" the traveler replies, glancing at Liam.

I hear a crash in the distance, as the mob of travelers struggling with the final feeler succeeds in smashing it to the ground.

I stand up next to Liam and stare down at David's strangely peaceful face. His cheek is already red and starting to swell from Liam's blow. Cass steps to my side.

I remember my first day on the wheel with David. I never thought it would come to this—him against all of us. Questions burn in my brain: *How did he even end up here? Why did he do what he did?* Perhaps I will never understand.

Gadya finally reaches us. Her knife is back in her hand. She has a bloody abrasion on the side of her face from where the tentacle hit her. "He dead yet?"

"No."

"Why not?" She lunges forward. Travelers stop her, holding her back.

"We need to question him," one of them says. He glances back at the distant remains of the feelers. "It looked like he was controlling these things somehow. He might have brought himself here on purpose."

"Why would he do that?" I ask.

"We don't know. That's why we can't kill him, even if he turns out to be who you say he is."

"He's a spy for the drones!" Cass says. "There's no debate!"

The traveler looks at her. "Your kind of politics doesn't interest us. Right now, he's just a person who's arrived in our territory. He's in a situation that we need to deal with, and try to understand."

Cass stares the traveler down. Finally, she sighs and looks away. "Fine. Just don't trust him, or you'll get burned like we did." Then she stalks away, as if the sight of David is too much for her to bear.

"Controlling the feelers?" Liam asks the traveler. "Is that even possible?"

"We've heard rumors," the traveler says.

"But David only got to the wheel when I did, less than two months ago," I say.

The traveler shrugs. "Maybe there's an easy way to do it, and David learned it from someone."

We're silent for a moment.

"David escaped from a feeler on the way to the archive," I finally say, trying to puzzle it out. "He said that he pulled out its battery, and it fell down from the sky. But he could have been lying. Maybe he knows how they work."

"Maybe he's known all along," Gadya adds.

We keep looking down at David, weapons drawn. He's in for an unpleasant surprise when he wakes up. This time it won't be like when he was captured back in the village and I spoke up for him. *This time he's on his own.*

Emma joins us, eyes wide. She stares down at David too. "I can't believe he's here."

As I look down at David, I see him start to stir. Everyone watches him cautiously. His eyelids flutter. Then his dark eyes open a bit, squinting. He stares up at us, and at the sky beyond.

"I'm alive . . . ," he murmurs.

"Hopefully not for long," Gadya says, glaring at him. But travelers keep their hands on her arms to keep her from doing anything rash.

David looks around at the gleaming spear tips and blades pointed right at his face. He reaches up a hand and rubs his eye and cheekbone where Liam hit him. "I wouldn't have expected anything else," he murmurs. He shuts his eyes. I wonder if he's delirious. I'm guessing that he'll try to stand up, but he just lies there.

"Did you get sent here? Banished by the drones?" a traveler calls out. Now that the final feeler has been brought down, more travelers are joining the circle of people around David. Cass joins us again, pushing her way up front.

"Tell us who you really are!" Cass prompts. "And whose side you're really on!"

David opens his eyes again. He sees Cass, and for a moment, a look of surprise passes across his face at her words. "You don't understand." He pauses. "None of you do."

"Then explain it to us," I say to him coldly. "You owe us that much."

"Yeah, explain how you live with yourself, with so much blood on your hands!" Gadya hisses.

"There's blood on your hands, too, Gadya," David says tiredly.

"Why did you sabotage our plan to rescue everyone on the wheel?" I ask, determined to make him answer me. "Why did you betray us?"

David moves slightly, like he's preparing to sit up. Everyone shifts, ready to strike him with fists or weapons if they have to. He notices and pauses.

"I didn't do this to sabotage you, Alenna." He looks right at me, staring into my eyes, ignoring everyone else. "I did this to save you."

# 19 DAVID

HALF AN HOUR LATER, all of us have moved back to the settlement under the highway. The remains of the feelers have been cleared away, and taken into the forest. Travelers work in the underbrush, dismantling them for parts.

Liam and I still can't get close enough to David to talk to him. After his cryptic words on the road, travelers instantly surrounded him despite our angry protests, and took him away with them. I assume they are interrogating him right now. Maybe they're even torturing him, given that they won't let us watch.

But I'm thinking about what David said. *That he did this to save me.* How is that even possible? I'm amazed at his audacity. I can't let myself believe in him again—not after what he did.

Liam and I now sit on the hanging wooden platforms beneath the road, with Gadya and Cass. Alun is lying down a few platforms away from us. The travelers have brought him up here and given him herbs to help with his pain and blood loss. He moves in and out of consciousness. Emma is at his side, helping tend to him. Dabbing his forehead with a cool, wet rag. She's also fashioned a new eye patch for him out of cloth.

Gadya is seething about David. "I should have killed him! He's a scourge." She looks at me. "He just claimed he's doing this to save us because he doesn't know what else to say."

I nod. "Probably. But the travelers seem to think he might know something. Let's find out what it is."

"What do they know?" Gadya scoffs openly. "They spend their lives trying to avoid conflict, in a place where fighting is the only thing that keeps you alive!"

"But they've been keeping *you* alive," I point out, startled by the sudden turnaround in her attitude.

Gadya glares at me. "Yeah, well, today has just reminded me what the wheel is really all about! Violence and war."

"I hate David, but Alenna's right," Cass interrupts. "Let's wait and see. Back in the resistance cell—"

"I'm sick of hearing about resistance cells!" Gadya snaps. "We're not back in the UNA. We're on the wheel! Different rules apply."

"Fine," Cass retorts, rolling her eyes. "Whatever."

"Either way, we know we can't trust David," I say in the tense silence. "So let's just let the travelers figure out what to do with him, okay?"

Liam nods. He's been listening to Gadya and Cass bicker this whole time. "If David was banished by the Monk, the travelers will get that out of him. And if he can control the feelers, I'm sure they'll figure that out too. That'd be a pretty useful skill to learn."

I nod. "Exactly. David might not matter. But his knowledge still does."

We sit there in uneasy silence, waiting.

Eventually, we see a group of travelers heading toward us on the platforms.

Startled, I see that David is walking freely among them. Liam and I stand up, on guard. So do the others. Gadya's hand is already on her knife. Liam unsheathes his blade.

"He's all yours. He's safe," one of the travelers says.

"Safe?" I ask. "What does that mean?"

"Are you serious?" Cass spits. "After what he did?"

"Has David fooled you guys, just like he fooled us?" Gadya calls out.

"No," the traveler says. The group keeps heading our way. David is staring right at us, completely unfazed. "By 'safe,' I mean he doesn't have the ability to cause us any harm right now," the traveler clarifies.

The travelers walk closer with David. I sense the nervous energy bristling all around me.

The travelers can sense it too. One of them looks at us and says sharply, "Leave David be. Put your weapons away. There will be no violence among us today. Sit and talk with him. You have a lot to discuss."

They stop moving.

But David keeps walking, heading directly toward us. Gadya and the others stand their ground, glaring at him. I think I detect a sliver of fear pass across David's face, but it's hard to tell in the gray light.

"Don't come near me, traitor!" Gadya hisses at David.

"Listen, I—" he begins.

"Quiet!" I snap. "Let us ask the questions. That's the only way this is going to work. Okay?"

David nods.

"Sit," Liam commands. David slowly takes a seat across from me and the others. His glasses are back on, but now one of the lenses is cracked.

We face him like interrogators. If it weren't for the travelers nearby watching us, he wouldn't be alive right now. And I can tell that he knows it.

"What did you mean when you said this was the only way to save us?" Liam asks. His voice is as hard and cold as steel. I clasp his hand. I can tell that he's working hard to suppress his anger and give David a chance.

David looks at us and sighs. "The drones knew about the rebels' plans all along."

"From you, probably," Cass says.

He shakes his head. "No. From their new Monk. He found out somehow and told them. The Monk knew that you were coming in airships from Southern Arc—I don't know how. At the time, I was being pursued by drones and feelers in the jungle. It was only a matter of days before I got caught." He pauses. "So I let the drones catch me and take me to the new Monk. And then I pretended to work with them. They knew I was talking to the scientists via satellite. That's the only reason they didn't kill me. Because they wanted to use me. But I was also using them."

"You're such a liar," Gadya mutters.

"Yeah, you're just saying this stuff now because you got caught," Cass adds.

"Tell us more," I say to David. "But you know that everything you've said and done looks really suspicious, right?"

David nods. "I know. There's a reason for that. Just listen."

"It better be good," I tell him.

"I realized I could control every detail from the inside of the Monk's camp," David continues. "Set up the landing site. Make the Monk think I was telling him everything that was going on. But I wasn't." He gazes at Liam. "Who do you think put those weapons and that map in your cell? It was me. I did it to help you and your dad get free. I knew you'd rescue Alenna and the others."

"Keep talking," Liam says warily.

"I picked a landing site that was near that cathedral, and the highway as well. I knew that you could get outside through the tunnel and into the forest."

"We barely survived," I say.

"But you *did* survive. So I was right."

"You couldn't know that we'd make it. Not for sure. You took too many risks with other peoples' lives," Liam says. "I don't even know if my dad is alive."

I nod, staring at David. "A lot of people died in that cathedral. Scientists. Guards. Kids. What about them? Didn't they even matter to you?"

"That was going to happen anyway," David says softly. "Did you think you'd land here and the drones would surrender peacefully? Throw you a welcome party? No chance. They wanted a war. So I made sure they didn't get one. They thought they were one step ahead of us. Many more people survived than if we'd gone head-to-head with them." He pushes his glasses up his nose. "A battle would have meant thousands dead within a few hours." He pauses. "And yes, I saw what happened to Dr. Barrett. I couldn't stop it. The Monk wanted to make an example out of him."

"Is he alive?" I ask.

"I'm not sure." David looks down.

Some of his words have the ring of truth. But after what happened, I'm not going to grant him my trust easily again. He's clearly an excellent liar.

"So who is the new Monk?" I ask.

He looks back up. "Someone who knew that with Minster Harka gone, he could harness the power of the drones. And someone who knows a whole lot about the UNA. I don't know who he is, or where he came from. The weird thing is—" He breaks off.

"What?" Gadya snaps.

"I think— I think he knows who I am. He never said anything, but I got the feeling that he did."

"Did you ever see his face?" I ask.

"Never. Only the mask."

"It's possible that Minister Harka had an understudy," Gadya says. "Someone who was shadowing us, watching and waiting in the wings this whole time."

"We have to figure out who he is," Liam says. "He's doing a much better job controlling the drones than Minister Harka ever did."

David nods in agreement. "Definitely."

"Stop that!" Cass says to him angrily. "You're not part of our group. You're not going to insinuate yourself that easily."

David stops nodding.

"So how did you get here?" I ask David. "I mean, out on the highway?"

"As you probably suspect, I've figured out a few things along the way, with the scientists' help."

"The feelers, right?" I ask.

"Exactly. This whole time we were focused on getting off the wheel, rather than controlling the parts of the wheel that we could. I knew if the UNA didn't care that so many airplanes were getting hijacked, they wouldn't care—or even notice—if some of the feelers didn't act like they were supposed to."

"But how did you do it?" Cass asks, looking at him with narrowed eyes.

"The scientists read the technical specs to me, and then they talked me through the steps," David says. "They showed me how to turn the receiver I'd taken from the crashed feeler in the gray zone into a transmitter." He reaches into the pocket of his jeans, under his black robes.

Everyone flinches, and knives are instantly raised.

David pauses.

"Slowly," Liam cautions.

"If you want to live . . . ," Gadya adds.

David sighs. "The travelers already searched me."

He tentatively extracts a black box the size of his palm. It has crooked wires sticking out of it, and rows of tiny white switches on its smooth metal surface.

"What the hell is that?" Cass asks.

"This box came from inside the crashed feeler, but I've modified it, based on what the scientists told me to do. The feelers work off radio signals. It's possible to intercept the signals, and make the feelers do what you want. The scientists locked on to this box and downloaded codes into it, so that by pressing different switches, certain codes are activated, and the box is able to control nearby feelers. We can even send out a signal to call feelers to us if we want."

"And the travelers let you keep that box?" I ask.

He nods. "They told me they didn't want it. They don't really care about technology. Only nature. They said it would bring them harm if they kept it."

"Sounds about right," Gadya mutters.

"How far is its range?" Liam asks. I can tell that his mind is racing. "If you're telling the truth, we could use the feelers to free the scientists and Dr. Barrett's guards—and everyone else from the cathedral."

"They don't work that far, unfortunately," David says. "A couple hundred yards."

"Why didn't you do anything when we first landed on the field?" I challenge him. "You could have brought feelers in to kill the new Monk right then, and to fight for us."

"There weren't any feelers around," he answers. "Dr. Barrett's men were using similar devices on the airships to jam the signals and keep the feelers at bay. I couldn't reach any."

An idea occurs to me. "It's not too late to do it now."

"What do you mean?" Gadya asks.

But Liam instantly understands. "She means we go back to the cathedral with David and some feelers, right? By now, I bet all of Dr. Barrett's stuff has been destroyed. No more jamming signals."

I nod. "We could get within a hundred yards of the cathedral, and then use the feelers to attack the drones."

"It would be a bloodbath," David says.

"Worried about getting hurt?" Cass sneers at him.

"Better someone else's blood than ours," Gadya points out.

Liam is still thinking, his eyes burning with passionate intensity. He gestures at David's box. "How precise can you get with that thing? How does it work?"

"You point it at a feeler, lock on to it, and then flick different combinations of switches that trigger various codes. You can then point it at another feeler. You can basically link them together in whatever pattern you want. It takes some practice, though. I can show you when we find another one—"

"No, stop," Liam interrupts. "I'm asking because I want to know if we can go in and use the feelers to extract one person. Not fight an entire battle for us."

"The Monk," I say in the ensuing silence, locking eyes with Liam.

He nods. "If we take out the Monk, we take them all out. At least temporarily. We can step in and stop them from regrouping."

"Or not," Gadya says. "Look what happened when Minister Harka died."

"If we use the feeler to kidnap the new Monk, at least we'll get some answers," I say. "Why does he want to create an army? We need to find out."

"It's worth a try," Cass muses.

Liam turns to Gadya. "Can we count on the travelers to help us?"

Gadya shakes her head. "I doubt it."

"We need to ask," I tell her.

Gadya looks at us. "It's never gonna work. They've survived much longer than we have. We can't convince them that their way of doing things is wrong. I've been here for a month, and I know how they think." She looks glum. "The travelers are never going to become the army we want them to be. I tried when I first got here. I wanted them to go back to the archives to get Rika, Markus, and the other frozen villagers. They wouldn't do it. And they wouldn't go back to Meira and our village to protect it either."

"They're holding a meeting tonight," David says softly. "I heard them talking about it on the way back from being interrogated. We could ask them then."

"Good. We'll talk to them tonight," I reply. "Explain the situation. Tell them our plan to use the feelers to kidnap the Monk." I pause. "But David, we're going to be keeping an eye on you. We can't take the chance that you're lying to us. Or that you're going to betray us again."

"I'll watch him," Cass volunteers.

264

"Me too," Gadya says, fingering her knife.

"We all will," Liam says.

We look around at one another in the gray light. No one disagrees. I know that none of us trusts David at all, but right now, we need to keep him around to use whatever information he's willing to tell us.

Right then, I see a group of travelers heading in our direction. Walking across the platforms toward us, making the wooden beams shake. We start standing up.

"Sit," one of them says, unsmiling. He looks at Gadya. "We need to talk to you, alone."

I keep standing. So does Liam. "What's going on?" he asks.

"It's okay," Gadya tells us. "Don't worry."

"Are you sure?" I ask.

She nods.

"It won't take long," one of the other dreadlocked travelers tells us. His voice is monotone, and his weathered face is hard to read. It's unnerving.

I'm glancing back and forth at the travelers. Liam is too. They just stare back at us with their firm, unblinking gazes. Completely inscrutable.

"I'll be fine. Just don't go anywhere," Gadya half-jokes. Then the travelers surround her. Before we can ask any more questions, she starts walking away with them.

I stare after her retreating figure, perplexed. I wish I knew exactly what was going on. The travelers definitely don't seem too pleased with Gadya right now.

Slowly, Liam and I sit down again on the wooden slats. But I'm ready to leap up at any second if I have to. I keep watching until Gadya disappears from view into the shadows.

"So, that was weird," Cass says.

"The travelers don't like having us here," David speaks up. "We're causing too much commotion."

"How do you know that?" I ask.

"Just a guess." David falls silent as Cass glares at him.

"We're going to have to work hard to convince them tonight, if we even have a chance at all," Liam says finally.

I lean forward. "They haven't seen the new army of drones. If we explain it to them, maybe they'll understand." I pause. "We'll *make* them understand."

Everyone nods. I know that our survival might depend on enlisting the travelers. If we can get them on our side, we have a chance of defeating the Monk and his army. But without them, our last chance at saving the wheel might just slip away.

At dinner that night, the travelers gather in the trees and on the platforms under the highway. The travelers easily number six or seven hundred—more than I thought. But they are silent and still. They are constantly cautious, aware of every noise. The sun has set, but the moon is full and it illuminates the trees by the side of the road.

The silence makes me edgy. The only noises are the sounds of the forest at night, and the creaking of the wooden beams supporting us.

Some travelers move nimbly across the platforms, passing around buckets of fruits and vegetables. There is no cooking fire. Only handheld lanterns that cast a constant shifting glow around the space. Sentries remain hidden on the ground, watching for trouble.

All of us sit there, not sure what to do or say. Emma is helping take care of Alun on a nearby platform, trying to nurse him back to health. I can hear him moaning. I eat some bites of langsat, glancing over at Liam. I'm looking around for Gadya, but there's still no sign of her.

"Where's Gadya?" I whisper to Liam. "I thought she'd be back by now."

"I was wondering the same thing," he says. "We'll ask the travelers if she doesn't turn up soon."

"You think she's okay?"

"I hope so."

A female traveler steps over to us, ladling water from a canteen into wooden cups. Liam and I fall silent so that she doesn't overhear us. All of us are thirsty. I grab a cup and let the traveler fill it for me. I suck down the cool liquid, feeling it trace a path from my throat into my stomach.

Finally, a voice rings out in the dim light.

"New friends!" the voice says. It has the trace of a Spanish accent. I glance in its direction.

The voice is coming from an older traveler, maybe twenty-one, standing in the center of the nearby octagonal platform. He's average height, but muscular, with the sunburned skin that so many of the travelers have. He's dressed in hoofer skins, with his long dreadlocks tied back with black twine. He's looking right at us. "Your arrival today has caused a stir." He pauses. "You are the first people to find us in a long time."

Everyone's eyes are on him.

"As you know, our tribe has no official leader—and no use for one," he continues. "Today, I have been elected to talk to you and share our feelings. My name is Ramiro Gutierrez."

We nod. I don't know if he expects us to introduce ourselves. I just take another bite of langsat.

"So, please understand that while I speak for the members of this tribe, I am just their voice, not their leader." He smiles.

I smile back, but I'm still wondering where Gadya is.

"We already understand what you want from us," Ramiro continues. "We know that one of you has the means to control the UNA selection units. And we also know that you want us to go with you and locate some of the selection units. To find them in order to kidnap the Monk."

"Gadya must have talked!" Cass hisses. "I knew it! That snitch!"

"Maybe she just asked the travelers for help," I whisper back. "Come on!"

"That wasn't the plan," Cass retorts.

I keep listening to Ramiro. *There's no way the travelers could have guessed our plan.* Either Gadya talked to them or they overheard us somehow.

"We understand the rationale behind your actions," Ramiro continues. "However, you must understand that we do not wish to become entangled with your warring tribes. We stand outside those battles and we always will. Transcending conflict is the only key to long-term survival on the wheel."

"You're wrong!" Cass cries out.

"Let him talk!" I hiss at her.

Silence falls. I'm aware of hundreds of eyes watching us. For everything positive that Gadya said about the travelers, I'm not so sure these people are as peaceful as they claim. *And now there's no sign of Gadya at all.*

Ramiro smiles gently at us. "If you seek trouble on the wheel, you will always be able to find it. That is what we have learned." He pauses again, holding out his hands in a beseeching gesture. "I am sorry, but our decision has been reached. We cannot and will not help you. Your determination to save your friends is admirable, but your warlike passion does not belong here among us."

I turn to Liam. This is our time to talk. To try to make the travelers see things our way.

I'm about to stand up, but for some reason, I feel a wave of dizziness pass over me. "Should I talk or should you?" I ask Liam, trying to shake it off.

He looks back at me. "You." His speech sounds slightly slurred. "I'm not feeling . . . too good." He grips one of the wooden beams to support himself.

"Me neither." The dizzy sensation is getting worse. It feels like seasickness. Ramiro and the travelers are watching us closely.

Startled, I look over at David and Cass. David's eyes are half closed. He's struggling to get up. Cass has managed to make it all the way to her feet, where she sways unsteadily, like she's drunk.

*What is happening to us?*

"Listen, Ramiro," she begins. Then she staggers a bit. "You have to—" She nearly falls, and catches herself, sinking to the floor, her words becoming an incoherent murmur.

I get to my feet feeling terrified, using some hanging chains to support my weight. The world feels like it's spinning around me. I'm exhausted too, like I'm about to fall asleep for no reason.

I peer down at the cups of water and at the uneaten bits of langsat sitting on the platform. Then I look back up at Ramiro.

"Ramiro?" I ask. My tongue feels two sizes too large for my mouth.

"Yes?"

"You put something . . . in our food . . . ," I manage to say. Liam is trying to get up next to me, but his legs are giving way, like they've just turned to rubber.

269

"You are not wrong, Alenna," Ramiro replies. "In both your food and your water. Our way of doing things is not to argue. We have made our will known, and there is no need for further discussion."

"Gadya . . . ," I murmur, still struggling to believe that she would play any role in this.

"It was not your friend's decision. It was ours, as a group." Ramiro pauses. "She wishes you to know that."

I sink to the wooden floor again, dragged down by whatever drug the travelers have poisoned us with. My body is going numb.

*Am I going to die?*

Have we made it this far only to be poisoned by people we thought would help us?

I want to scream at the travelers and curse at them, but the world is quickly slipping away from me. My arms and legs feel like they have weights attached to them. My ears are ringing.

No one moves to help us. The travelers sit there, silently watching as we collapse and writhe on the platforms.

Ramiro is still gazing at me. "You never should have come back to the wheel."

I crawl toward Liam, desperately reaching out for him. He's barely conscious now. His eyes are shut, and he's taking shallow breaths.

*Liam*—I try to gasp, but my lips can barely form his name.

My hand grabs his arm. There's almost no sign of life. The world is swirling and spinning with increasing velocity.

I cling to Liam as I start to lose consciousness myself, sinking into the abyss. The whooshing sound of blood gets louder in my ears until it blocks out everything else. My vision goes gray and constricts to a narrow circle. I struggle to take a breath, my chest shuddering.

And then everything goes black.

# 20 ABANDONED

I HEAR A VOICE calling my name from the darkness. It sounds like it's reaching me from a long tunnel. My head is pounding, my mouth is dry, and my muscles are burning like I've run a marathon. I feel like I want to go back to sleep and never wake up again.

"Alenna!" the voice says sharply. I want the voice to stop bothering me. I curl up into a ball with my eyes tightly shut. But the person won't leave me alone.

I feel strong hands moving me onto my back. Brushing hair out of my face.

Then I realize, even in my stupor, that the voice belongs to Liam.

I use every ounce of energy that I possess to force my eyes open.

"Liam!" I gasp, struggling upward when I see him, choking and coughing.

I find myself in his arms. He wraps them around me tightly. I press myself hard against his chest. I can barely breathe. My hands and feet are still numb, and my lips are tingling. "I thought . . ."

"I know," he says. His voice is rough. "Me too. But it wasn't fatal. Probably just some kind of toxic herb. Enough to knock us out for the night." He pauses. "It's already morning now."

I cling to him for a few more seconds. Then I turn my head.

We're no longer up on the platforms. In fact, we're out in the jungle somewhere. I'm lying on dirt and pebbles in a small clearing surrounded by giant mangrove trees and underbrush. Gentle morning sunlight filters through the branches down toward us.

I can't see the highway from here, let alone the travelers or their camp. They've just taken us out to the middle of nowhere and abandoned us.

I look up into Liam's eyes. "I can't believe we let this happen to us."

"Same here."

"We're lucky to be alive." I gaze around. "Where is everyone?"

"Out cold." He leans farther back so that I can get a good view. David, Cass, and Emma are sprawled on the forest floor behind us.

*And Gadya too.*

"So they left her as well," I say. "She's got some explaining to do."

"No kidding."

Liam helps me to my feet. I stand there swaying for a moment next to him. The feeling is slowly coming back into my hands and feet, and they tingle wildly, just like my lips. I shake them to get the blood flowing again.

"Where's Alun?" I ask.

Liam gazes around. "Maybe they took him with them. At least that's what I hope. He was too badly hurt to leave out here."

I nod. I know it's possible that he's dead.

"You okay?" Liam asks me.

"I'm getting there." I rub my hands together.

Liam smiles a bit.

"What?"

"We're back to where we started. All alone in the jungle."

It's not funny at all, but I can't help smiling either. Then I look down at the ground. My smile fades. The others are so motionless, it looks like they're dead. "They're okay, right?"

Liam nods. "I checked them when I woke up. They're fine. Just sleeping it off."

I lean up and kiss Liam quickly. But there's no time for romance.

"So what do we do now?" I ask. My head is still fuzzy from the poison. "We need a new plan—and we're starting from scratch. Yet again."

Liam slowly takes something out of his pocket. It's David's black box. The one that controls the feelers. "The travelers left this with us. I found it next to me on some leaves. The travelers didn't want it. I'm guessing they thought that someone could track it, and use it to find them."

"Or else they're just crazy," I say.

Liam nods. "That too."

He holds out the box. I take it and stare down at the many tiny switches. It's amazing to me that this small object could control something as large and terrifying as the feelers.

"I wish we'd had this back in the village," I say, turning the box over in my hand. "Why couldn't the scientists have helped us sooner? Right at the start. Things would have been so different then."

"I know." He looks at me. "But we have the box now. David finally turned out to be useful for something."

"Now we just need to find some feelers," I say. "I mean, if we continue with our plan to kidnap the Monk."

Liam looks up. I see the spark in his eyes. "It won't be easy without the travelers' help, but it's possible."

"Then let's get started." I brush dirt and leaves out of my hair, and off my jeans. I look around at the others, who are still asleep. "I almost don't want to wake them up," I joke.

"Yeah. I know what you mean."

For a second, a look passes between us. A glimpse of what it would be like if Liam and I could just be together, without this madness surrounding us. If the UNA had never descended into fascism, maybe that could have been the case.

I suddenly check my back pocket. "I've lost my book," I say. "*The Myth of Sisyphus*." I feel oddly sad. The book was a connection to my dad, and it was also something that Liam gave me. I look around but I don't see it anywhere. It must have fallen out at some point.

"C'mon," Liam says. "Let's wake everyone up and let them know they're alive."

We move over to the others, side by side, starting with Emma because she's the most peaceful. One by one, we wake each of them. Until all of us are sitting there in the jungle.

I can feel the lingering effects of the poison. My head feels heavy. I try to ignore the feeling. I know that the others are doing the same thing. We are exhausted and bedraggled-looking.

"I don't know what to say, guys," Gadya finally mutters, staring around at everyone. She's resting against a fallen tree. Her blue-streaked hair is a tangled, spiky mess.

"Did you know they'd leave you too?" I ask her.

"Sure, I thought there was a chance." She rubs her eyes, trying to wake herself up. "I told them how I honestly felt—that we should fight the drones and snatch the Monk. I guess they thought I'd become a liability." She gazes at Cass, looking annoyed. "This is actually all your fault for agitating them and asking too many questions." She looks over at David. "And your fault too!"

David doesn't respond, but Cass looks angry. "My fault? What are you talking about?" She sounds dazed, but also ready to fight. "We're the ones who just got tricked. Your friends left us out here with nothing! And they took Alun, too."

"For peaceful types, they don't seem very concerned about our safety," Emma points out softly, blinking behind her glasses. "Is Alun even okay? I'm really worried about him."

"They took Alun to help him," Gadya says with a sigh. "Just like they did for me. They never leave injured kids behind. It's part of their philosophy."

"Well, their philosophy sucks," Cass retorts.

I lean forward. "Come on. No arguing. At least we're not dead."

Liam raises the black box so that everyone can see it. "And they left us with this."

David perks up. He's been quiet so far. Either he's brooding, or he got harder hit by the poison than we did. Or he's plotting more secret treachery. "Let me see that."

Liam hesitates. "Why?"

"It's okay," I tell him. My head is clearing, and it's getting easier to talk. "David, you won't do anything weird with it, right? Remember, we outnumber you. If you try to stab any of us in the back, then you'll have to answer to all of us."

David slowly nods. "I know."

Liam reaches out and reluctantly hands him the black box.

We all keep our eyes on David in case he makes any sudden moves.

"Alenna and I think we should continue with our plan," Liam says to the group, standing up. "Find a feeler that we can use to capture the Monk."

"But how do we find the Monk?" Emma asks after a moment's silence. "We don't know that he's back at the cathedral. He could be anywhere on the wheel by now."

Silence falls again.

"Can't your magic box locate the Monk for us?" Gadya asks David sarcastically. He's checking the box to make sure it's not broken.

"No," he admits.

I stand up next to Liam. "Then there's only one way to find the Monk. If we don't know who he is or where he is."

"What's that?" Cass asks.

"We bring him to us."

"Seriously?" Emma asks.

I nod. "If we want to find him, what other option do we have?"

"Alenna's right," Liam says in the ensuing silence. "We're going to have to lure him out somehow."

"That's a pretty scary plan," Emma says.

"No, it's actually a great plan," Gadya declares, standing up too. "I'm game. If we can think of a way to do it, then we should try. If we get the Monk to show himself, we can use feelers to come in and grab him." A look of fire and determination drifts into her eyes. "We went one-on-one with the previous Monk— and we won! We can do it again."

"So how do we lure him to us?" I ask.

David speaks up. "It might not be as hard as you think." He brushes down his matted black hair. "The Monk is already looking for us, actually."

"What? Why?" Gadya asks.

"Because of me," David answers slowly.

"Figures," Cass mutters.

"You should have mentioned that earlier!" Liam says to David. "I thought you care about Alenna so much. But you keep putting her life in danger."

"All of our lives," Gadya points out.

"Why does the Monk want you?" I ask David. "What does he care about you, now that his drones have managed to stop Dr. Barrett and our entire plan from working?"

David raises the black box. "The Monk wants this back. He suspected I had something like it, but he wasn't sure. I kept it well hidden in a hollowed-out tree. But then he saw me use it to escape from him and the drones, so now he knows it exists." He gazes around the forest that surrounds us. "To the travelers, this box was a useless hindrance. But to the Monk, it's the key to total domination of the wheel. With the feelers linked and under his command, he might even be able to head off any attacks from the UNA. The Monk could start his own nation on this island, if he wanted. A psychotic kingdom."

His words hang in the air.

"So they've probably sent an army after us already," Liam says. "No wonder the travelers wanted to get rid of us so fast." All of us are standing up now. David's revelation has increased our sense of urgency.

"Any more secrets you want to share?" I ask him.

"No, that's everything."

"Yeah, right," Gadya spits.

"The drones might not even be that far away," I say. "They've had the entire night to travel."

We're scanning the forest. It's silent and still.

"Do the drones have any way of tracking us?" Cass asks David.

"Probably," he answers. "It's best not to underestimate the Monk—whoever he is."

"Then the travelers left us out here to die!" Cass snaps, eyeing Gadya.

"They didn't know the Monk was coming after us!" Gadya retorts.

Cass raises her hands, balling them into fists. "You sure about that? How do I know you're not in on this just like David."

"Cass—" I begin. "Gadya—" But they ignore me.

Gadya grins at Cass. "It's been a while since I've kicked a drone's butt, but I'm ready to do it anytime you want. Just let me know."

"I'm not a drone, but I'm happy to shove your face in the dirt and dance on your head!" Cass snarls back.

"Stop fighting!" I yell, stepping between the two of them before it can escalate. Liam joins me.

Both Gadya and Cass glare at each other around us.

"Knock it off!" I call out. "We need to find a feeler. Not fight each other!"

"Yeah, we can schedule that for later," David murmurs from behind us. Both Gadya and Cass turn their angry glares toward him.

"You're lucky they're not coming after you," I tell David.

"Very lucky," Liam adds. He gazes around at the group. "Alenna's right. It's time to stop arguing and go feeler hunting."

Gadya nods. She slowly lowers her fists. "Good idea."

Liam and I step back. Gadya heads in our direction, without a second look at Cass. Cass goes over to Emma's side.

We start walking back the way we came, in tense silence, divided by hostility. I keep my eyes on David.

It's surprisingly simple to find the path that the travelers used to take us here. That's because the underbrush is flattened, like they just dragged our unconscious bodies across the ground. There's no sign of their tracks leading anywhere else, unless they went back the same way that we're going now.

We are right in the middle of the thick jungle. And I'm assuming that we're completely lost.

But twenty minutes later, to my surprise, we stumble out of the trees and see the elevated highway right there in front of us. For a moment, I think that the travelers are still going to be there underneath it. That this was some kind of test, or lesson for us.

Liam and I pause, squinting at the platforms under the highway. I don't see anyone up there right now, but that doesn't mean the travelers aren't around.

"Don't waste your time," Gadya says, brushing past me. "They're long gone."

"How do you know?"

"I just do."

"They'd leave their whole camp?" Emma asks.

"They'll build another," Gadya says. "Like us villagers used to do."

"That's crazy," I mutter.

"That's the kind of thing that keeps them alive. They don't take any chances. They're miles from here already."

"At least they didn't get us lost," Liam says. "Could be a lot worse."

David nods in agreement, scanning the sky as he clutches his black box. I still don't know what motives really drive him. He seems so different from the boy I met on the wheel nearly two months ago.

We keep walking. I can't believe that the travelers would have abandoned their whole camp just because of us. But that's clearly the case. I see the remains of their wooden platforms under the road and in the trees. They are desolate and completely empty.

"They left the ropes," Liam says, pointing. "Look." I follow his gaze and see them hanging down like vines. Some lead directly to the platforms, and some lead up to the road, farther along where the barricade is.

"You sure that box still works?" I ask David.

"Pretty sure."

"We need to get up on the highway and see if we can find a feeler," Gadya says.

We keep heading through the underbrush. "What if no feelers come?" I ask Liam.

"We could walk back closer to the cathedral," he says, then pauses. "Or we could clear the barricade and go forward on the tram until the road gives out. Hope that we cross into another sector or something and that the hidden motion detectors trigger a feeler to show up then. If it does, we can point David's box at it and try to control it."

I nod. I never thought I'd be eager to find a feeler. Not after I spent so much time fleeing from them the first time I was on the wheel.

With a feeler in our control, we have a chance at plucking the Monk into the sky. And revealing his true identity. Knowledge is the key to surviving the wheel, and right now Liam and I need to find out what's really going on. *Killing Minister Harka should have ended the drones' reign of terror.* Who else would dare to take on his mantle and continue leading his deranged flock?

I wish I had the Camus book with me to get more insights on what to do. I try to remember quotes from the book, but the text merges together in my head. I remember reading something in it about how society always disintegrates and becomes a wild jungle in the absence of personal freedom and culture. This is literally what has happened here on the wheel.

I keep trudging forward. I stretch out my hand and find Liam's. I hold it tightly. I notice that he's gone silent. I glance over at him and see that his eyes have a faraway look.

"You okay? You thinking about something?"

"Naw. It's nothing." He pauses. "Just my dad."

I squeeze his hand. "He'll be fine. I saw him fight. The drones are the ones who should be worried."

"That's what I keep telling myself."

"Maybe we'll find him out here in the forest. Stranger things have happened on the wheel. I'm sure he and his men got away from the cathedral."

Liam nods. "I just don't want him to think that I abandoned him. Like I let him down."

"You didn't." I brush back a coil of hair, looping it behind my ear. "He knows that we're the best chance of figuring out the wheel and helping take it over."

Liam squeezes my hand back. "I hope you're right." He pauses. "You worried about your mom?"

"All the time," I admit. "I hope she made it back to Southern Arc, but there's no way to know for sure."

"If we get back to the scientists, maybe they'll have some

means of contacting her. Besides, Southern Arc's definitely safer than the wheel."

"True." We stare out at the ropes swinging down from the road in front of us.

I'm surprised the travelers left anything here. Maybe it was their way of trying to help us without getting too involved. I can already hear Cass complaining about having to go up the ropes.

"Ready to do some climbing?" Liam asks, with a crooked grin.

I smile back, with a resigned sigh. "I'm ready for anything."

# 21 THE FEELER HUNT

SOON WE'RE BACK UP on the highway. The six of us stand there in the sweltering heat under the sun. It's much warmer today than it was yesterday.

The tram is parked on the side of the road, where we left it.

But the barricade that the travelers made has been removed. The only signs of it are greasy bloodstains left by the hoofer carcasses. The metal track has been cleared for us to continue, if we want to.

Still, I know that the road supposedly cuts out ten miles from here. We'd end up in the same situation as before. At least here, we have the abandoned platforms nearby to hide in if things go wrong.

Liam walks up ahead a few yards to check out the track.

"Alenna," I hear David say softly. I turn and see that he's come over to my side. "You still trust me, right?"

I'm not sure why he's even asking me this right now. Why does he care? I look him in the eye. "I don't know what to believe anymore," I tell him honestly. Deep down, I'm not sure I can ever risk trusting him again. "I don't want to get hurt. I have to protect myself."

He looks wounded. "I thought you knew me better than that."

"I thought I did too."

I look away from him and see Liam already heading back toward me. David moves away again quickly, off to the side with his black box. It's like he doesn't want Liam to hear him talking to me.

"I wish we had some fireworks to set off," Gadya says. "That'd get some attention."

"That would bring drones instead of feelers," David muses, fiddling with the box.

"Shut up," Gadya snaps at him.

"What are you doing with that box?" Liam asks David.

"Searching. Trying to find any feelers in the area. I think I can get this box to emit the radio signal to draw them to us. The scientists gave me a code and it's stored in here somewhere. I just have to remember the right sequence of switches."

"Try it," Liam says. "But if you screw up, or if you're lying, then things are going to get pretty unpleasant for you."

"Fine, but I just can't control how many feelers turn up," David continues. "Should I still try? Because if the transmitter calls the feelers to us, a hundred might show up. Maybe more."

We're all looking at David. Maybe he's working for the Monk and this is some way to call the drones to us faster? The thought makes me shiver, despite the heat. But we have to take the chance. I look up at the peaceful blue sky, dotted with clouds, and at the lush treetops around us.

"From up here, we'll be able to get to the ropes in time if any feelers show up," I say. "Like the travelers did. We could hide under the highway and try to control them from down there."

Liam nods. "David, how many can you control at one time?"

David looks at us. "I don't know. According to the scientists, they're programmed to operate off a sequential algorithm. Once they're linked in a chain we can get them to hang in the sky. Totally harmless. That's what I did with the three that accompanied me here—I just used them for protection while I traveled."

"Press the switches to call them then, and let's find out what happens," I say.

We stand there, watching.

"Yeah, do it," Gadya urges.

David slowly flips some switches, then some more, his fingers moving faster and faster. My eyes are glued to the box. "There. I think I got it," he finally says. "The transmitter should be like a homing signal now. Hopefully something will be headed our way soon."

"Let's hope it arrives before the Monk and his drones get here," Emma says.

I stare back up at the sky again. We stand there for a few moments. Waiting and watching. Looking out in every direction.

Liam and I stand next to each other. He's scrutinizing the horizon. He suddenly pauses. I can feel his whole body tense.

"You see something?" I ask.

"Over there." He points back down the highway, in the direction we originally came from. "Just above the treetops."

I squint. "I don't see it yet."

"Me neither," Cass adds.

Liam is still watching the sky. "Look closer. Something's definitely there."

Then, as I keep staring, an object coalesces into view. It's floating over the trees in our direction, several miles away or more.

"I thought the range was just a couple hundred yards!" I say.

"I did too," David replies.

"Let's not make the same mistake we did at Destiny Station," I say to Liam. "It's time to get off the highway now, in case things go wrong."

"I still don't see anything," Cass says.

"I see it," Gadya tells her, pointing out the object.

"C'mon. Let's go," Liam says. "Better safe than sorry."

Liam and I head over to the side of the highway. Gadya, David, Cass, and Emma follow closely behind. I glance back at the black dot in the sky. It's getting closer fast.

I can already hear the churning sound of its rotors, heading in our direction. We're watching the sky as we move.

"Now I see it—" Cass finally declares, but she's interrupted.

"Oh my god!" Emma yells as we reach the edge of the road.

Startled, I glance down.

*The ropes have been cut.*

They dangle there, hanging just a few feet down into thin air. After that, they've been cleanly sliced in two with a sharp blade. I see their coils lying far below us in the underbrush. Without the ropes, there's no way to reach the platforms, or to get down to the jungle floor. The side of the highway is just sheer concrete and empty space.

I stagger back from the edge.

"Who did this?" Gadya screams, looking around furiously. "Which one of you?" Her eyes find David. "Was it you?"

"Are you kidding?" David yells back. Even he seems startled for once.

The noise of the feeler is even louder now.

"It couldn't have been any one of us!" Liam calls out. "I was watching everyone! Especially David!"

"I bet it was the travelers," I say, reeling in fear and panic. "They did this, didn't they?"

"Why?" David asks. "And how?"

"One of them must have sneaked onto the platforms, got up there and cut these ropes, and then used their own rope and grappling hooks to get back down," Liam says.

"Damn them!" Cass curses.

I stare at Gadya. "Why would the travelers cut the ropes?"

"I'm not sure that they did! But if it was them, they must have wanted to trap us up here. But I don't know why . . ."

Her words trail off. The only reason to trap us here would be if the travelers wanted us to die. Perhaps for them, that was the easiest way to avoid dealing with any future problems. But if they wanted us dead, they could have just given us a fatal dose of the poison when they had the chance.

David suddenly holds up his box, flicking switches as he points it at the incoming feeler. "We've got bigger problems than the ropes!" he calls out, sounding worried. "I can't control this thing. I'm trying to make the feeler slow down, but it won't respond!"

"How could this be happening?" Emma says, close to tears. "David, are you lying? And why would the travelers strand us like this?"

"They did this because they only care about themselves," Cass replies. "And Gadya thought the drones were bad. At least the drones fight for what they believe in—even if it's totally insane. The travelers probably killed Alun and threw his body into a ditch."

"Don't say that!" Emma cries. "He's your friend! How can you be so callous?"

"Yeah, shut up, Cass," Gadya says.

The feeler is clearly visible now. Just a mile away and moving fast. And we're out here with no shelter. If David's box fails to make the feeler do what we want, then we'll have to fight it.

I spin around, trying to figure out a way to escape the situation. Liam is doing the same thing. Our eyes light upon the answer at the very same moment.

"The tram!" Liam suddenly yells out. "Let's get in it and go! Until David figures out how to control the feeler."

We start racing back toward it. I know that the track only goes ten more miles. But the tram will give us some kind of temporary shelter. And the ability to quickly move farther down the road. *Maybe that will buy us enough time for David to get the box working.*

When we reach the tram, we pile into it, slamming against the metal hull. Liam slides the door shut behind us. Emma presses the buttons in sequence. Now that there's no obstruction in its way, the tram starts up again instantly and begins to move.

I hear the clattering thrum of the feeler above us. David is flicking switches on the box and raising the crooked antenna up. "I can't get a good signal in here!" he yells. We're moving faster and faster, but the feeler is getting louder. It's coming in low, like it's about to attack the tram with its tentacles.

"Brace yourself," Liam says, grabbing me. "This could get rough."

Everyone other than Liam and me has started screaming and yelling. David is pounding on the controls of the box. The feeler is getting closer.

"What's wrong? Make it work!" Gadya and Cass are both yelling at David, sounding uncannily similar in their anger and fervor.

"Maybe the travelers did something to sabotage it!" David yells in frustration. "Like how they cut the ropes! I don't understand why it won't work!"

"Or maybe you're lying, like Emma said!" Gadya yells back. "Maybe you're trying to trick us again!"

"I swear that I'm not!"

Our tram is picking up speed, but it's not going fast enough to avoid the feeler. At any moment, I'm expecting the first metal tentacle to lash down and knock us off the rails.

I try to see the feeler out the windows, but it's hovering above us. Deliberately hiding itself from view.

Something suddenly cracks down above our heads. It sounds like a gunshot, but I know that it's the tip of a tentacle. The tram sways on the tracks a little. It wasn't built to withstand this kind of assault.

I grab on to the seats. Liam keeps an arm around me. I know it's possible that the feeler could push the tram right off the highway, and send us plummeting to our deaths below.

Another whip crack detonates above our heads. The entire vehicle shakes, sliding from side to side. I look up and see that a large dent has appeared in the roof of the tram. We're moving too fast to get off the vehicle now. *We're trapped.*

The feeler strikes us a third time. There's an angry screech of metal shearing away as we nearly get dislodged from the rail. A hole opens up in the roof, letting in sunlight.

Then David yells, "I've got it! I've locked on to its signal!"

The rotors are still hammering overhead. But David is right. The attack has ceased. I'm about to breathe a sigh of relief. But then I look out the front windshield.

"Oh no," I whisper.

We've been so distracted by the feeler above us that we haven't been watching the road.

Several hundred yards ahead, the highway disappears.

It just drops out of view, like it falls into a chasm. This is where the road is broken, but it's much closer than ten miles. The concrete is demolished. Jagged pillars are all that remain until the highway appears again, about thirty yards beyond the gap. Nothing separates us from a forty foot fall here straight down to the ground. The tram is not slowing down.

But that's not all. Writhing and churning inside the chasm is one of the most terrifying sights I've ever seen.

It's a mass of feelers. *Hundreds of them.* Floating there so close together that their blades almost hit one another. I don't understand how this is even possible.

I hear voices screaming around me. But I'm too numb to scream. We must be moving at about fifty miles per hour. And we're headed straight into the pit full of feelers.

David is still wrestling with the box. But it's too late.

I wonder for an instant if there's a way to get the feeler to pick up our tram and hoist us into the air. But we'd be way too heavy for it. We'd just drag it down into the abyss with us.

I doubt that the tram is going to stop automatically like it did at the barrier. This time there is no object blocking its path. Just empty space. I see Gadya banging on the tram's buttons. They do nothing to slow us down.

Suddenly, wind is whooshing through my hair. Liam has thrown open the vehicle's door.

"Out!" he yells at me. "Now!"

I'm about to protest, but then I realize that he's right. Jumping is our only chance.

"Go!" Liam yells at me.

"You first!"

But before either of us can do anything, David flings himself right out the open door. He curls himself around the black box as he jumps, so it doesn't get shattered. I glance back and see him rolling away from us down the highway.

"Together!" I yell at Liam.

Gadya is right there with us now. Cass is forcing Emma toward the door too. I know we only have a few seconds left.

"Ready?" Liam asks.

"Yes!" I scream.

*Liam and I jump.*

For a moment, I feel like I'm flying. Air rushes all around me. My hair blows across my face, and dust and grit whip at my eyes. I lose sight of Liam.

And then I hit the road hard with my shoulder, in a flare of agony that steals my breath. I roll sideways to absorb the blow, but the impact is hard enough that it rattles my whole body. I get thrown across the road, away from Liam.

The world spins as I keep moving, slamming against the unforgiving concrete. I feel it scrape my arms and legs. I try to keep my hands around my head, with my elbows up to protect my face.

For a moment, I think the force of the impact is going to kill me. That it's going to tear me apart. But eventually, I stop rolling.

I lie there for a second on my side, stunned. I listen to the sound of the feeler in the sky—and the roar of the feelers ahead of us in the chasm where the highway is broken.

I struggle to sit up. My elbows and knees are skinned, completely raw, and my clothes are torn. My forehead aches. When I touch it, I feel a lump. My shoulder and ribs are throbbing. Every breath hurts when I gasp for air.

The others are scattered across the road. Some are lying there prone, and some are already standing up. Liam rushes over to me, limping. He has a gash across his cheek.

He reaches me and kneels down. I cling to him, struggling for air. I feel his strong hands supporting me, holding me up.

He's about to speak, when there's a huge crashing sound nearby.

I glance over to see the tram sailing off the road and slamming into the feelers below. It smashes down into some of their blades, demolishing them instantly. But within half a second, other feelers are rising up and tearing at it with their tentacles, as the tram continues falling. Then it disappears from view.

I look up, afraid. The feeler that David has locked on to with the box is hovering in the sky above us. Just floating there, looking oddly peaceful. Its tentacles hang straight down, limp, as though it's sleeping.

But the same is not true of the other feelers in the chasm. They keep rising up from the broken road, buzzing and humming.

"David!" Liam yells across the road. "Get up and help us!"

I look over and see that David is just lying there. He's not moving. Probably unconscious. I don't see the box anywhere. Both of his hands are empty.

Liam and I start scrambling toward him. The others aren't far behind. All of them are awake, although I see blood dripping from Emma's nose and from one of her ears.

Liam and I reach David first.

"David, c'mon! Wake up!" I yell.

Liam grabs David's wrist and checks his pulse. "He's alive. But he's hurt."

We both start searching the road around him for the black box.

The noise of the feelers is deafening now. A cacophonous roar. I'm guessing that soon they will come straight for us. We have no way to fight back. Not against so many of them. *They will take us and freeze us in the archive.* I'd rather die than let that happen.

I spot the black box off to the side of the highway. I race toward it with a yell.

"Alenna!" Liam calls out, startled. But then he realizes what I'm doing, and he follows after me.

I reach the box and snatch it up with one hand. I glance down at it. Its casing is slightly cracked, but it appears to be working. Its switches are intact.

I start flicking them up and down, but nothing happens. We never asked David how to operate the box, or what the codes were in case something happened to him. Then again, I'm not certain he would have told us.

Gadya is at our side, too. "Make it work!"

"I can't!" I point it at the feelers heading toward us, and desperately flick random switches. But the feelers keep coming.

The only feeler that responds to my efforts is the one above us that David locked on to. Its tentacles open up and spread outward. I play with more switches and its tentacles twitch violently. I have no clue what I'm doing.

I press another switch on the side of the box and the feeler moves forward. I press it again, and it moves forward a second time, like it's following us. I realize I've figured out what one of the switches does, at least. If I can do that, then maybe I can figure out the others. I just need more time, and that's one thing we don't have.

"I'll be right back," Liam suddenly says. He races across the highway to David's body. I watch him hoist David over his shoulder. David remains unconscious. Cass and Emma are heading our way too.

"We have to get off this road!" I say to Gadya.

"I know!"

For some reason, the feelers from the broken road aren't attacking us. At least not yet. It's like the strange chasm in the highway is where they come to rest, or perhaps to recharge. Maybe David's box agitated them, and drew them to that part of the road. Or maybe they'll only get activated if we cross one of the invisible sector boundaries—and the broken road is preventing us from doing that. Anything is possible.

Liam is carrying David. Liam signals at us to start moving back down the highway in the direction that we came from. Back to the travelers' camp. Gadya and I nod.

We start running across the road to join him. Cass is helping support Emma.

I watch the feeler above us as I run. I keep pressing the switch that seems to move it in our direction. The switch must make it follow the box. Although the odds are slim, I hope that if we can get off this road without the other feelers attacking, there's a chance we can continue with our plan.

But as we keep running, I hear a sound directly in front of us. Coming up from the curve of the highway ahead. The source isn't visible. For a moment, I think it's the clattering of more feelers.

*But it's the sound of footsteps.* Thousands of them. I freeze and stagger, turning sideways.

The feeler above us almost collapses to the ground as I accidentally hit the box, but then it stabilizes again. It floats in the air far above our heads.

Gadya and I reach Liam. We help him put David down gently on the concrete. He's still unconscious. The footsteps keep advancing.

"Drones," Liam says grimly. "A whole army."

The others reach us, breathless. Emma's head is lolling back a bit. Without Cass, she wouldn't be standing. I'm not sure that she's going to be okay.

I stare at the highway, which shimmers in the heat and sunlight. There's nowhere to run. The road is just a sheer forty-foot drop on either side. And behind us is the swarming mass of feelers from the chasm. Soon the army of drones will come into view.

I stand there with Liam, knowing that this could be the end. Maybe this was a trap. Set by David, or by the travelers.

Our feeler hangs above us, and a bit behind. I hope the drones just assume it's one of the feelers from the chasm, and don't know that we can control it.

I feel like we're pawns. Stuck in a game that we don't know the rules to. Maybe the travelers were working with the drones the whole time, in some kind of secret alliance. Or maybe the drones knew that the feelers were here, and were waiting to corner us.

As I watch, the first battalion of the drone army emerges. It stretches the entire width of the highway, in a line at least fifty kids across. Behind each of them is a seemingly endless column of other kids. All of them have spears, or bows and arrows. They wear their homemade black robes. Their uniformity is frightening.

Liam leans in close. "We might have to jump after all," he whispers. "Off the edge of the road. Hope that the underbrush cushions our fall. I noticed earlier that there are some trees and thick bushes directly below the highway here, to our left."

Jumping terrifies me. "What about David?"

"I can try to wake him up and take him with me. It's risky, but better than staying up here if the army attacks."

I nod. Anything is better than having the drones get us. But I don't know if we'll survive a jump—especially David. "We still have the feeler," I whisper back to Liam. "If David wakes up, maybe he can use it to do some damage first."

The five of us stand there with David at our feet, as the army stops perfectly in place, a hundred paces away. From here, I can see their faces. Their eyes look blank and brainwashed. More mechanical than human.

I can hear the buzzing of the rising feelers behind us. Including the one that we control. I hide the black box deeper inside my pocket.

"What do you want with us?" Liam calls out, his voice bellowing across the landscape.

The drones don't reply. They act like they haven't even heard him. I look down at David. He isn't moving.

"We'll fight you!" Gadya screams at the drones. "Every last one of us, until we're dead!"

Again, the drones completely ignore her words.

I gaze at the army, sensing sudden movement.

Then I see a drifting figure, being carried by six drones on a large covered platform draped with golden fabrics. The figure's wooden mask is unmistakable.

*The Monk.*

"He's here!" I gasp.

My hand instantly slips back down to the black box. *I have to get David to wake up somehow.* Only he knows how to control the feeler, and what switches to flip to activate the right codes.

The army of drones parts down the center as the raised figure drifts closer toward us.

We stand our ground.

I kick David hard with my boot. "Wake up!" I hiss at him. Cass crouches down by his side, trying to rouse him by yelling in his ears and pinching him. Emma sways under the sun, but manages to stay standing.

The Monk comes even closer, protected by his ocean of drones.

"Coward!" I yell at him, trying to draw him out farther. "You let other people do your fighting for you! Come here and face us."

I hear a slow chuckle begin to build. It's electronically amplified and distorted, so that it drowns out my words. There must be some kind of amplification system hidden in the platform that carries him. Just as there was back at the cathedral.

The Monk casts his gaze across us. Taking me by surprise, he begins to name us, one by one: "Liam, Alenna, Gadya, Cass, Emma, and David."

I'm startled. All of us are.

The Monk chuckles again.

*Who is behind that awful mask?*

"You didn't think I knew who you were?" the Monk asks, his voice an electric squeal. "I know everything." He turns to each of us in turn. "Liam, I know that your father is dead! I killed Octavio myself, with great pleasure back at the confinement house. I want you to know that he suffered a thousand agonies before he died."

I grab Liam's arm. I don't know if the Monk is telling the truth, or trying to demoralize us.

"Alenna," the Monk continues. "I know that your mother is stuck in Southern Arc—a dying station, about to freeze to death alone. Soon, she will join Octavio and the other heathens in hell!"

I can barely breathe now.

"Gadya, the travelers betrayed you," the Monk continues, turning his gaze yet again. "Just like Liam betrayed you when he chose Alenna instead of you. How does that make you feel? And Emma, so weak and frail. Do you deserve to be alive?" The Monk looks at Cass. "And Cass, I knew your brother Vincent. He was a pathetic coward, loathed by everyone who met him on the wheel. A slave and a nobody."

The words hit harder than blows. It's like listening to the devil speak. The voice is mocking and sadistic. Hypnotic in its cadence. How can the Monk know any details about us?

"Don't listen to him," I say. "It's all lies."

The Monk peers down at David's prone body. "Looks like David got what he deserved, doesn't it? I doubt he'll ever wake up."

But the Monk doesn't know that I've just felt the first stirrings of David's body at my feet. I crouch down instantly. Hopefully, the Monk will just think I'm overwhelmed by his words. But I have a plan.

"David!" I whisper. "Wake up! You have to!"

He mumbles something incoherent in response.

"Come on! You can do it!"

I slip the box out of my pocket, secretly in my palm, and press it into his hand, desperately hoping for a miracle.

*Then David's fingers close around the box.*

That's when I realize we actually have a chance.

The Monk is so distracted by his desire to hurt us that he doesn't seem to notice what's going on.

"I did spare one life!" the Monk cries out. "Behold!"

As he speaks, a group of four drones drags a wicker cage forward. An old man wearing a tight leather leash is inside. I instantly recognize him as Dr. Barrett. His hands and feet are bound, and circular red wounds dot his grizzled, bearded face. His eyes burn with complete rage. I feel sick. Death would be a better fate than this.

"I keep Dr. Barrett alive as a reminder of the failure of science over faith," the Monk sneers.

"You're a demon!" Cass yells at him, revolted.

"Fraud!" Gadya seconds. "You're not the real Monk anyway! He's dead." She looks at the army of drones and addresses them. "The real monk was Minister Harka from the UNA! We killed him. You're following an impostor!"

The drones stare back, completely unconcerned. They must be drugged. Nothing else would explain the hold that this man has over them. The group of drones with the cage hauls Dr. Barrett away again, out of sight. But I can't get the image of his agonized face from my mind.

"One of you has something that I need," the Monk says after a pause. "Something that David stole from me. I propose a trade. You give me what I want, and I will kill you quickly. Not like what I did to Octavio." I can hear the smile behind the mask. "You can avoid that fate if you wish." The Monk turns his masked face to survey the drones. "Or perhaps, if you work hard, you might even convince me to spare your lives. You could join my devotees in a life of selfless devotion."

"Never!" I scream back at him.

I see David's hands move slightly on the box, as his fingers probe the switches. I know he's awake now, but pretending to be knocked out.

"You're a liar!" I yell at the Monk to distract him. "You'll lock us up like Dr. Barrett!"

The Monk just starts chuckling again.

"It's time," Liam whispers. He's realized what's going on.

"What if David can't make it work? Or doesn't want to?" I whisper back.

"Then we run and jump. Take our chances."

I nod. Gadya has heard what we're saying. She's telling Cass and Emma.

"Resistance is a waste of your time," the Monk intones. "Submit to my glory . . . or face my wrath!"

Drones start aiming their arrows at us, preparing their onslaught.

There's a split second of silence.

Then David sits up and his fingers fly across the surface of the black box, flipping switches, activating programmed codes, and unleashing the feeler. He points the box's antenna at the feeler and then aims it right at the Monk.

"Take that!" I scream.

The Monk notices what's happening. "Guards!" he cries out.

Drones flood around him.

But the feeler flies forward, moving at full speed. David has somehow managed to get it locked directly on to the Monk.

The Monk is caught up in his platform. He's trying to move backward, but this was clearly not what he expected. He's yelling at his drones angrily. They start moving him back. But they're not fast enough for the feeler.

I'm trying to watch the drones and the feeler at the same time, and also help David manipulate the box. The feeler is zooming in, aimed right at the Monk.

"Attack!" the Monk suddenly cries out to his drones. "Make these heathens pay!"

The army of drones instantly starts rushing straight toward us, throwing spears and firing arrows. But some of them are also busy attacking the feeler—pointlessly, because their weapons are no use against it.

I fling myself to the concrete. Liam shelters me as well as David. But then Liam cries out in pain. *He's been hit.* I feel panicked.

"Liam, are you okay?" I scream.

"Yes!" he yells back. "David, keep control of that feeler!"

And then I glance up to see that the feeler has found the Monk.

Tentacles coil around the flailing robed figure, as David flicks another sequence of switches. Tangled up in his robes, the Monk can't get away quickly enough. The tentacles contract, and pull the Monk right out of his gilded platform. The feeler sails high into the sky, carrying the Monk with it.

Then a spear flies through the air at my face. I duck, but the tip plows into the concrete surface of the road. The shaft smacks David across the side of his head. All of us are screaming.

Liam spins off me and David. The drones are firing arrows, but most of them saw what happened to their leader. They are stunned. Dazed. Gazing up at the feeler with slack mouths.

"Off the highway!" Liam yells at me. "Go!"

But David is slumped over onto the concrete. He's been knocked out again by the blow.

Liam bends down to pick him up, but then flinches in sudden pain. He's been struck in the back by another arrow.

"No!" I yell, scrambling to my feet.

Cass and Emma have pressed themselves flat on the concrete near Gadya, not far away. Cass is trying to shield Emma from the arrows.

"Liam!" I gasp, as he shuts his eyes for a second, in pain.

"It's okay," he says, between gritted teeth.

But he doesn't look okay. He's bleeding everywhere, although I can't see the arrow from here.

More arrows fly at us, preventing anyone from grabbing David. There's no way we're going to be able to get him off the highway. I reach down and yell at him, trying to rouse him. But nothing happens.

"We have to run or we'll get killed," Liam says into my ear, trying to drag me along.

He's right. There's no other way. We've obviously disrupted the drones' entire hierarchy, but they're still willing to fight us. Violence is like an automatic response for them.

I reach down and snatch the box from David's fingers. I call out for Cass and Emma, but I'm not sure that they can hear me. If David survives this attack, then somehow we'll come back for him. Traitor or not, at least he did the right thing in the end when it came to helping us catch the Monk. We can't abandon him.

Liam and I race to the side of the highway. I'm clutching the box in my hand. We reach the low concrete wall at the edge. I glance down over it. Far below us is brush and low, dense trees. *This is going to break some bones. Maybe even kill us.* But we have to do it. I can't be afraid anymore.

I grab Liam's hand. We scramble onto the low wall.

"I love you!" I say to him quickly.

And then I let go of his hand and jump.

I sail through the air, moving faster than I thought possible. The drop feels like it lasts for forever. A million thoughts and images race through my mind, spanning my first day on the wheel to the present moment. It's like watching a movie—I see the village, Gadya, Veidman, Meira, Rika, the drones, the feelers, and everything else flicking past in my memory. Then I'm slamming through trees limbs, feeling them tear viciously at my skin.

And then I hit the underbrush.

Everything spins and goes dark for a second.

Slowly, my senses return. The trees and brush cushioned my fall, but I can barely move. My legs throb. I try to get to my feet, but I just fall over.

Liam is right next to me, already helping me up. He must have jumped a second after I did. "We did it!" he says, sounding jubilant. "C'mon!"

The black box is still in my hand. And it seems to be working. From down here, I can see the feeler in the sky. The Monk remains in its clutches.

I look back up at the highway. There's no sign of Emma, Cass, or Gadya following us. Or David. It's just me and Liam now.

"What do we do?" I ask Liam in pain.

"We try to bring the Monk down here to the forest. We'll rescue the others later if we can. Including Dr. Barrett."

"There's no 'if'! We can't leave them behind."

He stares up and yells at the road. "Gadya! C'mon!" There's no response. "Cass! Emma!"

Then I catch a glimpse of something lodged in his back. "Turn around!" I say.

"What?" He turns.

My hand goes to my mouth. Now I see the thick, broken shaft of the arrow protruding from right below his left shoulder blade. It's worse than I thought. The wound is bleeding heavily. "You're hurt!"

"As long as you're okay, I'll be fine." His hand goes up to the broken arrow. He winces as he contorts his body to touch the shaft. He lowers his hand. "I've been hit worse." He looks at me.

"The others have a chance at survival too, if the drones are distracted enough. We just need to focus on the Monk."

"I'll help you get the arrow out later." I touch his arm. I know he must be in agony, but pretending that he's not. I can't tell how deep the arrow has penetrated his flesh. It looks pretty bad.

I hear pinging noises in the foliage around us. I glance up and see a row of drones at the edge of the highway, firing arrows down at us. They've appeared unexpectedly.

"Run!" I yell, although neither Liam nor I am in any shape to run anywhere. My legs throb from my shins to my hips. We stagger forward anyway, into the cover of the trees, helping each other along as we look for shelter.

I grip the box. The feeler moves farther overhead into the forest as I keep pressing the one switch that I understand—the one that moves the feeler along with us somehow. The metal tentacles are keeping the Monk locked in place in the sky. I catch glimpses of his mask staring outward.

"We'll bring him down in the trees if we can figure out how," I say. "Far away from his drones."

Liam nods. I see that his shirt is becoming slick with blood. I want to pull the arrow out of him, but I know it could make the wound bleed more. My heart races faster. Liam is badly hurt. David is unconscious. And our other friends are stranded on the highway—probably getting attacked by drones.

We never should have come back to the wheel. Just like the travelers said. If we hadn't, then Liam and I might still be safe. And Gadya would be safe too, with the travelers. Nothing has turned out like I hoped it would.

Liam and I keep moving, heading into the dense jungle where the arrows won't find us. We just need to reach a clearing that's large enough for the feeler to descend. I stare around us, searching as we run.

Out here, we will finally have the Monk to ourselves. And if we can bring him down to the ground, we can begin to unravel the mysteries that have plagued us since our return to the wheel.

# 22 THE UNMASKING

As we run, there's a distant crash behind us. For a moment, I think it's a drone. Maybe a brave one is giving chase after all.

But then I glance back and see that it's Gadya. She stands up unsteadily in the thick underbrush, as arrows rain down around her.

"Gadya!" I scream, racing back toward her.

She stumbles through the brush and into the trees. She's headed our way, limping badly and dodging arrows. I don't know how she's managed to make it without being hit.

When she gets close enough to us, I race forward and grab her. She nearly collapses into my arms. I hold her. Liam rushes over too.

"Are you okay?" I ask, helping her stand.

She nods, looking dazed. "I messed up my ankle again."

"Let me look," I say.

She shakes her head. "I don't even wanna see it."

"What's going on up there?" Liam asks her.

"Some of the drones are fighting," she replies. "It's like they don't know what else to do! Cass and Emma are stuck—I couldn't get to them. And the drones have surrounded David. I couldn't reach him either."

I feel sick. "We need to keep moving," I tell her. Above us, the Monk hangs in the sky, at the mercy of the feeler. "Liam's hurt."

Gadya sees the arrow sticking out of his back, and her eyes widen. But she doesn't say anything. We just start hiking into the jungle as fast as we can on our wounded limbs.

"So, we've got the Monk," Gadya says, as she glances up through the branches at the feeler. She's using a tree branch as a staff to help her walk. "I can't wait to be alone with that bastard."

"Remember, we can't kill him," I say. "At least not right away. We need answers. And we need to figure out what codes to use on the box. Or else he's gonna be stuck in the sky forever."

We keep hiking, pressing even deeper into the forest, stumbling forward. I try not to think of Cass and Emma back on the road, fighting for their lives. Or David. Or even Dr. Barrett, who looked so close to death.

We reach a small clearing, strewn with leaves and dead branches. Above it is a circle of blue sky. My chest is heaving for air. Liam sits down, looking pale. He's losing way too much blood.

"Let's try to bring the Monk down right here," I say.

"Okay," he agrees.

Gadya comes over to my side.

"How does this thing work?" she asks, gesturing at the box.

"No clue," I tell her.

She leans in and starts flicking random switches.

"Careful," I warn her.

"Look!" she yells, glancing up. The feeler is moving back over to the highway.

"That's the wrong way!" I tell her, grabbing at the box. I flick the switch to bring him back over to us again.

"Trial and error," Liam calls out to us. "There has to be some code to bring the feeler down to the ground. Just keep working on it. . . ."

Fifteen minutes later, after struggling to understand the box, we finally manage to get the feeler to start descending from the sky by toggling one of the central switches downward. Now that the Monk is closer, I can see him struggling against the tight, unyielding grasp of the metal tentacles.

I feel no pity or remorse. This charlatan deserves his fate. We are about to expose the source of so much evil on the wheel. The Monk has been outwitted. There are no drones to protect him now. And the UNA drugs that he relies on to keep his followers in line do not affect us.

The feeler drifts lower.

"I'm going to cut your throat!" Gadya yells up at the Monk.

The feeler is now about fifteen feet above the ground, its rotors dangerously close to hitting tree branches. The Monk keeps writhing, but he remains curiously silent.

"It's time," I tell Gadya. I stop toggling the switch. The feeler stops moving. It just hovers there like a mechanical hummingbird. "Now comes the hard part."

It takes another few minutes of playing with switches until we get the feeler to uncoil its tentacles and release the Monk.

When it happens, the Monk is taken by surprise, and so are we. He plummets straight down to the earth, landing in a heap in front of us with a thud. Dirt and leaves scatter everywhere.

Despite his wounds, Liam is already back on his feet. The three of us stand there, watching the wretched figure lying on the ground. I toggle the switch upward, and the feeler drifts back into the sky, to hover loudly in the air again.

The Monk lies there for a moment, shrouded in his black robes. None of us say a word.

Then the Monk begins to move, drawing himself inward. As we watch, he smoothly pulls himself upward to his feet. He seems uninjured by his fall. Then he stands, facing the three of us.

His wooden mask is tightly locked on to his face, completely obscuring his features. Blue eyes burn out from behind the eyeholes. The whites of these eyes aren't mottled and red like Minister Harka's were, but I can see raging fury in them. The Monk remains silent.

"Now it's our turn to ruin your day!" Gadya taunts. She tosses her tree branch to one side and takes her short knife out of her ankle sheath. "Bet you didn't think you'd end up here with us."

The Monk still doesn't reply. He just keeps watching us.

"Take off your mask," Liam commands. "Slowly."

The Monk doesn't move. He just keeps staring at us with eyes filled with raw hatred and contempt.

Gadya holds out her knife. "I can make you take it off. Even if I have to carve up your face in the process."

The Monk just glares back at her.

"Say something!" I yell. "You had so much to say to us before. Why not now? Why won't you speak?"

The Monk's blue eyes find mine.

A moment passes.

And then the Monk speaks.

"You think you've accomplished something?" the Monk hisses. "You've done nothing but seal your own fate!"

I step back, startled despite myself.

*The voice coming from behind the mask is distinctly female.*

Liam and Gadya look equally surprised.

It never crossed my mind that the Monk could be a girl. I realize then that we've never heard the Monk's voice unamplified before now. It must have been run through some kind of electronic alteration to lower its pitch, as well as to increase its volume.

"Who are you?" I breathe.

As I gaze at the masked figure, she raises her hands and unclasps the mask from her head. She reveals light-blond hair pulled back in a bun, and a pale, sweaty face. Her full lips are curled into a feral snarl, distorting her natural beauty.

I recognize her instantly. It feels like the air has been sucked out of my lungs. I stand there, stunned.

She tosses the wooden mask to the ground disdainfully.

It rolls, and lands at my feet.

*The Monk is Meira.*

"Traitor!" Gadya screams. She rushes right at Meira with her knife raised, ready to slit her throat. Liam steps between them, holding Gadya back.

"No!" he yells. "Don't!"

Meira just stands there. She reaches up a hand and lets down her hair. It isn't pristine and sleek like I remembered. Now it's dirty and unkempt. And her face is marked with red pressure lines from where the mask has rested on it. She looks deranged.

"How could you do this to us?" I ask her angrily.

"Do what?" she retorts.

"Betray everything that you stood for!" Liam says, still struggling to keep Gadya from killing her.

Meira ignores him.

"The scientists said you were a spy when we got to Destiny Station," I tell her. "You and Veidman both. But I didn't really believe them."

Meira sticks out her tongue. To my shock, I see that it's been cleaved in two. She smiles when she sees me recoil in disgust. Her teeth have also been filed into sharp points. Just like so many of the other drones.

"Do you believe the scientists now?" she asks.

Liam gets Gadya under control, at least for the moment. We stand there facing Meira. Her life is in our hands, although she doesn't seem to care about that.

"Explain yourself!" I tell her. "Have you gone crazy? Why did you do this?"

"Why?" she spits back like she's possessed. "I don't need to tell you. You're going to kill me anyway."

"You owe it to us," Liam says. "I fought for our village. All of us did. We would have given our lives for you and Veidman. What would Veidman think of you now, or was he in on it too?"

"Of course he was," she sneers. "We both were. We were sent from the UNA to control things in the blue sector, and make sure the villagers never succeeded in anything they did. We sabotaged many missions. We were nothing like you." She pauses, her crazed eyes darting back and forth. "I was never a villager. No more than I am a drone. I am whatever the situation requires of me to stay alive. And in control."

"You're not in control now, and I doubt you're going to stay alive much longer," I tell her calmly. I notice that she doesn't have any trace of a Canadian accent, like she did in the village. *That must have been an act too.*

"Just tell us why," Liam says. "That's what we want to know. Why did you do this to us?"

"Because the GPPT actually works!" Meira cries out. "Because you are scum. You are disruptors who have no place in the golden society of the United Northern Alliance!" Her eyes are burning with savage glee. "It took everything I had to hide my true feelings back at our village."

"Then why did you get sent to the wheel?" Gadya snaps. "I mean, if you love the UNA so much." I know she's dying to lunge at Meira again. Liam and I are too. But our desire for answers prevents us from doing anything.

"I didn't get sent here, you moron!" Meira says to Gadya. "Veidman and I volunteered. To serve our nation." She pauses. "You really don't get it, do you? The GPPT tests for genetic mutations—like the kind all of you have—that make you less susceptible to mind-control drugs. But it also tests for perfect psychological subjects like me and Veidman. Kids who would make the ideal double agents. Diamonds among the coals. Kids that the UNA can train to work for the good of the nation and—"

"You mean sociopaths!" Gadya interrupts. "That's what the two of you are. Two-faced soulless monsters. I always thought you were a phony, Meira! Now I know that I was right!"

"Why are you leading the drones now?" I ask Meira coldly. "What is your agenda?"

She laughs. "To turn them into soldiers for the UNA. That's what the wheel is all about now. Creating an army. Those were my new orders, as of nearly five weeks ago. The UNA is going to use the drone army to invade and conquer Australia. They'll be sending an armada of ships soon to pick them up. I'm just doing my job."

"An invasion of Australia?" Liam asks. "Was the destruction of Destiny Station the first step in that plan?"

"Of course."

"Why are the drones acting so differently?" I ask her. "How are you making them follow your orders?"

"New drugs. Ones that work better. That's why the selection units aren't picking up as many kids. The units have been busy dispersing the new chemicals everywhere. The chemicals shut down most of the drones' frontal lobes, and create a temporary chemical lobotomy. It works on ninety-five percent of them."

I'm horrified, but it's what I already suspected. I vaguely wonder what happens to the other 5 percent of kids. I'm guessing they just die from side effects, or get killed by the drones. I also wonder why this drug hasn't worked on the travelers. I assume they must be naturally immune to the UNA's drugs, or they wouldn't have lived this long anyway without succumbing to the Suffering.

"Why do the drones follow *you*?" Gadya presses. "Of all people?"

Meira smiles, like our questions amuse her. "As soon as I got word from the UNA that Liam and Alenna had escaped, and Minister Harka was dead, I was given this new assignment. A feeler delivered me the mask, the robes, a voice alteration device and speakers, and a document with instructions on what to do next. I went out and walked among the drones. I told them I had the power to heal myself—to control life and death. They saw my miraculous recovery and believed that I really was a god. Combined with the new drugs, they now do exactly what I want. They follow every word I say, without questioning me."

Liam, Gadya, and I are silent for a moment. I never would have thought that Meira would end up like this. No longer beautiful. No longer sane. I see her split tongue flick out and lick her swollen lips.

"Why are you telling us this now?" I ask.

"Because I want to suggest a trade," Meira continues. "What I've told you is only a fraction of what I know." Her eyes look disturbingly ferocious and maniacal. I wonder if the UNA drugs are affecting her in some way, even if she doesn't know it.

"A trade for your life?" Liam asks. "You want to switch sides again? No chance."

"Not just for my life. That you come back with me to my drones. I'll get metal masks made for each of you." She smiles at us. "You can be my council of spiritual advisers. You can join me in my power, and we can rule the wheel and the new army together for the UNA. I will tell you secrets that you've only dreamed of knowing."

I suppose that nothing should surprise me at this point, but I'm startled nonetheless. "You want *us* to switch sides? Are you serious?"

"Your cause is doomed. The wheel is mine. The army of drones is mine. So is Dr. Barrett. You will never win against the UNA. You will only suffer if you try to fight them—"

"Let's just kill her and get it over with," Gadya interrupts, turning to me and Liam.

Liam shakes his head. "No, she'll be valuable to us alive."

Gadya looks at me. "Alenna?"

"I'm with Liam on this."

"Of course she is," Meira says to Gadya with a crazed giggle. "You're out in the cold. A third wheel. You always were, even back at the—"

"Shut up!" Gadya snaps, spinning back toward her and raising her blade. "Do you want to die?"

"If I die, another trained spy will take my place. The UNA has a contingency plan for my disappearance or death. Someone has to lead the new army until their ships arrive. There are others waiting for the chance. Someone will wear this mask after me, just as Minister Harka did before me. The UNA now sees great use in the drones, and in the concept of the Monk. Minister Harka did them a huge favor by taking himself out of the picture."

We're silent for a moment.

"We're going to have to tie her up," Liam says finally. More blood has soaked through his shirt from the arrow wound. His skin looks as white as paper. I go over to him.

"Are you doing okay?" I whisper. "For real?"

"He's dying!" Meira cackles. "Look at him!"

"Stop talking!" I yell at her.

Gadya advances on Meira with her knife. "If you say another word, I'll cut your throat and pull your tongue out the hole."

"She trying to upset us," Liam says softly. "She wants to get under our skin. She's been trained by the UNA. She can't fight with weapons right now—only with words."

"You think you know me so well, Liam Bernal?" Meira taunts him.

Gadya moves even closer to her.

"I know your kind," Liam says tiredly.

"Really?" Meira asks. Gadya keeps getting closer, her knife raised. "Then what do you think about this?"

Out of nowhere, there's a sudden flash of light and an explosion of noise that sounds like a firecracker.

Gadya stumbles back. So do I, blinking. Where Meira once stood is just a drifting pillar of dark gray smoke.

"It's a flash grenade!" Liam yells. "She's on the run!"

Despite his injury, he's already chasing after her. Gadya is rubbing her eyes frantically. She was closest to the explosion. "I can't see!" she yells.

"It'll fade! You'll be fine!" Liam calls back to her.

"Let's go!" I yell, dragging Gadya along with me, despite her ankle. I know we can't let Meira get away.

We race through the trees, following after her. I see her robes flapping in front of us. She's much faster than I would have expected. Liam is in the lead, not far behind her. Gadya is still cursing and yelling, limping along behind me now.

It's clear that Meira is never going to be anything but a traitor and a spy. We should have killed her when we had the chance. But at least she gave us some important information—assuming anything she said was true.

I dodge a tree branch and keep running.

Liam's injury is slowing him down. There's a chance Meira will get away. She's darting through the trees like she knows this landscape well.

I keep running.

Liam is still ahead of me, with Gadya trailing farther behind us. Meira is slowing down a bit too. Perhaps she didn't count on our perseverance. Or maybe she's planning on unleashing more flash grenades.

Then, as I watch, I see her nimble stride get rudely interrupted. She stumbles over a tree root and falls to the ground face-first, her robes flapping up around her.

Liam bursts forward, going as fast as he can. I'm right behind him now.

Meira gets up and glances back, wide-eyed.

But it's too late.

Liam and I are on her, both grabbing at the hem of her robes. She tries to pull away from us, but the robes refuse to tear. She falls onto the dirt again, kicking and clawing like a wild animal.

"Stop it!" I yell at her.

Liam manages to grab her from behind, and he drags her to her feet. She stands there swaying as he presses his knife against her throat.

Gadya finally reaches us, staggering up with her knife too. We're all gasping for air.

"No more running!" Gadya says to Meira. Gadya's eyes are red and painful-looking from the flash grenade. Their lids are swollen to twice their normal size.

"There's something you should know," Meira hisses, baring her pointed teeth at us. She's not smiling anymore.

I gaze right back at her. "Tell us."

"The specimen archive? What you're trying to save so desperately?" She pauses. "It's already been set to self-destruct."

"What are you talking about?" Liam asks.

Meira stands there, panting. "Now that the UNA has found their new drug, they don't need the archive anymore. They're going to blow it up. It's part of their plan to reduce the wheel to rubble, so no other country can steal their technology once they abandon it. Acquiring Australia and dominating the globe is their only focus now. The archive has served its purpose."

"You're lying!" I say.

But the gleeful look in her eyes lets me know that she's definitely telling the truth.

"Our friends are in there!" Gadya yells.

Liam tightens the blade even more. I see a thin line of blood appear across Meira's throat. *Does Meira want us to kill her?* It almost seems that way.

"Why are you saying this stuff?" Liam asks her. "Why would you give us a chance to stop the destruction?"

"There's nothing you can do to stop it."

"How long do we have?" I ask her.

"It's already too late. In four hours, the archive will be in ruins. The charges are set. And you will all be dead!"

"That's where you're wrong," I tell her. "We're not only going to stop the archive from blowing up, we're going to stop you from causing any more harm."

"Nothing you do will ever stop me," she says, between gasping breaths. Liam's knife is constricting her windpipe. "Don't you understand? I am the UNA. I cannot be defeated!"

She suddenly grins, opening her mouth wide. Between the two halves of her split tongue, I see a small, clear capsule. It's filled with white powder. She holds it there for a second. It must have been hidden under her tongue this whole time.

"No—" I yell, lunging forward to grab it out of Meira's mouth.

Meira bites down on the pill instantly.

Liam tries to grab Meira's jaw and force the pill back out. Gadya rushes up and we struggle with Meira together.

At first, I think she's fighting back. Her hand knocks out and hits me hard in my mouth with a closed fist. I stagger back. I bring my fingers up to my face. One of my lower teeth feels loose, and I can taste the copper tang of blood.

I'm about to charge back into the fray, when I realize that Meira isn't fighting us at all. She's convulsing.

We step back from her.

She falls to the ground, twitching like she's in the grip of a grand mal seizure. Her eyes roll back in her head, showing their whites.

Liam crouches down at her side, trying to keep her mouth clear. Trying to keep her alive.

But Meira has stopped breathing.

There's nothing we can do.

"Damn it!" Gadya yells, flinging down her knife in frustration.

Within seconds, Meira's body goes limp as the seizure finally stops. The life has gone from her now. Her eyes have the glazed sheen of a corpse.

"She killed herself," I say.

"Cyanide pill," Liam says. He's checking the body to see if she has anything on her that we can use. But there's nothing. "The UNA must have given it to her."

"I'm glad she's dead," Gadya mutters, rubbing her eyes and trying to clear her vision. She looks down and picks up her knife from the dirt. "I'm not gonna cry any tears for her."

I stare down at Meira's corpse, feeling nauseous. "She was probably brainwashed like her followers."

"Either way, now it's over," Gadya replies.

"Is it over?" Liam asks, glancing up at us. "Like she said, there's another person set to step into her place. And the archive is about to self-destruct."

My mind is racing. "Do you think the drones know what happened to her yet? I mean, that their leader is dead?"

"Maybe," Liam says. "But hopefully there hasn't been enough time for the UNA to step in and activate her backup."

A terrifying plan is starting to form in my mind. "Then we might have a chance to stop everything. If we move fast."

"A chance at what?" Gadya asks, looking puzzled.

But I can tell that Liam understands. "To send one of us back in her place," he says softly. "Right?"

Gadya just looks at him.

"We could take Meira's mask and her robes, and send someone back up to the highway. Using the feeler to take them there and drop them off."

"That's crazy—" Gadya says to me, but then she falls silent. I can tell that she's considering my plan, turning it over in her mind.

319

"Meira claimed that the drones follow her every word," Liam says. "They're practically programmed to. If one of us went back, there's a chance we could control the drones in her place and make them stand down."

"And then we could use them to break into the gray zone, and try to free everyone in the archive before it self-destructs," I continue.

"We could also send drones back to help the scientists in the cathedral, and find my dad," Liam adds. "I don't believe what Meira said about him. I think he's still alive. Either way, we would be in charge. We could release Dr. Barrett. The drones would do the bidding of the Monk, without even knowing that it was actually one of us."

"If it works, we could liberate the wheel!" Gadya says, nodding. "Like we always planned."

I stare around at her and Liam. "That's assuming no one knows what happened. There could be cameras watching us right now. But we could pull it off if we get back to the highway fast enough."

"We just need to figure out how to make the black box do what we want," Liam says.

I nod. "There must be a simple way. David used the feeler to bring himself here and drop himself off."

"We need to learn how," Liam says. "We can strip the robes off Meira's body. Then we run back, find the mask, and bring the feeler down. I'll get dressed and we—"

"*Wait*," Gadya and I say at the same instant.

Liam looks at us. "What?"

"It can't be you," I tell him. "You've got an arrow in your back! Besides, you're a foot taller than Meira."

"She's right," Gadya says. "Meira's robes won't even fit you."

"The drones are brainwashed. They won't be able to tell the difference," Liam argues. "There's no way I'm letting either of you go."

"Liam, you have to. You're bleeding." I gaze into his eyes. "Trust us."

Gadya stares at Liam hard. "If you go, and you bleed out and die, it's going to be your fault that our whole plan fails. Are you willing to risk the lives of the kids in the archive?"

"It's a risk no matter which one of us goes," Liam says.

I take Liam's hand. "I let you put your life in danger when you went to save your father on the hydrofoil. I'm not letting you put yourself at risk again. Stay here."

He looks over at me. His skin is pale and waxy. I know he's badly hurt. "If I stay, which one of you will go?"

"Me, of course," Gadya blurts out.

I turn to face her. "Oh really?"

"Yes."

I shake my head. It's time that I stood on my own. The wheel has taught me that I'm stronger than I ever thought. But I've relied on others to help keep me alive too many times already. I think of my lost book by Camus. He wrote that only by facing the harshness of existence head on, can a person live their life to the fullest. I want to step up and be a leader when the occasion calls for it. In all senses of the word, I want to live.

"No," I tell Gadya firmly. "This was my plan. If it fails, then I should be the one to suffer the consequences. And Gadya, you sacrificed everything so that Liam and I could escape from the specimen archive and get to Destiny Station together. I can't ask you to do that again."

She looks aggrieved. "Who's asking? I want to do it!"

"I know. But it's my turn." I stare her down. "Besides, I'm

shorter than you. Closest to Meira's height. And I don't have a busted leg and ankle, or blue hair."

"There's no way!" Gadya snaps. "I'm a better fighter! I can—"

"Let her go," Liam interrupts.

I look over at him, relieved and grateful for his support.

But in his expression, I see a mix of emotions. I see the torment of him letting me go. The pain and hurt of knowing that I might not come back. But I also see the love and respect.

He understands that I will do anything to free the wheel from the grip of the UNA's tyranny, just like he would. That's one of the things that brought us together in the first place.

"I can't believe you're letting her do this," Gadya snaps at Liam. "You're supposed to be in love with her, aren't you?"

Liam stares at her. "That's *why* I'm letting her do it, Gad."

"But—"

"But nothing." Liam cuts her off. "She has the best chance of any of us. You know it. So do I. She can blend in better than either of us can. And I know that the flash grenade hurt your eyes. I'm betting you can't see right yet."

Gadya looks away. "Fine," she mutters. "Just tell me how that stupid box works, so I know which switches to push."

I nod. "I'll try."

I hand her the box.

Then I bend down and start pulling the black robes off Meira's corpse. Liam leans down to help, despite his injuries. Meira's limbs are already starting to stiffen from the aftereffects of the cyanide. "We better hurry," I say, as we pull the robes from her body. "We don't have much time."

# 23_THE RETURN OF THE MONK

FIFTEEN MINUTES LATER, WE'VE run back through the jungle and found Meira's wooden mask. It was resting on the forest floor in the clearing where Meira threw it. I already have it on, latched at the back of my head, along with Meira's flowing black robes. My hair is in a bun like hers. The feeler still hovers above us, ready for when we need it.

The mask feels horrible. It's tight and suffocating, and it pinches my face. I can feel it pressing hard on the sides of my head. It also restricts my peripheral vision, making me more vulnerable to attacks.

I don't know how Meira could stand to wear this thing for so long. I wonder if she ever took it off for a break. I remember that the drones are prohibited by their religion from gazing directly upon the Monk's naked face. Maybe Meira took advantage of that rule.

"How bad is it?" I ask, staring at Liam and Gadya. "Is this even gonna work?"

Liam is resting now against a fallen tree trunk. He smiles at me. "I've seen better looks on you."

Gadya stares at my masked face. She doesn't smile. She just

tilts her head, evaluating me. "You look just like Meira," she says finally. "And Minister Harka, too."

"Perfect," I reply.

"All except for the eyes," she continues. "They're not the same color as Meira's, but there's nothing we can do about that."

I nod.

"You ready?" she asks me.

"Yes," I tell her. I feel butterflies in the pit of my stomach. "Bring down the feeler."

I've already shown Gadya which switches to toggle to bring it down, and which ones to flick to send me back up to the road. We've figured the rest out together. Our understanding of the box is primitive. Like Liam said, we learn only through trial and error. We can't make it do anything as specific as David could, let alone manipulate individual tentacles. But hopefully an elementary understanding of it will be enough.

I move over to Liam. His skin is even paler than before from blood loss, and he has broken out in a light sweat. "I'll be back soon," I tell him, running a hand over his forehead. "Do you know how much I love you?"

He grips my hand. "Of course."

"You guys make me wanna throw up," Gadya mutters behind me. I turn and glance at her and see her rubbing her swollen eyes. Then she looks down at the box, and starts flicking switches.

The feeler begins to descend, rotors churning noisily as it comes down into the clearing.

I take a deep breath and then exhale. The last time I was taken by one of these machines, Liam risked his life saving me. My heart is really pounding now. I can hear it loudly in my ears.

Liam struggles up. I hug him.

"I don't know if I can do this," I whisper. I don't want Gadya to hear me express any doubt.

"You don't have to," Liam replies over the sound of the feeler. "We can find another way."

It's so tempting to agree with him. But I know that this is the best and fastest plan. We might never have an opportunity like this one again. I shake my head. "No, I have to go."

Liam holds me tight for a second. Then he releases me.

"Move back!" Gadya yells at him. She's still bringing the feeler down.

I glance up. The feeler's tentacles are descending gently. Now they're just ten feet above me. The noise and the wind from the rotors are nearly unbearable.

I reach up my hands, trying to grab the tentacles as they get near.

Liam steps forward again to help, as I feel the first tentacle brush across my wrist.

I recoil. I can't help it—it's a gut reaction. I feel another tentacle brush my shoulder.

"It's okay," Liam calls out, sensing my panic. "You're gonna do great!"

He grabs one of the tentacles and puts it into my right hand. More and more tentacles are dropping down around me.

I clutch the tentacle, feeling its cold, dead surface, like a limp metal rope. But I know that soon enough, the black box will bring it back to life.

Liam puts another tentacle into my left hand. I start wrapping them around my arms to give me some support. The feeler's rotors are thundering away above me. The blades create gusts of air that lash the tree leaves.

"Ready?" Gadya screams over the noise. "Get a good grip, okay?"

Liam moves over to her side. The whole back of his shirt is drenched with blood now. I feel a pang of fear. *What if I make it, but Liam doesn't?* Maybe I'm selfish to be going. Maybe I should just let Gadya do it. But it's too late now to change my mind.

"I'm ready!" I yell back to Gadya.

"We'll be following you! Tracking the feeler with the box!" Liam calls out. "We'll try to find a way up to the road to join you as soon as we can."

I nod, wishing there was a way to communicate with them once I get on to the highway.

"Here we go!" Gadya yells, flicking more switches on the box. "Watch out!"

A second later, I feel the tentacles begin to tighten and wrap around me. They bite into my flesh through the robes. It's like being enclosed inside a wiry, metal cocoon. I can feel my feet still on the ground. But the tentacles have wrapped themselves around my torso, as well as my arms and legs.

I clutch on to the tentacles as best as I can. They are my only lifeline now.

I stare at Liam. He's just a few paces away. It's too noisy to speak anymore.

Liam touches his heart with his hand, taps it twice, and points back at me. Then he steps forward and kisses me on the lips. But he's forced to lean back pretty quickly, narrowly dodging one of the stray tentacles.

"I'm gonna start moving you up!" I faintly hear Gadya's voice call out to me. "Liam, get out of the way! C'mon!"

Liam steps back even farther. I'm about to say more to him. To

326

tell him that if I don't make it back alive, he meant everything to me. That he gave my life meaning, even in an absurd and terrible universe.

But the feeler yanks me upward right at that moment. The tentacles cut deeply into my wrists, startling me. I'm pulled a couple feet off the ground.

I dangle there vertically as I let out a startled yelp.

"Sorry!" Gadya yells. "This thing is hard to operate!"

"It's okay!" I call back, but my words get drowned out by the noise.

I start moving upward again. Faster, but more smoothly. I shut my eyes for a second. I'm scared and disoriented. I have no idea if this plan will actually work.

I open my eyes again. Trees are rushing past me. I try to look down to see Liam and Gadya in the clearing, but the tentacles are rigid, and I can't move my head.

I continue rushing upward. Within seconds, I'm out of the trees, hovering directly above them. The feeler just pauses there for a moment.

Now I can see the forest in a panoramic view. It's just an ocean of treetops in every direction, except for the elevated highway off to my left. I look for the gray zone, but I can't see it from this angle. The highway isn't far away. Maybe a quarter of a mile at most.

I gaze down at it.

The road is packed with the army of drones. The people look like specks, but I can see exactly what's going on. The army is even larger than before. There are at least ten thousand of them here. The drones seem to have endless numbers.

Some are just standing there in the center of the highway.

Some are at the edges, peering over it. But some are now looking up at me and pointing, as they hear the noise of the feeler. I don't know if they can see my mask from here, but it's possible.

I try to search out David, Cass, and Emma. I think I see them on the road, alive but surrounded by a large circle of armed drones.

I wish I could talk to Gadya and tell her to move me closer. But I just hang there in the sky for another long moment. I see more and more drones staring up at me and pointing. The mask feels heavy and tight on my face.

And then I start moving forward again. Air rushes across my body, and through my black robes. Gadya and Liam are steering the feeler in the direction of the highway. I cling to the tentacles as hard as they cling to me. If something happens, and the feeler malfunctions or Gadya screws up, then I'm going to have to hold on to them for my life.

I move in even closer, sweeping down toward the road.

I'm terrified now that the drones will start peppering me with arrows. *If they figure out that I'm not their Monk, it's possible I'll be killed before I even reach the highway*. I just have to hope that I can fool them for long enough.

I get closer. Now I wish I had control of the feeler. I want to bring myself down as close to the Monk's platform as possible. It's vital that I get to the voice altering device, presumably hidden inside it, so that I sound like the Monk when I talk. Until then, I'll have to rely on my silence, my mask, and my robes to play the role.

I keep moving. The road is quickly rushing up to greet me. I'm just about to cry out, when I start slowing down. The rotors churn above me, as the feeler brings me gently into position. I'm about fifteen feet above the concrete.

I stare at the drones. They cover the highway in every direction. I'm being brought down near the center of the crowd. Gadya is doing a good job navigating. Drones move back slowly to clear a space for me. Their heads tilt up in wonderment and awe.

By now they can definitely see my wooden mask. I gaze down at them, trying to cloak the fear that I feel inside.

And then the drones begin to kneel. It's like watching a human tidal wave. They move back, falling to their knees and pressing themselves onto the concrete. Prostrating themselves in front of me.

I feel horror, and pity as well. But I also feel a huge sense of relief. At least so far, the drones think that I'm their leader. Returned from the dead to continue giving them orders.

And then, all at once, the tentacles open up. They whip out of my hands and away from my body, spiraling upward and outward much faster than I expected.

I instantly drop down onto the road, my boots slapping hard on the concrete. I bite my tongue not to cry out. I nearly fall over. But somehow I manage to keep my balance. I stand there, arms outstretched, swaying as I stare out at the army of drones.

They are silent. And they are still bowing down to me. Thousands of them. I pass my eyes over the crowd, searching for David, Cass, and Emma. I can't see them from here. But I do see the Monk's platform, visible over the bowing bodies. It's parked a few hundred yards away. I need to reach it immediately.

I take a tentative step in the direction of the platform. The drones shuffle aside to make room. There's no question that they think I'm their Monk. *After all, why wouldn't they?* They've been drugged to accept whatever they are told. My inexplicable disappearance and reappearance doesn't seem to trouble them. But I don't want to do anything wrong and tip them off about my true identity.

Overhead, the feeler begins moving away. Liam and Gadya must be pulling it back over the trees so it doesn't distract the drones.

I take another step.

Then another.

I begin to fake a deranged kind of confidence, striding forward more quickly. I can only guess how weird I look, wearing Meira's wooden mask and her robes. I feel hot and claustrophobic inside them.

I keep walking. No drones block my path. My mask is enough to convince them. Liam—or anyone—probably could have turned up in the mask and been accepted.

I glance around as I keep walking. I notice that now the heads of a few drones are sticking up. And then a few more. They are starting to rise to their feet behind me.

I'm nearly at the platform now. At any moment, I fear that someone is going to yell out at me. Or challenge me. But no one does.

I keep thinking about what I'm going to say when I reach the microphone. I need to keep control of this army somehow. Get them to put down their spears and bows and then give them the task of finding the gray zone, and freeing everyone before it's too late. I'll have to put it in language that they'll understand.

I reach the Monk's covered platform, and climb up into it. Instantly, six drones rise up from the crowd on either side of it and lift me into the air. I'm startled, but I don't let it show. They hoist the platform onto their shoulders.

As if on cue, the remaining drones stand up too. Everyone faces me, an entire army looking at me for direction.

I search for the microphone. I don't see it. I feel a moment of total panic. I won't be able to tell the drones what to do if I can't talk to them.

But then I see a small black wire, almost hidden in the front of the platform. It sticks out, like a strange, crooked tube. *This must be it.* I tap the end of it once with a fingertip.

And then I flinch, as a loud booming noise explodes out of the speakers hidden beneath me. It's so loud, I feel it vibrate the soles of my boots.

I sink down onto the silk cushions on the platform, adjusting myself. I take hold of the tube-like microphone and bend it into position.

My mind goes blank for a second. I don't know what to say. My very first word could ruin everything. I try to think about Meira and the Monk. What would they say?

I lean forward. "Greetings . . . ," I murmur.

I hear a voice very different from my own emanate from the speakers. It's distorted and guttural. *Just like Meira sounded.* The drones stand there, watching me with their blank faces and eyes.

"I have returned . . . ," I continue. "From the dead." There's no response from the drones. But I take this as a positive sign. I stare around at the masses before me.

I don't feel happy about having this kind of power. It makes me feel sick to my stomach. If these kids weren't susceptible to the new UNA drugs, they would never be acting like this. The power I have is just an illusion. I take a deep breath.

"We must find and travel into the gray zone at once," I declare, struggling to imitate the cadence and speech of Meira and Minister Harka. "We will leave this road the way we came. Continue our journey into the forest." I pause. Still no response.

I keep going. "A task of great importance awaits us inside the gray zone. . . ."

I hear some shuffling sounds now. *Are the drones getting uneasy? Do they even understand what I'm saying?* It's hard to tell.

"This is a task that means eternal life!" I lie.

The crowd keeps shuffling even more. I'm getting increasingly worried, until I see four robed drones dragging someone toward me. Someone with a black hood over his head, and his hands tied behind him with rope.

The crowd parts so that the four drones and their prisoner can reach me. For a second I think it's Dr. Barrett again, but then one of the drones speaks.

"Master," he says. "We found the heathen who fled from us into the sky." His voice is a dull monotone.

I already know who he means.

*David.*

I hide my relief at the fact that he's alive. "Bring him closer!" I instruct. The drone does as I say. "Take off his hood! Undo his hands!"

The drones around him follow my orders.

Within seconds, I'm staring right at David. He's only ten feet away, and he doesn't have his glasses on. His face is bruised, and there's a swelling on his left temple, but his eyes are surprisingly alert. He stares back up at me, squinting. The drones hold him upright.

I have to find a way to let him know who I really am. "David," I say into the microphone.

"Meira," he snaps right back.

I'm shocked.

*So he knew who the Monk was all along?*

I don't know what to say for a moment. Has he been in league with Meira and the UNA this whole time? But of course he probably isn't on Meira's side, or he wouldn't be tied up right now by the drones.

"I was hoping the feeler killed you," David says. His voice is hoarse. "Maybe it did. Maybe you're Meira's replacement." He squints at me harder.

"Keep talking," I say. I can tell that David hasn't figured out it's me behind the mask. I can't believe he kept his knowledge about Meira secret from us. Why would he do that? Why wouldn't he tell us he knew who the Monk was? Maybe he didn't trust all of us. But yet again, his actions confuse me and make me even more suspicious of him. It's like he's playing the different groups on the wheel off one another. I just don't know why yet—or even if there is a why.

"I wanted you to find me, you know," he continues. "That's why I ran in the first place and left the cathedral."

I stare at him. "You will be punished for running," I manage to say, trying to keep up my façade.

"No, I don't think I will be," he replies. "You see, I've led you and your drones into a trap. It's checkmate time, Meira."

"A trap?" I ask.

"I'm sure you've heard of the travelers. They've been building a secret nomadic army far greater than yours for years. Since kids started getting sent to the wheel. Right now, you are in the heart of their territory, and they knew you would be coming. They've traveled here from all over the wheel. You are completely surrounded." His voice is calm and matter-of-fact.

I can tell that he isn't bluffing.

I want to tear off my mask right then and there, and let him know who I really am. But I can't do that yet—not when we're surrounded by these drones. The mask is the key to my survival.

"Bring him closer," I say sternly to the drones. They obey unhesitatingly. Now David is only three feet away, staring up at me from the base of the platform.

"You only have a few minutes left before the travelers begin their assault," David continues. "You're going to pay for betraying everyone. You're going to—"

"Look into my eyes," I interrupt him hastily. "Look into my eyes!"

There's something about my tone that startles him. He stares up at me more closely, scrutinizing me.

"Look into my eyes, David," I say softly, one final time.

He fixes his eyes on mine. He cranes forward. And then his vision slips into focus.

"Alenna!" he gasps, recognizing me despite the mask. I can see him figuring everything out within a fraction of a second. "Of course! You took Meira's place after the feeler snatched her!"

"Can you call off this attack?" I hiss, covering the microphone with my hand.

"No, it's too late! I had no idea." He sounds frantic. "Make the drones surrender! Tell them not to fight!"

"The specimen archive is set to self-destruct in less than four hours!" I blurt out, as I decide to risk telling him the truth in front of all the drones. "Did you know that? Meira told us. Before she committed suicide."

"Then we have to get there right away! The travelers know a way to free everyone in the archive. They just didn't want to do it until the drones were defeated, in case some of the frozen drones decided to join the new Monk!" David is looking around.

"The battle is going to start soon! The travelers are going to kill everyone!"

"Why now?" I ask him, still covering the microphone. "Why fight after so many years!"

"They were waiting until their numbers were large enough—and for the perfect opportunity. Now they have it."

"Why didn't you tell me this stuff earlier?"

"I just couldn't!"

"Why not? You've made it impossible to trust you!"

"I'll explain when we're safe!"

I grab hold of the microphone as fast as I can. "I have received news," I begin saying into it. "You must put down your weapons right now. Onto the ground. Or toss them off the road."

Without hesitation, the drones begin doing what I commanded. Many of them start laying their weapons down on the concrete. The drones near the edge of the highway simply drop their spears and bows to the underbrush below. I should have told them to do this sooner, but I feared they would resist it.

"It's working!" I whisper to David as I watch in relief. More weapons tumble to the ground and fly off the highway.

But then, a second later, I see something shooting through the air near the edge of the highway. It's a line of sharp grappling hooks on the end of ropes.

*The travelers have arrived.*

We were just a way for them to lure the Monk and the drones to them. Nothing more, and nothing less. Their talk of peace now seems like a ruse.

I see the travelers in their hoofer masks and skins burst up and over the edge of the road. There are thousands of them. Waves of arrows start raining in all directions.

Most of the drones have put down their weapons, but some still have them in their hands. They pause, confused.

An arrow plunges through the roof of my covered platform. I realize that the travelers think that I'm Meira, and they are coming after me.

I reach out for David, but he gets knocked backward by the surging crowd.

At the same moment, my platform is suddenly hoisted up even higher. The drones carrying me start racing forward.

"Surrender!" I yell at them, but the microphone has cut out—maybe because we're moving so fast. They can't hear me anymore, so they keep running. I lose sight of David.

Even though the drones are brainwashed, they're astute enough to defend themselves when attacked. Or maybe this is a plan that was put into place long ago. *A plan to always defend their Monk, no matter what else happens.*

The drones are swarming around me. Rushing me sideways to the edge of the road. They climb on one another's shoulders to provide a human shield. Arrows keep pelting us.

One of the boys carrying my platform is struck right through the chest. He topples backward. The platform lists sideways and almost falls. I cling to it until another drone takes his place and it stabilizes.

I need to get off this platform. There's no way to let the travelers know who I really am. Or to stop them from fighting the drones. I see hordes of travelers clambering over the side of the road. Some of them have climbed up into the few trees higher than the road, and fire arrows down from above. The drones are not so silent now. I hear gasps of pain and screams as they get hit by arrows and sliced by spears.

The platform pauses for a moment as we run into a mass of drones, getting backed up by the travelers in the chaos of the battle. *This is my chance!*

I instantly leap off the platform and into the crowd. I land hard, crashing down on the concrete and tumbling into drones.

The drones try to help me up. I feel their urgent hands on me, trying to bring me to my feet. I brush them off, staggering upward. "Get away from me!" I yell.

They keep coming. Most of them are chattering crazy prayers that sound like evil incantations. They reach out, gently probing me with their fingers. They're desperate to sacrifice their own lives for mine.

"Alenna!" a voice cries out.

I look up, staring through the mask's eyeholes.

David is staggering toward me, followed by a group of travelers. I struggle toward him. The drones around me are engaged in battle now. Travelers with massive iron blades strike them down.

The travelers are already overwhelming the drones. Without a Monk to lead them, or many weapons, the drones are going to get brutally defeated. *Or at least that's what I hope.*

"This way!" David screams. "Follow us!"

I need to rip my mask off now. If I don't, the travelers might accidentally kill me. I reach my hands up and grapple with the straps affixing it to my head. Within seconds, I manage to tear it off.

I push strands of hair back and stare around, gripping the mask tightly in my hand. None of the drones even notice. They're too busy fighting.

"Come with us, Alenna," one of the travelers intones over the noise of the battle, as I reach him and David. Around me now is madness and destruction. The drones and the travelers are locked in combat.

I scramble forward, ducking arrows and blows. I keep the mask in my hand. I don't want to discard it in case I need it later on.

"We have to get off this road!" I call out. It's just a writhing sea of people. All fighting and screaming and scrambling over one another.

I stare up, trying to find the feeler in the sky. I don't see it anywhere. I hope that Liam and Gadya are okay in the forest. Maybe they've already been found by the travelers and rescued. I keep moving toward the side of the road.

If I can survive this battle, then—together with the travelers—we can conquer the drones once and for all. But we still need to reach the specimen archive before it self-destructs. If we don't, then this day will be a victory for the UNA after all. I run faster, determined that this time we are going to win.

# 24_THE PATH TO FREEDOM

WE REACH THE EDGE of the road, and I slam into the low concrete wall. I stare down over the side, peering into the forest to look for Liam and Gadya. Rough hands yank me back from the edge.

"Careful," one of the travelers cautions. But there's no time to be careful.

David is right there next to me. "I should have known you'd do that with the mask," he says, shaking his head. "I passed out again, right after the feeler took Meira. But you could have been killed!"

"Hurry up!" one of the travelers calls out urgently, before I can ask David more questions.

I stare around for Cass and Emma as we race along the side of the highway with the travelers. We can't leave them here on the road. But there's no way to find them in the battle. "Have you seen Cass?" I ask David. He shakes his head.

We keep running. A traveler helps David along; he's weak from his injuries. I keep looking for Cass and Emma, but I don't have any luck. The travelers are now herding the drones toward the center of the highway as they continue their relentless assault. I duck my head and keep moving.

339

Occasional arrows hit concrete nearby and splinter. Spears and blades slam against one another in a clash of metal. I constantly duck.

"Here!" David yells.

We stop moving. I nearly fall into the traveler in front of me. I glance down over the side of the road and see fresh ropes hanging there. I also notice that these ropes have metal loops to hold on to. Loops that grip the rope and control the speed of descent.

Everyone starts grabbing the ropes and getting ready to slide down them. I grab one of the metal links firmly. Then I loop my foot around the rope twice. And I begin sliding down it as fast as I can. David is nearby, hanging on to the back of a traveler.

I hit the bottom thirty seconds later with a crash that knocks the air out of my lungs. I stumble backward and regain my balance. David and the traveler land a few seconds later, slightly more gracefully.

I stand there for a moment, listening to the battle raging above us as I search for Liam and Gadya. The travelers rush around us everywhere in the forest. David and I get caught up in their wake, and we start moving too. Heading toward the trees.

"So what happens now?" I ask as we run. I still don't know if I can fully trust him, or if there are more surprises along the way.

"The travelers conquer the drones," David replies, struggling to keep up.

"Did you always know it was Meira? Behind that mask?"

"Yeah."

"How?"

"The scientists told me they thought she and Veidman were high-level spies, trained for years. It didn't take me long to figure out who was already on the island who could have stepped into

Minister Harka's place so quickly. So I went to her and pretended to be on her side. I offered her information so it seemed like I was spying for her."

"Why didn't you tell me?"

"I was afraid you and Liam would have tried to reason with her."

"That's doubtful."

"I couldn't take the risk."

We keep running.

"I need to get back to Liam," I say. "He's hurt. Gadya's with him. She's hurt too." I look up at the sky. There's no sign of the feeler that transported me onto the road. Maybe it crashed.

"We've done it," David says, pausing for a moment as he struggles for breath. "This battle will be the final major one on the wheel. I mean, there will be skirmishes and stuff, but without the Monk around, the travelers will be able to control the drones and defeat them. Of course we have to get to the archive in time. But we're not that far from the gray zone."

"You sure about that?" I ask.

I startle when there's a thud behind us. I glance and see that the body of a drone, peppered with arrows, has landed a hundred feet away from us. Someone has thrown him off the highway.

We start running again.

"I just don't want to underestimate the UNA," I tell him. "Meira said that the UNA valued the drones. That they wanted to build a new army to invade Australia."

A group of travelers suddenly bursts out of the trees in front of us. David signals to them. They're heading toward the ropes behind us. Probably planning on joining the battle.

Then I see Liam and Gadya in their midst.

"Liam!" I yell, racing straight toward him.

Liam sees me and instantly breaks away from the group.

He runs over to me as fast as he can. I fall into his arms. He grabs me and hugs me tight. I hug him back, pressing him against me.

Then I worry that I'm hurting him. But I see that his wound has already been covered by a bandage, and the arrow has been removed. The travelers have taken good care of him. I hug him tightly again.

We don't say anything. We don't need to. We both know how close we came to never seeing each other again.

"C'mon. I knew you'd be okay," a voice says behind me. I turn and see Gadya standing there, leaning on a stick, feigning nonchalance. "Liam was worried, but I told him you were a fighter. After all, I trained you. How could you not be?"

I smile. She leans in and we hug as well.

"You did it," she whispers.

"For all the good it did," I say. "I didn't know the travelers had their own plan!"

"Me neither. How could we? But if it weren't for you, Meira would have been up there on the road. She definitely would have commanded the drones to massacre everyone. But because you told them to put their weapons down, the travelers got the upper hand, and we're safe. Think about the lives you saved."

When I pull back from Gadya, I see David standing there watching us. "It's time to go," he says.

I glance at Liam. "What's the plan?" I ask.

"Most of us are heading forward into the gray zone," he replies. "It's nearby. But some of the travelers are headed back to make sure everyone gets free from the cathedral. They're going to look for my dad as well."

"The travelers said there's another path into the gray zone from this sector," Gadya adds. "A way to get into a master control tower and free everyone at once. While there's still time. The travelers are going to come with us."

I nod. But something in my gut makes me feel that it can't be this easy.

"We should keep our guard up," I say, gazing around at the group. "Meira gave her life to protect something. There's probably more going on here than we think."

"There always is," Liam agrees.

"So how do we get into the gray zone?" I ask. "I mean, without nearly freezing to death like last time."

"Secret tunnels," David says. His brow furrows a bit. "Or at least that's what the travelers believe. No one's ever been through these exact tunnels before. But apparently they exist, as part of an old subway line that was constructed by the UNA to transport materials when they were building everything on Island Alpha. But we're going to have to go by foot. The subway cars got destroyed a long time ago."

I nod.

"What are we waiting for?" Liam asks, staring around. "We need to go there right now. Let the travelers finish up this battle while we get to the archive. We can thaw out the villagers first."

"I don't know if the travelers will let us do things that way," David says. "I'm not sure if—"

His words are interrupted by a loud rumbling noise nearby. I see a look of surprise flit across his eyes.

"Feelers!" Gadya says, voicing my thoughts. And I know exactly where they're coming from: the chasm where the road is broken. I'd nearly forgotten about them in the fear and excitement of the battle.

I stare up at the sky as feelers begin rising into the air, one after another like a swarm of angry bees. They keep coming. I've never seen so many on the move at once.

I keep looking up, horrified. The feelers are headed straight toward the heart of the battle.

"Who's controlling them?" I yell as travelers around us rush toward the ropes leading up to the road. Prepared to fight and help their fellow warriors.

A couple of them pause and toss us spare knives. The blades are long and sharp. I take one in my hand and grip it firmly. I discard the Monk's mask. "Whose side are the feelers on?" I ask again.

"I don't know!" David yells back.

Liam has taken the black box out. He and David are trying to get it to work, but there are too many feelers in the sky. It's useless right now.

The sky is getting dark with the shadows of these machines. The feelers are ignoring us down here in the trees. They are only focused on the highway. I'm worried about Cass and Emma—not to mention the travelers who are fighting for our freedom.

I see the first few feelers dart down from the sky and pluck kids into their metal embraces. I see drones getting taken, but also travelers as well. The feelers don't seem to be discriminating between the tribes. *Is this some sort of automatic response?* I can't tell.

"The tunnels!" voices are yelling. "To the control tower!" A small contingent of travelers is heading in the opposite direction, away from the road.

344

I feel Liam take hold of my hand. "We have to go now, into the tunnels before the archive self-destructs."

We both start running along with Gadya and David and a group of travelers. I don't know exactly where we're headed in the forest.

Above us come the sounds of the feelers zooming down to snatch up even more kids from the road. I also hear more drones jumping off the highway, landing in the shrubs. Some of them scream in pain as their bones snap from the impact. Some make no sound at all, and I know they might not have survived the fall.

"This way! Faster!" one of the travelers yells at me. He's guiding us, still wearing his hoofer-skin mask.

We race after him as best we can. The feelers are directly overhead now. I'm afraid they're going to start plunging down into the trees and coming after us.

"There! Straight ahead!" Liam calls out to me. "I bet that's it!"

I see what he's staring at. It's a large stone archway built into the side of a low grassy hill. We race toward it, following the travelers. I wonder how many of these tunnels there are. I remember that before the drones blew it up, Liam used to use a tunnel in the blue sector to access the gray zone. But none of us have ever seen this one before, because the purple sector has been controlled by drones for many years.

Soon, we're inside the entryway. It's surprisingly spacious here, like the opening to a large cave. Travelers flood past us. We pause to catch our breath. It's dark, with stone steps that descend downward into musty darkness.

"This must be the old access tunnel to the gray zone, right?" David asks a passing traveler. "I've seen it on maps. The gray zone's not far—"

"Quiet!" the traveler snarls at him. "Maps aren't always made to scale." He stares at us. More of his men surround us. "It's a five-mile hike through these tunnels. At least. And we don't know what's waiting for us inside them. Or at the end. But this is the fastest way into the gray zone and to the control tower."

"What are we waiting for, then?" Liam asks.

We descend the steps rapidly, heading down into the tunnel. The noises of the battle and the feelers grow softer behind us.

"Where does the tunnel open up?" I ask.

One of the travelers glances at me. It's hard to tell them apart because of their hoofer skins and long hair. "Exactly where we need to be," he replies obliquely. Then he turns back and keeps heading down the stairs.

Clearly, the travelers don't trust us. We should be angry at them for lying to us and using us as bait. But I'm just glad to be alive.

"When we hit the bottom of the stairs, we start running," another traveler says.

We keep descending the steps.

They seem to stretch on forever, deeper into the darkness. White stains of efflorescence mark the damp stone walls.

Finally, we reach the bottom.

The tunnel is large and spherical here. I see subway tracks in the center, but they're corroded and covered in a layer of water. In fact, the whole bottom of the tunnel is flooded by about a foot of stale liquid.

"Those tracks aren't live, are they?" a traveler asks. "I don't want to get electrocuted."

"No. I'm sure they've been dead for years," someone else answers, sloshing down into the water without hesitation.

346

A few travelers start lighting dim lanterns. It's nearly impossible to see even with these lights, but I'm guessing that they don't want to risk using any bright lights unless they have to.

Liam and I reach the bottom of the stairs, and we step into the water. It smells awful, like raw sewage, or runoff from the wheel. I feel it soak through my boots instantly, making my feet cold.

I hear more footsteps coming down the stairs behind us. More travelers.

"Let's go save Rika, Markus, and everyone else!" Gadya bellows as she starts running forward, despite her injured leg.

Liam and I follow closely behind, weapons raised.

Our feet churn through the water. I glance back and see David lagging.

"Liam," I say, touching his arm. We both pause for a moment so that David can catch up. We need him and his knowledge to help free the archive. And we've also lost so many friends, I don't want to lose track of any more. I wish I'd been able to find Cass and Emma on the highway. *What if they didn't survive?*

As we continue running, I ask Liam, "You think this could be a trap?"

"Maybe."

"What if Meira told us we had four hours until the archive self-destructed, but it's going to blow up as soon as we get there?"

"Then we just have to get there faster than she thought we could."

"The bombs could be automated," David speaks up next to me. "Like the feelers. Our arrival at the archive could actually be what sets off its destruction. We have to tell the travelers to be careful."

"How do you even know the travelers so well?" Liam asks.

"I knew about them from rumors in my resistance cell. And

then I heard stories about ghosts on this part of the road while I was in the drones' camp. So I put two and two together. But when I landed that feeler on the road, I'd never actually met them before. They instantly understood how I could be useful to them, once they saw the black box and I told them about Meira."

I hear more and more travelers sloshing in the tunnel around us. I think of the freezing cold temperatures in the gray zone, and I shudder. It's cool down here in the tunnels, but nowhere near what it's going to be like in the zone. And this time we don't have any protection against the cold.

My only hope is that the tunnel opens into some kind of protected building. If it just opens into the gray zone outside somewhere, we'll freeze to death.

We keep running. Endlessly, down the wide tunnel. I wonder if we'll even be able to tell when we pass underneath the barrier to the gray zone. Probably not.

We just have to reach the control tower and free everyone before it self-destructs. If we can do that, then our mission will have been a success. *No more Monk. No more archive. No more different tribes fighting one another when we should be united in fighting the UNA.*

I wonder where the feelers will take the kids they capture, after the specimen archive is destroyed. Or perhaps they're programmed to self-destruct too. If they aren't, they'll eventually run out of power. Or else they'll be struck down from the sky by us, one by one. They might snatch a few more kids along the way, but their days ruling the skies will be over.

We keep running. My chest is heaving. My heart feels like it's about to burst. But I know we can't stop to rest now, not even for a second.

Liam is helping David along. Gadya is a few paces ahead of us. I just hope that we reach the gray zone soon.

But it's then that the first terrifying screams begin. And I hear the sound of travelers yelling in surprise—as something begins darting from the shadows and skittering across the water, down here with us in the darkness.

# 25_UNDERNEATH

I INSTANTLY STOP MOVING. So does Liam. He swings his body sideways to protect me. The water is churning all around us.

I realize that we're not alone. That something unseen is down here in the tunnels with us. I raise my blade. Liam does the same.

"Great," Gadya mutters.

David staggers sideways. Travelers are calling out to one another. I also hear more strange sloshing noises in the dark.

"What going on?" Liam calls out.

"I don't know!" a traveler yells back. "We didn't think anything was down here. No feelers. No machines—"

I hear the noises again. Eerie, chittering, cackling sounds.

"It's not feelers," I say dismally, staring into the darkness. These sounds are too raw and animalistic to be coming from machines. "It's drones."

"Drones?" David asks. "One's who've gone rogue?"

"No. Drones who aren't wanted," I say, in a moment of sudden realization.

This whole time it has bothered me that the drones all seemed so similar. I'd remembered them as a diverse group. Now I realize that some of them—probably the craziest ones who couldn't be controlled—might have been weeded out by Meira. *The 5 percent that the new drugs don't work on.* They might have been banished and sent far away, to a place where they couldn't cause any trouble. A place just like these tunnels.

Liam looks at me in the dim light. "What do you mean? Tell me."

"Gadya and I fought a huge girl last time we were on the wheel— nearly a mutant. And we saw a few kids like that at Minister Harka's camp. I think they'd been physically affected by the drugs here, or even back in the UNA." I pause. "But didn't you notice how uniform the drones seem now? How placid?"

Liam nods in agreement. "The drugs couldn't work perfectly on everyone. There had to be some kids who didn't fit in. Who stayed completely wild. Makes sense."

David stares into the darkness. "And now they're down here with us?"

For once, I can tell that something has taken him by surprise. It's clear he didn't know about this. Meira must have kept it from him. And now these crazy drones are going to form a human blockade between us and the control tower in the gray zone. If we can't get past them in time, then the specimen archive is going to self-destruct after all.

"We're going to have to fight them off," Gadya says.

"No problem," I say, sounding braver than I feel.

Gadya hoists up her spear. "Just another day on the wheel, right?" She forces a smile in the gloom.

Suddenly, I see a blazing flash of orange light. I shield my eyes. One of the travelers has lit a flare. I didn't even know that the travelers had any. He's standing about fifty feet ahead of us in the tunnel. I glance up and freeze.

"Hell no . . ." Gadya breathes.

I see that we are far from alone in the tunnel. Facing us down is a group of terrifying-looking drones, hissing and snarling. All of them look sick from the Suffering, pockmarked with bloody sores. But they also look completely insane.

I instantly know that my theory was right. These are the outcast drones. These are the drones that couldn't even be controlled by Meira and the new drugs. There are hundreds of them, staring at us angrily. Maybe thousands. They would be useless as part of an army attacking Australia, or anywhere else. But here in the tunnel to the gray zone, they work perfectly in preventing any progress. Meira put them here on purpose.

I see a couple of travelers already lying facedown in the water. Blood pools out from their bodies.

It's clear that we won't be able to reason with these drones. When Meira took control of the drones, she must have exiled any kids who didn't fit. *Just like the UNA exiled us when they sent us to the wheel.*

One of the nearby drones growls, displaying his pointed teeth. He's huge and menacing, with rippling muscles. But I see that his mottled flesh is rotting with infected sores. None of the kids have weapons, but their teeth and fingernails are razor sharp. They stare back at us, the light of the flare reflected in their dilated pupils.

The light seems to be keeping them at bay. But I know that this flare will burn out soon.

"Charge!" one of the travelers yells, as the flare starts to flicker.

A moment of pure silence follows his words. Our only option is to keep moving forward. We can't go back because of the feelers.

The travelers start rushing forward through the water, heading straight at the drones. The tunnel is plunged into near darkness again as the flare sputters out, and we rely only on lamplight.

"Stay next to me!" Liam says, clutching his blade. I hold my long knife up too, just like Gadya taught me.

I hear screaming. Something thuds into me and I instinctively leap back, swinging out hard with my blade. But I don't catch anything—only empty space.

"Keep moving!" voices yell.

We race forward in the near darkness. I see a traveler trying to light another flare, but it's knocked from his hands by a large drone who leaps onto his back. Both the traveler and the flare go into the water. The drone holds the traveler's head down, trying to drown him. We sweep past them, unable to take the time to stop and help.

I hear the voices of the drones cackling and wailing. The drones keep coming at us relentlessly.

A crazed girl with a shaved head claws at me with her fingernails. I knock her back with my elbow, and she stumbles into the shadows, babbling to herself. It's like they've lost the capacity for speech. Their minds have rotted, just like their bodies.

"Don't stop, no matter what," Liam says. We're at each other's side.

I glance back for David. He's several yards behind us, keeping low to the water. "David, come on!" I call out. "Hurry up." He hears me and moves faster, heading toward us.

A traveler gets another flare lit behind us. Its orange glow illuminates the horrific scene. I see a drone crouched over the body of a traveler, using his pointed teeth to tear at the traveler's neck.

353

It's like watching an animal rather than a fellow human being. These drones seem possessed with fury.

I glance up and see even more of them heading our way. *How many could there even be down here?* Somehow, we have to get past them. I don't know how we're going to do it.

We keep pushing forward. The water is deeper in places, and the base of the tunnel is uneven. My feet sink into holes at least half a foot deep, making me stumble and nearly twist an ankle.

I see a huge, crazed boy lumbering out of the shadows right at Liam.

"Liam, look out!" I yell.

A second later, the boy throws himself on us.

I lash out with my blade. It hits the boy across his bare chest, slicing into his skin. He goes spinning sideways, falling into the water with a scream and a splash.

Another drone darts out at us. This one is thin and lean. His emaciated body is covered with weeping sores. His pointed teeth are bared, like fangs. He hisses at us like a snake and then leaps right at me. I hit him with my blade, and he plunges down, flailing in the water. Liam and I rush forward again.

But this thin drone won't leave me alone. I hear splashing sounds. A second later, tight fingers grab my ankle like a vise. I gasp in surprise and stumble, falling onto all fours in the toxic water. It sprays up, splattering my face.

I kick out with my boot, hitting the drone's face and knocking him backward.

"Liam!" I yell. He turns around to help.

But the drone leaps onto me before Liam can reach me. The drone is screeching as he scrabbles up my body, trying to push my head down into the water. I fight back as hard as I can, getting to my knees. Water gets into my mouth and makes me retch.

I fling my elbows backward, trying to hit him in the face again.

Then he's tumbling off me. Liam has slashed him across the face with his blade. The drone topples into the water, bleeding.

I stand up, grabbing Liam.

Before we can even move forward, the drone is up again, startling both of us with his demented vigor.

This time he goes straight for Liam, moving with surprising speed. His face is contorted into a mask of madness. Blood drips down his forehead from where Liam cut him to the bone.

He slams into Liam, gnashing and clawing at him. Liam hammers at him with his fists and with his blade.

I rush forward. If I don't do something, then this drone is going to hurt Liam. I lunge and stab the drone in his side, plunging the blade to its hilt.

With a howl of pain, the drone relents and lets go. He drops back down into the water, clutching the bleeding wound.

Liam and I rush away from the drone as fast as we can. I glance back and see him hobbling off in the other direction, into the darkness. Behind him and around us, travelers continue doing battle with these banished drones. The drones are screaming and grunting, but they keep attacking.

It's like they can't help it. Like they've lost any self-control.

More of them burst from the shadows.

If they continue to assault us like this, they're going to be able to halt our progress. And then everyone in the specimen archive is doomed.

"Up ahead!" Gadya calls out. "There's more of them!"

The travelers are being overwhelmed by the drones now. There are just too many of them here in the dark. They're slowing us down.

Liam and I race forward, fighting our way past them. I glance back to make sure David is with us. I see him staggering along in our wake.

"This way!" Liam yells, pointing at a gap in the horde of drones. We plunge into it, fighting to keep their claws and teeth away from us.

I keep running side by side with Liam. My only thought is that we need to keep going. If we stop even for a moment, I know that we'll be killed.

Finally, we reach a bend in the tunnel. A traveler sets off another flare. This one is blue, and it casts an eerie light. I stare around in despair. More crazed drones lunge forward. Others scuttle back and forth in the shadows, growling.

The travelers thin out here. The drones have decimated their numbers.

"It's getting worse!" Gadya cries.

I'm still gasping for air. We've run a terrifying gauntlet—one that doesn't seem to have an end.

"Don't stop!" Liam calls out. "The drones are following us!"

I glance back. He's right. As we continue to move through the tunnels, the drones give chase. So we keep racing through the water.

"You okay?" Liam asks, as he swings his blade, knocking a drone out of our path.

I nod. "Barely! You?"

"Yeah." I look at him and see that his bandage has come undone. The wound from the arrow is leaking blood again. "You're bleeding!"

"I'll be fine." He glances at my arms. "You're cut too."

I look down and see deep lacerations across my left forearm. Probably from where the thin feral drone gouged me with his fingernails. "I'm fine," I tell Liam, not wanting to waste any time.

Drones flood from the shadows. Terrifying figures that keep lashing out. I stare ahead down the tunnel as we race forward, swinging our weapons. "You think we'll make it?"

"We better hurry."

As we keep moving, I feel like it's getting lighter in the tunnel. It remains gray and dim, but it's a little easier to see. The light isn't coming from torches or flares. It's just like the level of ambient light has increased in general. And then, finally, as we turn another bend, I see some kind of light source up ahead of us.

Liam sees it too. "That could be the exit! Could be our way into the gray zone."

"It's getting colder," I point out, realizing that the temperature has dropped by several degrees.

Gadya reaches my side. "I must have killed twenty drones!" she mutters. "They're relentless. And they're still on our tail!"

I point at the light up ahead as we run. My joints ache. But we're moving forward.

I see a few remaining travelers ahead of us running forward too. They're calling back and forth to one another. I can't believe our group has been whittled down so quickly. There are fewer than ten of them left ahead of us.

"This is it!" one of them yells, turning back to us. Before we can ask him any questions, he just plows forward again.

We follow him and the others, heading toward the light in the distance. I can see now that it's embedded in the side of the tunnel, like some kind of opening in the stone wall.

It's definitely colder now. The air has a distinct crisp chill to it, and it smells fresher. The farther we go, the colder it keeps getting. We turn another slight bend.

When we finally reach the opening, it's not what I expected. Instead of stairs and a stone archway leading outside, there's a metal hatch. *Like the ones I remember from the specimen archive.* The hatch door is hanging wide open.

Beyond the hatch, I see a spiral staircase encased inside a cylinder of thick, curved glass. It looks as though the hatch leads into this strange, vertical glass structure. The stairs only head in one direction. Upward.

We race after the handful of travelers, a few steps behind them. I don't want to get caught by the crazed drones again. I can hear them in the tunnel battling the remaining travelers behind us.

"Where does this thing go?" Gadya yells from behind me and Liam. She's running next to David.

None of the travelers reply. Either they don't know or they're not saying.

I plunge through the hatch with Liam and onto the metal stairs. The air is much colder inside the glass tube. I'm hoping this is a good sign—that it means we're back inside the gray zone. But I also don't want to get hypothermia before we can free everyone.

I stare up at the staircase. I can see the stairs continuing on forever, past the feet of the travelers. I don't see a ceiling to the tube, although I know there must be one.

We start hiking, climbing faster and faster. The constant turning is making me feel dizzy. I stare out the glass, which so far, just shows a dim, gray blankness.

Then we rise above the level of the earth, and a harsh landscape comes into view. Even though it's cloudy outside, the brightness is overwhelming. I blink fiercely, desperate to see where we are.

"The gray zone!" Liam says. "We made it."

I stare out as we keep moving. Beyond the thick glass of the cylinder is the grim landscape that I remember all too well. I see sprawling industrial buildings and huge white pipes connecting everything.

There are no trees anywhere or signs of wildlife, only concrete and steel. The buildings look in even more disrepair than the last time I was here. There are gaping holes in the sides of some of them. Cracks in the concrete. And just as before, everything is clearly abandoned.

"I don't see the specimen archive!" I blurt out. There's no sign of that huge white and silver building that houses the frozen occupants.

"We might be inside part of it already," Liam replies.

"But this doesn't look like the archive," Gadya says, now a pace behind us with David. "Not like I remember."

"Could be a different section of the zone," I say. "We don't know what part the control tower is in."

"Let's just hope the travelers know where they're going," Liam says. Then softer, he whispers back as we climb, "If things go wrong, let's meet back here. On these stairs. We can even hide out in the tunnels for a while if we have to. Keep going forward, wherever they lead."

I nod. "What about the drones?" I can hear their howls beneath us. I wonder if they'll follow us right up the stairs.

"We avoid them if we can. Fight them if we can't."

"Sounds like a plan," Gadya says.

The higher we go, the more I can see of the gray zone. I see the ocean now, stretching out beyond the buildings and the rocky shore. And then the jungle, and beyond that, the sixty-foot barrier marking one side of the zone's perimeter. But there's still no sign of the specimen archive. Maybe we really are already inside some strange wing of it.

We continue moving upward. I feel scared and nervous about what we're going to discover up here. The last time I was inside a building in this zone, miniature feelers attacked me and Liam, right after I rescued him. For all I know, they might be waiting at the top of the stairs for us now.

Below us, the drones are clamoring. I wonder if they've entered the hatch and the stairwell. It sounds like they have.

I think about Clara—that strange computer program that controlled everything last time I was in the gray zone. Clara tried to block me from rescuing Liam. I can only hope that somehow she's been shut down, but I fear that she hasn't.

"Faster! Faster!" Gadya yells from behind me. There's real panic in her voice now.

For a moment, I wonder if our journey back to the gray zone was worth it. Every single thing we planned along the way has gone wrong. It's like we were doomed from the beginning.

But then I think about Rika, Markus, and everyone else frozen in the archive. If Liam or I were in there, we would want someone to come and rescue us. Those kids' lives depend on us. And we also need them to join us in our mission to take back the wheel and fight the UNA.

I hear travelers above calling out to us:

"Move it!"

"C'mon!"

"Go!"

I take a deep breath and tell myself that even if we fail, we've done more to affect the UNA than any other group of exiles in history. I grab Liam's hand, and we keep moving upward.

# 26 THE TOP

LIAM AND I EVENTUALLY reach the top of the spiral stairs. I'm freezing now. My teeth are chattering, and my skin feels numb. I can hear the drones howling and screaming below us. They're in the stairway. Soon, they will reach us.

Gadya steps out behind us. Her knife is covered with blood. David steps out next to her. I gaze around and see that the spiral stairs have led us into a large, circular domed structure, with a ceiling made from sheets of foot-thick glass. Above us are clouds and gray skies. This must be the control tower.

On the walls, I see computer screens flashing with blue streams of data. Cracked leather seats sit in front of them, long abandoned. Unlike the observation deck that Gadya and I discovered the last time we were in the gray zone, this place has none of the harsh utilitarianism of the archive. Everything here looks like it was once plush. The kind of place that the UNA's elite might have once come to visit.

I look more closely at the numbers and letters on the screens. They are all the same. It's like a countdown, repeated over and over. But it's in some kind of code, so I can't figure out what it means. The travelers rush over to the computer keypads beneath the screens.

"How do we know this is the right place?" I ask Liam.

"We don't," David says. Gadya has helped him farther into the control room. "But it's the most obvious one."

"Why?" I ask.

"It's the highest point. From here, complete destruction of the specimen archive could be orchestrated. It could even be observed if someone wanted to watch, although I think the place is abandoned except for us."

"Wait—I thought we might be in the specimen archive."

David shakes his head. "No. Look." He points. Far from us, way down below, I finally see the massive roof of the archive. "The archive is probably filled with hidden explosives—maybe even placed there when it was first constructed, in case of an emergency. But the controls that detonate it will be someplace distant. Like in this tower. That's why the travelers have led us here instead of directly to the archive."

Out the windows, I see dots in the sky. Distant feelers. Perhaps they're part of the contingent attacking the highway. Or maybe they know that we're up here, and they're circling around to get us.

I glance over and see the travelers still at the computer terminals. There are only six travelers in the room with us now. The others are on the stairs, defending us.

The travelers at the computers punch numbers into keypads, but nothing happens.

"It's not working!" one of them yells to another.

The screens continue streaming with data.

I hear a clattering sound, as well as deranged howls. The crazed drones are getting closer. I rush over to the stairway with Liam to help guard it. Gadya is right there with us.

362

I glance back and see that the countdown, or whatever it is, hasn't slowed.

The travelers keep calling back and forth to one another. They sound desperate.

"The controls are locked!" one of them calls out.

Then there's a loud electrical crackling sound, like a clap of thunder inside the room. A flare of white light bursts from the computer consoles, and their screens go black.

I stagger back, almost falling down the stairs. Gadya grabs my arm, and I hold on to her.

"What was that?" she yells.

I smell smoke. "I don't know!"

Liam is at my side. "You okay?"

I cough. "Yeah. What happened?"

I glance over at the travelers. To my horror, they are no longer on the seats. Their bodies are lying on the floor. One of them is twitching.

David stands there, like he's afraid to move. "I think it was a booby trap," he says. "An electric charge. Designed to electrocute anyone trying to tamper with the computers."

We look around at one another. None of the travelers is moving. I'm not sure whether they're dead or just unconscious. *Either way, it's just us now.* We yell down at the travelers on the stairs, telling them we need help, but they're too busy fighting the drones to hear us.

Then the computer screens flare to life again. Now I'm expecting the worst. I'm terrified that somehow we'll see a masked figure on them—a new Monk laughing at us. For a moment, I see only static. But then, a second later, a familiar face appears, gazing out at us with eyes that look so much like my own.

"Mom!" I cry out, shocked and confused.

"Can you hear me?" my mother asks as her image flickers and bends. Behind her, I see the shadowy figures of other scientists, ones I recognize from Destiny Station. And I also see the distinct tiled walls of Southern Arc. *She made it to the base.*

"Yes! Help us!" I can't believe this is happening.

"Are you safe?"

"Barely—there's just a few of us left! And drones are chasing us!"

"How are you talking to us?" Liam asks her.

"Our radios picked up the self-destruct sequence going into motion and we were able to cut into the video and audio feed. We can talk to each other, but we can't stop the sequence. You don't have much longer."

"Are there any more booby traps?" David calls out.

"No," my mother says. "We couldn't stop the electric discharge from the computers. That was manually set years ago, when the gray zone was evacuated."

I watch her, torn between the desire to know what she's going to say, and my fear of the drones coming up the stairs.

"Speak fast!" Gadya adds. "Please! The drones will be here soon!"

"Tell us what to do," I say to my mom. "How do we save everyone, or make the archive stop from self-destructing?"

The pounding on the stairs grows even louder. I can clearly hear the footsteps of the drones overrunning the travelers. And out the windows, I see that the black dots in the sky have grown larger. The feelers are heading our way as well.

"Mom, what do we do?" I call out again. "We're out of time!"

I hear the first of the drones reach the landing. I turn. He's standing there, hands stretched out with nails like claws. He's growling. It's an awful, subhuman sound. The sound of complete madness.

Liam is at my side, ready to strike down the drone.

"The drones are here!" I yell out to my mom. The signal on the screen is weakening for a moment. I don't know if she can hear me.

David is crouching down by the computer consoles now. They are completely fried, leaking wisps of smoke.

"Help us!" Gadya yells at the flickering computer screens.

More drones appear on the stairs. We're trapped up here. I glance back at the monitors on the walls. My mother's face has reappeared. I can see the fear in her eyes. And I see the scientists behind her moving around more urgently.

"There's an emergency exit that leads into the computer cooling and maintenance tunnels," she says to us quickly. "Go! I'll be able to talk to you inside. There's another monitor in there."

"I don't see an exit!" I yell back at her. Gadya and I start looking around desperately as Liam fends off the drones.

"Press the wall between the two center screens," my mom says.

Gadya and I do what she tells us. A section of the wall between the screens slides open with a hiss.

None of us needs a second to think about it.

We plow through the narrow opening, sliding into the maintenance tunnel. It's cool and dry in here, and the tunnel is small and round. The walls are made of metal. Liam hits a red button on the wall, and the door slides shut. Then he hammers the button with his knife, disabling it and knocking the button sideways. This means we might be trapped in here. But it also means the door is closed off to the drones.

We crouch there for a moment, breathing heavily.

The tunnel isn't tall enough to stand up in. In fact, where we are right now is just some sort of vestibule for the maintenance tunnels. Three of them sprawl off in different directions heading down and away from here, behind half-open hatches. They look small and dark, like burrows. They are lit only by green emergency lights.

I feel terrified—but at least we are still alive. I faintly hear the drones clamoring outside. More of them are in the control room now.

I look around for a computer monitor and see a small one bolted onto the wall. It's dead.

"Mom?" I call out.

Only silence answers.

"Hello?" David asks.

There's no reply.

"What do we do?" Gadya asks.

"We stay calm," Liam says.

I slam my hand against the monitor, willing it to come to life. Faint crackling static emanates from it, although its screen is dark.

"Alenna . . . Liam . . ." my mom's faint voice says. "Are you there? Are you all right?"

"Yes!" I yell back at her, as we gather around the monitor. "We're in the maintenance tunnel. The drones are blocked off from us, at least for now."

My mom starts talking rapidly again. "The way to stop the self-destruct sequence is to journey down one of these tunnels and disable the entire archive, by destroying its cooling mechanisms. That's the only thing that will stop the archive from being destroyed, and it will also automatically trigger a controlled release of the pods—freeing everyone who has been captured and frozen."

I eye the long, sinister maintenance tunnels.

"It will be a very dangerous journey," my mom's voice continues. "If you want to change your mind, the tunnel farthest to your left leads down and out, into maintenance tunnels beneath the observation tower that go underneath the barrier and out of the gray zone. But if you want to continue, then the tunnel in the center is the one that you need." My mom pauses. "I'll be proud of you all, no matter what choice you make."

Liam and I look at each other. A sudden banging on the door startles us. The drones know where we are and they still want to get us.

"Tell us more," I say.

David is staring into the tunnels, past their half-open hatches.

"I don't know if you have weapons, but you don't need them," my mom continues. "Just continue down the center tunnel, without stopping. You'll eventually reach the cooling center. You will see the neutron-chemical generator for the gray zone. It's a series of metal and glass pipes around a silver sphere. You must smash and disrupt this core. You must destroy it with anything you can." She pauses again, her voice breaking with emotion. "The core is filled with dangerous chemicals. You're going to have to smash it and then run back into the tunnel and close the hatch. You won't have long. One mistake, and you'll be overwhelmed by fumes." She pauses. "But if you succeed, everything will instantly cease working. The core is the Achilles heel of the specimen archive and the wheel."

"Are you asking us to sacrifice our lives?" Gadya says. She isn't angry. Her voice just sounds flat.

"No," my mom says. "You know that I could never do that, especially with my own daughter involved. But whichever one of you smashes the core is in the most direct danger. And there's a chance that even if you move fast, things will go wrong."

I'm about to speak. About to say that we'll do it—that we've come this far and would never give up now. That we can move fast and avoid the chemicals.

But suddenly, David ducks his head and starts racing forward on his hands and knees toward the center tunnel. I instantly realize what he's doing.

"No!" I yell. "David! Wait!"

Liam sees David too, and grabs at him, trying to get his ankle. But David has caught us by surprise. I didn't think he could move so fast.

"Stop!" Gadya screams, lunging after him.

We try to reach him, but he slips through our fingers, his momentum carrying him forward.

*It's too late to stop him.*

David grabs on to the center hatch and flings it all the way open. And then he dives into the center tunnel, slamming the hatch shut behind him as quickly as he can, and locking it.

"No!" I scream, kicking at the metal when I reach the hatch.

Liam races forward and tries to open the hatch, pulling on it with all his strength. But the handle won't budge.

"David, what are you doing?" I yell, horrified.

Through a thin glass slit in the metal hatch, I can see his eyes looking back at us. They look frightened but determined.

"What's happening in there?" my mother's voice cries out in a blast of static. But there's no time to answer her.

"David, stop this!" I call out to him.

"I took an oath . . ." His voice drifts back to us, as we cluster around the closed hatch. "In the resistance cell. To give my life when and if the right time came. For me, this is the time. But none of you needs to die or get hurt."

"David, no!" I cry out, tears flooding my eyes. "This isn't the right way! What are you doing? We can work together!"

"We need to talk about this," Liam calls out. "Think it through!"

"Please—" Gadya says.

"No," David answers firmly. He stares out at us, his eyes looking back and forth. I see the certainty in them. "This is what I have to do. There's no time for debate. If I do this and destroy the cooling core, my mission will be complete. . . ." He turns and glances behind him, as though he's preparing to leave. "I will have sacrificed everything I have to give. I will have proven where I stand."

"You don't need to prove anything!" I yell.

"Maybe I do, to myself."

"Mom!" I yell out. "David has gone into the tunnel and locked the hatch! He's going to do it on his own!"

I don't hear a response. Only static. The connection has been lost.

I bang my fist against the metal hatch door, feeling total disbelief. David is going to sacrifice himself to save us all. *Did we drive him to do this? By always questioning his motives?* I know that none of the others ever trusted him as much as I did, but even I lost faith in him for a while. But it doesn't have to be this way. "David! Come back!"

Gadya starts yelling too. This is happening too fast. We hammer on the metal until our hands are raw. Liam is right there too, yanking at the handle again.

David turns back around for a final time. His eyes find mine.

"Just don't forget what I did." His muffled voice echoes down the tunnel. "Don't let anyone say that I was a traitor. Let them know that I was on the right side all along, no matter what it looked like."

"Of course! David, I—"

"Keep me in your thoughts, Alenna," he murmurs. "You've always been in mine."

And then, stunning me, he turns his back on us and disappears into the darkness of the tunnel.

"No!" I scream out. I throw myself against the hatch.

It's almost too much to bear. And I could have stopped him somehow. Any one of us could. If only we'd known what he was going to do.

"He's gone," Liam says, holding me from behind. I'm sobbing. I can't help it. I don't want David to die.

"We could have gone together!" I cry. "We could have found another way! All of us!" I kick at the hatch. "David!" I scream one final time. But there's no response. David is gone.

I don't hear my mom's voice anymore either. I wonder if she's continuing to give David instructions, farther along the tunnel. But possibly not. The radio signal most likely just cut out. I feel like I'm going to throw up. It wasn't meant to end like this.

"What do we do now?" I ask.

Liam hugs me. Then he says softly, "We go back down and get out of the gray zone. And we hope that David succeeds."

Three hours later, I sit on the rocks outside the barrier to the gray zone, next to Gadya. We've made it out of the zone, through a complex network of maintenance tunnels. Hundreds of travelers now surround us everywhere.

They were victorious on the highway, and now they have come to assist us. And to liberate the inhabitants of the archive as well.

When we came out of the tunnel an hour ago, I saw a surreal sight. Feelers were falling out of the sky, plummeting straight down to the earth. Their whistling, screaming noises sounded almost human to me. They crashed down into the jungle around us, splintering trees as they fell.

It was then I knew that David had succeeded—both in stopping the self-destruct sequence and in automatically releasing the captured kids from the pods. Everything mechanical was coming to a halt, including the feelers, which must have been controlled by computers in the gray zone as some kind of automatic defense system.

*It was also when I knew that David was probably dead.*

None of us said anything.

For me, it was too painful.

I just staggered out of the tunnel opening next to Liam and Gadya, and into a large cleared area of the forest outside the gray zone.

Now, Gadya and I sit here on rocks, resting and watching everyone. Liam is helping the travelers guide shivering kids from the archive out of the tunnel, despite his own injuries.

I stare at these dazed kids shambling out of the gray zone through the tunnel. The travelers are draping them in their spare hoofer skins. Most of these kids look so shell-shocked that they're not causing any trouble. Only a few drones are violent, and they are easily restrained by the travelers.

I should feel victorious. But I just feel empty inside. David is dead. I cling to any shred of hope I have, but there's no sign of him. By going alone, he made sure we weren't in danger, but he sacrificed his own life to do it.

I glance over at Gadya. "I wish David were here," I murmur. "He fought for this day as much as we did."

"He escaped from the feelers once," Gadya says, trying to make sense of it. "When it didn't seem like there was any hope. Maybe he'll manage to survive again."

I nod. "This time feels different."

"I know."

We fall silent again.

I watch Liam. More than anything, I'm grateful that I still have him. Against the odds, we have both survived this terrible day.

The wheel is now ours. We are planning on heading back to the cathedral in the forest soon, to try to find Octavio and rescue the scientists—at least the ones who've survived. The travelers are also going to try to find Dr. Barrett and free him. With the specimen archive emptied, and the feelers defunct, we will soon be in total control.

From here we can build a new army and eventually mount an attack on the continental UNA. Just like we always planned.

Although the vessels that brought us here have been destroyed, I've heard the travelers talking among themselves. The plan is now to use the old, massive UNA airplanes in the gray zone— the kind that Liam and I once hijacked—to eventually transport us back to the continental UNA. According to the travelers, there are a lot of technological resources left on the wheel, both in the gray zone and hidden elsewhere on the island. If we can free the scientists from the cathedral, they will work to set up a defense system to protect the island from any bombs or missiles. I hope they can also somehow synthesize a new batch of antidote pills to help cure the drones and the Ones Who Suffer.

Most of the details of what happens next are being kept secret from us by the travelers. At least until the wheel is under control. But we've learned from the travelers that they believe the resistance cells inside the continental UNA are in communication with the scientists at Southern Arc already. Rebels living secretly inside the UNA will help us arrive, and we will attack the UNA from within simultaneously as we attack from without. Apparently, conditions in the UNA have worsened since I left it. The populace is rebelling against the endless wars with other nations, and against the increasingly harsh laws mandated by the government.

Hopefully, the UNA will crumble when we return, as its own citizens join us and fight back in an attempt to restore democracy. It's a risky plan but at least we have a chance. Still, I know we have a long way to go before we succeed in conquering the UNA for good. And taking over Island Alpha is the first step.

"We did it," I say to Gadya. "We won the battle, at least for now."

She gazes at me with haunted eyes. "I know. I just hope it was worth it."

I stare back at the streams of dazed kids flooding from the gray zone. "They don't even know that they owe their lives to David's sacrifice."

I scan the crowds, watching the different faces emerge.

Then, suddenly, I see a familiar figure appear from the tunnel. A short, freckled girl with her hair in braids. She's being led along by Liam. They're headed in our direction. I'm so startled that I can barely say her name.

I just point.

"Rika!" Gadya gasps when she sees the girl.

We stand up and begin waving wildly at our friend. We rush

over to her and Liam. She sees us, and her face lights up at once. She doesn't have her glasses on, but I can tell that she has instantly recognized me and Gadya.

"Look who I found," Liam says, smiling, as we reach them.

"Alenna! Gadya!" Rika says. "I never thought I'd see you two again!"

We hug her.

"I knew you'd come and rescue me," she says.

"You did not," Gadya retorts.

"I'm so glad you're alive," I tell Rika, shutting my eyes for a moment.

Then I lean back, searching for Cass and Emma in the crowd, and Markus as well, but I see no sign of them yet. If they survived, then we need to find them too. I'm hoping that Cass and Emma turn up soon with the travelers from the road.

"How long was I asleep for?" Rika asks us. "I'm starving!"

Gadya and I exchange a glance. "Not too long," I say to Rika. I figure there'll be plenty of time to tell her the truth later on.

I stare out at the line of kids. It's growing with every moment. By never giving up, and being willing to sacrifice our own lives, we have succeeded in taking over the wheel. But I also know that this is the start of a larger battle. One in which we must defeat the UNA on its home turf.

I know that between us kids, the scientists, the rebels, and the travelers, we can find a way. But first, we must return the drones to sanity—if we even can—and recover our strength before moving forward.

I lean against Liam. I feel his arms wrap around me. He kisses the top of my head. We don't say any words. There is nothing to say right now. I watch Rika talking to Gadya excitedly.

I know that we will keep fighting until we overturn the government, or die in the process. Where there was once just a handful of us, now there are thousands.

The UNA should be more afraid of us than we are of it. They have more power and resources, but we have the passion and the desire for vengeance. I refuse to let David's death be in vain. Not only have we conquered the UNA's main prison colony, we've killed the leader of it—twice over. Nothing can stand in our way now.

I gaze out at the kids in front of me, wishing David could be here to share this moment. Soon, we will return to the UNA. Soon, we will take back the country that was stolen from us, and put it back into the hands of the people. Where it has always belonged.

"I'm ready for whatever happens next," I murmur to Liam. Then I tilt my head back and glance up at him. Our eyes lock. "I'm ready for war."

Don't miss the heart-pounding conclusion to
the *Forsaken* trilogy.

# THE DEFIANT

# THE CRUCIBLE

A VOICE WHISPERS MY name: "Alenna."

I try to respond, but I can't. Besides, I don't even know if the voice is real. It's probably an auditory hallucination.

I have no senses. I can't see, hear, taste, or smell. I can't feel anything. And all around me is darkness. Blacker than any night you could imagine. I am totally disconnected from my flesh. My senses have been stripped away, like bark from a tree. My nerves are deadened, and I don't feel hunger or thirst.

I could have been like this for hours, or weeks, or months. Sometimes I sleep, and sometimes I'm awake. It's hard to tell the difference.

Often I want to scream. Other times, I want to break down and cry. But I am capable of neither.

I have no memory of how I ended up here, but I know that one of two things must have happened. Either I got captured somehow and placed in some sort of isolation pod, or else I died and now I'm stuck in limbo. It's worse than anything else I've ever experienced.

Over and over, I try to figure out the last memory I have before everything went black. It's a memory of a few weeks after we liberated everyone on Prison Island Alpha, the place also known as "the wheel." The specimen archive—where the captured kids were being held in stasis—was destroyed along with the flying machines known as "feelers," and we retook the island.

Most of the brainwashed drones converted to our side, once their minds were free of the government chemicals. Some didn't, and they formed guerilla groups in the forest that would attack us every night.

But even those attacks started dying down. Our plan was going well. Island Alpha was becoming our new home base, just like we intended. The different tribes on the island—the rebels, the scientists, and the travelers—were working together to turn the island into our staging ground for our assault on the continental United Northern Alliance, better known as the UNA.

But obviously something went wrong. *Was I captured and poisoned by rogue drones?* Maybe I hit my head, or was given some kind of drug along the way. My memory is so fuzzy. Trying to think about things too hard makes my head hurt, like looking through glasses with the wrong prescription.

The last thing I remember is helping build a cabin with my boyfriend, Liam, as we were working on a team constructing a new fortified village on the island. Liam and I were laughing and playing around. Things were good. I felt safe—for once.

My only lingering sadness was over David's death. David was the boy whom I'd woken up with the first day I'd gotten banished to Island Alpha by the UNA. He sacrificed himself by destroying the cooling core of the specimen archive, which halted the government machinery running the wheel. He did it so that the rest of us could live. And also so that the kids who were frozen in the specimen archive could survive. I still thought about him every night before I slept, and he appeared sometimes in my dreams. Often we were lost in the forest on Island Alpha together, on a dark hidden trail, and he was beckoning for me to follow him deeper into the darkness. Sometimes I would wake up crying.

I hid these dreams from Liam. I don't know why. Maybe I didn't want him to know how strong my feelings for David were. Maybe I didn't even realize how strong they were myself, until after David was gone. I was still sorting out my feelings, more than two months after his death. David and I shared a deep connection. When he died, it felt like I lost a piece of myself.

I will never know exactly how David felt about me. I suspect that he liked me more than he ever let on. His final words to me—"Keep me in your thoughts, Alenna"—linger in my mind. I keep wishing that we had done things differently, and that David was still alive.

Other than David, my other friends survived our massive battle with the army of drones. Liam, Gadya, Rika, and I found Cass and Emma alive but injured after the assault on the elevated highway. Both of them were still recovering but doing well.

I try to think past that final memory of me and Liam working in the village together, but there is only blackness. I'm suffering some form of amnesia.

I remember that our attack on the continental UNA was several months away. For once, I had felt so peaceful. It had seemed like we were free from worry—at least for a while. *Did someone attack us on that day?*

The final image in my head is that of Liam's smiling face gazing at me. After that there is nothing. No matter how hard I try, I can't bring any more memories to my mind.

Then, out of nowhere, I hear more voices crackling in my ear, saying my name. They are too loud and sharp to be imaginary.

"It's time to bring her up," a voice says.

"Alenna? Can you hear us?" another one asks.

"Say something if you're still sane in there!" the first voice commands.

The voices are familiar. Oddly reassuring. I realize that I must be wearing an earpiece. *Am I back in the UNA?* I try to touch my ear but I can't feel anything, not even my own hands.

*Yes, I can hear you,* I struggle to answer. But I can't speak. Then I try to say it again, and this time, I hear the words crackling back at me in my ear. My hearing is returning. "What happened? Where am I?"

"Hang on," another voice calls out. It's a girl. I recognize her voice at once. *Gadya.* She's one of my closest friends.

"Gadya?" I ask, confused. But as soon as I say her name, I feel a strong tugging sensation on my arms and legs. Other senses are returning. I'm floating in thick, warm liquid. And the substance around me is flowing and shifting, like a slow-moving river.

It startles me to feel any sensation. I must be in some kind of sensory deprivation chamber. I feel relieved to still be alive, but very confused about where I am—and why I got put here.

My sense of direction is skewed. I can't tell what is up, and what is down. Only that I'm finally moving.

My arms and legs start to throb, and my head begins pulsing. I'm being pulled up through the jelly-like liquid. It reminds me of the material that the barrier around the gray zone was built from. I struggle to kick and move my arms. I thrash and flail, and this time I can feel the motion. All my senses are returning at once, and they make my body ache. I see a circle of light appear directly above me. Shimmering and fluctuating. Growing larger as I'm pulled upward.

"Hey! What's going on?" I call out.

I feel wires tugging and pinching my flesh, like intravenous tubes. They feel like they're going to rip right out of my skin.

I cry out in pain.

"It's okay! Stay calm! You're doing great," I hear Gadya's voice say in my earpiece. "Don't mess up now!"

"Mess what up?" I ask, confused.

Air bubbles burst around me in the oily liquid. I realize there's a tube in my nose. I try to yank it out, but it hurts too much. I taste copper and realize that I'm bleeding.

I keep moving, wrestling with the tubes sticking into my body. I feel restraints and wires pulling away from me, setting me free.

And then I'm pulled out of the fluid and into harsh white sunlight. I yell in pain, as tubes whip out of my flesh one by one.

I'm in a bamboo hammock attached to a small metal crane. It's carrying my body up through a large metal hatch in the top of a giant isolation tank, and over to a stone walkway in a jungle clearing. *I must be on Island Alpha.* Rows of other isolation tanks sit next to the one that I was inside, monitored by scientists in white lab coats.

There is no sign of Gadya or my other friends. And my memory hasn't come back either.

The fresh air flays my skin. Every nerve feels like it's burning, as though I've been tossed onto a funeral pyre. The light is so bright, I can't even hold my eyes open. I clench them shut. Even with them closed, it's too bright for me. I see a burning red color on the inside of my eyelids.

"Gadya?" I call out, as I struggle to orient myself on the hammock. I put a hand to my ear and try to adjust the earpiece. "Where are you?"

"Right here."

"Where?"

"Watching you on a monitor."

I try to put the pieces together. I gasp for air. I feel like a fish from the river, thrown onto a rock and tortured by small children. I'm dressed only in my underwear.

"Stop flailing!" Gadya yells into my earpiece, her voice distorting. "Or else they'll fail you!"

"Quit helping her," another voice grouses faintly in my earpiece. "She has to do this on her own. If she fails, she fails."

"You mean like you did, Cass?" I hear Gadya retort.

*Cass.* Another friend. One whom I met at Destiny Station in Australia, when Liam and I first escaped from the wheel.

"I didn't fail the test!" Cass snaps back. "I was disqualified due to my injuries! There's a difference."

Their voices are loud and crackly in my earpiece. "Stop arguing!" I yell at them. "My head hurts!" *What test are they talking about?*

I finally manage to get my eyes to open again, into narrow slits. The crane is bringing my hammock to the ground. I keep shifting and writhing. It feels like my body has to keep moving, like I have insects under my skin, crawling around. I finally get deposited on cold stones. I curl up. Everything is throbbing.

"Surfacing is hard. But you need to stay calm," Gadya says. I adjust my earpiece to hear her voice better. "The scientists are judging you right now."

I take deep, shuddering breaths of air, lying on my side on the stone. I never realized how thin and cool fresh air felt before.

Suddenly a shadow falls over me. Startled, I try to get up, but my body feels too weak. Then I realize the shadow belongs to one of the scientists.

"How are you feeling, Alenna?" the scientist asks briskly. He's holding a gray T-shirt, jeans, and a pair of combat boots.

"Pissed off," I say. "Everything hurts!"

The scientist tosses the clothes and boots onto the ground in front of me. Then he checks my pupils with a small, piercing light. "Good," he says approvingly. "You're ready for the next phase of your test. Take out your earpiece and give it to me. Then get dressed."

"No," I tell him, as I struggle into the jeans and T-shirt. The earpiece is the lifeline to my friends.

"It's okay," Gadya says in my ear. She can hear our conversation. "Don't worry about it. You'll see us soon."

"Are you sure?" I'm scanning the jungle for them. There's no sign of anyone but the scientists.

"I'm certain of it."

"The next phase of the test involves physical combat," the scientist says with a sigh. "The earpiece might get broken, and we don't have many of them to spare. Give it to me."

Slowly, I raise a hand and pull out the earpiece. It's still glistening with fluid from the isolation tank. The scientist takes it from me. Then he closes the isolation tank and locks it.

I'm incredibly thirsty. My mouth and throat are burning and dry.

"How about some water?" I ask.

"Not yet."

"Why not?" I ask. "Where are my friends? And what's going on? What is this next phase exactly?"

He frowns. "You don't remember yet?"

"No. . . ." But as I say the word, memories start coming back to me in a rush. "This is some kind of test to figure out which ones of us can handle getting sent back to the UNA . . . which ones of us can handle being tortured. I'm right, aren't I?"

The scientist nods. "We put a tiny dose of a natural neurotoxin in the IV tubes. It's meant to blank out your mind for a while, and affect your short-term and long-term memory, like a strong sedative. Don't worry. You'll get your memories back."

"Why did you do it?"

"To see how you handle the stress, mentally and physically. These isolation tanks were discovered on the island, and we reconditioned them. The UNA uses torture tactics like this to break any dissidents. They use drugs and isolation to get rebels to give up confidential information. Isolation can be a much more effective form of torture than pain." The scientist glances at the tanks. "You were in one of them for seventy-two hours."

"It felt longer."

He kneels down to spray with iodine the cuts where the tubes came out of me, and he gives me small bandages to put on them. "Just imagine being in one of those things for a month or two. The tubes keep your body running, but without any stimuli, the human brain can go crazy. We had to know if you could deal with it. Most kids can't. Not even seventy-two hours. We pull them out early." He stands up again.

I get to my feet too, legs shaking. I slowly put the boots on.

"You said that the next phase is physical. I have to fight someone, don't I?"

"In a sense." The scientist starts walking away from me. "I can't say too much, or it will interfere with the test results."

Memories are flooding back now in a vivid rush. Only a few kids will be getting sent back to the UNA. Only the ones who are strongest, mentally and physically. My stomach lurches. Liam and I helped design this test, along with the scientists and the travelers. *How could I forget such a thing?* We wanted to make sure the test was as harsh and brutal as possible. But I didn't think it would be this bad. I wipe residual slime out of my eyes.

"Hey!" I call out to the retreating scientist.

He pauses. "Yes?"

"How long is this going to take?"

"That part is up to you." He starts walking again, disappearing into the jungle. The trees close around him. I realize the other scientists have left too.

I am alone.

I stand there, checking myself for weapons. But I have nothing. Just my clothes and boots. I look around for something to use as a weapon. I don't want to get caught off guard. I also don't want to fight with my fists unless I have to. I know that whoever attacks me will probably be armed in some way.

My memories aren't perfect yet, but I remember that for this phase of the test, I will be expected to fight and disarm an opponent within a limited period of time.

I scan the jungle in every direction around the clearing. Everything is completely silent and still. I wonder if I can use the crane as a weapon somehow, but it's too high up. Then I see a thick tree branch, like a baseball bat, lying nearby. I rush over and grab it, spinning around in case someone comes up from behind. But nobody does. I stand there, clutching the branch.

"Come on then!" I yell into the forest. "What are you waiting for?"

I don't feel too afraid anymore. I know this is just a test now. My opponent will probably be someone I know, or maybe some other kid from the archives, stepping out of the trees to frighten me.

After the battles that I've been through, I'm pretty sure I can take whoever it is, or at least give them a good fight. *Besides, the worst that can happen is that I fail the test.*

But more memories keep coming back, including one of Liam and me talking about the test. I'm sure that he'll pass it, if he hasn't already, and will be headed back to the UNA. So if I fail, I might get separated from him again, and left behind on Island Alpha. I can't let that happen.

I look around more urgently. "Hurry up!" I yell. My voice is hoarse from my time in the isolation tank. "I'm ready for you now!"

The scientists must be watching me. I look for cameras in the trees, but I don't see them. I know that they are there. I have to do well and impress everyone, and show them that I'm capable of fighting hard, so that I can travel back to the UNA with Liam.

Initially, I had expected that everyone on the wheel would travel back to the UNA as a massive army and fight the government soldiers there. I thought that the scientists would create new weapons out of the feelers, or other materials on the island, and build ships to take us back to the UNA in an armada. But I was wrong about their plans.

The scientists only revealed their true strategy after the island was brought under control. According to them, sending everyone back at once would be too dangerous. We can't afford to lose any major battles. So instead, the scientists will only be sending back a select number of kids, a group at a time, who will be given safe haven by the rebel cells already existing in the UNA.

Our plan is to work with the rebel cells, and use our knowledge to help them bring down the UNA from the inside and jump-start a civil revolution. It turned out that the scientists have been in contact with the rebels inside the UNA for years. They believe the most effective way to destroy the UNA is to slowly dismantle it from within.

The power structure of the UNA is decentralized. We know that Minister Harka is just a figurehead. There is no prime person or location that we can locate and easily attack. We must simply get the citizens to rise up against the soldiers and use their sheer numbers to overcome the government in every city and every town. That is our first and only order of business. Many lives will be lost, but the sacrifice will be worth it. Or so all the scientists and rebels hope.

After the citizens have stormed all the UNA headquarters and defeated the soldiers, a plan is in place for the European Coalition to swiftly move in and help us rebels rebuild, before chaos takes hold. The planet cannot bear the UNA's tyranny any longer, so the European Coalition is eager to give us aid. The UNA is fighting eight different countries at the moment, and they will never stop. The rest of the world can't tolerate its madness any longer.

This plan makes me nervous, especially the first part. I don't know if I'm cut out to be an enemy spy in a rebel cell. I was never in a resistance cell before being sent to the wheel, unlike David and Cass. I am used to battles and fighting, but not hiding and plotting. Those are different skills. Will I be able to urge the citizens to rise up? I'm not sure.

I also don't know if we can trust the European Coalition, although from what I've heard, they are a fair and relatively peaceful alliance of nations that do not subject their citizens to the violence and atrocities that the UNA does. They will supposedly help us reconstruct the nation, and help us put a new democratic form of government in place. Then, once the UNA is self-sufficient again, they will allow us to be a free and independent nation once more. Perhaps we will even be able to split back up into Canada, the United States, and Mexico, if the citizens so choose.

My thoughts are interrupted when I hear a noise from the trees. It's the sound of footsteps crackling on twigs in the forest. I spin toward the source of the sound. My fingers clench on my tree branch. I crouch low into a fighting stance.

I remember the shy, timid girl I once was. Before I got sent to Island Alpha, and before I met Liam and Gadya. Now I am no longer scared and weak. I am a warrior, tested by many battles.

"Let's do this!" I yell, banging my tree branch on the ground.

I expect whoever it is to yell something back, but instead I just hear a weird growling noise. Maybe the person is trying to scare me, but it's not going to work.

I keep hearing the branches crackle and the leaves rustle.

And then a figure steps into view.

There is a universe of possibilities in all your choices. You never know where they will lead … or whom they will lead you to.

d i s s o n a n c e

ERICA O'ROURKE